THE
BETRAYAL

Also by Sabin Willett
The Deal

THE
BETRAYAL

A NOVEL

SABIN WILLETT

VILLARD NEW YORK

Copyright © 1998 by Sabin Willett

All rights reserved under International and Pan-American Copyright Conventions. Published in the United States by Villard Books, a division of Random House, Inc., New York, and simultaneously in Canada by Random House of Canada Limited, Toronto.

VILLARD BOOKS is a registered trademark of Random House, Inc.

Grateful acknowledgment is made to Ice Nine Publishing Company, Inc., for permission to reprint twenty lines of lyric from "Ripple," lyrics by Robert Hunter, music by Jerry Garcia. Reprinted by permission of Ice Nine Publishing Company, Inc.

Library of Congress Cataloging-in-Publication Data

Willett, Sabin.
    The betrayal / Sabin Willett.
        p.   cm.
    ISBN 0-679-44853-5 (alk. paper)
    I. Title.
    PS3573.I4454W58   1998
    813'.54—dc21   97-45946

Design by Mercedes Everett

Random House website address: www.randomhouse.com
Printed in the United States of America on acid-free paper
98765432
First Edition

For my two Isabels, Claire and Catherine Willett,
and for their brothers, Hugh and Pete

ACKNOWLEDGMENTS

Though a poor student, I am a grateful one. First among my teachers was Jennifer Hillman, who labored mightily to teach me about the Office of the United States Trade Representative. Certainly the events in this book could never have happened during her tenure there. Mike Kendall (once a feared prosecutor) and Mark Pearlstein (still one) gave me tips about the lives of FBI agents and assistant U.S. attorneys. Michael Glen offered needed guidance on horsemanship; Philip Kemp, on aviation. My partners at Bingham Dana have, as ever, provided enthusiastic support. As a token of gratitude, I have vouchsafed them at least three cameo appearances. Thanks again to my agent, Stephanie Cabot, for unflagging encouragement. I am especially grateful to my editor, Susanna Porter, for advice, thoughtful scrutiny of creatures great and small, and a doggedness in negotiating the picayune that in my experience is unmatched even among lawyers. (I reached the last half-page of manuscript to find her demanding not one but two changes. It is, of course, a better book for each of them.) A tip of the cap to my other friends at Random House and Villard (who were *particularly* attentive on the matter of the title). Thanks also to my Isabel consultant, Miss Luned Palmer. Luned, Isabel is the best this groan could do. For everything else, heartfelt thanks to O.T.L.

In the councils of government, we must guard against the acquisition of unwarranted influence, whether sought or unsought, by the military-industrial complex. The potential for the disastrous rise of misplaced power exists and will persist.

—Dwight D. Eisenhower,
farewell address to the nation,
January 17, 1961

"Home is the place where, when you have to go there,
They have to take you in."

"I should have called it
Something you somehow haven't to deserve."

—Robert Frost
"The Death of the Hired Man"

PROLOGUE

Dubai, United Arab Emirates, November 1992. It was a mating dance, and the watcher studied it through binoculars. All around the gleaming machines on the runway, the dancers met and parted, while others thronged the viewing stands to watch silvery streaks high above the desert. For music they had the thunder of aircraft engines, and for intoxication, the pungency of jet fuel in the morning air. Young pilots, their flight suits as gaudy as prom dresses, strutted the tarmac, as if to say, "Dance with me!" Along the rows of fighter jets, the salesmen from Dassault, from Saab, from Lockheed and McDonnell Douglas, leaned up against their shiny aircraft like boys who lounge against the fenders of waxed muscle cars. Dance with us! And the objects of all this technosexual display were no blushing ingenues, but middle-aged men in suits and caftans, with briefcases and laptops, who trolled in clusters along the ranks of fighter jets, their eyes hidden chastely behind dark glasses.

From inside an air-conditioned hut a short distance away, the watcher's slim finger rotated the knurled wheel on his binoculars, tightening focus on one of the groups in this crowd. His stare was intent but patient. He watched the crowd the way a cat, motionless near a stone wall, waits for a small animal to appear. From head to toe, there was something oddly feline about the silver-haired man with the binoculars, all stillness and inscrutability, as though, without warning and without expression, he might pounce. Or purr.

It was early. The sun had not long since risen from the Gulf of Oman and still threw a pink light on the desert hilltops of Muscat, far to the southeast. At the world's largest open market for weaponry, the merchants liked to begin the day at sunup, before the deep blue of the cloudless sky faded to white, and a tyrannical sun fired the tarmac into refractory and heated the wings of the fighter planes into skillets. In the early morning, the colors were richer, too: the orange of the flight suits of the Italian pilots brighter, the horizon purpler, the gleam of the Hughes AMRAAM and Raytheon AIM-9X sidewinder missile arrays as white as vanilla ice cream.

Cats dislike heat, and prefer distance. The watcher had no desire to join the crowds outside, to touch the airplanes or see their aerobatics. Much of his life had been spent in places where only the prospect of money made the heat bearable. From his position in the hut, he had a better perspective on the dance anyway.

From the moment the watcher had arrived three days before, he had sensed more than the usual air-show buzz. Since the high-tech circus that was the '91 Gulf War, nothing had been selling better than American. Rumors of record deals were bruited all over the town. The Taiwanese would spend more than $5 billion for F-16s. And then there was the Saudi deal: 150 fighter jets, for a stunning $9 billion, enough money to make even the heart of an arms merchant skip. This was not a mere air show. It was a feeding frenzy.

The binoculars found their object, and the watcher sharpened the focus until he could see even the little drops of perspiration on the forehead of the McDonnell Douglas sales rep who was, at that moment, polishing the canopy of an F-15. Crossing the tarmac toward him, escorted by American pilots, was a party of three short Asian men in tan suits and open-necked shirts.

The watcher had long studied the dance. He knew the gestures that betray a man's desire, and that morning he marked them all from the air-conditioned hut. Oh yes, the Indonesians wanted the plane, that was clear enough. And they had the money. The plane wasn't the hard part. Nor was the money. Indonesia, that would be the hard part. Still, a deal to sell fifty jets, at $40 million apiece, ought to provide challenges. He watched the first businessman climb the stepladder and enter the cockpit. A faint smile appeared on his lips. Coitus.

That night, at the Hilton Beach Club, the smell of mesquite and the hail-fellows of the Americans were in the air as the steaks sizzled on the grills. Pilots and munitions merchants, buyers and sellers, generals and cousins to the emir, all mingled under the tents set out on the hotel grounds.

"Running your licenses and permits is going to be tricky, I don't need to tell you," the man from McDonnell Douglas was saying to the Indonesians at his side, raising his voice just a little to be heard over the growing rumble of the party. "Your country isn't Taiwan, if you know what I mean. There'll be a few nervous Nellies in Defense—Commerce too. You need Washington lawyers, you need consultants, you need access, you need a team of people who know what the hell they're doing, and frankly, if you want these airplanes in real time, you need your team up to speed—and fast."

"You have perhaps a referral?"

The American smiled. "Far as I'm concerned, if you want your deal done, the man who can do it for you is Claude Housez. I think he's here tonight, somewhere."

He was, somewhere—somewhere nearby. Now that the sun was down, the Cat had come outside. The expatriate Frenchman, then officially resident in Geneva but just as likely to be found in Martinique, or Vail, or, it being November, in Dubai, was there. And later he emerged from the crowd, inclined his head just so, smiled with feline inscrutability, and shook the hands of the Indonesians. Why a Frenchman should be able to arrange for the sale of American fighter jets was not a question that occurred to them, or at least was not one they were likely to raise. For in truth, the Indonesians had not come to the Emirates to window-shop. They had done their homework, and Housez was a name they had run into with surprising frequency.

There on the hotel grounds, gently, elegantly, Claude Housez began to midwife the Indonesian sale. Though not his largest, it was large enough to be outside the routine. It would be interesting, now, to know exactly what he was thinking at that moment. Perhaps of the money in the deal, although he didn't need it, not anymore. And it would be still more interesting to know whether, as he stood on a patio beneath a desert sky more gorgeous than anything in old Omar, even Claude Housez had any inkling of the collateral damage to come.

THE
BETRAYAL

CHAPTER 1

September 6, 1996: Everything since the convention has been a frenzy, a delicious panic, the high command now fevered and hyperventilating during the staff meetings as the final campaign is mapped and each post at the picket is allotted. The convention, like most everything else the Republicans do, had been staged, a dumb show for the television cameras. But tonight is actually something real. President James Breed's Republican insiders, who will be in the van, sweeping all before them and inexorably home to reelection in November, have come to party.

"Just us," she says to herself while brushing her hair that evening, "just us." Yet Louisa Shidler is no longer one of them, not really. Once, perhaps, when her mentor, Royall Stillwell, began his progression from the Senate to the top post at the Office of the United States Trade Representative, to president-in-waiting as Jim Breed's reelection running mate. But no longer. Life intervened: Isabel's adolescence, the drift of Louisa's marriage, and, to be honest, a certain discomfort with the retail side of politics.

Now she has become almost an afterthought of the Breed-Stillwell campaign. Her status is uncertain. She is rather like an old girlfriend invited to a wedding: everyone knows that she is no longer relevant, and yet a wary curiosity surrounds her, as the wedding guests wonder what ancient knowledge she brings with her to the reception.

Brushing her hair, she has all of those thoughts, but smiles anyway. For tonight, status be damned. Tonight is the campaign staff party. Tonight they will drink too many tequilas and vodka Collinses and dance to "Louie Louie" on the tabletops. Holding their ears, they will shout to each other over the noise of the band, and even Louisa will feel like one of the gang. She will relive earlier evenings like this one—for there have been many such evenings in Royall's career. By midnight the fillies will begin to stumble off toward hotel rooms with the happy drunken boys. And she will watch them with a smile, but not follow, for it is then that she will remember Isabel, and the carriage that awaits, and Toby. Toby—maybe.

But first, Dulaney Stillwell, or, as she is known to everyone, Doolie. (Like that of many southern women, her name derives from some distant male antecedent, but she is known by a feminized diminutive.) Louisa has been seconded to the candidate's wife to escort her to the party at the Willard Hotel. This assignment carries with it an unspoken duty.

Royall Stillwell's grand, white-brick home in McLean, Virginia, stands secluded at the end of a winding, private lane. If you arrive by day, you see, first, where a massive pin oak dominates a grassy island in the circular drive, and beyond it, the tall chimneys, and then you begin to make out the blue-gray shutters against the white brick. At night, you see little at all, headlights bouncing off the woods that crowd the lane. Louisa drives up about eight. A Secret Service agent trains his flashlight on her driver's license. They don't even know her anymore.

"Honey," Doolie is saying from somewhere up the carpeted staircase and around the curve of the banister rail, "I don't know what to wear to this party, I'm so old and fat and wrinkled. Whatevuh 'm I gonna do 'round so many pretty boys and girls?"

There is no fat, not a cubic centimeter of it, on Doolie. Louisa smiles.

But, like everything Doolie says in dizzy good humor, the remark contains an element of worry. A drop of the glue that holds Doolie's smile in place is that fear, that knowledge that she has used certain basic gifts to get herself where she wanted to be, and that holding her position calls for nearly as much artifice as achieving it did.

Doolie's position is well fortified. In part, it is the house itself: a three-story, six-bedroom, two-chimney whitewashed-brick redoubt in McLean. In part, it is the elaborate social network she has built and sustained with the dinners and the cocktail parties and the barbecues and the "at homes." Partners for tennis and golf are carefully selected. Doolie has laid out an architecture of social contacts that is deeper and broader and more intricate than anything Royall has achieved in public life.

Tonight is a special night, even for Doolie: a party to rally the select, the anointed, to the last big push for the Breed-Stillwell ticket. In a few months, her husband will likely be the vice president of the United States. A great thing, even on its own, and a great milestone, even for Doolie, but, nevertheless, only a milestone.

"Elizabeth, sugar," Doolie is saying, "get Louisa a drink. Get her a nice vodka Collins to have with her Aunt Doolie." Louisa protests, but without effect. Her assignment—unspoken, but clear enough—was to prevent this from happening. She supposes Doolie has guessed that. Elizabeth brings a wide cocktail glass on a silver tray, her dark face courteous but humorless, and Louisa avoids her eyes as she takes the drink. She doesn't even like vodka.

She stands on the checkerboard tiles in the foyer, the glass in hand, and listens to the disembodied Doolie talking to her through the floors and doors and walls above, honeying her and sugaring her. "That dreadful Cynthia Barnett, she'll be there, don't you think?"

"I think so," Louisa answers.

"Mustn't do anything without Cynthia Barnett's permission," Doolie says. "Cynthia, darling, would it be all right with you if we passed this law?" The voice fades as she clop-clops briskly into her dressing room but remains audible. "Cynthia, I'm supposed to give a speech. Would you look into your computer, honey, and see what it would be all right for me to say? . . ."

The voice trails off completely, and then returns. ". . . that charming boy of yours, sugar? I don't mind telling you how mashed on him I am. Frightful, a relic like me." She doesn't know that Toby has moved out. Happily, before Louisa can answer, Doolie moves to new territory.

"Can you believe that man Proctor and what he said about Jim?"

Sam Proctor is the Democratic party nominee. The campaign has gotten a little rough.

Doolie doesn't wait for an answer. "Honey, a man like that has got no class. And I'll tell you what, a short little pecker, I'll bet." For Doolie is wickedly profane, too—it is plain that she doesn't easily yield the floor in the ladies' locker room. Somehow they've come this far and she's never yet gotten Royall in trouble. Louisa wonders how long that will last as the intensity of the public spotlight grows.

Doolie pokes her head over the banister rail and wrinkles her nose. "A little bitty thing, don't you think, sugar? Are we communicatin'?"

Louisa smiles and Doolie winks at her. I'm not sure we are, Louisa thinks, as she hears the ice cubes clinking in the glass upstairs.

"Now, Louisa honey, tell me, be honest with Aunt Doolie, what do you think of this wretched hair of mine?"

Fifteen more minutes go by before Doolie descends the stairs. Although Louisa sees that she is done, really done, and that she has come without the glass, still, there is to be a little drama before departing. Always, always with Doolie there must be drama, and she puts her hand on Louisa's forearm and looks at her as earnestly as though she were about to ask if Louisa could introduce her to God, and she says, "Do I need a wrap, Louisa honey?"

So they debate the wrap for a few minutes, until Doolie trips back up the staircase and recommences her monologue. She hasn't got a thing, not a thing that will go, except just two or three of the rattiest old sweaters and that Chinese jacket Royall gave her the time we all went to Peking—"I know, I know, honey, it's Beijing now, and whah the Chinese cain't keep the same name on their capital, I do *not* understand."

She is still upstairs when she says, "Go on into Royall's study, honey, and get the invitations for Marilyn and Bill. Frank was here earlier to drop off Royall's things, I think. They should be in there. I meant to send them over, but then I forgot." Marilyn and Bill, friends of some kind, will need the invitations to get into the party.

So Louisa traverses the living room, past tables groaning under the holy of holies—the silver-framed photographs of gorgeous children (there are three: two gorgeous boys, Chip and David, both Duke undergraduates, and one gorgeous daughter, Kimberly, a student at Madeira)—and comes to the study. The heavy door yields noiselessly, and then she is in Royall Stillwell's sanctum. It is quiet. A clock ticks, but that is all. For the first time, she cannot hear Doolie.

Here, books prevail, floor to ceiling in the cases, and in stacks on the leather chairs. In piles before the French door that leads to the back garden are the briefing books, the three-ring binders with the answers to everything. Courtesy of Cynthia Barnett.

He has the desk facing the entranceway, with the chair back toward the French doors and windows, and it looks rather like the photographs of how the President's desk sits in the Oval Office. It is odd to be here, for she was this man's lieutenant for so many years, and yet has been in this place only twice, and never alone.

She fumbles hurriedly through the mess on his desk. A stack of mail has been dumped unopened there, and as her fingers are rummaging through the mail, it slides out.

It is a coffee-colored envelope.

Louisa stares at it stupidly, a feeling of dislocation coming over her. She holds it in her hands and makes mental notes. Postmarked June 15, 1996, Geneva. It was sent to a post office box in Washington. There is a return address: 4 Place du Bourg-de-Four, Genève 41-720, Suisse.

The brown paper of the envelope has a waxy feel to it. She can make out nothing when she holds it to the light.

In the distance are the brisk footsteps. Doolie is approaching. Louisa hunts swiftly for the tickets, and they are in her hand when the door bursts open.

"The country's in a state when it's about to elect a man who can't organize his own desk, but we'll just keep that between us, won't we, honey?"

Louisa looks again for her to wobble, but Doolie stands with perfect steadiness.

In the backseat of the car bound for the Willard, Doolie chatters on, and the stories are funny. As they approach the district, Louisa is thinking about the party. She has paid her nanny, Bridget, to stay late. She has resolved to put out of her head, for this evening anyway, everything but this party.

The Secret Service agent exits from the bridge and guides the car around the Lincoln Memorial. As Doolie chatters on, Louisa's mind drifts, for a moment, to the lonely marble man seated in the darkness. There is such melancholy in those sunken eyes. We never see melancholy in politics anymore, she thinks. Television has prohibited it.

Perhaps unconsciously, Louisa runs her hand across her lap. For the rest of the trip, she is thinking of the purse that rests there. Inside it is the coffee-colored envelope. After all, it was addressed to her.

Everyone is there, streaming in and out of the Potomac Room. The noise from the band is deafening. Everyone is kissing everyone else. The boys—so many of the men seem to be boys to Louisa—embrace her and dodge her cheek to plant big kisses on her lips. Their hands explore her back quickly and inappropriately and then the boys move on to kiss another. The women squeal and embrace and present their cheeks.

The boys and girls are whirling and gyrating on the dance floor. Royall and Doolie and Jim and Lacy are everywhere, with their blue-suited and earpieced attendants, and Doolie, of course, is the most dashing of all. The poor First Lady looks rather dowdy next to her, as Doolie embraces and laughs and touches and is everywhere surrounded by admirers.

The bright-eyed young boys are supermen. There is something nebbishy about most of these boys in the harsh light of noonday, but now in the darkness, fortified by intoxication, and communing with the thrill that is running through everyone here, their chests expand with confidence. By midnight they will be heartthrobs enough.

Not for Louisa, however. Tonight, as on most nights, she will be an observer. Childbirth and child-rearing make you a perpetual observer, a sleepless student of hormonal cycles, a journalist assigned to the gastrointestinal beat. You observe, note, file, and calculate; every hour, every day, every week. So Louisa spends the evening keeping clear of the loudspeakers and calculating what will become of the Breed-Stillwell ticket (a win, she thinks); what will become of Doolie (she handicaps her staying power as outlasting her drinking problem and Royall's flirtations); which of the merry boys and girls will catapult forward in this administration.

Everyone is there. There are the Three Amigos, as the press calls them: old political pals Bill Jaeger, the secretary of defense, Secretary of Commerce Peter Coburn, and, of course, Royall. Their friendship is said to trace to the days when the loser of their monthly poker game thereby paid the winner's rent. A lot of the big-money D.A.R. types from the early days have come—the "stringy tennis ladies," Louisa's friend Dominique calls them.

Over by the bar, Louisa sees Frank Ianella locked in conversation with Cynthia Barnett. Ianella has the head deputy secretary's job at Commerce now, and working his way across the room, he stops by with sheepish, uncomfortable small talk. Ianella, she has always known, is addicted to politics: ten hours a day for Commerce, another nine for the Breed-Stillwell campaign. But, honestly, sometimes Louisa thinks she could slap him. He's so painfully conscious of how far "ahead" of her he has moved in the Stillwell army that he thinks it must keep her lying awake nights. Frank, she thinks, relax: it's me, Louisa, from the old days in the airshaft office in the Executive Office Building.

"We should get together," Frank shouts.

"Sure."

Ianella pulls out a business card, then scribbles something. She holds it under a table lamp and looks at it. He has crossed out "Liaison Officer" and written over it "Deputy Sec'y." Great, Frank got another feather for his growing cap. She smiles, tucks the card into her purse, and shrugs.

"Afraid I haven't been promoted!"

Frank moves on, and his cloud with him. The night is from that point on a delight, until, late in the evening, Louisa looks up to see that Cynthia Barnett has her in range.

"Trick or treat, Louisa!"

Cynthia Barnett is a physical anomaly: petite, with birdlike features and puffed-up blond hair that makes her seem, at first, like a cartoonist's creation: an enormous head upon a tiny body. She looks almost fragile, as though she might be knocked over by a strong wind. And yet she has a voice that can cut through fog, a face and a gaze as determined as a terrier's, and a manner that pushes, pushes, pushes, until you back away. Cynthia is a political consultant—*the* political consultant, according to the people (whoever they are) who determine these things. Some long-forgotten aide gave her the nickname Smaug, which seems unfair, since her dimensions are more those of a wren than a dragon. But she does have a way of breathing fire, and she is vastly powerful and enormously clever. In the eyes of her clients' political opponents, at least, she is Tolkien's dragon come to life and patrolling Pennsylvania Avenue.

Her eyes fix Louisa like a specimen on the dissecting tray. She balances a drink and a cigarette. Louisa, feeling rather like Bilbo, shrugs back, further serving, she knows, to confirm the consultant's view that Louisa is a person of little consequence: a lieutenant, a stewardess with a law degree. "Excuse me?" she answers.

"Give me a treat, Louisa. Tell me something I want to know. How is the dear Dulaney?"

"She seems to be having a marvelous evening."

"Yes. We need to monitor that, I'm afraid. Have you talked to her tonight?"

"I accompanied her."

"Good. Best she have a lot of company, I think, don't you?"

Louisa doesn't answer.

"Be a dear and keep her away from the press, at least until after the election. She does get a little bit loud, sometimes, when she's left alone after lunch with a gin bottle. It could be a problem." Smaug brightens. "And how is Toby?"

"Fine." Louisa smiles brightly too, but only in order to say, ever so politely, "Next subject, please." Which Smaug understands perfectly, and ignores.

"He couldn't make it?"

Louisa shakes her head. We are not going to talk about this.

"Too bad. Give him my love." Louisa shudders. Smaug's love—it is a strange notion. The consultant peers at Louisa, unblinking, like a bird, and takes a pull on her cigarette.

"Louisa, your loyalty to Doolie is touching, but she could be . . . a complication. I'm starting to hear little whispers on the press bus. They don't know quite what to do with her. Yet."

Smaug looks across the crowded room at Doolie. "I give her six months of worship. Then they'll be baying for blood. She worries me, honey. Proctor has already gone negative, and they're looking for new material. Have you tried those cheese canapés?"

"No."

"A little disappointing, coming from Republicans. Almost what I might have expected from Dem— well, from those whom we shall not name in this place." She expels a stream of smoke to Louisa's side, but not quite far enough to the side.

There is mirth in Cynthia Barnett's eyes, a dark light there: she knows Louisa recoils at her manner, she knows it annoys her, and so she flaunts it. Louisa is praying for her to leave. She glances around, hoping someone will come to her rescue, but even a deputy press aide knows better than to interrupt Smaug when she is dining on a victim. All of a sudden in this crowded party there seems to be acres of space around them.

"Speaking of the evil ones, have you heard about Belakis and Diana Felotti?" Smaug asks.

Louisa hasn't, so Smaug tells her the newest rumor of infidelity that she has mined on the Democratic challenger's running mate, George Belakis. Her sentences run on even more than usual, a sign that Smaug is genuinely excited. She is, after all, being paid millions by the Republicans to destroy the Proctor-Belakis ticket. Perhaps, Louisa thinks, it is mean-spirited of me to begrudge her the relish she takes in the task.

"Cynthia," Louisa says, "people have been saying that kind of thing about Royall for years. Why not call them even and concentrate on the issues?"

Smaug scowls. "Louisa, please. The issues? These *are* the issues. They are the *only* issues. You catch the other fellow with his trousers around his ankles, turn a quick spotlight on the wife to watch her squirm, hand out glossies about his contempt for our Norman Rockwell values, and most of all, you keep the other team away from our little princes. And their ambitious wives."

"That's quite a testimonial for democracy, coming from one who makes her living from it."

"Democracy!" Smaug's little frame shakes, setting the diamonds or rhinestones or whatever they are spangled across her middle to quivering. "Democracy! Louisa, do you know what democracy is?"

She shakes her head.

"It's a client base! It's a client base, honey." Disgusted, the political consultant stalks off into the throng.

It is almost midnight when Louisa remembers the letter. She tries the ladies' room first, but it is abuzz with breathless confessions and giggling and confident announcements of imminent assignations, and so she settles for a lounge chair in a corner of the hotel lobby, where the noise of the party is a distant boom and thump.

Alone now, she sits with purse in lap and looks again at the smooth-textured brown paper, the typed address with her name and a Washington post office box that is not her post office box. An envelope that tumbled out of a stack of his mail, on his desk. It must have been recovered from a post office by Royall, or one of his people. So why is the envelope addressed to Louisa?

Now her fingers are tearing it open. She notes, before reading, the hue and texture of its contents. A cream-colored sheet of stationery, twice folded. Behind it, a computer printout of some kind, a printed form.

"Dear M. Shidler," says the letter, "We enclose account statement dated 30 May with compliments." Its valedictory is "Yours faithfully," and then there is simply a name, handwritten, which looks like "H. Racine, av." A lawyer.

The form behind it is a bank statement reporting on the account activity for May 1996 in account number 6614723–456. The statement identifies the bank as Duclos & Bernard, 12 Rue Hollande. Louisa does not know the name, but somewhere in the recesses of her memory of trade talks in Geneva is the Rue Hollande. It is the street where a few of the more secretive Swiss banks have their discreet offices. The account carries no name: merely the identifying number. Interest accrued since the last statement is 320,412 Swiss francs, making a total of Swfr 1,871,334 in interest accrued this year. The total current balance is Swfr 62,645,512. No other activity is shown.

Louisa was Royall's deputy in the Office of the United States Trade Representative, and has been its interim director since he left to campaign. Currencies are part of the stock in trade of her consular rank. She knows marks, lira, yen, pesos, escudos, pounds, francs, drachmae—and Swiss francs. Sitting in the gold brocade chair in a corner of the hotel lobby, she does the arithmetic. Then she does it again, in case she lost track of the zeros, but it comes out the same way, and so she does it a third time, first going to the desk and borrowing a pen and a piece of notepaper. At the end of the third calculation, she has the same figure, except this time it is written on the scrap of paper. She folds the bank statement and slides it back into the envelope and returns the envelope to her purse. She closes her eyes briefly, making a mental note to study this matter in the morning, when her mind is clear. For Louisa is a calculator, a creature of the left brain, and sometimes she even calculates when it's best to calculate.

It is not best to do so now. Now there is loud music and an electricity in the air, and there are shouts from the bright-eyed troops and the last assault of Campaign '96 is launching. She has had two drinks, and she might have another, and she positively never permits herself to do anything serious on those rare occasions when she exceeds two drinks. She may do that tonight. She may shut this party down. She needed this party, and nothing, not Toby, not this envelope, is going to stop her from being around those who are now as she once was.

Louisa Shidler gets up from the chair, the envelope restored to the purse, throws her shoulders back, and heads back toward the noise, leaving for the morning any further reflection on the curious fact that there appears to be, on deposit with Duclos & Bernard in Geneva, a numbered account—an account that is not her account but for which someone named H. Racine thinks she should receive account statements—and which contains something in excess of fifty million dollars.

CHAPTER 2

Why do people underestimate Louisa Shidler? Certainly not for her résumé.

One man describing her to another will struggle for the right words, because the obvious ones fall short. No one says that she is beautiful. She wears plain clothing and sensible shoes and little makeup, and she is businesslike in manner. Her lawyer's suits disguise more than they accent. She indulges little in herself.

And yet her person is still at odds with its own manner, as if it has never quite accepted it. There is her hair: too thick, too chestnut-brown, too long for a thirty-seven-year-old lawyer-mother. In winter she wears it in a ponytail and in summer she pins it in a swirl above her neck. Her hair is suggestive of another self, and perhaps it is that self which sometimes turns a man's head, and calls to his attention the pretty oval of her face, its full lips, her wide brown eyes set in a broad forehead, and leaves him grasping for what Louisa can so subtly suggest.

Unless the man has a good eye, an artist's eye. And then he will see it immediately. The same thing that makes her striking makes her a woman whom people do not adequately respect.

It has something to do with the quality of her skin.

Somewhere between powder and pink, like a baby's; still soft, still easily flushed, with only the trace-work of age, trace-work the world has yet to notice. Her skin is innocent or, at most, coquettish, but it is not sober—it is not serious skin. When she smiles, it is not the smile of a negotiator who has won a point. She might be a woman strolling outside a café in Montmartre, perhaps, who smiles as she catches sight of you, but not a negotiator. She might be from Renoir: a smiling ingenue, one of his confections of infant and woman, of pink skin and spheres. She is not fat, but she is concavity and convexity. You would draw her with a compass, not a rule.

Even when the table is at the World Trade Organization, not by the Seine, and the invitation is to expand the bauxite quota, rather than to dance, and when she asks only of the other government's negotiators that they debate the proposal in her document, rather than what the condescension in their gentle smiles says is on their minds, it is the same. She is a woman you do not take seriously, not at first.

Soon, she will learn to use this quality to her advantage, but in the past, it has sometimes led to great discomfort. Louisa is tough and can be unyielding on a point and is sometimes too quick-witted—seeing the conclusion early and then staking it out against all comers. When provoked, she has lashed out—sometimes too quickly. There have been uneasy moments in her career. There was that time with the Koreans, and it has happened with others. It is usually a surprise to those around her.

Renoir is in the hair and in the skin, in the eyes and the lips, but these days rarely in the expression: juggling the Trade Rep's office and her duties at home has made Louisa's expression rather severe. The frolic, the gaiety, are now a mere suggestion. There is a hint in the eyes, to be sure, but her manner leaves it unrealized. Upon her face, dappled light falls less frequently than fluorescent.

And Renoir's models rarely sat early on a Saturday morning. On this one, Louisa does not look like an artist's subject. She is in the kitchen with a cup of coffee and the *Washington Herald,* blinking off sleep and pushing strands of hair away from her eyes. She stares at the newspaper articles, loses the sense of anything more than headlines, and keeps finding herself rereading a sentence she thought she read minutes ago. To make matters worse, Isabel is interrogating her. It is a bright morning, too bright, in Bethesda, and the sunlight streaming through the window over the sink makes Louisa squint. Her head throbs dully. In the pit of her stomach is an ache, but it is not hunger, and it is not a hangover. The ache rises to her forehead. Of all people on earth, she thinks.

"Was Mr. Jeffers there?" Isabel asks, thumbing through the neat stack of Louisa's mail—her real mail—pulling out the catalogues and letting the rest topple over. Louisa is glad of the distraction, but with Isabel there is too much of it. She will not sit. She asks a question and then leaves the room before the answer. Perpetual motion, thy name is Isabel. God, Louisa thinks, she's a twelve-year-old Doolie. They have been through this, Isabel and her mother. She should sit, calmly and quietly, and converse. Instead she leans, leans on the fridge, leans on the countertop, darts to the sink, grabs an apple, paws through the mail, changes course, interrupts, moves, gesticulates. It is altogether too much movement, too much noise.

"Yes. Everyone was there," Louisa answers.

"And?" Her daughter adds a syllable or two to the conjunction.

"And?" Louisa echoes her and looks up. Isabel has discarded the catalogues and holds her hands on her hips with the heels of the palm forward and fingers back. Her head is cocked down and her eyes search out her mother's face. This is how the girls in the seventh grade pose when cross-examining their friends over imagined amours.

"Oh, Mother, come on."

Doolie. All Louisa can think of is Doolie, wondering if she was just this way when she was twelve. Isabel gets a lot of material out of preteen romances and girl-hero mystery stories. A lot comes from television, too. When Louisa sees her daughter affecting a pose, or a line, which happens about three times an hour when they are together, she wonders what its source is. About six months ago, for example, Isabel suddenly stopped calling her Mom and she became Mother. Curious, Louisa nosed into her room and found a broken-spined copy of *Restless Heart,* an aptly named work, as it seemed to her, since its fifteen-year-old heroine, at least in the ten pages Louisa managed to get through, behaved with considerable restlessness. (She spent most of them on horseback, and Louisa began to grow concerned for the horse.) She did notice, however, that Miranda Spendlove (for so she was called) addressed Lady Spendlove as Mother.

"Just what *is* coed naked field hockey?" Isabel has on that shirt, again, for which Louisa has little patience.

"Oh, Mother, it's just a joke, don't be such a nerd!" The room fills with adolescent exasperation.

"And what is it that you do, I mean, 'without obstruction'?"

"Mother!" She stamps her foot, folding her arms across her skinny chest, thus concealing the leering boast on her T-shirt, which is that aficionados of the game "do it without obstruction."

"You'd think," Louisa says to her, "no one *had* sex in this society, the way people are so eager to talk about it on their shirt fronts." She returns to her coffee, and the *Herald,* and her headache. Proctor is on page 1. In a speech in Michigan, he is flailing away against Republican indifference to the elderly. The Republicans are going to shut down Medicare and Social Security. We will take away their wheelchairs and leave them in withered heaps on cold street corners.

Louisa folds the newspaper in disgust. Who invented democracy, anyway, she wonders, and what was he thinking of?

"That's just the problem with you," Isabel goes on, the hands reverting to the hips. "You know that you're being a nerd and you're a nerd anyway. You're proud of it. You barely get home from a party and you go back to your wonted nerdliness."

"My wonted nerdliness?"

"Uh-huh. It means your customary nerdliness."

"Oh," Louisa answers. "Be careful what you call your mother. Oscar Wilde said that all women become their mothers. To answer the question you are really asking, Mr. Jeffers said hello to me last night, and he sent his fond regards to you."

"And that's all?"

"That's all. Did you have a bagel?"

"As if! Those gross onion ones? How was Doolie?"

"Mrs. Stillwell," Louisa corrects, "was in high good form. As always. You need to eat some toast, then. And some fruit. I think Royall's beginning to get worried."

"Why worried?" Isabel asks, turning up her nose at the fruit basket.

"Don't grimace. Have that banana. Isabel, a candidate's wife isn't supposed to have too much personality. Her job is to be photographed looking—up, preferably—in an adoring fashion at the man of the hour. She may have a pet charity as long as it makes no political statements. She is not permitted to give offense." Louisa goes back to the paper. "I want you to change that shirt, Isabel," she says. "Honestly, I don't know what Toby is thinking, sometimes."

"Isn't it enough that my mother should be a nerd? Does my father have to be one too? Do I?"

Isabel's hair is dark, like his, and Louisa thinks she will be exotic, as he is, when she gets out of her ungainly stage. She is ambivalent about that. Corn-fed and cute—which is how *she* would prefer to describe herself—has served Louisa well enough. She's not sure she is ready for dramatic in a teenager. Now Isabel, twelve, is all braces and coltish knock-knees and skinny legs and big dark eyes. But Louisa knows that will change. Judging by the number of posters of shirtless rock stars sprouting up on Isabel's bedroom wall, it will change soon.

"The thing," Louisa says, measuring her words, since her head seems to ache in direct proportion to the length of the sentences she utters, "about T-shirts with third-rate tacky sexual puns is that they appeal instantly to every third-rate, tacky person on the Metro platform." Louisa smiles brightly at her daughter before returning to the newspaper, and the girl stamps off up the stairs. But Louisa rather thinks she is going to change the shirt. For Isabel, like her mother, has a certain snobbishness about her.

Her mother listens to the footsteps on the staircase, listens to the ninety-six-pound adolescent who, changeable and mood-driven and mercurial as she is, is the one constant in her life. She folds the newspaper and pours herself a second cup of coffee, and then her mood turns dark, as she begins to think, again, about the bank account in Switzerland.

In the Office of the United States Trade Representative, Louisa Shidler negotiates trade agreements. What will be this year's quota of Malaysian flax? Of Chinese textiles? Of New Zealand apples? If there is another kidnapping in Chile, will we boycott or limit the intake of Chilean grapes or wine? How many American auto parts or computer monitors or mutual funds will the Japanese let in? If they won't let in enough, what will we boycott? If we boycott, will the Japanese threaten to quit buying U.S. government bonds? What will Treasury have to say about that? In other words, she deals with complex problems, of economics and politics interwoven, problems that require imperfect, predictive solutions.

This is a different sort of problem. It calls for cover.

Cover is a medium of exchange in Washington. Cover is insurance, reinforcements; cover is a memo in the file or a story leaked anonymously. Cover is a favor owed you, or knowledge of a public man's private indiscretion. It is an opinion letter from a law firm that says your agency, which is being forced by the administration to turn left, should be turning right. Whether right or left ultimately is the intelligent choice is irrelevant. If things go badly to the left, the memo can be leaked. If things go well, the memo is simply another insurance policy against which no claim had to be made. And the letter from the law firm may be from a junior partner— because the senior partner, like everyone else, needs cover.

Louisa has none. Where to turn for it is a problem she wrestles with for a few days that first week. Loyalty, she has learned, is rarely profound in Washington. Most often it is like Toby's: least reliable when most needed.

The lawyer in her catalogues and reviews the facts. It is an odd set of circumstances, for this is an unusual election year. Breed, like a man half dressed, entered the cycle with a running mate but no sitting vice president. On July 1, Vice President Patrick Finneran resigned, suddenly. The press went on highest alert, searching for a scandal, but could find none. Received wisdom was that the wise men had decided that Breed's campaign needed a dramatic lift, and Finneran was not the man to give it one. Old election hands thought there had to be more to this—just how *did* they force his resignation, they wondered—but in the craziness of election season, there was little time to think about it. History's footnote could be filled in later. For now, it was time to turn to Finneran's successor.

Once Finneran resigned, under the Twenty-fifth Amendment, it was for the President to fill the vacancy. But the same constitutional provision gave both the House and the Senate the power to vote on his choice. Approval meant hearings, and in July of an election year, giving the Democrat-controlled Congress the opportunity to hold hearings on the new running mate was an invitation James Breed did not care to extend.

So he simply didn't fill the post. The country was without a vice president. At first this struck everyone as significant, but the phenomenon of a vice-presidential vacancy, if unusual, was not without precedent. It had last happened in America after Spiro Agnew resigned, although at that time the post was quickly filled with Gerald Ford. Yet in the nineteenth century, four presidents—John Tyler, Millard Fillmore, Andrew Johnson, and Chester Arthur—had no vice president at all. In 1996, everyone understood. Rather than risk the hearing circus, Breed had made Royall Stillwell his informal deputy. Having resigned from his post as trade representative, now simply a private citizen from McLean, Royall Stillwell was named running mate. He swiftly became, in all but title, second in command to the President of the United States. Former Rhodes Scholar, Vietnam veteran, former junior senator from North Carolina, former United States trade representative, recently the author of a widely praised book setting out a blueprint for the success of American industry in the next century, at sixty, Stillwell was a risen star, widely praised as a successor to the unfortunate Finneran.

Now it is Stillwell who has somehow obtained a bank statement from a Swiss bank, addressed to Louisa and showing a small fortune in a numbered account. He has apparently recovered it from a Washington post office box.

It is September in an election year, and everyone is going to have an angle. The Democrats will smell an opportunity to pin a scandal on the ticket, and the Republicans, from Breed himself on down, will be most determined to see that there is none.

Where is Royall in this? He was Louisa's mentor, and now the brilliant officer has given his soldier the last lesson of the course. He has made her—once his favorite and most loyal aide—his cover.

CHAPTER 3

Tolkien's dragon had his mountain lair, and Smaug has her own redoubt. It is approached, like the dragon's, through tunnels. Tunnels lead beyond the receptionist—always an extremely decorative young woman. (Smaug calls them "chiclets," appraising them periodically, as she does the floral arrangements, and once every several years letting the office manager know that "it's time for a new chiclet." Her customers are politicians, and she knows how to appeal to the men among them.) The tunnels are bright, decorated with good art and Chippendale end tables: they veer off from the chiclet's desk past the cubbies of the research assistants, past the analysts, past the offices of the pollsters, now turning a corner and running along past the larger, windowed spaces of the media directors, the art directors and copy editors, until at last one tunnel ends at Smaug's gatekeeper, Mrs. Christian.

No chiclet she. The chiclets are antipasto; Mrs. Christian is the main course. Substantial, white-haired, patrician, her clipped accent that of a Brahmin, her clothing tailored, subtle, all her movements, all her mannerisms and intonations, measured, calm. Mrs. Christian tells no tales, and seems rather unconcerned, in a benevolent way, about yours. A client always feels a sense of triumph the day Mrs. Christian addresses him by first name, a day that often takes some time to dawn. For, at the first visit, her visage will tell the new client who has traversed the tunnels that he has reached what he craves: power.

Hovering near Mrs. Christian might be found an odd and solitary man named Ken Sauer. He is also known as the Crab, for he tends to walk and look and, in a very real sense, *be* sideways most of the time. His voice is low and gravelly and usually unheard. He talks to Smaug and Smaug talks to him, but few others engage him, if they can avoid it. He is a lawyer—or perhaps not. No one is quite sure. A fixer, a quartermaster, someone who can find you things quietly and quickly and without a lot of noisome scrutiny, and who can type up his own papers on his own computer and even photocopy them in his office on his private machine, and then go and get the papers signed, even sign them himself, so you don't have to do it. He knows all about corporations and things, keeps them like cupboards for storage, and can move money around the globe as handily as a croupier slides chips across felt.

The Crab is around and then he is not around. Not an employee, exactly—not *anything,* exactly—he is one of those for whom the word "consultant" does broad service. He has a small office where the light is likely off by day and likely on by night, for crabs are, of course, nocturnal, and this one scuttles in and out at unpredictable times.

Behind Mrs. Christian stand the double doors; beyond them the anteroom, with its thick white carpet, and flanking guardhouses for Jack and Jill. Jack and Jill are the twin special assistants. Always one Jack, always one Jill: their job requirements are to be brilliant, devoted, young, sleepless, discreet, and licensed to drive. Also, largely celibate. Had they been inclined to sex, it would have to be with each other, in the guardhouses, for there is no time to go home, or anywhere else unless it be on an errand to suit Smaug's whim at any hour of the day or night. Jack and Jill don't have windows, but then they rarely sit still long enough to look out of one. They have beepers and cell phones and laptops and modems and faxes at home and faxes in the cars, and well-thumbed airline guides. They have planes to catch and meet, places to shuttle Smaug and persons to shuttle to her, pails of water to fetch from up the hill. They are twenty-three when they sign on, work hundred-hour weeks, and make $38,500 a year. On the other hand, each one of them can get in to see the President of the United States.

Past the flanking guardhouses of Jack and Jill lies the special conference room, with its large-screen high-definition televisions, its computer monitors, its table with fourteen seats microphoned for conference calls, its faxes and printers. Past them stand the second set of double doors, and Smaug's private lair.

There are people who live in their offices for so long that those offices begin to look more and more like homes. Smaug is one of these, although the "home" she has created is on nothing like domestic scale; indeed, nothing like even grandest Washington scale. You might fit the Oval Office in one corner, the Speaker's office in another, and still have room for a party. You could throw a dinner for twenty there (as she occasionally does—the kitchen through the inset door is well appointed). Here are the getaway isles of couches and coffee tables, there the arcade of still more television screens arrayed before still other couches; across by the south windows, a granite table set with chairs; back to the east, a massive bookcase along one wall housing a fair collection of American political writing.

There is the daily table and the weekly table. Jack sets out the daily newspapers on the one; Jill, the magazines on the other; and they take turns arranging vases of cut flowers that Smaug requires each morning, when Jack and Jill must whisk out the old paper, and whisk in the new, digest the decrees of Smaug scrawled on Post-it notes, empty the ashtrays, pack away what must be packed away, discard what must be discarded, and live in terror of guessing wrong.

Over on yet another wall is what amounts to a museum exhibit of photographs of those lucky clients who owe their success to Smaug. Stillwell is there—Jim Breed, too. And though they have their places of honor, the places are not conspicuous. After all, presidents come and go.

Then there is the desk. The word must be applied loosely: it is sculpture to sit at, a creation of glass and wrought iron that was fashioned over the course of two years by an artist. The desk paid most of the down payment on the artist's house, although he would under no circumstance do business with Smaug again. She'd wrung him like a rag over every detail, and though she paid the bill, a prodigious one, it wasn't enough.

The desk holds Smaug's laptop, a telephone, and a vase of flowers. There must be no fingerprints on the desk, ever. Jack keeps the Windex in his office.

The office sketch is incomplete without a final detail, significant not so much for opulence as for pure geography. It lies beyond a set of French doors in the glass wall behind the desk, beyond Smaug herself. There, twelve floors above the corner of Pennsylvania Avenue and Tenth Street, is Smaug's last retreat, her observation deck. A patio is all it is, bounded by a three-foot wall, set with plants in cast-iron urns, a café table, benches. But, as the real estate brokers would say, "Views!" Away to the east, the Capitol dome hovers in the Washington night like a yellow moon. The White House, though obscured, lies closer by, to the west. Pennsylvania Avenue like a pulmonary artery links them, and the bulwarks of government stand guard. On the south side of the avenue are the great piles of stone and copper rooftops of Justice and the Internal Revenue Service. Just across Tenth Street, close enough to lob a tennis ball, stands the FBI building, the J. Edgar Hoover Building, with its bristles of antennae and radio dishes.

Smaug's patio belongs there, for hers, too, is an institution. She might even argue, silently, as she smokes a cigarette and looks out from that aerie, that her institution is stronger than those others. They serve at the pleasure of government. But government serves at hers.

She likes the deck, has a proprietary air about what she can see. Sometimes in the evening she goes there to be alone. Jack and Jill have seen her through the window glass, over where the wall makes a corner, peering eastward up Pennsylvania Avenue. Smaug leans up against the wall like a sort of capital mother on her porch, calling along Pennsylvania Avenue for the children to get home for supper. Up the avenue to the Capitol, down to the White House: when Smaug calls from the patio, the dark limousines rush to number 1005 Pennsylvania, and the children—as children everywhere—hurry home to be tucked in.

So much for the topography of Barnett and Associates. Its business is less easy to map. It began with Cynthia Barnett's political consulting practice, and that remains its mainstay. But it has moved into other ventures. Now the firm handles lobbying of all kinds, has a subsidiary in the home security business, others in private investigation and surveillance, yet another that makes a tidy sum preparing corporate videos. It has even bought a profitable "paintball" company. All of these ventures derive ultimately from Smaug's pervasive influence and contacts within the Republican party and the Washington and Pentagon elites.

But in September 1996, these enterprises are far from Cynthia Barnett's mind. If she has thought about them at all over the past months, it is to reflect that they all derive from influence, which depends on Republican ascendancy, which, in turn, depends on her holding President Breed on message and defending the reelection.

Today Jack and Jill are nervous as they attend the sovereign. She is smoking a cigarette at her desk, frowning. Her face looks tired. The orders are barked with a shortness that warns Jack and Jill away from conversation. They stand in silent obeisance before the desk, avoiding eye contact and waiting for the orders to issue forth.

"Where am I tonight?"

Jill has the daily schedule. "Senator Dunn's fund-raiser at six-thirty. Reception at the Smithsonian at—"

"Oh, *God!*"

"—eight," Jill continues without breaking stride. "Lanchesters for dinner at nine."

"Cancel the Smithsonian. Guest list at Lanchesters?"

"Commerce Secretary Coburn, Mr. and Mrs. Frontenac, Representatives Lewisham, Mandell, and Young—"

"Young will be drunk before the soup. So to speak. Admiral Benson?"

"Yes. Undersecretary Addison, U.S. Attorney Hanscom French, Mrs.—"

"All right, that's enough. I have to go. Did you pick up that suit for me, the white one—"

"Yes."

"With the—"

"Pleated skirt. Yes, I picked it up this morning," Jack says.

Smaug scowls. She always makes the Jacks pick up the dry-cleaning. It helps to emasculate them. But she grows a little testy when they respond well to the discipline and anticipate her whims. When they know to get the skirt with pleats. On the other hand, it is a bother to have the *wrong* clothes picked up. Life is difficult, sometimes, even when you are Smaug. "What time is my meeting at Commerce?"

"Ten-thirty."

She looks at her watch. "Have the car ready. And bring me the dailies. And a decent cup of coffee."

Jill throws a quick glance at Jack. She told him to brew a fresh pot, and he hasn't done it. Jill turns on her heel.

"Get me Maxie's latest numbers," Cynthia Barnett says to Jack, and he, gratefully, hurries from the room. "And the film on that new Breed Medicare ad. Did they finish last night?"

"Yes, Cynthia. I've loaded it on the monitor in the conference room."

She sighs, still in no mood for clever assistants to anticipate her, and waits for Jack to be gone. Jill is turning to follow him, but before she does, Smaug seems to soften, asks her, "Are we going to be reelected? Or is the New Jerusalem to be turned over to the heathen? What do you think?"

Jill has learned to resist flattery. She looks at the floor.

"I don't know," Smaug sighs. "The President is surrounded by fools. And Royall's been acting funny lately." She looks up at Jill. "Oh, never mind," she says. "Go."

CHAPTER 4

It is the air's heavy stillness that signals the onset of a storm. As three days pass at the office on Seventeenth Street, absolutely nothing happens, save in Louisa's head, where her views rotate, one after another. One hour she frets about the foreign account, feeling the storm's approach, knowing that it cannot possibly veer off course. The next she gives in to its inevitability, trying gamely to ignore it, to deal with the growing stacks of papers on her desk. Verna looks puzzled when she comes in with the morning mail: usually a model of regimentation, Louisa's desk lately is becoming a rubbish tip. This grows worse as the week wears on. Louisa has become obsessive about her problem. She is overtaken, and her mind can grasp nothing else. She needs cover. She *needs* it.

On Thursday, she leaves the office at lunchtime.

"Headed out today, Louisa?" Verna asks.

"Yes, Verna, I've got to run an errand at the post office," Louisa says.

It is true, after a fashion. Ten minutes later, the lunch-hour crowd has thinned as she hands six dollars to the cabdriver and steps out into L'Enfant Plaza. Glancing up at the pink stone of the edifice, she trots up the steps and into the lobby of the headquarters of the United States Postal Service. Simon Hawthorne, a distant law school acquaintance, now deputy chief counsel of the service, has agreed to see her at 2:00 P.M. She glances at her watch, sees that she is a few minutes late, and grows impatient in the lobby over the elevator's delay. No one else there appears to be in any kind of a hurry. It is, after all, the post office.

We deputy chief thises or thats, Louisa is thinking, have been popping up all over, now that we are twelvish years or so out of law school. Simon is a tall, stooping, fidgety man, with thick tortoise-shell glasses. He is going an appealing gray in the sideburns and behind his ears, although he still looks young to Louisa. His office is standard GS-15 issue: small, graceless, cluttered with files and cheap veneer furniture. Even the flags behind his desk (everybody who is anybody in Washington has flags) droop, faded and listless. Simon greets her, stoops to move the files from the chair, and remains fixed in an ungainly stance, holding the files, as he realizes there is nowhere else to put them down.

"Thanks for seeing me, Simon."

"Hey," he says, groping for words, "great! We . . . visitors here . . . not a lot, you know." Simon came on during the Bush administration. He doesn't do sentences very well.

He puts the files on the desk. There is a little small talk, equally uncomfortable. "Well," Louisa says when they are seated, and he has taken refuge behind his desk, "I have a favor to ask of you." And she launches into her speech, inwardly noting with some guilt how smoothly it flows. "Over at USTR we are negotiating a very delicate trade agreement. I'm afraid I cannot disclose more than that. We've received information that one of our trade partners' representatives may, well, may be doing things that he should not be doing. Sorry to speak so obliquely, but, let me just say, things that would greatly damage the relationship.

"The person in question is highly connected. This gives us something of a dilemma. If we seek information through formal means, or even if we involve the FBI in making inquiries, we risk our inquiries coming to light. They may prove groundless, and the fact of the inquiries themselves would probably greatly injure the relationship. So I have been, well, it falls to me to make the investigation, as quietly as I can. We have made use of some private surveillance, and it appears that this person is using a post office box in the district."

Simon looks a little puzzled, for his mind has jumped ahead to the question of why she would be seeing him about this. "Intercepting someone's mail, we . . . uh . . . I can't . . . you know, we prosecute people for that, Louisa."

"No—not the mail, I just need to know who owns the box. What it comes down to, Simon," she says, "is that the trade rep needs a little cover. He cannot openly poke around in this. On the other hand, if things are as we suspect, he cannot later be seen to have ignored matters."

Simon smiles, for Louisa is talking in bureaucratic Esperanto: the universal language. Like Louisa, Simon is someone's lieutenant, someone who needs cover now and again. Louisa explains to him that if they ask Justice to subpoena the records, they are afraid it will get back to the other side. He seems almost disappointed at this, as though he had hoped she was going to ask him for some more sensational disclosure.

"The owner of a post office box? Hell, that I can . . . you know, while you wait."

As he makes his phone calls, she glances nervously about the cluttered office, feeling a sort of sadness at it all, that this agreeable but ineffectual man is reduced to demonstrating his power to her by disclosing the owner of a post office box, and that she is reduced to preying on his desire to do so.

When he is finished, Louisa makes another modest show of chatting with him, but Simon is intelligent enough to recognize that the obligatory promise to get together is for appearances only. At last she is in the elevator, feeling dirty for having lied to an old acquaintance, having come into this seedy office with her seedy mission. But in her jacket pocket is a piece of paper, and on it, in his handwriting, is the name of a corporation.

It remains there through the balance of the afternoon, for Louisa absolutely must deal with the Argentinians. But she cannot concentrate. The print of the documents swims before her eyes. Heaven only knows what she says to the chargé who has flown in from Buenos Aires and arrives with two attendants from the embassy. After the meeting, Louisa wonders if she has exchanged pleasantries or committed her government to a billion-dollar exclusion to the beef tariff.

At five o'clock, Louisa makes another call. Marcy Mosseau, another Georgetown pal, is now a senior associate with Skidding, Arper's Washington office. Feeling a little silly about it, Louisa nevertheless walks to a pay phone on Seventeenth and places the call from there. Marcy is a brilliant, brash, beer-swilling project-finance lawyer. She loves football, waste-to-energy power plants, and men indiscriminately, and makes no apologies. These days Louisa sees her only once a year or so.

"Weezy Shidler!" she hollers, "how are you, girl!"

"Fine, I'm fine, Marcy," Louisa lies. "How are you doing?"

"Weezy, you'll never believe it."

"What?"

"Guess."

"What is it? Partnership?"

"Yeah, right, Skidding hands out partnerships like candy. No, better—"

"You're—"

"I'm—"

"Oh my God, Marcy, that's wonderful! Who is he?"

A pause. "Shit, Weezy, we're not talking marriage here. I'm *pregnant*."

"Oh."

"Don't say, 'Oh,' girl! Pregnant, Weezy! I'm gonna have a baby, which I want, and I'm not gonna have to have a man around, which I don't want but once every three nights!"

Later they meet at a bar on M Street, for old times' sake—with Marcy, you always meet at a bar. (Has anyone told her about the effects of alcohol on the fetus?) She has commandeered a booth, and when Louisa arrives two steins of beer have preceded her. Marcy is at work on one, and suggests that Louisa get started, lest she drink both.

Unlike Simon, Marcy looks her age. Pregnancy has put more than a few pounds on her, and did she always wear that much makeup? But her expression is radiant, and as the two chat for the next fifteen minutes—chatting rather loudly over the music, Louisa is nervously aware—it feels so reassuring to see Marcy again that Louisa's mission weighs less heavily.

It comes time for Louisa to lay it out for her. She needs to find out who's behind a corporation called Logos Resources, Inc. Articles of incorporation, public filings, and so on.

"That's all you know? Logos Resources, Inc.?"

Louisa grimaces, hearing the name yelled over the noise, smelling the beery breath. "That's it," she says.

"Where's it incorporated?"

"I don't know."

"Well, shit, Weezy, could be anywhere."

"That's why you hire Skidding." Louisa smiles sweetly.

"Great," Marcy says, "that's why you hire Skidding. When do you need this?" She sees the look in Louisa's eye and answers her own question. "You need this yesterday. That's also why you hire Skidding."

Marcy mulls it over for a moment before going on. "Weezy, you mind telling me what this is all about? I have to put on a trench coat and my Jackie O shades and meet you in a bar to get the top secret mission that you need a routine fifty-state secretary of state search?"

But, again, all Louisa really needs to do to lie in this town, she is discovering, is to say nothing. Imaginations will take care of the rest. So Louisa adopts, again, her straight, unsmiling face, the dear diligent sweet-eyed face of an honorable government lieutenant in just a bit of a pinch, and lets Marcy work out whatever will answer. Perhaps this is not lying. But it is abetting a lie.

"You can't tell me," Marcy says, and then gives herself a canned speech. "I'm to tell no one about this, not even my secretary, not even the odd delivery boy who wants to make it with a pregnant lady, not even Lord Whiskers. Strictly top secret. Memos in lemon juice, all paralegals to be issued cyanide tablets. When I'm done, report to Louisa on a park bench at midnight, flush name of corporation down the john, forget this ever happened, right?"

The music thumps. The crowd has swollen around them, so that drinkers, standing, begin to infringe on the booth. But Louisa is smiling as she asks her, "Who's Lord Whiskers?"

"My cat."

Louisa pauses with mock solemnity. "How discreet is your cat?"

"Well, she's never been pregnant." Marcy winks, takes another hit from the beer.

"You know, Marcy, you need to be—"

"Careful. Yeah I know. I am careful, just not paranoid. A couple of beers ain't going to hurt the little fella." She pats her belly. "Kick once if you like it, Lester!"

"It's a boy?"

Marcy beams. "Yeah, I peeked."

"We did those ultrasound things with Isabel. I could never tell what I was looking at."

Marcy pulls two films from her bag and grins. "On this guy you can tell what you're looking at. Hung like a bison."

Louisa can only smile; truth to tell, in the dim light of the bar, she can't make much of Lester out.

"So, Louisa," Marcy sighs, at length, after placing an empty beer glass on the table and leaning across as conspiratorially as her girth and condition will allow, "let me guess one other thing. The last thing I can do is bill you for this, because, like you didn't just tell me a minute ago, none of this ever happened. So I need to lose all the search fees and other assorted bullshit in some new business development account. Right?"

The beery breath, the noise in the bar, the eager faces of the yuppies pushing in at the door: it is time to go. Louisa looks across the table and nods again, trying to smile sweetly, but afraid, now, that her worry over the matter is too plain.

"Weezy, honey," Marcy says, as they leave, "that's *not* why you hire Skidding."

Marcy is loud and she is obnoxious and, frankly, Louisa fears for the child, but there's one thing about Marcy. She and her law firm are good. They get things done right, and they get them done yesterday. They do cost a fortune but, on the other hand, only if they send you a bill. At eleven-fifteen the next morning, Marcy phones.

"Louisa Shidler," she says, just as if they haven't spoken for years, "it's Marcy Mosseau. Been too long. Lunch at Jason's?"

Small talk, silly stuff—she's been meaning to call Louisa, going to have a baby. She tells her she's buying. "Be there at one. Aloha!"

She is good. Maybe she is in espionage. Anyone listening to that call would never guess the two had met in a bar the previous evening.

And at half past one, after the plates of blackened snapper have arrived, Marcy Mosseau hands Louisa facsimile copies of a certificate of incorporation from the office of the secretary of state of the state of North Carolina, a good-standing certificate, and the original filed articles of incorporation for a North Carolina corporation known as Logos Resources, Inc.

Louisa looks at the document in disbelief. "Did you look at this?" she asks.

Marcy nods. "You could have saved me some time, Weeze."

"No," Louisa says, her voice taut with concern, "don't you see, I couldn't. I couldn't!"

On the way back to the office, Louisa stops at the Copy Kop center and waits while they make the photocopies of the North Carolina articles of incorporation, dated April 20, 1993. Their typewritten boilerplate declares that the corporation may carry on any and all business permitted under North Carolina law, all as duly authorized by the facsimile signature of its sole incorporator: Louisa C. Shidler.

The house in Bethesda is dark, and upstairs there is silence from Isabel's room. No cars pass outside. Louisa sits on the couch in the living room and withdraws from her purse the documents: the bank statement, original and two, the corporate documents, original and two. She spreads them before her, collating them into three neat piles on the coffee table. She stares again at the signature, a good forgery. Who had access to her signature? Royall, of course.

She studies the document more closely. Other than her signature, the only handwriting on it is the notation "Sec'y of State" in the upper right-hand corner, indicating, apparently, that this was the copy for filing. She focuses on those three words. The handwriting looks familiar, but she cannot place it. It is not Royall's, however; she is sure of that. Everything else is typed, and all the typed words are routine. The corporation shall issue one hundred shares, par value $.01, all issued to the sole shareholder and incorporator—herself—and there is no clue to its actual business purpose. Her signature is well forged, and the address shown is hers, the home address in Bethesda. She can make nothing of this.

Later, her mind is laying out the possibilities. At her office, the documents would be found. Here, they would be found. If she opens a safe-deposit box, they will find the key. She could hire a lawyer, leave a set with a lawyer. Her face retreats to a frown. A lawyer: that is the obvious thing. And they will find out: a phone record, she thinks, the check she writes him for a retainer. Something. Can they subpoena lawyers? She read something about that recently, although Louisa pays absolutely no attention to what goes on in courtrooms, for it has nothing to do with her.

Perhaps that would be the best, but she sighs, uneasy with any solution that involves her own profession. Besides, she has a sense that the people who have engineered this will not trouble over legal technicalities to gather information. A thought comes then. One set for the finders to find, left somewhere not too obvious. In a file folder, bottom of the desk drawer, under a heap of other stuff. Another set for herself. The third, a fallback.

Then she thinks of Mac. She will leave one set of the papers with Mac. Of all professions, his is the last that suggests itself for the role, but there is only one Mac, and you can trust him.

A long time passes as she sits lost in thought, distracted by thoughts of Royall. There must have been signs of this, early signs. She searches her memory as one gropes in a darkened basement for the string from an overhead light—knowing it is near, but unable to grasp it. They went to Switzerland once, to the World Trade Organization, but it seems in her memory that they were there only for the afternoon, before flying on to Rome. Or was it Athens?

She sighs, returning to the problem of the last set of papers, Louisa's own bit of string to clutch in hopes that it will someday lead her back out of the labyrinth. But where to clutch it? When the time comes they will turn this house upside down, she reminds herself. For a while, nothing except absurdity comes to mind. She pictures herself with a shovel, in the moonlight, burying a canister in the flower beds at the back of the yard. And then she imagines the wide-eyed look on Cheryl's face when she looks out of her bedroom window—the sentry post, Louisa calls it, for Cheryl maintains a ceaseless vigil—to catch Louisa burying something under the snapdragons by the light of the waning moon. Louisa smiles wryly. Cheryl would conclude that she has unmanned Toby as he sleeps and is burying the evidence. She sighs. Maybe the thing to do is buy a few spy novels and study up on the problem.

Later Louisa is in Isabel's room, two of the stacks of papers still sitting downstairs on the coffee table. In sleep, Isabel retreats almost to the fetal position. The adolescence subsides and her face is purely a child's. Louisa tucks the comforter back to where it has slipped from her daughter's shoulder. As she turns to leave, her eyes fall on the dark silhouette of Buster, sprawled on the top of Isabel's bureau amid a heap of girl clutter. Buster bears old wounds, and his pelt has been rubbed almost bald, but his sleepy eyes are still as loving as they were the day he arrived. He is the survivor of many a field hospital: at least two of his limbs have been restored after accidental amputations.

How did we get here, Buster? Didn't we imagine, you and I, that we'd find the golden mean by now? That we'd be wife and mother and professional, that we'd serve the public by day, study with our perfect child by night, find time for the soccer matches and the Girl Scout hikes in the late afternoon, and nuzzle up to a faithful husband after the last light had been turned off? Louisa has done none of it right, she thinks. The husband, the profession . . . well, the daughter—*that,* she reassures herself, *that* she has done right. Buster consoles her with his gentle smile, and she returns to kiss Isabel one more time, with the germ of an idea.

Ten minutes later Louisa has settled back on the couch in the living room. Before her is the last stack of papers, a cup of chamomile tea, her purse, her sewing scissors, a needle, and a roll of brown thread. And Buster.

CHAPTER 5

Tuesday morning, September 17, at about ten A.M., the call comes through at USTR. Louisa is immersed in a redraft of the agreement on wine and spirits the office has been trying to hammer out with the Spaniards for more than a year, when Verna's voice comes through on the intercom. "It's Mizz Stillwell, Louisa, on two."

She lifts the receiver, more with surprise than any other emotion, because she can't remember ever receiving a telephone call from Doolie.

"Sugar," Doolie says, "I'm sorry to bother you. Did you have fun at the party? I hardly saw you after we got to the hotel and wondered wherever had you got to? That poor boy, who was he, Timothy, I think Royall said to me. I believe he had something on his mind, honey, didn't he?"

"Ah, I'm sorry, Doolie, I don't remember who you're talking—"

"Oh, sugar, I expect you do. Well, we never took vows not to tease just a little, did we?"

"No, ma'am. No, we didn't—"

"You know, honey, I said to Royall at the party, why on earth must you play the music so loud no one can talk to one another, and he said to me that was just the idea, y'all don't do nothing but talk to one another all day and all night, and political people are such yaps you have to turn it up that loud to stop them. Besides, he said, what kind of a party would it be if everybody was just talking to one another? And I didn't dare ask the old fool whatever he might be suggesting for fear he'd say it in front of a news reporter. Louisa, honey, I don't know how I'm to endure being so discreet. Anyway, Aunt Doolie's rattling on and I know you've got a thousand treaties and things to write and fuss about and whatnot over there, sugar, so could you tell me, you remember when you went and got those invitations for Bill and Marilyn from Royall's desk?"

Louisa's pulse leaps and she feels her throat catch. Ten thousand synapses fire at once, so much so that she has difficulty even hearing Doolie. She stammers out an acknowledgment.

"Well there seems to be some sort of *business* about the mail. Frank Ianella—my dearest friend—telephoned this morning and said he'd brought over Royall's mail that evening, and now Royall needs something he'd left here, some kind of bank statement or something that was on his desk. Well, honey, you've seen the desk—land sakes, you leave something there, who knows who'll *ever* find it. I said to him, have the silly old fool call the bank for another one, but I don't know, Frank said they needed the original one. You know how het up they get in these campaigns. Anyway, I remember I'd sent you in there to fetch those invitations the night of the party. Did you see any kind of bank statement?"

Which is a polite way of saying "Did you *take* the bank statement?" Oh, no, Doolie assures by her confiding manner, she knows Louisa didn't have anything at all to do with this silly business. That's why she softened her up with small talk about the party. That's why she is marking, with her perfect pitch for human relations, the sound of Louisa's voice; its timbre, tone, its modulation. She is waiting for Louisa to say that no, she didn't take his mail, but the blood is pounding in Louisa's neck and she cannot say anything at all. It is beginning: now, so quickly, before she has even thought through the matter coherently. Things like this break furiously in Washington, Louisa knows that, and they careen to resolution at Mach speed.

Louisa turns reflexively to look over at the leather handbag on the credenza that holds the last copy. Doolie is silent still, awaiting a response. Louisa has always had a weakness in negotiating—a strange admission, given her job, because indirection is unnatural to her, and ambiguity too, and so the best she can manage is "I'm sorry, Doolie, I can't help."

As Louisa replaces the receiver, she can almost visualize Doolie's lips pursing thoughtfully as she punches out the numbers for Royall's line. He is to be in New Jersey today, but they can find him anywhere for Doolie, and she will tell him about the call. Louisa is staring at her purse, as she realizes that the last set of papers is the only cover she has. She gives herself another five minutes to play it through in her mind, but she has been in Washington for years now, and she knows that now there is absolutely no time at all. And she knows that, urbane as he is, placid as his manner seems to be, caring and empathetic, Royall is a man quietly determined to succeed, a man whose enemies have dropped, one by one, by the wayside.

She fishes out the last set of photocopies of the bank statement and the Logos Resources incorporation papers, and then fifteen minutes go by as, in a shaky hand, she writes out three pages on a yellow pad. She folds the handwritten pages with the photocopies and tucks them all in a manila envelope with the USTR return address printed on the upper left. Telling Verna that she will be back after lunch, Louisa takes her handbag and leaves the office.

At half past eleven, Louisa is peering through the glass wall of the *Washington Herald*'s city room. It remains much as she remembers it, although the computers are new. There is not much activity at this hour. Reporters for morning dailies are night owls, mainly. They ease slowly into consciousness toward midday, nursed by several cups of coffee and shying like deer away from noise or even sudden movement. Around the room are only three or four of them, scattered among the dozens of monitors. Newspapers, telephone books, notepads, and files litter the desks. A woman hunches forward in a desk chair, the phone cradled on her shoulder as she types at the terminal. Across the room, a boyish young man squints at his monitor, hunting and pecking on the keyboard. Louisa watches for a moment, until he drains his coffee cup and then stands up and begins to walk toward her. Just inside the glass she can see the kitchen door. As the young man approaches, coffee mug in hand, she comes around the glass and asks to see the managing editor.

The reporter shrugs. He asks for her name, which means nothing to him, and he figures that the quickest way to end this exercise in civility is to dump her in Mac's office. Louisa had hoped for a familiar face, someone who would recall her brief passage as a reporter here. Her days of glory, covering the Silver Spring Planning Board hearings! But there is no one.

They go into the city room, and then, off to the left, Louisa looks at the row of glassed-in offices. In the central office, the lights are on; she sees Mac's white mop of hair first. He sits at his desk reading the paper, with a cigarette between index and middle finger, his brow resting on his fingertips, and a cup of coffee by his elbow. Mac's face is an active one, his jaws and lips alternately pursing and then stretching, his eyes squinting, the face now pouting, now frowning, now smiling, as he works his way through the *Herald*. She knows, from experience, that he will read every line.

"Mac, somebody to see you," says the reporter when they reach the door. He shrugs and shuffles back toward the kitchen.

"Yeah," says Mac, taking a moment before he looks up. When he does so, his eyes narrow, and he says, softly, "Well, for Chrissake."

"Hello, Mac."

"Ambassador Shidler, come to see her old companions the newspaper hacks." Louisa smiles, thinking that Mac must be one of only ten people on earth who can remember, or care, that her job carries ambassadorial rank. She hovers uneasily at the door.

"Here," he says, "sit down. Whom are you here to see?" He has calculated that she must be here for an interview, and is wondering which of his political reporters would have scheduled a meeting for this hour. But he has figured it wrong.

"You," she answers. "I'm here to see *you*, Mac."

Now Mac is interested. Mac is always interested in something new, something unexpected. It is part of what has made him a legend in his business. "Well, for Chrissake," he says again, "in that case, I'll get you some coffee."

He leaves her for a moment, returning with coffee, which she finds better than the quality she remembers. Better coffee, he explains, is the one positive legacy of the Ephram acquisition. They commiserate for a few moments about the sad day two years ago when Washington's most prestigious daily sold out to the Ephram Newspaper Group, a division of Ephram Media, Inc., subsidiary of Finch-Ephram, Inc., the vast film, cable, and newspaper giant.

"Oh, yes," he says, "we're in entertainment now. Photos of the journalists next to their copy, as though every one was a columnist. Hell, every one *is* a columnist, these days, so I suppose it's appropriate. Limited news hole. Snappy art. Graphs, charts, photos. Blood and guts, tits and ass. Interactivity. Whatever that means. So whatever happened to facts?"

Even after these many years, she finds Mac intimidating. Beneath the unruly mop of thick white hair, his brow is lined with thoughtful furrows, and his pale blue eyes do not waver when they find a subject. Mac's face is demarcated at the level of his temporomandibular joint, like a sort of horizon between sea and sky on a calm summer's day; the aspect above is serene and motionless, while below, the regular, tidal rush of the surf busies the shore with movement. His mouth has all the usual activity, as his cheeks puff in and out and the lips expand and contract, and as his mandible grinds up and down and from side to side. She used to wonder if Mac's face did that in his sleep. His mind must need the whole of the night to digest the day's intake of facts. His fingertips are stained with mustard-colored streaks, and they run along the pale skin between his index and middle finger. Mac's fair skin looks to have burned here and there over the summer, or maybe the blotches of red are the inevitable consequence of his taste for scotch whisky.

The little office is rank with cigarette smoke and ash. The walls are glass, but on the pillars between the panes hang frame upon frame of memorabilia. Most of it consists of letters or articles, and almost all of them—one night, many years ago, she checked—accuse Henry MacPherson of high crimes or misdemeanors. A letter that says, in its entirety, "If you love the Northveitmese so much, commie asshole, why dont you move there!" A Joseph Alsop column, dated October 13, 1963, blasting "certain of our press contingent who spin the rumors of Saigon's gin mills into six-alarm exposés," and then citing the "unmistakable evidence that President Diem's regime is strong and growing stronger." Next to that, Mac has framed the Washington News Service Flash from November 1: "Diem Toppled in Midday Coup!"

As a young reporter, Mac lived through the glorious days of telegrams. They had their own elegance and are, in their quirky combination of ciphered informality, the spiritual ancestors of e-mail. Many have found their way to his wall. Among Louisa's favorites are the exchanges between Mac and his boss, the Tokyo bureau chief, a WNS lifer so absorbed by bill collecting, it was rumored, that it was many years before he became aware that there actually was a war going on down there in Indochina. Under glass on Mac's wall she sees it again, the fading yellow paper—crinkled where he balled it up, and then later unballed it for posterity—of a teletype message from his bureau chief in Tokyo. SEND EXPENSES SOONEST OR POSITIVELY REPEAT POSITIVELY CANNOT ACCOUNT FOR CONSEQUENCES NEW YORK STOP LAST WARNING STOP HODGE. Below it in the frame is Mac's response. HODGE EX RPT FOLLOWS STOP YOU FUCKERS OWE ME $552 STOP END EX RPT STOP SEND SOONEST STOP PS POSITIVELY REPEAT POSITIVELY FUCK YOU STOP WARM REGARDS MAC.

On another pillar, a quotation, attributed to Kennedy, circa May 1963, refers to "the anti-American propaganda machine" in Saigon and brands "the WNS bureau reporter the worst of a very bad lot." Another quote, attributed to Johnson. A third, this one almost a page in length, from Nixon: all blasting Henry Stevens MacPherson. A handwritten letter, in flowery script: "Dear Henry, I think you owe me an apology. Yours sincerely, Maggie." It is a letter from the famous reporter Marguerite Higgins. Another note from David Halberstam. "I tip my cap to the worst-paid, best-laid of us all. I never had your sources. Thank God I didn't have your deadlines. Last one to leave, turn out the light. David." Another note from Sheehan of UPI. One from Browne of AP. A third from Mohr at *Time*.

Newspapers are heaped here and everywhere, and there are piles of correspondence, magazines, papers, files, photocopies, offprints, books on the floor and in the corners. Rust-colored carpet lies beneath the piles of papers, splotched here and there by a darkened coffee stain or cigarette burn. Mac has a little stand next to his desk that holds the Smith Corona where he bangs out his famous one-line notes. He has a computer behind him. He uses it, of course, for, as with anything new, he was immediately fascinated by it, but every reporter who has ever worked for him has heard his dirge for the passing of the typewriter.

"It is the history of this country to discard the aesthetic in favor of the convenient," he likes to say to them, "and the aesthetic of the typewriter was vastly preferable to the sterility of the plastic key. The noise, the syncopation, the clatter of the teletypes and the typewriters gave this place the air of deadline, of pace, that makes this wretched, ill-paying trade endurable. Now," he'll say, rolling his wrist in the air, the cigarette between the fingers, "now this." He ends by shaking his head. "Plastic, for all its utility, is alien to romance. And romance is why a man used to take up this trade."

Louisa is still not sure how to approach Mac with this. So she asks about his family, how he's doing.

"Bede," he says, frowning, "is an *investment banker.*"

She infers that this is not a good thing, not to Mac, anyway.

"Of my seed born, fruit of my loins, an investment banker. Thus does an implacable Yahweh punish the miserable MacPherson for his lifetime of sin."

"Duncan?"

"Duncan has not yet finished impoverishing his father at Harvard College. He sleeps fourteen hours a day, beds his classmates with Polynesian guiltlessness, and studies, as far as I can see, not at all. More evidence that the soul of Henry Stevens MacPherson is destined for eternal hellfire." He smiles at me. "You have a daughter, Isabel, I think?"

"Yes," Louisa answers.

"She must be . . ."

"Twelve. Almost thirteen."

"Lord," he replies. "It seems like you only just whelped her. Beware of puberty, Louisa," he goes on. "It is the invasion of the body snatchers. It looks like your kid, that angry lump of protoplasm, but trust me, it isn't. Puberty will gray your hair. Puberty is why God created boarding schools, distant boarding schools in the frigid north."

It is silent for a moment.

"Mac, I have a problem," Louisa begins. "May we speak off the record?"

Mac frowns. Louisa is a news source: highly connected to the Republican reelection campaign. She may be privy to information, which is

Mac's stock in trade. It is unfair for her to try to secure confidential source status.

"For Chrissake, Louisa," he says, "you know the rules."

She does know the rules, and sits in silence.

"Does this have to do with Breed or Stillwell?"

He can see that it does.

"Louisa, don't come in here to hide your man's dirty laundry under an off-the-record deal. If Stillwell has a problem, it's my business to write about it."

"Mac, he's not my man. Not anymore. It's me who has the problem."

"It is I, for Chrissake." Rapid movements now dance across his lips. "How big a problem?"

"I don't know. But I'm, I'm concerned. I'm scared, actually."

He frowns again, looking off into the newsroom. "Wait a minute," he says. He has seen a reporter, and he steps around Louisa to poke his head out the door. "Hey, Greenberg," he hollers. "You've got the NTSB hearing on Dallas, right?"

There is some conversation from the man Greenberg. Mac tells him to read the *Dallas Morning News,* as they are reporting that the board knew about wind-shear reports as long as six months before some plane crash or other. "And," he adds, "where the hell were we on this?"

"Jesus Christ," he says, returning to his desk. "The *Dallas Morning News*?" He shakes his head as if to add, "To think that I should have lived to see the *Dallas Morning News* beat us on a plane-crash story."

"Louisa," he says, "you ask that goddamn guy what his job is, and you know what he'll tell you? You know what he'll tell the mother and the father and the aunts and the uncles and the cousins around the seder? 'Ma,' he'll say, 'I'm a writer.' They all, they all think they're goddamn *writers.*" His mouth purses as he spits out the word, and then he apostrophizes: "Excuse me, but I'm a writer. Please don't intrude upon my muse with such sordid things as facts."

Louisa smiles. She has heard this before.

"They're not goddamn writers at all. They're reporters. The sonofabitch's job is to find out about the NTSB before the *Dallas Morning News—that's* his job. Now, what the hell is *your* problem?"

He falls silent, with just the jaw working, and his eyes measuring her from beneath that pronounced brow. She begins again. "I think that I'm being set up. Scapegoated. I don't know. This has all happened very quickly."

She speaks very softly. "Mac, I need to leave something with you. Confidentially." Now she is fumbling through the handbag for the official

USTR envelope. Her hands are shaking as she places it on his table. "I want you to keep this," she says. "If something happens to me—"

"Louisa, for Chrissake, what the hell is this? If something happens to you?"

"I'm afraid I can't say any more. But I need you to keep this. And I need for you not to open this unless, unless . . ."

"Unless what? What constitutes 'something happening'?"

"Mac, I have no idea. You'll know. And I want you to remember what you told me about this town. About not trusting anyone in public life. I don't think anyone will know I've been here. I don't think they'll guess that I would come to see you, or that you would know. That may be important. Don't give that up."

"Louisa Shidler, save the cloak and dagger for the movies, and call the fucking police."

But she shakes her head.

Mac stares at her, in silence, with his jaw working around and around and his lips pursing, and then he says, quietly, "This is about the goddamnedest thing . . ." as he takes the envelope. He unlocks the credenza and places it inside.

As Louisa rides the Metro back to the office, she is sure she has done the right thing. In Washington, D.C., there are only two human beings in whose loyalty she has an absolute faith. One of them is twelve years old, and Mac is the other.

CHAPTER 6

Ianella comes for her. Louisa wasn't sure how Royall would do this, whether he would call himself, whether he would come himself. But it isn't surprising that he should send Ianella. Frank is his oldest lieutenant, his fixer.

He is the deputy campaign chairman now. They can't make him chairman because he doesn't do well on television. He has no pretty face or reassuring manner to present to the public. But Ianella knows everyone, and he catalogues the favors owed and paid, and he arrives to deliver the payments and to collect the debts. And he is hungry, hungry, day by day, week by week, month by month, ceaselessly, tirelessly hungry for Royall's political triumph. It is an odd pairing: Stillwell, the cultured Virginia aristocrat, and Ianella, the Italian borough politician from Queens.

Frank and Louisa go back to the beginning with Royall. But in the last year, so many more camp followers have attached themselves to her former boss that if she sat in the anteroom and watched the traffic go by, she wouldn't recognize but one in three people coming out of his office. There are the class marshals of the Christian right, men in hopsack jackets with paste-on smiles who wear their hair in pompadours and carry fistfuls of pamphlets. Then come the Thought Police: the media gurus and the political consultants, Smaug and her train, with their studies of demographics and their polls, TV ads, and canned position papers reducing the electoral exercise to the application of prescribed stimuli to laboratory animals in order to secure a series of predicted behaviors. There are the Investors: the Wall Streeters and the Rotarians who look at the campaign as they look at business investment, expecting that it will require cash but wanting to see a return on equity. And there are the military men, the Toy Hawkers, she calls them, because of their ceaseless fascination with the latest antisubmarine device or hand–held rocket launcher. Their business suits cannot conceal the buzz cuts and the predatory way of looking at you. They're the worst of the lot. At least she feels she can understand the other groups. Since January, she has felt herself slip to the fringe of the camp. Frank remains at its center.

He sits uncomfortably on the couch across from Verna's desk, his dirty raincoat all bunched behind him and too tight across the shoulders. Louisa can see instantly that he makes Verna nervous. She looks up gratefully when her boss returns to the office. Frank is frowning. He looks heavier when seated. He has been at this too long, living on the road, eating junk food, getting calls at any hour from his boss with instructions to rush off on an errand that must not wait. Where his jacket opens you can see that his belly spills into his lap. Men can hide some of that when they're standing, as Frank had been when she saw him at the Willard. It is harder when they sit.

"Louisa," he says, as she enters.

"Frank." She nods stiffly. "How are things at Commerce? You're the new . . . what was it, deputy?"

Ianella doesn't answer. A few days ago he was handing out cards. Now he doesn't want to talk about his promotion by Royall's old pal Coburn. Whatever Frank does there doesn't seem to get in the way of the campaign: here he is at midday. Oh well, Royall got him the job.

Louisa is ambivalent about this man. She ought to be frightened by him, and to a certain extent she is, since she knows his power, and has heard tales of its exercise. But she was also a kid sharing an office with him for Royall's Senate campaign, and she remembers him from those days, with his ambition, his desperate desire for success so plainly worn on his sleeve. He seemed, then, almost a puppy to her, in his slavish, affecting desire to serve Royall. Sometimes she can forget that the puppy has grown into a dog, and the dog is all business.

They leave Verna and step into Louisa's office, the door closing behind them. There they engage in no pleasantries, no pretense of interest in each other's families. Frank has come into the office only for privacy. "He wants to see you," he says.

"Apparently."

Louisa sits behind her desk, and looks down at a stack of papers there. "When would he like?" she asks, evenly.

"Now."

"Must be important."

Frank does not answer, so she says, "I thought he was in New Jersey."

"He's on his way back in the next fifteen minutes. He'll be at National by two forty-five. Photo op, five minutes of questions, back in McLean at three-thirty."

"I thought he was supposed to go to Cleveland tonight, for that dinner, what is it?"

Frank does not answer.

"Boy Scouts of America? Something like that? And he wants to see me—at home?"

Frank nods. "Girl Scouts," he says. "He canceled."

She tells Frank that she has to be home at six to prepare dinner for Isabel. Frank can now catalogue another fact, the fact that she did not want to meet with Royall. Because Frank knows that Louisa has a nanny.

Royall canceled. He let a lot of Girl Scouts down and missed a photo op in Ohio, a key state. "You can wait," Louisa says, weakly, "in the other room."

Again the Stillwells' checkerboard foyer, only this time Louisa stands like a felon, flanked by Ianella and a tall, expressionless man wearing a blue suit and an earpiece. She saw the Secret Service plates on the car in the drive and thought, That's what I need. Somehow she doubts she'll be getting an escort.

She looks and listens as they stand there, waiting for the return of the unfamiliar man who showed them in. Louisa cannot hear Doolie, but there is the muted voice of conversation away through the living room, and she can make out Royall's voice. He seems to be on the telephone. Then the footman returns and she is led through the living room to Royall's study.

The Republican nominee for the vice presidency of the United States is seated at the couch that flanks his desk, and he smiles as Louisa arrives at the threshold. "Frank, if you'll excuse us," he says, rising. She hears the door shut behind her as, like an automaton, she finds herself taking his outstretched hand.

He returns to his seat on the couch, placing a blue briefing notebook to one side. Louisa stands, uncertainly, for a moment, before he beckons toward a wing chair that faces the desk, and bids her sit. "Thank you for coming," he says, gently, as though she did him a favor, rather than submit to an arrest. He looks at her with concern. Royall is handsome in a regular way, with features that appear ordered, his graying hair short but still thick, and neatly combed. His blue oxford shirt—they tell them to wear blue for the television cameras—still appears pressed, even after a day of speech making and airplanes. He is as slim as Doolie, fit, trim, with the sort of nondescript attractiveness of a TV anchorman. His face is one of those that some men have—faces that look fresh even when darkening with a five o'clock shadow, faces without dry skin, without pimples or grease or any irregularities at all: television faces. If his hair were longer, it would be television hair.

"How are you, Louisa?" he asks her in his gentle, courtly way, and she does not mean to, but she fears that she expels a breath of fatigue, or tension, when she lies and tells him that she is fine.

He smiles coolly, the way a candidate in a televised debate does when he has been accused of molesting an acolyte. "Louisa, is there something you want to tell me?"

"No. Why don't we start, Royall, with what you want to tell me?"

It comes out too sharp, too strident, too defensive—every woman's fear in a negotiation. Already he has the advantage, with the soft, unthreatening, comforting tone of the Virginia aristocrat.

"What I want to tell you?"

"Yes."

"Well, what I want to tell you is deeply troubling to me. You know the affection I have for you, Louisa. But I have come upon very disturbing information."

It is quiet. She hears the gentle ticking of the clock on the mantelpiece above the fireplace.

"Honestly, Royall." She wants to say more, but is uncertain about him, mistrustful. She wants to ask him about the letter, about what he has done to her, about how he could do it—whatever it is—and mainly she wants to ask him how he can wear such an expression of concern when he is being so, so false. After so many years! But she suspects that he knows this, and that it is why he is baiting her this way. He knows her weakness as a negotiator. "Louisa," he once said to her in a hotel lobby after a disastrous session with the Koreans, "how much did we learn from them today, and how much did they learn from us? You see, information is precious. Don't think of it as something you give, but as something you spend. And you can spend it just by asking questions. Husband it, Louisa," he had said. So she bites her lip.

"Louisa, I have the deepest affection for you, you know that," Royall goes on. "And I want to help you. But I have a duty to the American people, and to the law, which must come first. If you have made a mistake, and Lord knows we're all subject to temptation in this line of work, it would be best for you to face up to it as soon as you can."

He has been around the religious fanatics for too long. He is taking on their oily hypocrisy, attempting to lecture her gently, like a loving but concerned grandfather.

"For heaven's sake, Royall, it's Louisa, remember? Your faithful deputy, the one who has earned your loyalty, and who now has the feeling that . . ."

"That what, Louisa?" he asks, still gently.

She sighs. To think that it will be like this. Not even a shouting match to punctuate the end of the relationship. Once he was her mentor. Now? It is over, and he could be speaking to the Rotary.

Frank Ianella pops in. He is sweating profusely in his dark suit. He looks at Louisa, but away from her eyes, his face stony. Maybe he thinks that the boss is having an affair.

"Frank," says Royall, "give us a few minutes, would you please?" Frank seems hesitant to leave, but does as he is bidden. The door closes softly behind him.

"Now shall we talk about it?" she asks.

"By all means."

"Why has the United States Trade Representative set up a numbered Swiss bank account?"

He looks off through the windows, pondering, almost saddened. "That is how you intend to avoid this. Well, given my position, I can see that you might imagine such an allegation would be an effective weapon. It is the sort of false allegation that could become a great distraction to the President," he says.

"Not to speak of you," Louisa says.

"Not to speak of me."

She waits, listening to the calming tick of the mantel clock. But he outwaits her, his hand gently massaging his temples, like a father in the waiting room who's just been given terrible news.

This act—surely it's an act!—is getting to her. "Royall, would you mind explaining why?" Louisa asks.

"Oh, Louisa, please," he snaps. "Frankly, I would like *you* to explain why. How on earth did you become this person?"

"Royall, why was the envelope on your desk?"

He looks away from her. "Louisa, why was it addressed to you?"

"However did you get a key to that post office box, Royall? Perhaps there's a search warrant that will explain it?"

"I don't see how that's very important."

She looks at him and feels her frustration grow. He is such an actor about this, for heaven's sake.

"I'm the cover," Louisa says, at length. "I was your loyal servant, your water carrier, your fidus Achates. Now I'm the cover. God, Royall, how can you look at yourself?"

His face is impassive. "Of all the people I have known since my return from Vietnam thirty years ago, Louisa, you were the last I would have suspected this of. But if you, and this, must be treated as just another political problem, another enemy who must be dealt with, then I am very sorry but so be it."

"Royall, what happens now?"

"I shall have to think very closely about it. The timing is not helpful to the campaign, of course. You were top of your class at Duke, as I recall. Perhaps you can think of an elegant solution to this problem." It is almost a plea, she could swear it.

"I'm more interested in your solution," she answers.

"Louisa, I've been looking, and I can't find the solution." He says this very quietly, then rubs his eyes.

"How did you come by the money, Royall? Was it the Koreans? The Chinese?"

"Please, Louisa, I gather the nature of the defense. It is unnecessary to rehearse it now."

Louisa collects her thoughts. There can be only enmity between them from this point forward. But she thinks that her instincts were right, from the moment of Doolie's call. And so she must come to her own defense, mark it out. "Royall," she says, "it was you who taught me the value of contingency planning. Of belts and suspenders, as you like to call them. Well, I have belts and suspenders. I've got cover of my own. Your fingerprints are all over this money. I have a few things, bank records, corporate records, other things of that kind. I have copies. Other copies are in safekeeping. If something were to happen to me, those copies would be unsealed. Do you understand?"

"Louisa, I understand that you believe it is appropriate to threaten me. I simply cannot understand why—"

"No. It is you who have threatened me. I have listened most carefully to the threat and you have succeeded in intimidating me, in forcing me to this. You have used me very badly. I am here to tell you that it would be a mistake for you to underestimate my resources of self-defense."

She stares at him, waiting for him to flinch, but he never flinches when provoked; she knew that before. Either he has had the best of this negotiation, or he simply has disengaged from it. What she sees as his hypocrisy has pushed her beyond any negotiating skill he ever managed to teach her. Before she leaves, she has to say it: "You are a coward, Royall, and since you have used me I know that there is no one on this earth, not Doolie, not your own children, whom you wouldn't use if it served your purpose. You may excuse me if I do not care to banter with you any further regarding elegant solutions."

They leave her in the foyer, next to the blue-suited man with the earpiece, waiting for her ride. Elizabeth comes around the corner, glares frostily at her, and leaves in silence. Royall remains closeted with Ianella. At last Ianella emerges, and they go to his car. During what seems an endless ride back to Bethesda, he remains silent.

That was extremely foolish, she is thinking, as they labor northward through rush-hour traffic. She hasn't identified his fingerprints on any of this yet—she just knew they must be there. And it was Royall who taught her never to end a negotiation without having planned the alternative.

Jack and Jill are chameleons. As the campaign has wound down to its last furious weeks, and Smaug's tension has risen day by day, they have practiced blending into the background, practiced speaking without tone, answering without words. In the mornings sleepy Jack casts a furtive look at bleary Jill, or at the carpet: anything but risk the eyes of Smaug. The ashtrays have to be emptied twice before lunch now. Jack and Jill do their jobs with shoulders hunched and eyes averted. They scurry like mice. And when they are not scurrying, they *become* the curtains, the carpets.

The Crab lurks in more corners, now. Late at night with his satchel of papers he has been seen by Jack and Jill scuttling in to see Smaug. When he is not with Smaug, he sits in his office with the door shut and talks on the telephones, talks to the people he knows in Washington, people who know people, who know other people, who can get things done. Doors close behind him—his office door, Smaug's.

And Smaug herself? She is fretting more than usual. The President is ahead, but she knows it is a soft campaign, the way Bush-Dukakis was, when everyone's support was a mile wide and an inch deep, where stupid trivialities undid the opposition: a cartoon helmet on top of a tank, a waffled question in a debate. A stupid triviality can undo either side. Bush was lucky. She is fretful because the electorate is, because Mr. Couch Potato is. He may be tuned in, but his hand is on the remote, poised to change channels. She can feel this.

Within hours of Louisa's departure from McLean, Royall takes a call from Smaug. And in the evening his man Ianella comes to Smaug's sanctum, remaining alone with her there late into the night. When finally he departs, he spares not even a glance for Jack and Jill as he hurries out of the office.

Smaug is on the intercom to Jack. "Get me Sauer," she says.

CHAPTER 7

It begins with a phone call, a disembodied voice, calm, deliberate, southern in its phrasing, a man's voice in the darkness, when she is blinking sleep from her eyes, a message that is over almost before it was begun, and that remains somewhere in the half-imagined frontier between dream and reality.

And if Louisa wanted another signal of her antagonist's potency, one as to whose reality there can be no doubt, it is delivered scarcely an hour later, just after dawn on that Sunday, September 22. She was never a prosecutor, but she is a lawyer, and so she knows something about the process. She knows that to gather the evidence, to obtain the approval of the chief himself, as you must in any case with such obvious political ramifications, to prepare a case, to get the necessary papers drawn—to do all of this takes time. To accomplish it in a week is extraordinary. But it is done in her case. And there is no clearer manifestation of Royall Stillwell's raw power than the blue-jacketed FBI agents on Louisa's front stoop at six A.M.

Her first thought is to thank God that Isabel has slept over at Lauren's house and that Bridget has the weekends off. That is what she is thinking as the agents come through the doorway and one of them tells her that she is under arrest. He begins to recite the charges, enumerating the sections of 18 United States Code that Louisa stands accused of violating, but in fact she hears not a word of it, and later, at the U.S. Marshals' office, she will have to ask that they be read to her again. Now the agent is reciting Louisa's rights to her. He has a little card that he pulls out of his wallet and reads from. Blood is rushing to her ears, and she hears the sound but does not perceive the sense of the words. She came to the door in a half sleep, wearing only a T-shirt and her underwear, and now she is surrounded by them, FBI agents in blue windbreakers with guns and radios and what seems like pounds and pounds of metal and plastic. Outside, she sees the cars in the driveway and in the street. The break and crackle of the radios fills the air. In the kitchen, one of them—the black one, a middle-aged man who moments ago looked at her with a searching expression as the younger one read out the rights—is on the radio and he is using the word "secure." The house is secure, or Louisa is secure, or the scene has been secured, or something, as though this were a terrorist bomb factory, rather than a brick-front colonial in Bethesda. The word "secure" sounds bizarre to Louisa, for she has never felt less secure, never more naked than now, with these people, these strangers with their pounds of plastic in her front hall and living room and tramping all around her. They are everywhere. She can't count them: is it four, five, six?

The voice, she is rehearing the voice in the darkness. *You will not mention Royall. Not to anyone.*

With the house breached, it is as though she too is breached, penetrated. Their tramping about the house is like physical violation. Louisa's body shivers and her back curves over as her arms fold across her chest. One of them, a woman, says, "Come with me, ma'am," and leads her upstairs, up her own stairs to her own bedroom. She is going to stand and watch her dress, with a holstered gun, a huge thing of ugly steel, on her hip. Louisa lives in Bethesda, in a $650,000 house, and she has a law degree from Duke, and her greatest offense in life has been the willful tampering with a college fire door, and this beefy woman in a blue windbreaker, whose name she does not even know, is going to lean her backside up against the dresser and watch Louisa dress.

Louisa looks warily at the agent, who stands next to the dresser. She is a tall woman, on the heavy side, with thick thighs straining her trouser legs and meat in her cheeks. Her curves are indistinct, her pale bread-dough face oval in shape beneath red hair; she looks big and sturdy and ill-defined, a Chevy Suburban of a woman idling in Louisa's bedroom. It is warm; why doesn't she take the silly windbreaker off? But she doesn't. Louisa looks for a ring—she always looks for the ring, but the agent wears none except what looks like a man's college ring on her right index finger. She doesn't smile. She has Louisa sit on the bed and tell her where to find the clothes. For fear, Louisa supposes, that she might have a weapon, she will not let Louisa retrieve the garments from the bureau, but does so herself. And then she stands and watches Louisa dress as though she were a laboratory animal.

What do you wear to an arraignment? Louisa has her get out a blue skirt and a cream-colored blouse. "My daughter is supposed to be back at eleven this morning," she says. She explains that Isabel has been at a sleepover, thinking that perhaps the mention of a twelve-year-old away at a

sleep-over will touch some common chord with this woman. But she can
see none.

"We'll telephone them from the Marshals' office," the woman says
woodenly, "and make arrangements."

Telephone them from the Marshals' office? "Oh, hello, Jane, would
you mind keeping Isabel for a little while? It seems her mother is being
held to answer for defrauding the United States of America." Make
arrangements! What arrangements will these people be making for her
daughter?

"You will telephone my husband," Louisa says sharply, "and leave the
arrangements to him."

By her shrug the agent conveys that nothing could be less interesting
to her than Louisa Shidler's trifling domestic concerns.

Downstairs a new indignity awaits, for the special team detailed by the
FBI deputy director, Jim Fitch himself, has arrived to execute a search
warrant. They are going to spend six hours poking through everything in
the house, every closet, every box, every envelope. Long after Louisa has
been carted away, a team of them will be making a painstaking handwritten inventory, twenty-eight pages of items, which she later will stare at for
hours on end, marveling at the appetite for small details. They will take off
with them boxes of her files, her old love letters from Toby (not too many
of those; he was never much of a writer) and from the other dear historic
beaux, every grocery list or handwritten note, the drafts of the upcoming
Uruguay Round accords she had brought home, the answering machine,
the PowerBook, of course, and all of its discs, the tax returns, the pay
stubs, the checkbooks, the account statements, the ledger statements, the
address books. She has some correspondence in a file from Levine, the divorce lawyer. They take that, too. "What about the attorney-client privilege?" she will later ask her criminal-defense lawyer, and he will shake his
head and laugh at her naïveté. The college and high-school yearbooks, the
baby books, Isabel's report cards, the photo albums, everything will be
bundled off. The special team arrives at the home of a deputy United
States Trade Representative: they leave the house of an illiterate.

One thing the searchers do not take—at any rate, it doesn't appear on
the inventory—is the manila envelope with the photocopies she made of
the bank statement and the Logos Resources, Inc., incorporation papers.
It is gone, but they did not take it, not according to the inventory. That
she will learn only later.

Louisa is placed in handcuffs. "For heaven's sake," she says, as the
metal clasp clicks shut. Louisa is five feet, five inches tall and weighs 120
pounds, perhaps 125 if she's been traveling and hasn't been so careful

about her diet, but any one of these FBI agents could swing her over the shoulder like a garden tool, and the notion that they have to handcuff her, like some kind of criminal . . . but they make no exceptions. When they lead her from the house to the car at the curb, she sees Mrs. Gelico across the street, watching from her kitchen window, and Maxine Feldman is in the front yard, with her jaw hanging slack. She doesn't need to turn to feel Cheryl's eyes on the back of her head, and Louisa can picture her, with her hand to her mouth, up in the sentry post. As they pull away from the curb, Louisa sees Maxine in the rearview mirror of the agent's car: a dentist's wife, standing beside the boxwood shrubs on the postage-stamp greensward of her Bethesda brick-front colonial, watching the neighbor whom she had trusted more than once to watch Joshua and Sara being lugged off by the FBI.

In the back of the FBI sedan, the voice visits her again, just as clearly as if the driver were speaking.

You will not mention Royall. Not to anyone. Not your lawyer, not anyone. If you do, we will know. And if we know, Isabel will die.

They take her to the U.S. Marshals' office at the United States Courthouse in Alexandria. Royall Stillwell must have moved heaven and earth to secure Louisa's arrest. It was arranged as a dawn raid, and prepared and carried out like a military operation. But now there is no hurry. Louisa is to be booked. Now it is a normal Sunday morning and they can't find someone called Lamott, and for some reason nothing can happen without Lamott. They could come to Bethesda, and put handcuffs on her, and ransack her house without Lamott. But they can't fill out the forms without Lamott. So they leave Louisa in a tiny cell. At the rear there is a metal door. The walls are institutional yellow brick, like those of an inner-city high school, and before her there is a wire screen, through which she can see the desk and chair.

At last the door rattles and they let Louisa out and they have found Lamott, who frowns at her across a desk, as though it is she who got him up on a Sunday morning, as though all of this is her doing. She keeps asking to use the telephone because she knows that she must reach Toby before he gets up and goes off who knows where. If he is even home. Lamott tells her, impatiently, that she can use the phone when they are done. And each time she asks, he seems to resume the typing of the form a little more slowly.

Finally, they let her use the telephone, and Louisa Shidler telephones her estranged husband, Toby Higginson, to tell him that he must pick up their daughter from her sleep-over because his wife has been arrested and is being held to answer charges for what amounts to treason.

CHAPTER 8

Louisa spends the night in the women's lockup. Toby brings Isabel to see her and says he has found a lawyer. It seems to her, afterward, that she doesn't handle the visit very well at all. Isabel doesn't say much.

The cell is clean, and when night finally comes she is left alone. They bring her sandwiches, potato chips. The corrections officers, all women, look at her stonily. It is a look that brings panic to her, a look that says with certainty, You belong here. Louisa does not eat the meal.

She wakes long before dawn and cries softly in the darkness. Today she will have to call her parents. At six she rises. They give her ten minutes to shower. At seven-thirty she boards a van with four other women and is taken back to the federal courthouse. The van makes its way unhurriedly, through the familiar rush-hour traffic. She looks out through the wire mesh at the lines of cars.

She is marched in a line with the others into the Marshals' office. The other women look like prostitutes who have overslept. Their clothes are outlandish, and they giggle like children caught playing dress-up. For a moment, the lawyer in Louisa wonders why they are there, wonders whether perhaps they ply their trade on federal property or something.

Louisa is told that she is to be arraigned at eleven before Magistrate Judge Ernest Lithgow, and they leave her to wait, once more, in the holding cell. She asks for a newspaper, and a young man says he will look for one, but he does not come back. She asks if she can telephone her daughter, and a woman says no.

The attorney, Joel Krasnowicz, arrives, breathlessly, at about ten. He is overweight and huffing and puffing, and when he opens his briefcase she can see through the screen that it is all jumbled in there, a notepad and a copy of the complaint and the other papers all higgledy-piggledy. She does not approve of this. But Krasnowicz has come highly recommended. He was in the D.C. public defender's office and was very successful, Toby said. Krasnowicz would not meet with Louisa until Toby delivered a check for five thousand dollars. Deputy United States Trade Representative or not, she is a criminal defendant, and lawyers don't work for people like her unless the money is paid up front.

The meeting has started badly with her first impression of him. It degenerates as he lectures her about how he can appear only for purposes of bail, given the retainer. Does she understand this? he asks her with painful deliberation, as though she were an idiot. She can only nod.

"Mark," he says—referring to the prosecutor, Mark Roth, though it comes out as "Mawk"—"must've been in a hurry."

"Why?"

"They arrested you on a complaint instead of direct indicting."

"I'm sorry, I don't understand."

"There's two ways to do this. You can arrest on a criminal complaint, or you can indict. On a complaint, they have to have a preliminary hearing—gives us a little chance to look at their evidence, which they don't like. They don't gotta do that with an indictment, except that it takes longer to get an indictment. You gotta go to the grand jury, bring in a witness or two, that kind of thing. You buy any plane tickets recently?"

"No. Why?"

"Sometimes they'll rush to complaint if they think you're about to leave town. Funny, doesn't seem likely here. You with a daughter and all. Why d'you think they were in such a hurry?"

An answer to the question would require that first disclosure in the relationship of trust which is supposed to exist between lawyer and client. She looks at him carefully through the wire mesh. He is a fat man, and the folds of his neck seem to overwhelm his shirt collar, drawing it in so that the collar points thrust outward like twin lances. A thread of rayon—something unnatural, anyway—runs away from his print tie, a loud filament trailing from a ghastly tie. The man has a gold bracelet on one wrist and a gold watch on the other. On his fingers are gold rings, a thick band on the ring finger with stones set around it, a smaller ring on each pinkie. A man with stones set into his wedding ring is to be her advocate?

Krasnowicz waits a moment for an answer, doesn't get one, and then begins to tell her about Sunday. There has been, he tells her, a long negotiation all through Sunday afternoon and Monday morning with the United States Attorney's office. Krasnowicz tells her triumphantly that he has secured their agreement to a pretrial recommendation of house arrest.

She will be "on the collar," as he puts it. His accent distresses her. "Collar" sounds like "cawlluh." "Pretroil," he says.

The collar is a unit they attach to your ankle. Then they wire your home. If you try to take it off, or if you leave, even to step outside for a moment, it sets off an alarm. She must wear this thing and be confined to the house. You cannot take it off or it triggers the alarm. You wear it to bed, to shower, at all times. Krasnowicz smiles at her through the mesh. He regards this as an achievement.

"You'll be able to take care of Isabel," he says.

He has used her daughter's first name as though he knows her and has a right to. The anger surges within her, anger at this obese stranger who makes himself familiar with her household. Louisa does not yet know that this is what happens to a criminal defendant: she becomes public property. Ranks of strangers—prosecutors, defense lawyers, probation officers, reporters—dig into everything about her, from her clothing to her marriage to her grades in high school to her daughter. They dig in and they gossip about it to the press and they write motions and briefs full of it and they stand up in public courtrooms and talk about it. It is unnerving, and it has started with Joel Krasnowicz.

This is a bad thing, this deteriorating relationship with her attorney. It is the snobbery again. Louisa is used to elegance, to cultured diplomats who resolve disputes in a certain mannered fashion. She has not been in a courtroom since law school and has not the slightest interest in nor empathy with those persons who frequent such places. There are no gold bracelets on the wrists of the men whose hands she shakes. She tells herself again that she does not like this Joel Krasnowicz.

His eyes seem too small, or maybe it is that his cheeks are too fat. The eyes nestle above the cheeks and mustache. He is waiting for her response, but she finds herself distracted by the folds of skin over his shirt collar, the points of the collars, the brown eyes over the fat cheeks, the little beads of perspiration at his hairline.

Krasnowicz smiles. He wants her to tell him that he has done well to secure such a plum as house arrest.

"Mr. Krasnowicz, I have no criminal record. I am a mother from Bethesda. There is no evidence of anything. I thought there was supposed to be a presumption of innocence. What about bail?"

His face falls, and then quickly recovers, adopting a look of condescension. "Louisa," he says, "you wouldn't"—*wunt*—"be here if there weren't evidence of something. Let's deal in the realm of the possible. If you want to litigate bail, we can do it. It will cost you another ten grand, and you will probably"—*probly*—"lose, but we can do it. It won't matter for today, anyway, because Lithgow doesn't have room on his calendar for an evidentiary hearing, and Mark"—*Mawk* again!—"isn't ready anyway. Today the options are incarceration or the collar. If you want, I can go in without an agreement and ask for bail, but . . ." He shrugs.

Louisa makes further mental notes. The prosecutor is "Mark"—her lawyer's buddy, apparently. The question of whether she is to be jailed will turn not on evidence, but on whether Judge Lithgow has room on his calendar, and whether "Mark" is ready. She wonders how much room Attorney Krasnowicz has on his own calendar today, but she does not ask.

" 'Mark' was ready to arrest me," she says. "He was ready to handcuff me in front of my neighbors. Isn't that ready enough?"

"Louisa," Krasnowicz says again, in the manner of a nurse with an hysterical patient. He shrugs. He's really not very interested in criticism of the system. He is here to take what bits and scraps the system offers. And right now the system is offering the collar.

The courtroom is a small one whose windows look out on the building's air shaft. It has only a handful of pews behind the enclosure, blond wood without ornament, the walls white and bare of decoration. Here the magistrate judge takes questions of bail. The little courtroom is packed with reporters. They spill out into the hall, and their chatter falls quiet when they see Louisa coming. In the corner of the last pew is a young woman no one notices. She would be recognized by the President of the United States, but neither the face nor the name of Smaug's Jill are familiar to the courthouse clan.

The marshals take a post by each of Louisa's shoulders, dwarfing her, and shepherd her along the corridor and into the courtroom. Looking past them she recognizes one or two of the television people among the three rows of spectators. She has not seen the morning newspaper. Where is Toby?

Not there. Louisa and Krasnowicz turn sideways, edging into the courtroom, bumping and jostling. Toby is not there. *Not there.* How could he . . . ? She sees Mac at the back of the room. He nods at her, and she can only turn back forward. Joel Krasnowicz has her sit at counsel table and then he steps a few feet over to the prosecutor's side. The room seems so tiny. She sits only a few feet from the clerk's desk. The bench is right above that. Next to the defense table is what looks like a stand for the witness, and it occurs to Louisa that if a witness testifies, she will be able to touch him.

Krasnowicz and the prosecutors chat, smiling. There are two dark suits from the U.S. Attorney's office, a man and a woman, and it appears that all of the lawyers are friends. Louisa hears something about one of Krasnowicz's clients, someone who "flipped." She gathers from the tenor of the conversation that this means the man agreed to incriminate someone else in exchange for a favorable sentence. "Oh yeah, Charlie had big ones," Krasnowicz says, and the lawyers laugh together. Ha ha. Charlie had big ones. Louisa sits in silence, thinking that she is to be arraigned before a United States magistrate judge, and her attorney, to whom she has paid five thousand dollars, is guffawing with the enemy, in the manner of boys in the junior-high locker room.

Louisa gets to her feet and says "Not guilty" when the clerk asks her how she pleads. She wanted it to sound more resolute, more forceful, more disgusted, for her anger has grown with the interminable recitation of the charges. But power drains from her the instant she takes her feet, and her voice sounds tinny and halting. The major charges, Krasnowicz warned her, were the two counts of 18 United States Code, section 201(b). "That the Defendant Louisa Catherine Shidler, being a public official, did directly and corruptly receive, in separate installments in July and October 1993, the total sum of approximately fifty million dollars in return for being influenced in the performance of an official act, to wit, execution of a certain rider to the 1992 Pharmaceutical Trade Agreement," the clerk reads out. But there are other counts: unlawful and secret acts as an agent of a foreign principal; conspiracy to defraud the United States; wire fraud in foreign commerce, money laundering. Money laundering! Her head spins with it.

Then an FBI agent is sworn and begins to summarize the evidence against her. It is the black one again: she recognizes him from the arrest. He says his name is Eugene Phillips.

Phillips is smooth. When the assistant United States Attorney asks him questions, he turns and answers directly to the judge. The bank statements, he says, show that a numbered account was opened at Duclos & Bernard on May 17, 1993, a day she was in Geneva, in the amount of 600 Swiss francs. Into that account a total of $50 million worth of Swiss francs was wired in separate transactions in July and October. They have a witness who says she took the bribe to arrange for an about-face on the United States position on the pharmaceuticals deal that summer. She made the deal in Paris, and it meant more than $10 billion in sales of French products in the United States. The drafts of the accords show the about-face in her position at the time the funds were deposited.

Louisa is no trial lawyer, but isn't this all inadmissible? Isn't it all that some undisclosed informant has told some FBI agent thus and such, and that this or that inference can be drawn from this or that document? "Isn't this hearsay?" she whispers to Krasnowicz.

"It all comes in at this stage," Krasnowicz whispers back.

"Who is this witness? This person they have?"

He shushes her. What is the point of "this stage"? she asks herself. It is all hearsay, you can't test it, and they are going to put the collar on her anyway, so what is the point? Is the point so that the press will have something damning to say? She turns and looks at them, seated in ranks behind her. They are scribbling intently.

"What do we say?" she leans over, pressing Krasnowicz again. "None of this is true."

He shushes her again. "We don't say anything."

Why? Why don't we say anything?

Mark Roth finishes with Agent Phillips, and Krasnowicz gets up to ask a few questions. It sounds perfunctory and disorganized; trifling details about the bank statements, and Lithgow looks sourly down from the bench, as if to say, "Mr. Krasnowicz, would you kindly finish this little pantomime so that I can get on with my finding of probable cause?" Krasnowicz seems to get the message. He sits down.

Now the agent has resumed his seat in the gallery, and Roth is making his recommendation to Lithgow. "Mr. Roth," the judge calls him. Mr. Roth says that the charges are serious. They could result in a fifteen-year sentence. (Fifteen years! Lord, Krasnowicz didn't say that!) Roth goes on about the serious breach of the public trust at issue in this case. Everyone is talking about Louisa as though she were not present. Although the defendant has no prior criminal record, the seriousness of the charge, the sophistication of the defendant, the defendant's contacts abroad and access to foreign funds, creates, in the government's view, a serious risk of flight, Roth says. The defendant this, the defendant that, the defendant the other thing.

He comes to the point. Accordingly the government is recommending that the defendant be fitted with a monitoring device and confined to her home pending trial.

"Mr. Krasnowicz?" Lithgow says.

"Your Honor, I have had an opportunity to review the recommendation with my client this morning—"

"Has the defendant had sufficient time to consider the recommendation?" Lithgow interrupts.

No, Louisa is thinking. Of course not.

"Yes, Your Honor," Krasnowicz answers. "The defendant joins in the government's recommendation."

The lawyers and the judge discuss dates for a pretrial conference. Louisa listens silently. It all turns, again, on Mark Roth's schedule, and Joel Krasnowicz's. No one asks Louisa about *her* schedule.

A half hour later, the little courtroom has cleared. The marshals have led Louisa back to the lockup, there to rejoin Joel Krasnowicz. Judge and clerk have hurried back to their burrows. The prosecutors, the agents, the press, have returned to the elevator lobby. The mob of press: vanished. Even the young woman in the corner is gone. But two people remain in the courtroom.

Henry MacPherson has been watching Agent Phillips for some time now, for the face was vaguely familiar to him the moment MacPherson entered the courtroom, and he grew sure when he heard the man's voice on the stand. Mac has been puzzling it out since they took Louisa away. The agent's age is unclear: he is a middle-aged black man whose hair, flecked in gray, receding, august even, seems at odds with the youthfulness of his face. You might guess late forties, or early fifties, and he has the un-ruffled look of a man whose job brings few surprises. His shoulders hunch over the small yellow spiral notebook in which he has been writing, de-liberately and unhurriedly, for some minutes. He wears a tweed jacket and a red tie.

He continues writing, oblivious to the fact that he is being watched, until Mac says, "Gene Phillips?"

The man looks up. "Yeah?"

"Henry MacPherson, *Washington Herald*. Been a long time."

Phillips's face betrays no recognition.

"Gambelli and Tillotsen, remember? Coke trafficking in Pensacola? The congressional aides?"

Phillips shakes his head, and then catches himself. It has been a long, long time since he thought of that file. "Oh, yeah, guy with the glass eye, right?"

"Tony Tillotsen, that was him. I covered that case."

Phillips cannot place Mac's face, but has a vague memory of a prying reporter who kept calling him at home. He shrugs, finally, and extends a hand. MacPherson sits next to the agent. "So, this your case?"

"This your story?" Phillips answers, still writing in the notebook.

"Yeah, we're covering it, but it's mainly personal. I know Shidler pretty well. Years ago she worked for me."

Phillips turns over a page. "Do tell."

"Hey, Gene, I'm not here to give a statement. She had some talent, but I couldn't persuade her to stay out of law school."

"Looks like you should have. Might have kept her honest."

"Oh, she's honest," Mac says.

A few minutes later, they walk together toward the elevators through an empty corridor, and their shoes squeak off the highly polished tile. Phillips doesn't seem to be in a hurry.

"Gene," Mac asks, "how old are you?"

"Fifty-two."

"Well, I'm fifty-six years old myself. Suppose I asked you for a list of honest people."

"Don't follow."

"People to whose honesty you would swear. People you've known. Absolutely incapable of dishonesty."

"Well, suppose you did." *Squelch, squelch,* go the shoes on the waxed floor.

"Know any?"

"Not too many in this building."

They chuckle together. "How many make your list? Absolute certainties. You'd vouch for their honesty against any claim, no matter how strong the claim looked, because you know that they are incapable of dishonesty. How many?"

The two men come to the corner of the corridor and into the lobby by the elevators. Phillips pushes the button.

"I don't know. Five?"

"Yeah, five's about right. About what I'd have."

When the elevator arrives it is crowded, and the two men squeeze into it, riding to the ground in stiff corporate silence. They emerge into the jostle of the courthouse lobby.

Phillips says, "Funny question."

"What?"

"The list."

Mac nods. His expression is not an advocate's, not at all. It is rather that of a man who is genuinely confused, genuinely uncertain, like a spectator watching the kind of speed chess in which hands bang the timepiece before one can even register the move on the chessboard. "I asked because I agree with you. I only know five or so. And she's one of them, Gene."

Mac shakes the agent's hand and wishes him a good day. As he heads for the door, he leaves Eugene Phillips standing in the midst of the rush of lawyers and clients, witnesses and families, staring at his notebook.

Phillips remains behind for a few minutes. He has been a little un-comfortable about this assignment. He is what they call a brick agent, and this is a paper case. It is high-profile: public corruption involving a fairly senior official. It will require tracing international funds, and it includes a staggeringly big bribe, one that dwarfs by many orders of magnitude any-thing he has ever heard of. It is the kind of case he wanted for all those years in the seventies and eighties, the early years they had him doing Pan-thers undercover, and the years and years after that of street-corner heroin buys in drug cases.

For all of those years, Gene Phillips wanted this kind of case and didn't get it. Now, with retirement in sight, they've put him on one. He has grown more than a little cynical, and he's not betting there's a good rea-son this has happened.

Because, despite what most people think, J. Edgar Hoover didn't really die back in '72. You had to walk under his name every time you en-tered that monstrosity of a building, and the white boys continued to get the best assignments, just as they did in the old days. The white boys and girls got the paper cases and the public corruption cases and the bank frauds, while the black boys and girls—such few of us as there were at all, Phillips thinks—why, we seemed to get nothing but drugs. Undercover buys where you were never quite sure of your backup, doing deals on street corners and in the backs of Lincoln Continentals with crazy, jacked-up paranoiacs armed to the teeth.

The bureau didn't have a better brick agent, not one better at reading a man in the street, at pushing him to that zone beyond incrimination. That's what they told him, back in the days when he fought it openly. It was true, after a fashion, but somehow being good at what he did never kept a white man from being promoted to do something else.

So the agent who has judged character at sight for almost thirty years reflects on the strange encounter with the newspaperman. For Mac has touched the right chord. When Jim Fitch, the deputy FBI director, called Phillips to make the case, Phillips had doubts; and when Fitch sent a spe-cial team to do the search, he felt more disquiet. The morning of the ar-rest, when Phillips first saw Shidler standing in the foyer in her T-shirt blinking sleep from her eyes, the doubts returned. This morning, up in the courtroom, the doubts were back. Even as Gene Phillips played the mag-istrate like a fiddle, he began to mistrust the tune.

But the fact is that Eugene Phillips has doubts about most things: de-fendants, judges, lawyers, the bureau, the press. He goes into the canteen to get a cup of coffee. Only three years till my pension, he is thinking, as he stirs in the creamer. Not so long. Not so long at all.

Upstairs, things have gone from bad to worse. Lithgow has adopted the government's recommendation, of course. Whatever was the point of this silly five-thousand-dollar exercise, Louisa is left to wonder afterward. And to crown it, to let her know how utterly preposterous and false it was, they can't fit her with the collar today. Jim Ferarro, the probation officer, is busy. Krasnowicz explains sorrowfully to Louisa that wiring the house for the collar is a two-to-three-hour job, a "pain in the ass," he puts it, and "Jimmy" is on another case. Jimmy doesn't have time to fit the collar this afternoon. Ferraro isn't sick, or testifying in front of Judge Duncan; he hasn't been called to the bedside of a dying aunt. He's just busy. Louisa is to spend another night in prison because Ferraro hasn't got time to fit the collar.

This is when she loses her temper with Krasnowicz. "A 'pain in the ass'! A 'pain in the ass' is what you call it, Mr. Krasnowicz? I am to be jailed because it is a 'pain in the ass' for some probation officer to do his job? Mr. Krasnowicz, I suggest that you go out there and find another probation officer! Or perhaps a judge to instruct him. Did we have an agreement with your friend Mark or did we not?"

He tries to interrupt but she cuts him off. When the Koreans cheated on the semiconductor accord she turned on their senior trade representative, a man who looked twice her age and, so she was told later, was a second cousin of the president, and let him have it with words the translators wouldn't translate. You work hard to hammer out a deal, and nothing infuriates Louisa like a welsher. She let the Korean senior trade rep have it in front of fifty diplomats and a half dozen interpreters, and she certainly is not going to sit still to see her own deal welshed on by a probation officer. "My agreement was for the collar, not for incarceration, not a single further night of it! Go out there and fix this problem!"

But he won't. He can't, he says. It won't work. The judge won't do it. The judge will take Jimmy's side.

"And forget due process, forget an agreement with the United States Attorney, forget all of that? The world has to screech to a halt because some probation officer named Ferraro is *busy*? All right, Mr. Krasnowicz, you are the lawyer, and I am the client. Here are your instructions. Go back to your office and place two telephone calls. The first is to Attorney Roth. You tell him that you are shocked that the United States Attorney's office is in breach of your agreement. You tell him that no one told you this Ferraro would be too busy this afternoon, or you would have asked for, and obtained, a court order that the monitor be attached today. You tell him these people could conduct an investigation and obtain a complaint and arrange for an arrest in one week and you will not accept, not for one moment, some pusillanimous, backsliding excuse from a *probation officer*—"

"Louisa—"

"Be quiet, Mr. Krasnowicz, I'm talking. You tell him, and you use these words, sir, you tell him that he, this Mark, has no big ones, no big ones at all, if he can be made a fool of by a probation officer, and you intend to advise the criminal legal fraternity of that posthaste. I want you to say it precisely as I have said it, because it is on that level that you people communicate, apparently. Is that clear?"

Krasnowicz fiddles with his tie, waiting for her to be done.

"You tell him your entire opinion of him has changed and that you cannot believe a man of any character would submit to this. You tell him that you will file an emergency motion for rehearing and sanctions at three o'clock today if this matter is not sorted out—"

"Louisa—"

"Shush! You have taken my retainer. You have appeared for me. I am giving you instructions. You will make that call. You will then place your second call to Roger Goldman at Latham and Watkins. As my agent, you will tell Mr. Goldman that I would like to retain a competent lawyer to represent me, one who is not intimidated by probation officers, and I would like him here at two o'clock—"

"Louisa—"

"Those are your instructions, Mr. Krasnowicz! Now get going!"

He leaves. The only thing Louisa knows about Roger Goldman, a name she's heard mentioned in the Senate Banking Committee's televised hearings on the Ventura Securities scandal, is that she cannot possibly afford him. Fortunately, it proves unnecessary. They find Ferraro—a little ferret-eyed man, whose ears seem too big for his head, and who wears a shiny suit and some kind of incongruous orthopedic shoes. He keeps her waiting all afternoon while the house is being wired for her electronic confinement. At last Ferraro spends fifteen minutes sulking while affixing the monitor to her ankle. At half past five, she is released.

"You owe me one," he says, as Louisa is leaving the probation office.

But she is still angry, and she whirls on him. "Mr. Ferraro, I owe you nothing. You owe me compliance with court-approved agreements, sir. You will find that I keep my bargains!"

Oddly, as it will happen, he will not.

"Call me when you get home," Ferraro answers, more a mouse than a ferret now. "Call me within an hour."

CHAPTER 9

Oh, Toby, she will think, why must this night go so badly, like all the others? Why couldn't we retreat, even for an hour, to the past, in the midst of this nightmare?

When he arrives, he says he is going to stay at the house. That should be interesting. Which of us gets the couch? He paces from the kitchen to the living room; he remembers a telephone call that he needs to return and that, it seems to Louisa, he prolongs. He won't stop, he won't hold her, he won't even sit by her.

Her estranged husband comes back to the room and begins, without even looking at her, "Louisa, this is a problem. I mean this is a—"

"*This* is not a problem, Toby. *I* am a problem. That is what you are saying."

He hates it when she tells him what he is saying.

"They want my resignation."

"And they want *my* confession. Look what a bother I am to you."

Sometimes she can't quite keep the scorn from her voice. Louisa can see—could always see—through Toby, always except when she chose not to. His presence at the house this night is not animated by love, not even by the better sort of duty, but by naked compulsion. He's there so that whoever was on the phone will think he is doing the right thing.

Toby has a post in the office of the White House counsel, more a political than a legal job. The job means more to him than the marriage ever did, and now the marriage may be the end of it. So Louisa wouldn't have minded the knowledge that Toby was only pretending. It would have been enough for her to fancy that it was for love, even an old and immature one. Why couldn't they just sit and hold each other on the sofa, listening to the night sounds, the tick-tock of the mantel clock, Isabel's occasional stirring upstairs, the buzz from the fluorescent light over the sink in the kitchen? Why couldn't he play with her hair and softly stroke the back of her neck, and lie to her, tell her that he loved her?

Now when Louisa thinks of how handsome Toby is, it is with a physician's emotional detachment. "Well-developed male presents with symptomology of delayed maturity of unknown etiology." He is dark, like Isabel, with the features of a film actor: dark eyes, dark hair as thick as his daughter's, perfect white teeth, and a sexy shadow across his cheeks, even when he is freshly shaven. If she had a nickel for every time a friend had whispered, breathlessly, "He's such a hunk!" she could have retired long ago.

But the handsomeness, and a certain social wit, and a way of standing, and looking, and sending out these flirtatious waves—that is the beginning and pretty much the end with Toby. He is a lovely pool, but a shallow one.

He returns to the kitchen and makes another phone call. For some reason, Louisa's mind goes back to the night he proposed. She was, at the time, infatuated with him. Never had she strolled along a city street with so dashing a man before; never in Durham, never in Washington, and she experienced the intoxication of a schoolgirl as she suddenly found, at twenty-three years, the feeling of being a princess, of being the one people watch. When they walked, it was as though they made a wake upon dry land, a wake of turning heads. There had been no dramatic change in her appearance, of course: she was still a Renoir girl, the sort of dairymaid who looks as though she has just collected a blue ribbon for showing her prize horse at the county fair. But when she was with him they were a couple, and that dizzy, absolutely novel sensation had captured her on the night when he asked her to marry.

It was over dinner, in a small Italian restaurant in Georgetown called Francesca's. He was wearing his heather Harris tweed, a jacket she loves, rich and complex in color, of wonderful texture, and they laughed about the antics of a classmate in Hayes's secured transactions class. Toby had the waiter bring a special dessert—there was a lot of nervous whispering among the wait staff about it, and at last it arrived on a tray, beneath a silver cover. Louisa was surprised to see dessert arrive with such a flourish. She had not guessed his plan, perhaps because even at that moment the prudent side of her, the calculating side, never imagined that she would long content this man. When the waiter lifted the cover, there on the platter, on a little cushion of blue velvet, was a ring. He had even arranged for a violinist to arrive at that moment, and a tubby waitress with iron-gray hair wiped away tears with a handkerchief as Louisa told Toby that she would be his wife.

Later, as they walked along Wisconsin Avenue toward his apartment, she chided herself for failing to feel giddy. She had accepted Toby's proposal of marriage, but was unable to transport herself. And even, perhaps especially, during their prodigious lovemaking that night, her mind was at work, calculating, and a small, hard-edged, farmer's voice was saying that it was a mistake.

Toby is as nervous as an ant on a hot stove. He alights briefly at the mantelpiece, but he cannot look at her while he is suggesting that maybe Isabel should stay with him until all of this "settles down." His eyes stray to the living-room window.

Damn it, Louisa thinks, look at me! It will not settle down anytime soon. He knows that. Besides, with this house arrest, it looks as if for once she can be a full-time care-giver. Oh, yes, Bridget quit this morning, too. Louisa's voice is taking on a sarcastic tone that she regrets even as the words cross her lips, but she has grown too tired to disguise the deeper frustrations.

"What are you really saying, Toby?"

"Louisa—"

"No, what are you really saying? Never mind that I am, I am in the middle of this, this nightmare, what you're really saying is, once again, this marriage is a real damned inconvenience to you—"

"Louisa!"

"Isn't it! Isn't that what you're saying?"

He relents, and departs at about ten. Isabel will stay with Louisa "for the time being." It makes Louisa grind her teeth even to think of her "victory" on that point, for all it signifies is her husband's insufficient spine: enough to anger you, but never enough to stand the response. Besides, it has probably occurred to him that it will be easier to get laid without a twelve-year-old around. Louisa thinks, sometimes, that his capacity for long-term commitment is set by the time it takes his testes to manufacture a unit of sperm.

The sound of his car has faded away, and it grows quiet again. Louisa realizes that she has been nothing but bitchy since morning—bitchy with Krasnowicz, with Ferraro, with Toby—and so she climbs the stairs and raps gently on Isabel's door and asks if she can come in. They sit together on the little-girl bed in the Laura Ashley room, the little-girl room that is stretching its elbows with adolescent rebellion, so that posters of rock stars leer at the ranks of teddy bears on the dresser. It feels reassuring to be there, as if no real harm can come to a person in such a refuge of pillows and frilly comforters. They sit together on the bed with legs crossed, and Isabel listens while Louisa tells her what has happened.

"Why would he betray you like that, Mother?"

"I don't know, Isabel. I suppose it was too much money for him to resist, and I was the obvious cover."

"That's a disgrace."

Louisa smiles a little bit. There is at least one person in Washington who equates betrayal with disgrace, and who believes, without a glimmer of doubt, that Louisa is guiltless in this.

The telephone call goes badly. How do you tell your parents that you've been arrested and charged with betraying the nation? Louisa's mother sobs and has to break away. Her father says nothing at all.

This is like them. Emily Fielding Shidler is prone to mood swings. No one is more fun at a party, and no one can become more hysterical over a default notice. John Shidler is quite her perfect opposite. His first reaction to adversity is almost always like his first reaction to a joke: silence. When Louisa was ten, the family lost almost the entire corn crop in the drought, and the very next summer, when she was eleven, was the summer of the weevil infestation. They lost about half the crop, and because of a surplus from the Midwest, prices were lower. Only when she was much older did she discover how close they had come to foreclosure. Emily shut herself in her room for what seemed like days on end, while John was in the fields. At night, he would sit at the kitchen table with a pencil and a spiral notebook, figuring. He'd figure the grain prices and the fertilizer costs and the interest payments. Every so often he'd turn the pencil in a little finger-held sharpener and then he'd brush the shavings into a pile and then go back to his figures. His face didn't show any expression at all, and somehow when he was done with the pencil he'd devised a plan to sell the road forty (always with an option to repurchase) or pledge the alfalfa field or something to the bank, or sell the combine and rent Gaddy Nelson's, and he'd worked his way through it.

John Shidler is short and wiry—Louisa wishes she could be so wiry—and he has to cinch his belt to the last notch to keep his trousers up, but he has uncommonly big hands. Many are the times she has seen her mother or her brother Will unable to open a jar or loosen a rusted nut, and John could always do it easily.

He'd always wanted Louisa to come back and run the farm for him. He knew from early on that his eldest, Will, who is a banker in Winston-

Salem now, wasn't cut out for farming. "See how Will mows that field," he said to Louisa once, as they stood together on the bluff where the dirt track comes down to the river field. "Look how he'll miss a little sliver of grass as he comes around." They were watching Will turn loops on the tractor, pulling the old rust-colored mower behind. Wisps of grass popped up after the mower passed. "You can see, he's in such a hurry to get that field done, he's calculating how few laps he can do. He's thinking about where he'd rather be. Like his mother." He shook his head. And then he turned and trudged on up the red-clay road toward the tractor barn.

The farm means a lot in the Shidler family: nine hundred and eighty rich acres along the Yadkin. In 1876, Louisa's great grandfather Wilhelm Shidler moved out from Salem and bought a hundred acres, the river field and what they called the live-oak field, when Louisa was a girl. Wilhelm and his eldest son, Louisa's granddaddy Otto Shidler, prospered as tobacco farmers, growing the rich blue-green leaf in the red-clay soil of the Piedmont, selling it by the bushel to the Reynolds company down in Winston, and buying up adjacent fields as less industrious farmers moved off. By the time John Shidler took over the farm in 1954, it had reached its present size, and Otto Shidler was one of the prominent farmers in the county. The winter Louisa was eight, Granddaddy Shidler died of lung cancer. That spring John plowed the fields under and put them all into corn and soybeans. "There's less work in corn," he used to say, "and corn never killed a man." There is less work in corn, but there's a lot more money in tobacco. And during the sixties and seventies there was a lot more market reliability, too. Louisa's father had some close calls keeping the farm. But he never planted tobacco again.

Louisa holds the telephone tightly, guessing what her father is thinking. All of this Washington lawyering, all of this consorting with lawyers and bankers and diplomats and other such fancy people, has been her undoing. There is not a great distinction, for her father, in whether she took a bribe, or whether she has been scapegoated by associates. It all comes of the same thing: going to work in a world where success is measured against human beings, instead of the seasons and the soil.

"You ought to farm, Louisa," he said to her when she came home for the summer after her freshman year at Duke. "You ought to do it. You got the orneriness for it, you got the self-reliance, and you see a job through. That's it, mainly, and studying up on your crops, not buying what you can fix or borrow from your neighbors. You ought to do it. Farm's been in the family three generations." And when she turned away or tried to change the subject, he'd say, "Louisa, the thing of farming is that there ain't too much other people can do to you. Mostly a farmer's in his own hands, and God's. You can trust both of those, long as you're patient. You can trust a cow or a corn crop or a hay rake to do like it should, and you can trust the good Lord, long as you're patient and got a sense of humor. But other people, no trusting what they'll do to you."

But she hadn't listened. She had gone up the drive to the mailbox on the Yadkinville Road, and put in it the application to the Georgetown Law Center, and raised the flag. And she went off to law school and to Washington and she married into politics and led a life her father couldn't understand. And now it has come to this. He lets her do the talking, and so she sits in her kitchen, telling him that she will get a good lawyer, that she is being scapegoated for something political, and that it will all come out all right. He doesn't say much, but Louisa can tell he is thinking that her reassurances all sound like things that will depend on other people.

"Tell me what happened at the arraignment," demands the voice in the darkness, even before Jill is awake to answer it. Not "Hello," not "Sorry to call at this hour." Just the demand for information. What happened at the arraignment?

Poor Jill. She is still shaking, startled from sleep by the ring of her phone. She stares at the little blue digits on the clock radio. "It was routine," she says. "They read out the charges. An FBI agent named Phillips gave a little background."

"Anything about Royall?"

"No."

"Did Shidler speak? Her lawyer? Anything said about Royall at all, about Shidler working for him?"

"No. Nothing. The FBI agent talked about her getting a bribe, and then the judge set a date for a conference. That was it."

"Nothing at all about Royall or the campaign?"

"No."

"What do the first editions say?"

Jill bites her lip. It's 1:49 in the morning. Is she supposed to go out and find the early editions on a newsstand somewhere? Yes, she is.

"Get them," Smaug says. "Get them and call me back."

In Bethesda, Louisa remains in her living room through the night. Sleep still will not come. She is thinking of Toby again. He had an affair with a White House aide several years ago. Louisa met her at a party—

before the affair, as far as she could gather later—and she seemed to Louisa very Jewish: New York City sophisticated, very brassy, confident, loud, and terribly smart. She was so put together—her hair, her nails, her face, her body—and Louisa felt old and dowdy and very unlike everything this young woman was. When she deduced the affair, some months later, she went through a period of near despair, a manic time when she swung between depression and a forced and unlovely giddiness. And then she tried to get him back. She would lie in the darkness, naked beneath the bedcovers, waiting for the sound of the car in the drive, of the key in the kitchen-door lock, of the little creaking the banister made under a man's grasp. Her eyes shut, feigning sleep, she would listen for his breath, sense his smell, thinking that if, just once, he might take note of her, become excited by her, run his hand across her flank and pull her toward him, then they could manage all the rest of it. If his toe might brush, even accidentally, across her calf, and if it might return again . . . but it never did. He would slip silently into the bed, clinging to its edge, and in minutes be asleep.

Now, on the couch, she wants to see him; she wants to think of him not as he was a few hours ago, but as she remembers him from years before. Louisa hunts through all of the shelves to see if maybe they've left one, just one of the photo albums. But they have taken every single one. So she wanders through the house and gathers all of the framed photographs of him, the ones in Isabel's room and the one that she has never been able to remove from the silver frame on the bedside table, and the one on the fridge that shows him mugging with her at the National Zoo.

She concentrates on the photographs. There it is in all of them, his I'm-gorgeous-and-I-know-it grin. If he'd shown any grief when they had separated, even a little, even one night of it, she might feel better, somehow. Feel better about the decision to marry, better about the marriage, more accepting of its failure. But he remained utterly in control. He showed about as much emotion as a traffic cop writing a ticket. He never cried. And if she'd been the one to have an affair, would he even have cared? Would he have asked for her lover's name? If she had written a book about it, would he have read it?

She sits with the small collection of photographs left to her and stares at them under the pale illumination of the living room lamp until the lamplight has faded into the gray of dawn.

And then it is Tuesday morning, an absurdly sunny September morning, a morning like a day in May. For one brief moment, it might all have been a bad dream, the past forty-eight hours. For there are no FBI agents, no probation officers, no defense lawyers with bits of filament trailing from their ties, no jostling newspaper reporters; there is no Toby. Nothing at all greets Louisa but quiet, and sunshine, and the morning routine: get Isabel up, pour the water into Mr. Coffee, get the breakfast going. She stretches, slides her feet to the floor, and then stares for a stupid moment at the strip of plastic around her ankle.

Two things arrive that day, both of them hand deliveries. At four o'clock, Isabel comes home from school with a letter. It is from Amanda Crane's mother, and Louisa opens it to discover that Sheila Crane has re-voked Isabel's invitation to Amanda's birthday party on Saturday night. "All things considered, I think this will be for the best," the note says.

Louisa shakes her head.

"What is it?" Isabel asks, suspiciously.

"Oh, Isabel," Louisa says, "the silly woman doesn't want you at Amanda's birthday party, because your mother is an undesirable."

Isabel's face clouds and her eyes begin to well, but it is with anger, not disappointment. "That is *so* lame," she says, and she is trying to summon up something biting, but it will not come. "That, that . . ."

"Was there more of this sort of thing at school?"

"No, Mother, nobody said anything, really."

"Are you okay?"

"Course I'm okay." Isabel strives to change the subject, and squats by her mother's ankle. "Does that thing hurt?" She examines the collar pro-fessionally.

"Don't pull at it, Izzy. I don't know what might set it off."

"Awfully *stupid,* if you ask me," she says, on her way to the kitchen.

The other delivery had come earlier, before Isabel's return from school. When Louisa tore it open, she felt relief to discover that its con-tents, an odd assortment of items, appeared innocent. She examined the three books and the scrap of newspaper Mac had written on. One of them was a legal thriller, another the Collected Works of Yeats, the third an autobiography of Vinson Adams, the war correspondent. And there was a note, handwritten in a black marker in a close script on a sheet torn from the *Herald*. She read:

> *Sorry to here about your troubles. I'm sure things not as they look.*
> *Enclosures perhaps of some help: Yeats ever a solace, Adams a lousy*
> *reporter but what a writer! The thriller may kill a few hours.*
>
> *Best, Mac*

Now Louisa looks at the books again, paging through them to see if there is a note hidden in the margins, but there is none. Hmm, she thinks, dear old Mac. The legal thriller—something about a mortgage, a misprint—she decides she will get to that later. Yeats is lovely but she already has his collected works. Didn't they used to talk about Yeats? Didn't she tell Mac she'd written her undergraduate thesis on Yeats when, one night over a glass of bourbon, he recited "When you are old, and full of sleep" to her?

"What's that?"

It is Isabel, returning from the kitchen with an apple, and with the child's sixth sense for the arrival of a package. Louisa tells her that Uncle Mac has sent some books. They sit together for a moment, the silence broken only by the crunch of Isabel's apple, until Isabel snorts.

"I thought he was the publisher of the *Washington Herald,* or something."

"Managing editor."

"Well, he can't even *spell.*"

" 'Here' for 'hear,' yes, I saw that," Louisa says, paging through the Yeats.

Isabel's remark brings her up short. He *can* spell. No one spells better. For a moment she calls to mind old tirades from the managing editor. "You cannot use a word unless you know it, and if you cannot spell it, you do not know it!" he used to holler whenever he saw a misspelling in the copy. "A man who misspells a word commits an assault upon the English language!"

Louisa remains silent, the memory of Mac's rantings against poor usage reverberating in her head, and then she looks at the note again. This note is wrong, all wrong. Mac types notes, he doesn't write them. And then, as she rereads it, she remember what he used to say to his young reporters about Vinson Adams. He used to hold Adams up as a model. "Read this!" he'd say, handing them a pile of old stories from Adams's tours in Iran and Vietnam or the presidential campaigns of the fifties and sixties. "Read this and what do you see? Not Pulitzers, not self-conscious writing, not even good writing! What you see, people, is reporting! News, facts, dates, times, people, quotes! And what would you see if you read the competition on the days of these stories? Nothing. Sweet fuck-all! Adams got the facts and he got them first. If Madame Nhu had bad gas after tea, this sonofabitch knew about it before Diem did. If Johnson made a deal with George Meany, Adams was under the table! The man was a reporter, the best there ever was!"

Everyone who ever worked for Mac remembered that speech. And what did the note say, no reporter but a *writer*? Mac has *contempt* for writers.

"All right, Isabel, what is the evidence?" Louisa asks. "A man who loves words misspells an ordinary one. He sends me one book he knows I have, and he writes that Adams, whom he venerated as a reporter, was 'no reporter.' "

"Mother," says Isabel, "look, he wrote, 'Things not as they look.' "

Louisa studies the note again. Things are not as they look. Mac has misspelled "hear," thus calling attention to the word "here." What is "here"? Literally, "here" is a page ripped from today's *Herald*. But it is not any page. Louisa chuckles as she notices, for the first time, the obvious: it is a page torn from the personals.

It takes her almost fifteen minutes to find the message, but that is because he has placed it in the section with which she has some trouble associating Mac. It is filed under "Men Seeking Men."

> OLD NEWSHOUND seeks European companion for
> one last adventure. Hefty bank account a must!
> You must be of good cheer and a faithful reader.
> Ref. 9024.

"Dear old Mac," she says, and for the first time in two weeks, she laughs out loud.

As September 24 fades into night, Louisa will drift off to sleep thinking of Mac, thinking, for the first time since she opened the letter in the lounge of the Willard Hotel, that perhaps, just perhaps, everything is going to work out all right. On that night, of all nights.

CHAPTER 10

Louisa, who can hear everything, Louisa who wakes four, five, a dozen times a night, she who has not slept soundly since before she was pregnant—she does not hear them. She does not sense a thing until a nightmare has melded seamlessly into wakefulness. Then, in the confusion of half sleep, blinding lights stab the darkness, and along her arms and legs the fingers are like C-clamps. Before she can summon a scream from her diaphragm, thick duct tape is across her mouth. She screams, but the sturdy, unyielding tape silences her, and the scream is choked off; the acrid taste of adhesive is on her tongue. She struggles, but the C-clamps tighten their grip on her limbs, and she can see nothing but the flood of white light in her eyes. Louisa's panic is animal. She would bite, she would claw and scratch, she would kill. She is terrified and enraged and she knows that she is going to die.

Where is Isabel? What will they do to Isabel?

There are three of them, three dark man-shapes in Louisa's bedroom, shadowy spelunkers with headlamps. One of the headlamps bores remorselessly in on her retinas. Behind it are two more playing over the room as the shapes move. When her struggling ceases, they raise her to the side of the bed and she can hear the thick tape as it is wound about her wrists behind her back. It hurts her shoulders. She hears a click and feels cold metal against her throat.

She can see nothing but the dark shapes beyond the blinding intensity of the headlamp, until the hands have hoisted her to her feet and are pushing her toward the door. She tries to break toward Isabel's room, but they push her roughly to the unlit stairwell.

Downstairs, the pairs of viselike hands guide Louisa into the darkened living room and seat her on the couch. Then the figures stand, three of them, forming a menacing huddle around her. The light from the center headlamp is still trained on her, but her pupils have adjusted now, and she can see the second man give a hand signal to the third, and then point upward. They wear dark gloves, dark body suits of some kind, and hoods.

"Louisa, you must be calm and listen very carefully to me," the one in the center says. It is the first speech, the first sound of any sort, she has heard from them. It is a quiet voice but authoritative, possibly that of a southerner. "I am about to give you very important instructions. I say it again. Very important instructions. Instructions that are vital to Isabel's safety. Do you understand? Signal by nodding."

It must be that the mention of her daughter's name has made Louisa hysterical again, because she is grunting against the duct tape, and her ears are filled with the sounds of the grunts and of panicked breathing through her nostrils, and maybe she has risen, for suddenly the C-clamps are on her arms again.

"Calm yourself and signal your understanding by nodding your head," the voice says.

The voice is calm, rational, clear. It is compelling. She realizes that she has heard it once before. Also in the night, also without warning. It was the voice on the telephone the morning of her arrest. Louisa nods to the man.

"Isabel is frightened but unharmed. She has been bound, as you have. She is upstairs, in her room. In a moment you will see her. Do you understand? Signal by nodding."

Louisa obeys, and the voice continues.

"Listen carefully. We are going to take Isabel with us. She will be safe, she will be fed, she will be protected, so long as you cooperate. I require utter, complete, unthinking obedience from you. If you comply, she will be safe. Do you understand? Signal by nodding."

Louisa does so, and now her vision is blurred by tears.

"Today you will announce that you wish to plead guilty to the charges that have been lodged against you. You will give the following account to the United States Attorney. You recall the Paris negotiations for the 1992 Pharmaceutical Trade Agreement. One morning during the May negotiations, you were approached by a man as you left your hotel. White, about thirty-five, dark hair, medium height, a small pair of sunglasses, wearing a light sports jacket and gray slacks. He knew your name and said his name was Edouard. He spoke English. The accent was difficult for you to place. You guessed it was European, but could not be sure. No last name, no announced affiliation. Was he from one of the French ministries, was he from Glaxo-Wellcome, from Smith Kline or Ciba-Geigy? You have no idea. He said he recalled you from a meeting several years ago. You did not recognize him. Five minutes, a passing greeting, nothing of substance was said, and you put it out of your mind. Do you understand?"

Louisa nods.

"Then you saw him again—you are not sure of the date, but you think it was a Saturday, which probably means May eighth—at the garden of the Tuilleries, at about eleven A.M. You had gone there to take a morning walk before an afternoon session. He appeared. You were surprised at first. You conversed. At first you exchanged pleasantries, trifles, nothing important. But by stages the conversation moved to the proposed pharmaceutical annex. He said it was of the highest importance to continued strong trade relations. Something like that. Do you understand? Signal by nodding once. Nod twice if you wish for me to repeat this."

But he does not need to repeat it, because they have woven this account from details that Louisa does remember. She did take the morning to walk in the Tuilleries, a lovely spring morning, although she walked alone and met no strange men. The calm voice goes on with the rest of the account. How Edouard outlined the arrangement as they sat on a park bench by the fountain. How Louisa was to open an account at Duclos & Bernard in the Geneva branch. She was to contact an attorney, Racine by name, to handle the arrangements. Edouard gave her an address, which she memorized. She would take a personal day to travel to Geneva when this round of negotiations was completed. She would take the morning train from the Gare du Nord, meet Racine in the afternoon at his office in Geneva. He would accompany her to the private bank, where she would deposit six hundred Swiss francs upon opening the account.

Here the voice pauses. "Six hundred Swiss francs to open the account. This is very important. It is essential to Isabel's well-being that you are correct as to these details." Another pause to let this remark sink in, another command that she acknowledges with a now docile nod. The voice proceeds. "You opened the account on the seventeenth of May 1993. A numbered account. You remember the date because you are sure it was the Monday after the first round of the Paris talks concluded. That was the fourteenth. You deposited six hundred Swiss francs. Racine assisted you with this. You met him at his office.

"Now you recall nothing save that the office was in the old quarter of Geneva, off a square, and you had to walk up several flights of stairs. You understand?"

She nods again, and he proceeds: Louisa opens the post office box in Washington, she receives bank statements and destroys them. Early in July

1993, a statement arrives that shows the deposit of thirty million Swiss francs. In September the talks resume, and she reverses her position.

This part is true. Louisa did reverse the American negotiating position during the September negotiations on the over-the-counter drug allotment. Because, she now recalls ruefully, Royall instructed her to do so.

"You receive, in October, a statement confirming payment of the balance: thirty million Swiss francs.

"Do you understand? Signal by nodding."

The disembodied voice from behind the halogen headlamp has fallen silent. The lecture will now shift its focus, slightly. Behind the leader, one of the man-shapes is in the kitchen. Louisa hears the sounds of some kind of physical labor, a quick whir like that of a drill, but somehow quieter, then another, then a clattering of small objects on the countertop.

The voice begins anew. "You did this," he says, "for two reasons. One, you expected that the rest of your career would be spent in public service. Your marriage was beginning to founder, and you did not know whether you could trust your husband to support you and your child in the manner that you insist you be supported. Two, you wished to ensure that the family farm be preserved at all costs. You knew that your father had had difficulty managing it, and as he grows older, you were afraid that it might be split up or sold. And finally, the position you were asked to take was one which you felt, in genuine good faith, was the right position on the merits. You did not believe that you were disserving the interests of American industry or your government. They offered the money. It seemed like a lot to you. There was no negotiation about it. You said yes.

"Now," he goes on, "you are sorry. You are sorry about this, although you know it is too late for that. You have not withdrawn any of the money. You have been uncertain as to how to deal with this problem.

"Do you understand?" he asks. "Acknowledge."

She nods.

"This is the statement you will give to the United States Attorney. You will express regret to your family, your friends, Ambassador Stillwell, and the United States. You will regret, particularly, any difficulty this revelation may cause the President and Mr. Stillwell at this time. You will say that you concealed this matter from him and that your shame is most acute because of your feeling that you have betrayed his trust. Acknowledge."

Louisa does so, nodding her head now for what seems the hundredth time under the glare of the headlamp, feeling small and powerless and insubstantial in her tattered cotton nightgown before this faceless lecturer, her shoulders now aching, her wrists sore from the chafing of the tape.

His hands signal to two of his companions, and they softly mount the stairs. When they return, one of them carries Isabel. She wears only one of her father's lacrosse jerseys and her underwear, and she is clutching something. They have bound and gagged her with the tape, and rage fills Louisa again when her interlocutor's headlamp swivels to illuminate the girl. She sees the width of her eyes. Her gangly legs, her T-shirt, her eyes, and something—what is it she is clutching to her chest in the darkness?

Buster. She is holding Buster.

In a moment Isabel is gone. Following another hand signal, two of the men slip softly outdoors with her. Louisa begins to sob.

"You must comply with every detail of the instructions. If you do so, Isabel will be returned to you unharmed. If you do not do so, or if you report her missing, or if you contact the authorities, or, indeed, if anyone discovers that she has been kidnapped, we abort this plan and revert to our contingency plan."

He pauses. His tone is matter-of-fact, businesslike, but he waits for her to raise her eyes, and when she does, he continues. "Under the contingency plan, only her body will be discovered. It will be found in a culvert, somewhere far from here, and it will be in such a condition as to make plausible the theory that she was abducted by a rapist and abused. Do you understand? Acknowledge."

Louisa is weeping now, gurgling sounds and sobs choked by the wretched tape, and tears stream from her eyes.

"Acknowledge!" he demands, and she nods her head, submissively.

"As necessary, you will permit it to be given out that you have concluded, in light of your unfortunate circumstances, that Isabel should spend some time away from Washington, with your parents, in North Carolina. You will advise her school of that in the morning. We will be listening, of course."

On he goes, with more detail to account for Isabel's absence, and Louisa is trying to listen, but she cannot suppress the sobs. She is to keep this secret from everyone: from Toby, from her parents, from her attorney.

"I want you to understand something," he says. "My people are professionals. They are not criminals. They harm her only on my orders. Whether she is to be treated like a hotel guest or eliminated will be up to you. In neither case will it be a matter of the slightest emotional interest to us."

Louisa has recovered her self-control and listens submissively. "Keep in mind that your telephone is monitored here. We have also installed listening devices throughout the house. If the recording devices are tampered with, if you fail to comply with instructions, if you attempt to do anything other than as you are instructed, we abort and pursue the contingency plan. When you have complied with instructions, Isabel will be returned to you.

"Thereafter, if there is any report, by you or her, of a kidnapping, or if any statement is made with respect to the subject of the account which is inconsistent with your guilty plea, we will find Isabel, and kill her. Do you understand? Acknowledge."

She acknowledges again. The halogen light is still in her eyes. The man waits, and it is just the light. "My associate," the man says at length, "has almost completed installing the listening devices. Now, as your obedience is vital to your daughter's well-being, do you wish for me to repeat the instructions?"

Louisa nods her head.

"That is very wise," he says.

They have been in her house for almost an hour when he is finished repeating them. With almost a gentle touch, he removes the tape from Louisa's wrists and mouth. Her eyes have finally adjusted to the light, at least a little, and she can see his hands as he folds the tape and tucks it into a zipper pocket on his breast. He says, softly, "Provided that your obedience is scrupulous, your daughter will be entirely safe. I give you my word on that. But if you violate the rules in even a minor particular, her life is forfeit. I give you my word on that as well. Now return to your bedroom. Do not watch from the windows as we depart."

"What about Toby?" Louisa asks, calmly now. "I can't keep my daughter's kidnapping secret from her father, can I?"

The halogen headlamp does not move, and the voice responds calmly. "Do not worry about Toby. Do precisely as we have told you."

He turns, but she says, "Wait." And then the light is in her eyes again. "She's going to need a bag."

They walk upstairs in single file. The dark man-shapes hover by and in the door, illuminating with their headlamps the closets and dresser as Louisa gathers a few items of clothing for Isabel, a pair of sneakers, underwear, blue jeans, and a sweatshirt, and puts them in her backpack. In her mind she is cataloguing the items, committing them to memory.

They descend the stairs and return to the living room. She stares resolutely at the silhouette. Most of all Louisa finds that she wants to see his eyes, this man who has taken her daughter, who assaulted her in her bed and who gives cold-blooded instructions. But the halogen headlamp continues to shine from his forehead, and she can see nothing where his eyes should be.

CHAPTER 11

At 10:30 A.M. local time, Wednesday, September 25, Henry MacPherson debarks from Swissair Flight 1042 at Geneva's Cointrin Airport. He runs the gauntlet of neon billboards for Chopard, Baume & Mercier, Patek, Swiss watches, Swiss jewelry, Swiss chocolate, finds his overnight bag, and passes through customs under the "Bienvenu à Genève" sign. The customs officer looks him over briefly, noticing only a wrinkled raincoat and the bleary eyes of an American businessman. He waves him through. Mac has slept fitfully on the flight over, and wants a shower and a nap, but first he places a call from a public telephone. He is in luck: the woman says that he can come in at three o'clock.

Outside, he finds the cab rank and tosses his bag into the rear seat. "Something near the station," he says.

The carillon rings out with its Wesleyan melody, and then the bell in the Cathedral of St. Pierre booms like a cannon three times, the sound echoing through the streets of the old town. It fades, and in the adjoining Place de la Taconnerie, the sparrows swarming in a linden tree resume their fierce debates. Perhaps they gossip about the rainstorm that threatens; perhaps about the white-haired man clutching a tourist map who passes by them, picking his way over the cobbles. He traverses the square, and pauses to reorient his street map and peer at one of the royal-blue street signs set high on the building walls at each corner. Apart from the sparrows and the clop of shoes on the stones, there is little other noise, as only foot traffic is permitted in most of the narrow streets of the Old Town. Mac looks up at the faded green of the cathedral's bronze spire. It shines with prestorm luminosity against the lowering sky. He turns the corner past a small tobacconist's shop and into a short street.

Around the corner, in the Place du Bourg-de-Four, near a popular café called La Clémence, he finds the address. It appears to be a respectable if not opulent row house of sober, stolid limestone construction. Centered in a dark, oaken door is a knob of polished brass, and beside the door are three brass plaques and a blackened spot on the limestone where one has been removed. "H. Racine, avocat" says the bottom one and, underneath that, "3ième ét." Mac looks at the sign and then up at the building. On the first and second floors, the shutters are thrown open inside the grillwork, and he thinks he can just hear a man talking on the telephone. The shutters are closed on the third floor. Mac pushes the door open.

In a few minutes, still catching his breath, he has given his name to a graying receptionist inside the third-floor office and taken a seat in the attorney's tiny waiting room. No noise from the square is audible here.

The door to the inner office opens at ten past three. A man in a dark green suit nods. Tall, slim, stooped, of indeterminate middle age, the Swiss attorney is rather like an old palm frond someone left in the hall closet during Holy Week, long and dry and curling at the edges, and in coloring more vegetable than animal. He is fair, his hair not so much blond as yellowing, and there is a sort of greenish-gray pall to his long face. Mac shakes the attorney's hand, which droops a little. "Thank you for seeing me on such short notice, Monsieur Racine," he says in English.

Racine inclines the head. Mac opens his money clip and withdraws ten one-hundred-franc notes. "Will this be sufficient for a consultation?" he asks. The attorney shows no expression as he watches Mac hand the bank notes to the receptionist.

A moment later, the door closed on his sanctum, the reedy man opens the shutters ten or twelve inches, looks out for a moment, and then returns to sit, expressionless, behind his desk. His long torso curling out above it, he stares across the desk at his new client with the bushy white hair.

"May I rely on your absolute discretion?" Mac asks him.

"Of course, Monsieur . . ."

"Smith."

"I'm sorry, I thought my receptionist, Madame Willenstein, has called you—"

"Yes, I know. But, for the sake of convenience, let us say Mr. Smith, Monsieur Racine. Let us merely say I speak for a principal and I seek advice on banking matters. I understand you have some experience in such matters?"

The attorney looks away to the window. "I have assisted clients from time to time in cases such as you describe." He speaks English fluently, if a little stiffly.

Monsieur Racine has seated Mac in an office about ten feet square, a cluttered, unlovely room. On inspection, it seems at one time to have been spacious, but in the recent past to have been bluntly partitioned, so that the moldings on the ceiling end in mid-pattern. Behind the desk, what is visible of a grand pair of floor-to-ceiling windows is gray with grime. Facing the window are inset bookshelves, but they, too, are dusty and cluttered. On the floor is a threadbare carpet. There is no artwork, nothing to soften the harsh appearance of the room. The desk is cheaply made, its back scuffed with footmarks, a corner showing where the veneer has peeled away. An ashtray spills over onto the desktop.

Mac looks through the narrow gap in the shutters. He can just see the two smoke deflectors on the chimney pots across the square. Outside, it looks darker. It will rain soon.

"How is it that you come to me?" Monsieur Racine asks, still looking at the window.

Mac waves off the question with a smile. "You were referred by someone who recommended you for discretion."

"You are American," the lawyer says, now looking back at him. "I have not many American clients."

"But some, surely? A few?" Mac grins. "Just the occasional one or two, Monsieur Racine?" He invites Racine to laugh, or even to smile, to revel conspiratorially and turn his eyes away to acknowledge that yes, he is a devil of a fellow. Racine's guard is up, and he does not yield to the visitor. Mac's expression hardens just a little. "Monsieur Racine," he says, "don't underestimate your reputation. It is international."

"Very well," says Monsieur Racine, without smiling. "What is your inquiry, please?"

"Well," Mac says, and expels a breath, "my principal wishes to safeguard a sum of money. A considerable sum of money. He wishes to establish an account."

"Then he is free to visit one of our city's many private banks," the attorney answers, with an expression indicating that Mac had better come to the point. He stands at the window, pushes the shutters open wider. Stray raindrops begin to pop against the stonework.

"For various personal reasons, my principal would prefer that this account not be associated with him directly."

"Our private banks are most discreet. It will be a numbered account, if he likes."

"Yes, but bank records . . ." Mac looks away and shakes his head. "Confidentiality is simply not what it was. Not even in your country."

Racine returns to his desk. "I see. Monsieur . . . Smith, this money your principal wishes to safeguard, it is of course the proceeds of legitimate activity?"

"Of course."

Polite smiles are exchanged. "Of course. As I imagined. Your principal is simply discreet, and wishes to avoid annoying scrutiny." Racine says this with perhaps a touch of irony. Outside, the rain begins to fall harder.

"That is precisely right, Monsieur Racine. Precisely right. Annoying scrutiny. Anyhow, I had heard that you are a creative attorney. That you can help clients find creative solutions to problems."

No reaction, as the lawyer remains impervious to any flattery. "Well, Monsieur Smith, perhaps. An account ordinarily is opened in the name of its owner." He swivels to one side and looks out the window at the buildings across the square. The patter of raindrops gives way to a steady drumbeat. Monsieur Racine's expression hardens and his eyes narrow. Softly, he says, "Schedule B formerly provided an alternative."

"Schedule B," Mac repeats.

"Yes, this is quite right. Schedule B was permitted under the Banking Secret."

"The Banking Secret?"

"Bank Secrecy Laws, you would say. Here in Geneva this is known, simply, as 'the Banking Secret.' It is this which obliges a private banker to maintain confidentiality. In the old days, one's agent opened the account. He identified the beneficiaries on Schedule B. But now Schedule B is not permitted."

"Ah. Then that is a problem for us."

A dull cast has come over the reedy man's eyes, as he looks out at the rain spattering his window. "This all depends. You see, it is not necessary that the beneficiaries of an account execute the account informations."

Silence inside, for a moment, as the men listen to the rain falling against the grillwork outside the window and thrumming against the windowpanes. "I don't understand," Mac says.

"Suppose, Monsieur Smith, your principal has children. He wishes the funds to be transferred to the children. For their well-being. But he does not wish the children to know of this. Not until they reach maturity, for fear they will squander the money. You see? The names are recorded as the beneficiaries of the account. But they do not know this, they have not signed this. Now, are the children really the beneficial owners of the account? No one knows except the father. There is no way to—comment-dit-on?—inspect? Their agent receives instructions in the name of these beneficiaries, he disburses the funds as directed. However the instructions direct. This is Swiss law. The owner may direct that withdrawals be made in favor of another."

Mac considers this. "So if a person were to establish the account and identify my principal as the beneficiary, and to give you a standard power of attorney and instructions, then you could disburse the funds to, to my principal?"

"To whomever I am directed per instructions. This is Swiss law, yes." Yes, of course this is Swiss law. Perfectly regular, the lawyer is assuring himself.

"I see," says Mac. "Very interesting. Tell me, when the account opens, Monsieur Racine, how will it be recorded by the bank?"

"By attorney such an one, as agent."

"As agent for the beneficiaries?"

"No, simply agent. Although the bank will have the informations, the"—he pauses, frowning, searching for the word—"the applications, you say?" Mac nods. Racine continues. "Identifying the beneficiaries. It lists them, their names. But they are not signing this. So far as Swiss law is concerned, it is as though they retain ownership of the corpus, and have simply delegated the power of its administration."

"Whom would you recommend as a . . . discreet bank?"

Racine pauses, shrugs, says, nonchalantly, "You may wish to investigate Duclos et Bernard. I have the forms here and can make the arrangements. The introductions. It is necessary to have an introduction."

Another polite exchange of smiles. One cannot simply walk into a Swiss bank: it would be like walking into someone's home. One needs the introductions.

"Duclos et Bernard, yes. Yes," Mac says, making notes for a moment, and then looking up. "Well, then, Monsieur Racine. I believe that my principal would like to go forward."

Racine rocks forward suddenly and begins to make notes.

"This is all right. Yes, very well, I shall open the account in the morning. Now, how much will you wish me to deposit into the account, Monsieur Smith?"

"Sixty million Swiss francs."

Racine stops writing. He stares, blankly, for a moment, at the page, and then looks up at Mac. Mac gives no hint, asking after a moment, "Is that acceptable?"

Racine is on the point of saying something, but he does not. He returns to the notepad, his fingers fidgeting. His hand steals away toward a desk drawer. He opens it and withdraws a package of cigarettes.

"Would you care for a cigarette, Monsieur . . ."

"Yes, thank you," says Mac.

A moment or two go by as the men smoke in silence, and Racine stares blankly at the window. Push a little harder, Mac is thinking. And then Racine asks, "Who will be the agent?"

"You will, Attorney Racine."

No answer. He fills in the little blanks on the forms. "Monsieur Smith," he says, "in light of our discussions, will you be executing any further instructions with respect to my administration of the account?"

"Yes. You will list me as a beneficiary. But you will take instruction from a Mr. Royall Stillwell."

Racine looks up sharply, but only briefly, and Mac cannot be sure. There is a pause, and then he resumes writing, demands a series of facts: name, address, American passport number. Mac supplies them, guessing at the McLean address, inventing a passport number. Racine draws up the application, and signs it. He fills out blanks in a form of Swiss engagement letter. Mac signs that as well.

The Swiss lawyer rises and turns again to the window, watching in silence as the rain falls heavily on the cobbles in the street below. "That is enough for one day, I think, Monsieur Smith. Perhaps you come back tomorrow morning, and we notarize the papers? Nine o'clock will be agreeable, yes?"

Mac nods. "Yes, that will be fine." He smiles innocently.

"You may go now, Monsieur Smith."

Mac smiles, and as he listens to his footfalls thudding on the treads of the old stone staircase, his mind replays the way the attorney paused and checked himself, the way the pencil dropped to the page, the way the hand reached for the desk drawer. "Gin," he says softly, triumphantly, to himself.

At that moment, Racine is asking Madame Willenstein for a telephone number.

Mac has one other errand before returning to his hotel for the evening. It is not an important errand, really, but it is in the reporter's nature to want to see things for himself.

Guidebook in hand, he threads his way downhill through the rain and out of the Old Town into the Rue de la Corraterie, where he dodges a streetcar while a solitary passerby stares indignantly at this contempt for traffic laws. He tries to shield the book from the rain under the open flap of his coat, and makes his way through a dripping arcade of yellow, red, and black cantonal and city flags, past the opera, and into the quiet limestone haven of the private banks. The rain has driven most of the pedestrians indoors. An occasional man or woman hurries past beneath an umbrella.

One by one Mac ticks off the discreet plaques on the walls in the darkening streets, the Rue Hesse, the Rue Hollande. Some of them go so far as to boast their name—Banque Pasche or Banque Privée Edmond de Rothschild S.A.—while others, the epitome of discretion, confess themselves only by a bare initial in darkened bronze: B&Cie—Bordier and Company; L&Cie—Lombardier. The doors are forbidding, opaque: there is nothing like a teller's window visible inside, and on this rainy afternoon no one seems to be going into or leaving these banks. And then, at 12 Rue Hollande, Mac arrives: D&B&Cie, the sign advises. Duclos & Bernard.

The building is built of heavy, sooty limestone: it does not look quite so impressive as the others he has passed. Six steps up from the street is a door lacquered black, with tiny mullion windows. As Mac is trying to peer inside, the door opens very suddenly and a short, gray-headed man in a tailcoat asks cautiously, "Monsieur, que puis-je faire pour vous?"

The rain is falling harder now, and has soaked through the old raincoat. Raindrops gather on Mac's brow and fall from his chin.

"How about a loan?" Mac asks, smiling absurdly as the rain drips from his head, craning his neck to peer past the doorman, who looks at Mac without comprehension and makes no motion to admit him. A Swiss bank can offer many services, but the one thing you absolutely cannot do is walk in out of the rain and ask for a loan.

"It's nothing," Mac says in English, and points at his tourist guide. "Just looking." He can see nothing but a receptionist's desk and an elevator beyond the man in the tailcoat. He shrugs and grins, while the doorman stares at him, still uncomprehending. Clutching the now soaking book, Mac walks briskly away, through the puddles gathering on the street.

CHAPTER 12

On September 25 in Bethesda, it is as though Louisa is sleepwalking. She bumps into furniture, not seeing things; she stares as though into space even when an object is before her. At dawn she goes back to Isabel's room to see if she has awakened from the dream and if, perhaps, the child is there, stirring and stretching, kittenish on the bed. But Isabel is gone. In the kitchen, a spoon falls from Louisa's hand and clatters to the floor. She looks at it for a moment, distractedly, and then leaves it on the tile. She wasn't hungry anyway. Outside she hears the front doors bang shut and the automobile engines turn over as another day begins. She listens again for the morning sounds in her own home, the shuffle of bare feet on the carpet, the burble of water in the sink, the shower, the familiar soothing voices on NPR. There are none, of course.

Later, after the neighbors' morning sounds fade away, and the day slips into its midmorning suburban quiet, Louisa seems to climb out of her paralysis. She begins then to carry out the instructions with precision.

First she telephones the school, repeating the account by rote. Next the lawyer. At ten-thirty she has reached Krasnowicz.

"I have decided to plead guilty," she says.

There is a silence at the end of the line, but only a brief one. "Okay."

"Please advise the assistant United States Attorney of that. I want to schedule a plea hearing and get on with the sentence."

"Okay," Krasnowicz repeats, without surprise, without comment, just as a waiter in a lesser sort of restaurant says "Okay" when taking down an order. Louisa has prepared herself for misdirection, for explanation, but none is wanted, and for a moment she feels anger—it doesn't strike this man as absurd, as unjust, as ridiculous that she should declare herself guilty of these charges? Krasnowicz and Louisa have never yet sat together to discuss the background of the case. But he expresses no surprise. Perhaps, in his profession, you must expect the worst of people, she thinks, and his next words show that she is on the mark: the worst must be expected not only of clients but of the government.

"Louisa," he says, "we need to talk."

"There is nothing to talk about. I intend to plead guilty."

"I understand that. The question is, do you have anything to trade?"

"Meaning?"

"Information. I mean information, Louisa. Was anyone else involved in this? Under the sentencing guidelines, we can reduce your sentence if you cooperate with the government."

"Our government does that?" she asks.

"Of course."

She measures her words, reminding herself that the listeners will hear them too. "That is no government," she says, "of which I was a part. Mr. Krasnowicz, please call and arrange for the plea. I have no such information."

For a brief moment, Joel Krasnowicz hesitates after replacing the phone in its cradle. So far there is nothing about this self-important client that he has liked, but still . . . He looks out his window, across the street, to the window of an office building through which he sees a bald man in blue suspenders gesticulating at a woman. Life is going on, oblivious of Louisa Shidler. Two people, he thinks, who've never heard of her. And in five years, will Krasnowicz himself even remember the name? It was a good fee. The man is gesticulating, the woman shrugging. "So I'll deal with it, don't have a hemorrhage," he imagines her saying. Staring blankly out across the street, Krasnowicz's thoughts turn back to the case file on his own desk—a new bank fraud. Krasnowicz has long ago given up mental assays of good and evil. He has a job to do, and, he notices on his desk calendar, a twelve o'clock pretrial.

Pretrials, he thinks, the bane of the fixed-fee existence. Absolute waste of time.

Later that afternoon he carries out Louisa's instructions, placing the call to Mark Roth, not even bothering with pretense. "She wants to plead," he tells him.

And Joel Krasnowicz isn't thinking hard, hasn't scripted the call as he usually does. No romancing, no what-will-you-guys-do-if-I-could-only-get-my-gal-to-consider, none of the usual periphrasis. He'd just plead her, he had thought. It was a big bribe, sure, so she'll get four to five years, six months served, maybe, the balance suspended, a big fine, okay, fine, that's what she wants. And a shitload of community service. Shidler will do so much community service she'll drive fucking probation crazy. Krasnowicz pictures his client camped on their doorstep each morning demanding a new park to clean, and better rakes to clean it with. He chuckles. We'll plead her out and go on to the next case and let probation deal with her cheery face each morning. Krasnowicz is on cruise control. But it has been a simple case and a fair fee, and that's what pays the rent.

Then Roth says, "You know, Joel, we're going to need serious time on this one."

Silence. Serious time?

"I would regard *any* time as serious," Krasnowicz says, deliberately.

"Joel, I want to be straight with you. I need ten years served."

The reverie is gone. Mental balances of hours and fees vanish. Ten years? He might as well have asked for Joel Krasnowicz's firstborn. "Mark, get a clue. I can't go for that."

"Joel—"

"Mark, this is true bullshit. I mean, I'm pleading Anne of fucking Green Gables here to her first and only five-year felony. You and I may not be fond of her, but that ain't grounds for the gulag. Come on. You know that I can't go for that."

"It's a serious crime. Fifty million dollars, for Chrissake. She was a United States ambassador. Is one, I guess. She put the entire nation up for sale."

"Twenty-eight points, tops," Krasnowicz answers. He is referring to the arcane points system of the federal sentencing guidelines. Byzantine in complexity, the regulations form a kind of statutory bridge game by which Congress tried to rein in free-wheeling plea bargains. There are points for everything: seriousness of crime, maximum statutory sentence, presence or absence of violence, prior record, remorse. There are points added for this and points subtracted for that and upward adjustments and downward adjustments. Lawyers can snuffle in the points for hours and hours of hearings and then for more hours of rehearings and after that in the court of appeals for yet more mountains of hours. But however you slice this case, there aren't enough points. They both know that ten years can't be forced down an unwilling throat here. Not if she pleads.

"That's not how I count them," Roth says. "But we won't oppose a camp." He is referring to the lowest-security federal penitentiary.

"A camp! Mark, we are definitely not communicating. Because I'll oppose a camp. I'll oppose a suite at the Ritz with room service and a personal valet! Okay? I cannot accept ten years and hold my head up in this city. And you know that is the truth. The lady is ready to plead, to acknowledge responsibility in a case where frankly, I think there are defenses, and you're gonna make me try the thing?"

"What defenses?"

"You keep up with this bullshit you'll find out what defenses."

"Joel. Please. There are no defenses. Sorry. This is coming from upstairs."

"Well, put upstairs on the phone!"

This has annoyed Krasnowicz. He has his reputation to think of here. Pleading a first-offense, nonviolent felony to ten years? He puffs out his chest just a little bit, catches his reflection in the mirror. That's a sharp tie, he thinks.

"You don't even have to indict," he says. "We are walking in and fucking surrendering on a complaint, Mark. All you assholes have to do with this file is throw darts!"

"Sorry."

Krasnowicz protests for a few minutes longer, and then hangs up, punctuating the call with a loud expletive. He won't do it, he thinks. He can't do it. He'll talk her out of it.

And then Krasnowicz sighs, a long sigh of resignation. No one talks this self-righteous, contrary, pestiferous woman out of anything. He has been instructed to arrange a plea. He not only can go for that, he will have to. What the hell is going on here?

Joel Krasnowicz is thinking hard as his anger cools. Across the street, the woman has left the office, and the man in the suspenders sits at his desk, looking at his computer screen. Krasnowicz's own phone interrupts his reverie, and he looks at the handset, then lets it go. Mark isn't trading, doesn't seem to care if the government's hard line blows a plea. And what about that business about defenses, he wonders? It was bullshit, but Roth seemed concerned.

Krasnowicz rereads the complaint, and he reflects, again, on how little sense this case is making. Everyone's in a hurry. The government can't wait to arrest, the shiksa from Bethesda can't wait to plead. And then he thinks of something else. Forget Shidler. Forget the sanctimony, the holier-than-thou "That was no government of which I was a part." I got a top gal at USTR here, he thinks, apparently up to her eyeballs in the biggest bribe in history and sitting at the Trade Rep's table—the same rep who is now running for the White House—and nobody at Justice wants to ask me whether she's got information? He stares out the window and continues to work it through his mind.

Late at night, the lights are burning at Barnett and Associates. Jack sees Jill hesitating in the corridor, by the double doors.

"Don't go in there," he whispers.

"What? What do you mean?"

"What I said. Don't go in there."

"I was supposed to bring her the print on the jobs ad."

He beckons her, still whispering. "Let Mrs. Christian do it tomorrow. She's nuts tonight."

Jill looks once at the doors, then slips into Jack's guardhouse, shuts the door behind her.

"So tonight should be different?"

"I don't know. She's been in there with the Crab all day. Canceled all meetings since noon. I went in there with her tickets for the Wallace opening and she screamed for five minutes. I thought she might throw something. I am totally worthless. Totally. I am an affirmative liability. That was as good as it got."

"You're an affirmative liability too?" she asks, looking at Jack the way one death-row prisoner looks at another—with sympathy, but not quite enough to volunteer to go ahead of his neighbor. "What is it, the new tracking poll?"

"Must be," he answers. "We've dropped two points from last week."

"God." Jill rubs the back of her neck, shuts her eyes. "All right," she says, "you talked me into it. Mrs. Christian can bring her the ad in the morning."

"We've made the big time, huh?" Jack asks, as Jill leaves.

CHAPTER 13

It was Marcy's idea for me to write the story of what happened to Mother and me, the part I know about, before Mother disappeared. I had nothing to do for days and days but wonder where she was, and whether I would ever see her again. I had to stay inside Marcy's apartment all the time, and Marcy never got home from work until the middle of the night. So she gave me a Dictaphone, which is this little tape recorder, and said I should record it just like it happened and she'd get the secretaries at her office to type it. She's an attorney at a law firm called Skidding, Arper, somebody, somebody, and somebody else. Skidding and Arper and all them, they're all dead. But the attorneys there now, they all went to Harvard and they charge you, like, two hundred dollars just for a phone call. Really. Anyway, Marcy said, tell it just like it happened. And I asked her, would the secretaries type the swears and all? She just laughed. "Secretaries, they hear it, they type it" is what she said.

Well, I didn't know. I thought it was like this major law firm and they didn't do that sort of thing.

When you get used to a Dictaphone you can just record and play back with your thumb and you can get it all down without having to wait for all that time it takes to write. It makes it a lot easier.

I was asleep when they came, so I can't tell too much about that part. I just remember waking up, and all this confusion, and tape over my mouth so at first I thought I couldn't breathe, and these lights in my eyes like the ophthalmologist has, and then I was in the back of this car, and there were two of them in the front seat, and we were driving on the highway. Oh my God I was so scared. First I thought they would kill me. Later on I thought maybe they would be nice, since I'd read about nice kidnappers before. And then, later, when they punished me for the phone call, I was sure I was going to be killed again. In *Ride Like the Wind* when they kidnapped Sophia, they threatened to kill her because she would tell the king. And they would have done it, too, except for Lord Elveroth snuck in the tunnel. Anyway Smokes at first seemed like he might at least be a person who would talk to you, but the Beak never said anything to me, she started mean and got meaner as time went on. I called her the Beak—I mean, I didn't *call* her anything, it was just the word in my head—because her face made me think of a bird, all narrow and sharp and kind of pinched. And Smokes I called Smokes because of how, as soon as he finished a cigarette, his fingers would start to stray up toward that shirt pocket, start to be drawn up there, to have another one, and pretty soon he'd be lighting it up. It was gross in the car with all those cigarettes he smoked, and it seemed like forever we were in the car.

But all of that happened later, and Mother would say I should do this in order or I will forget things. Which would be just like her—mustn't forget anything, must we! She would have, like, made a list first and then an outline and then it would be the most organized story you ever read.

I wonder where she is now.

Okay. First things first. The very first thing was when Dad came to Lauren's house one morning in September—I think it was the twenty-second—and we were still eating blueberry waffles, only me and Lauren weren't really supposed to on account of our braces and we hadn't got dressed or anything and Mrs. Lindwall just said, like, don't worry about it, let's have the waffles, what does the orthodontist know about it anyway, and she wasn't dressed except in her night shirt without a bra or anything. It was on a Sunday. Mrs. Lindwall is really natural and cool. One time she took us to a Brad Pitt movie which was way sexy. You'd never see Mother without a bra on or at a Brad Pitt movie. And Dad came to the door and said come on, we have to go, and so I had to get dressed in a real hurry, and at first I was scared because Dad was so serious and he wouldn't say anything except we'll talk about it in the car. So I thought someone had died. I was really freaking out about it and then when we got into the car Dad said that Mother had been arrested.

And I'm like, "Arrested? Mother?"

And he's like, "Yes."

As if! You would have to know Mother. She could have been held over in Brussels because some treaty was going to take longer, maybe, but not arrested. My mother makes treaties, you know, that say how many cars the Japanese can sell here? I've seen them and they are pretty boring and about a thousand pages long. I tried to read one once and I read about five pages and I said forget about it, they can sell a million cars here for all I care rather than have to read this.

Anyway, Mother might be late. She could have to finish something at the office after I go to bed, you know, or maybe even she could be killed in a plane crash because she used to fly everywhere all the time. But be arrested? I don't think so. One time when we were kids, Stacey's brother Billy got a whole box of Creamsicles off the back of the Good Humor truck when the man was in the front. He just reached up and unlatched the handle and grabbed the box, and the man never saw and Billy took them to his and Stacey's porch, and me and Stacey and Billy and Hughie Maxwell and Victor Isselstine and some other kids ate the Creamsicles and it was no big deal, just a few Creamsicles. Hughie was like, "Creamsicles, Billy? This is the best you could do?" Then Mother heard about it somehow and oh my God it was a major felony. She had to call the Good Humor people and on a Friday she took me out of school and we had to drive to this office in College Park to meet this gross man with these like pimples on his forehead and she wrote out a check for the Creamsicles and I had to apologize to the man. And I didn't even take them. My mother can be so honest, she's just a total nerd. You know, if someone would have said, "Barbara, I love your hair, isn't it wonderful," Mother couldn't just say, "It's wonderful." She has to like, consider, is it really wonderful? Is wonderful exactly the right word to describe Barbara's hair? She has to be a dork and say, "I don't know, I liked it better without the bangs," or something, so that Barbara feels terrible about her hair. Mother can be such a nerd sometimes and she never even knows it.

But anyway it was true. They had arrested her and they had her in a real jail. You could see barbed wire on top of the brick walls when you drove into the parking lot. The guards had to buzz us through this like airport metal detector and my braces set it off. They all laughed. Then we went into the room with Mother and she had on like scrubs—you know, that the nurses wear in the hospital? It was very clean and the linoleum squeaked and we sat at the table, me and Dad and Mother. Through the wall there was this racket, shouting and yelling and a lot of amens! and I asked her what it was and she said some kind of religious service. For the born-again prisoners. Mother was crying and she told me it was all a big mistake and I needed to be brave. Honestly, sometimes Mother can be such a nerd. I didn't need to be brave. I knew she was innocent.

Well, that's enough for one night. I haven't seen her for a long time. Nobody has. She's all alone out there.

I miss her.

CHAPTER 14

It is 5:30 A.M. on September 26 in Geneva when Mac comes suddenly awake, lying in a sagging twin bed in the Hotel Bernini. The rain has stopped. He knows that he will not sleep again, and reaches over to the night stand, pushing aside the Lucite plaque that says "Defense de Fumer" to reach for the day's first cigarette. He lies in the darkness, flicking cigarette ash into a water glass.

Not a mile from MacPherson's hotel, an old watchman named Hugo Broillard is at that moment shuffling along the darkened frontage toward the SIG hydroelectric plant on the Rhône, a quarter mile downriver from Lake Geneva. All remains dark; just the palest light illuminates the sky above the mountains east of the lake. Broillard hears the river churning powerfully beneath his feet as he crosses the bridge to the plant. The overnight man grunts a good morning to him at the guardhouse.

Broillard nods to him. "All is well with you this morning, Jean?" he asks.

Jean shrugs, yawns.

Inside, after Broillard has stowed his coat in the locker and his lunch in the cupboard above, he starts the routine with which he begins every day. First, the urinal. Then, change the stinking grounds in the coffee maker, which Jean always leaves a mess. Next, brew and drink the coffee, look at last night's log sheet. Then, just before six, as the sun is coming up, put on a hard hat and begin the first tour.

He exits the guard station into the plant, walking slowly along the upper catwalk, waving a greeting at the crew below. Next he tours the ground floor, inspects the fire doors. Broillard uses a rear door to begin his tour of the turbine intakes and discharges. As he reaches the catwalk, he hears the last booms of the bells from the cathedral up on the hill, announcing the sixth hour, and then the rush of the water beneath his feet. Dawn is coming up. The river is faintly visible now, black water hurrying to France.

Broillard rounds the corner of the building and walks out along the lock. Halfway along, he stops, peering ahead into the dim light. Sometimes a dinghy gets loose up at the yacht club, and makes it all the way down this far, and other flotsam is found from time to time. He stares ahead, his step quickening. It is a rounded shape, bobbing by the far stone pier, hung up on the wire guides. And then, twenty yards away, he stops again. It is not a boat, not a buoy or an old tire. He knows precisely what it is. With a sickness in his stomach, he remembers the day, almost twenty years ago, when he found the man who had fallen in the night, drunk, from the Pont du Mont-Blanc, and washed up against the screens. Shuddering, he turns and hurries back to the plant.

A half hour later, when the police have pulled him from the river, the dead man is easily identified. He is Henri Racine, a lawyer who practiced in the Old Town.

Eight-thirty A.M. Mac is finishing his breakfast in a café that adjoins the Bernini, the morning breeze whipping the tablecloth against the plastic clips. He has not slept well and feels, again, the sharp lower-back pain that has been growing in intensity over the past nine months. It is a gray morning in Geneva, and he watches gray people hurrying to work from Cornavin Station across the square. Although they bustle, they do it without chatter. No one laughs; no one smiles, even. The people move briskly. To Mac it seems as if there is a curious pall over the city, an emptiness.

Mac finished the preceding evening drinking vodka in the hotel lounge, talking to a travel agent from Ipswich, England, on holiday with his wife. They sat at one end of the bar; at the other, an old prostitute drank alone. Mac was surprised at the notion that there are prostitutes in Geneva, but he knew that even the travel agent would make better company. Now his head thumps. Thankfully, the morning is gray, and he sits sipping the saucers full of coffee until it is time to rise and walk to the Place du Bourg-de-Four.

But when Henry MacPherson arrives at H. Racine's third-floor office an hour later, everything has changed. There is none of yesterday's Swiss order and precision in it. The receptionist, Madame Willenstein, looks pale, and is in conference with two police officers.

"I'm here to see Monsieur Racine," Mac says.

"No, I'm afraid you cannot," she answers, looking up. "That is not possible."

"I had an appointment."

"I'm sorry. Monsieur Racine has been in a . . . in a terrible accident and is yesterday killed."

"An accident?" Mac says, "but I—"

The voice, cracking and distraught, says again, "No, no. I'm afraid I cannot help you—"

"But, what sort of accident?" he asks.

"He is drowned, he falls in the river. His body, they, I'm sorry, I can say no more, Monsieur MacPherson. You must find another attorney, yes?"

A distraught woman and two police officers whose stares are distinctly unfriendly. Mac takes a moment to digest this, but only a moment, because he has long ago learned that the most ground can be gained where the field is broken.

"That's awful. I'm terribly sorry," he says to buy time, his mind racing. His jaw works up and down, his eyes squinting. "Madame," he goes on, "I have a problem. Yesterday I consulted Monsieur Racine on behalf of my principal, Mr. Stillwell. Mr. Stillwell had important business that I must transact. You remember the engagement papers we drew up? I am sorry for Mr. Racine's terrible misfortune, but I must have Mr. Stillwell's file and find a new attorney."

"This cannot wait, monsieur?"

The two police officers stare at him. Surely this can wait, their stares are saying.

"I'm very sorry. My plane leaves this afternoon, and these matters are essential to a closing scheduled to begin tomorrow in Brussels, involving parties from five different countries in Europe, Korea, Malaysia, and the United States. The file contains powers of attorney. We can't close without them."

The woman is distraught. She says something in French to one of the policemen. She turns back, brushing her hair from her forehead. Her eyes wander about the room, as if frightened that someone might leap out of a cupboard at any moment. "Yes, yes, you need the Stillwell file," she says. "I don't know any such file."

"It was confidential. It may have been kept under the name L. Shidler."

"Yes, yes. . . . As you can see, the police are here and I . . ." She sighs, and goes toward a back room, stumbling slightly, then turning the corner.

When she returns, the woman is so distracted that for a moment Mac thinks that she will simply hand over the file. But Swiss professionalism asserts itself at the last, and before she yields the folder, she says, "I'm sorry, sir, I don't even know you, except from yesterday. I cannot give you a confidential file."

The policemen take a keener interest. But Mac, in his day, has brassed it out with policemen before, in Saigon, in Watts, even in Tehran. "Madame Willenstein, listen to me, please. This matter was highly sensitive. The file belongs to my principal, Mr. Stillwell, but I very much doubt you will find his name in the file. However, if you check the file you will see the client identified as Ms. L. Shidler, with the following address." Here he reads out the Washington post office box. "You will find that authorizations for disbursements for Monsieur Racine's fees were sent by Ms. Shidler from that address. You will find in the file a power of attorney in favor of Monsieur Racine. For heaven's sake, madame, here is a copy of Monsieur Racine's last letter to my principal! Please see for yourself the copy in your file." Mac shows her a copy of the June letter that Louisa Shidler has given him. The first policeman is now looking over her shoulder, straining to understand. Madame Willenstein's eyes wander, looking at the paper he holds out for her, squinting at it. She looks down at her file, pages through the spindled correspondence, and finds it.

"Excuse me," says Mac, "but these are confidential files." He is looking at the first policeman, shooing him. "Are the police permitted to inspect them?"

The two, Madame Willenstein and the policeman, confer rapidly. The policeman withdraws behind the desk.

Again, from some storehouse, somewhere, comes Madame Willenstein's Swiss professionalism. "Where is your passport, monsieur?"

He hands it to her, and begins to feign exasperation. "Please, prepare a receipt and I will execute it." And then he changes his tone. "Madame Willenstein, I am sorry. This must be a very bad time for you, but my client's work must go on. Please, make a photocopy of whatever you wish, and I will find successor counsel to correspond with you to assure you that everything is in order. Perhaps you can recommend such counsel?"

This is the thing: to be an intrusive, demanding American businessman. That is credible everywhere. So nothing will do but that she must write down the name of another attorney—the name, the address, the phone—and then Mac turns to the policeman. "Can you direct me to this address, sir? Should I take a cab?"

The policeman shakes his head. There are no cabs in the Old Town. And then the three of them are peering over the address. Mac smiles an inward smile when the Swiss begin ever so politely to disagree about the best route to the new attorney's office. When the pantomime has finished, Madame Willenstein gathers up the file, sighs, and steps to the photocopier.

In the Place du Bourg-de-Four once more, Mac hesitates, then crosses the square—to get a cup of coffee at the café there, he tells himself, but the truth is that he wants to see what is in the file. Curiosity like a head-waiter leads him to the café table, and sets the coffee before him, and opens the file for him as though it were a menu. His life may thereafter be owed to curiosity. Had he walked down the hill toward the lake instead of stopping immediately at the café, he might not have guessed at his own pursuers.

They are Americans, he can tell that for sure, when he looks up from his table a few minutes later and sees three men by the door to Racine's building, across the square, about seventy-five yards away. Two of them look like military—broad-shouldered men in ill-fitting blue blazers. And it is an awfully gray day for sunglasses. They stand together but don't look at each other, scanning the buildings, the streets, rather than the people. The tallest of the three trots up the front steps and enters the building. The others wait outside, one with dark, closely cropped hair by the door, the second, a shorter man with a dirty-blond brush cut, pacing off toward the fountain at the far end of the square. Mac watches him as he reaches the fountain, turns on his heel, and returns, like a sentry on guard duty. The third man emerges from the building moments later. The three turn and stride off at a brisk clip down the hill.

For a moment, Mac's instincts are at odds with his senses. It is a gray morning, but the breeze is not a cold one. He sits at a café table, in a pleas-ant square in a charming corner of the old quarter of Geneva; the coffee, if absurdly priced, is good. Three men who look like Americans walked up to the building—so what? There were at least three other office doors he passed on his way up the stairs. And yet Racine is dead, dead within hours of Mac's visit. Mac has an unsettling recollection of Saigon in the days before Diem fell. So many rumors, and yet the cafés in the Rue Cati-nat did a brisk business and the waitresses smiled in the same disingenuous way just hours before the end.

A little schoolmaster's voice is dictating to him, as he tries, without success now, to go back to the file. They came for him. They came for the person whom the nervous Swiss lawyer reported to someone, a report that itself justified murder. They have Mac's name, in all likelihood. They will be covering the airport and Cornavin Station even now. Mac has checked out of the Hotel Bernini, checked his bag in left luggage at Cornavin, where he's booked a ticket on the high-speed train to Paris. They may al-ready know that. There isn't much time.

He looks across the square at the pay telephone.

A moment later a voice is saying, "Hotel Bernini, bonjour?"

"Bonjour. This is Mr. MacPherson. I checked out this morning, and I think I may have missed a message."

"Oh yes, monsieur. Your friends inquired this morning, just after you left."

"Friends? Mr. Smith and Mr. . . . Jones, was it?"

"I don't know. The one gentleman, monsieur, he says he is a friend of yours."

"Big fellow in a blue blazer, about six foot two? Short brown hair?"

"Yes, monsieur, one is like that. The other one has fair hair and is not so tall. Very broad fellow. And another darker one, I think. One wore a blazer. Yes."

"How many were there?"

"Three men."

"Well, thank you very much."

"Yes, monsieur. I hope you will meet your friends. Bonjour!"

I hope I won't, Mac thinks, replacing the receiver. He opens his wallet and frowns. Two hundred Swiss francs, five hundred dollars, and a driver's license. He rifles through the bills, trying to think of the here and now, of Cornavin Station and the airport at Cointrin. Three of them. Three and how many more? Fifty million dollars is a lot of money. And a man is dead, very quickly.

In Saigon, Mac learned never to rush when someone was looking for him. Arrive in a hurry, but leave in diffidence. Rushing draws attention. So Mac goes back to the café. He lights a cigarette and returns to the file. His heart is racing, but there is a smile on his face.

Mac has to calculate as he pulls the rental car into traffic ninety minutes later. How soon will they have the credit card number, the license plate? Soon. Still, a man could drive a rental car to anywhere from Geneva: Milan, Munich, Lyons. Or Paris. Paris. In a few hours, he decides, he will find a phone and call Archie Pierce.

He lights another cigarette. You can drive from Geneva to Paris, but it is a long drive.

"Well, for Chrissake," he says out loud a half hour later, as he pulls the Ford Cortina onto the motorway. He is thinking of the suit in the overnight bag he left at Cornavin Station. It was one of his favorites, and the day before he flew to Geneva, he had it pressed. Mac is descended from Scotsmen: his grandfather emigrated. He hates waste.

CHAPTER 15

Archie Pierce is a lifer, a wire-service man who inhabited every two-room bureau from Port Said to Lisbon, from Bangalore to Buenos Aires, before coming to rest in Paris. Wire service requires only that he exploit two things that come naturally to him, the knack for remembering everyone he's ever met, and the ability to type who, what, where, and when accurately, and at speed, when under the influence of alcohol. (It is said, without undue violence to the facts, that Archie Pierce can type seventy-five flawless words per minute even when too drunk to see the keys.)

He can also get a table at Taillevent or Lucas Carton on short notice, and is perhaps the only man of moderate means in the city who can make that claim.

By 1996, Pierce is perhaps past the point where he can say that he knows everyone. But he still knows almost everyone, and absolutely everyone who used to matter, and he can get you the facts fast. In Paris, that is almost enough for a wire-service man. *Why* he leaves to the younger, keener sort of reporter, the ones with the horn-rimmed glasses and the earnest expressions and the graduate degrees from Harvard or Columbia. He is past caring for why. For thirty years he has watched men and women, some of them very wise, seek for why, and not a one of them has found it. Who, what, where, and when is enough for Archie.

He wants no Pulitzers, no awards from the National Press Club, no invitations to host the talk shows. A little money is a good thing, surely, enough to dress well, to drink a better sort of wine, and to take a nice boy out to dinner once a fortnight. The Associated Press gives him that. It gives him little else but that and freedom, and the combination is enough.

He does like to dress; likes to spend his mornings—late mornings, of course—cruising the more fashionable sort of haberdashery, picking out here and there a new foulard, perhaps a shirt, one with loud stripes and a gleaming white spread collar. Archie looks after his body as well as he can: going regularly to the gym, fighting to keep the waist in goodish trim, lifting weights to prop up the first signs of sag in his chest, running on the weekends. He is in good shape for fifty-three: still slim, his angular face still lean; admittedly with just the suggestion of a bit too much of the bottle, but as yet no outward trace of the sleeping killer that, he learned eighteen months ago, is floating in his bloodstream.

He maintains an enforced diffidence about that, and has resolved to live his life according to its past until it is time to cut it short. There is in him no welling dismay, no urgency to confront the deeper philosophical riddles. He has no appointment with his Maker yet. Perhaps that will come later, with the sickness, and all the horrors he chooses not to dwell on. But for now he remains Archie. And he is careful about grooming: careful to keep the nails manicured and his hair—thinning now, sadly—cut short, and his beard (Archie is proudest about this) closely trimmed. You have to be observant to keep up with what is fashionable in Paris, and with what isn't, and Archie is the sort of fellow who might be walking with you in the morning crush of the Boulevard Haussmann, in the tumble of bodies all streaming from the Gare Saint-Lazare, and as you are consumed with trying to fend off the rush and elbow your way through the crowd, you might hear him say, "Did you see the shoes on that guy?"

Archie Pierce was floored by Mac's call. Even he has enough of the journalistic zeal to admire those in the pantheon of great foreign correspondents, and MacPherson is one of those. More important, though, is that Mac and Archie are of the same generation. For all their professional inquisitiveness, each fundamentally venerates the days when the press and the politicians understood the line between the public and the private: when any brand of chicanery was acceptable in the pursuit of a public matter, but no scandal would induce a reporter to cross the line to the private. Each abjures the current trend toward eliminating the line. Each can remember when there were unwritten rules, when whom a politician slept with or whether he said something off-color after too many bourbons was information for the brotherhood, not for the television camera or the broadsheet.

Almost as soon as he heard it on the phone, Archie remembered the voice: not its pitch or timbre, particularly, but the pungent diction, the odd way it had of accenting the unlooked-for syllable, or dropping and falling without warning. Mac, whom he had not spoken to for ten years, would be in town tonight. There was a little small talk—not too much, for

Mac sounded a bit rushed. But one thing Mac was very particular about. Archie was to bring the best man in the city on international trade.

As it happens, the best man in Paris on international trade also happens to have a legitimate claim to the short list for the all-world team. He is Ian Nevins, of *The Economist*. "Sounds rather a lark," Nevins offered, when Archie called. "Where do we dine?"

We dine at Lucas Carton. And on hearing this, Nevins could only say, "You dear old sod, Archie."

Now, in the late Parisian afternoon, Archie's mind has wandered from the story he has to file, and from the New York editor on the phone looking for it.

"Archie, when are you filing on the Chunnel refinance?"

Regretfully, Archie comes back to the present and sighs. Who really cares about the Chunnel refinance? he asks himself. Once you've written the blackened submarinian faces of the miners shaking hands beneath the English Channel, and done the bar car and maybe a piece or two about how a stockbroker can lunch in London and be on time for hors d'oeuvres at Guy Savoy, the story's done, isn't it? Who cares which bank is being paid the interest?

Archie listens to the voice of the annoying young woman in New York. This fixation on money is so, so eighties, he thinks, so *over.* "In an hour," he says, when she finishes caterwauling. "Maybe two."

"We don't have two, Arch, gotta move it."

"Babe," he says, "be patient. You'll have the sexiest Chunnel refinance story on the wires. Now go away for just a few minutes so Archie can get to work, okay?"

He hangs up the phone, and smiles, but he knows she'll have the story in an hour: maybe less. For Mac is coming into town, and that means the *Washington Herald* is going to stand the best wine, the best dinner in Paris for three at Lucas Carton. Wine to take a man far away, and stories of the wonderful old days, when you could afflict the comfortable by day, and comfort some afflicted boy by night, the glory days before the plague, before the great ones, the Henry Macs, had been pastured to editorships and the wire services stripped clean of giants. And no occasion, not even a tumble with the nicer sort of broad-shouldered blond, is more cheering for Archie than company from the past at a three-star restaurant.

It is just before six-thirty when Archie looks up to see him there in the doorway to the AP bureau, with one hand on the knob and a questioning look on his lined face. Mac is a little more stooped than Archie remembered, his skin a little grayer than is appropriate for an American, his tan raincoat stained and wrinkled, that mop of white hair in disarray. The visitor stands uncertainly for a moment, his eyes scanning the room, the Mac mouth ever in motion, pursing and grimacing, the jawbone sliding from side to side.

Archie rises and beckons to him. "Mac," he says, "good to see you."

"And you. How are you, Archie?"

"Rotting by degrees from the inside, Mac."

"You'll bury me, Archie."

"I wouldn't bet on it." They shake hands. There are two others in the bureau that night, Fritz Powlson and young Beam, an intern. From the way the two men greet each other, they can see that this visitor is from the old guard, the elite, as Archie likes to call it.

"Let's get out of here," Archie says.

But Mac is not ready to go for a drink, not yet. He insists on sitting Archie down in the bureau chief's tiny office first, and handing over, as if they were secret agents, the contents of a gray file for photocopying. Archie nods with amused detachment as Mac, perched in the cheap metal-frame chair pulled up by Archie's desk, gives his earnest instructions.

"I want you to send one copy of these to me at my home, express mail, and the second to an attorney named Joel Krasnowicz, in Washington. Do you have envelopes?"

Mac seals a set in an envelope and writes on it: "Hand-deliver, personally, to Louisa Shidler. Do not open. Do not discuss by telephone." Then he dictates the address as Archie, chuckling, writes it down.

"Anything else, Double-oh-seven? Shall we go down to Q branch for an exploding lighter?"

There is no answer. Archie fidgets a little; he is anxious for a drink and for the real business of the evening, which will be to revisit the old stories, not live a current one.

But Mac's eyes don't respond to the joke. "Did you find someone?" he asks.

"The best. Ian Nevins. He joins us at nine."

"From *The Economist*?"

Archie nods.

"Thanks. I'll meet you there."

"The hell with that, Mac, I'll follow you—"

"No," Mac says, and something in his distracted manner gives Archie pause. "No, let me go on my own. I, well, I need to wash up. Meet me there." He smiles. "Thanks." And then he is gone, the dirty raincoat clutched in one hand, the other rubbing the back of his neck.

Mac's eyes looked so tired to Archie. His jaw worked furiously. Perhaps this was not going to be a pleasant evening after all.

Ian Nevins is a man who at an early age must have rejoiced to throw off any pretense of youth. Stout, a little stooped, his hair thin on top and too long about his ears, dark and stringy and gone a bedraggled gun-metal color but still powdering the slopes of his shoulders with dandruff, his lips a little thick, his glasses inclined to slip down his nose, his complexion pale, Nevins holds his head at an odd, bemused angle when he looks at you, his eyes narrowing. He dresses donnishly in a tweed jacket and a mismatched patterned shirt, his tie somewhat askew, and manages to look older than he is: the sort of man who began looking as he did at age thirty, and would continue doing so until fifty-five, and might at this time be almost anywhere between.

"Hullo, Archie," Nevins says, as he reaches the table at the back of Lucas Carton. He extends his hand with perfect Oxonian diffidence, and his words with equally Oxonian elision, contriving to collapse them, somehow, into a single elongated syllable.

Pleasantries are exchanged. "Just in from Geneva, then?" Nevins asks.

"Yes," Mac answers.

"Not the place it used to be, really."

Archie cuts in. He wants his friend to know how impressed he should be, and spends a few minutes summarizing Mac's exploits, with due emphasis, of course, placed on the years in Saigon. The object of this essay feels a tinge of embarrassment to hear himself described in such swashbuckling fashion. Nevins looks away, and smiles almost apologetically.

"Sorry," he says, at an appropriate interval. "Before my time. Sounds all rather adventurous. Vietnam and so on. Was it a terribly monsoony sort of place?"

Mac smiles. "You could say that."

"Couldn't bear it," says the Englishman.

"Ian," says Archie, continuing the introductions, "is our man at the negotiating table, high priest of eurodollars, professor of trade, learned in the tongues of finance. You know his column?"

"I've seen it," says Mac.

"Read *The Economist,* do you?" Nevins asks, perking up.

"The 'American Survey,' anyway, which is about the best column on us I know," Mac answers. "I don't get through a lot of the pure financial stuff."

"Oh, well, 'American Survey.' Can't be helped, I suppose."

They begin with champagne. Not because there is anything to celebrate, but because hard liquor dulls the taste buds in a way that champagne does not. And at Lucas Carton, it would be an expensive folly to impair the sense of taste.

The men chat, staking out ground. A journalist is preoccupied with the strength of his source. One of them meeting another wants reassurance that he meets a colleague of some experience, a colleague worth his time and observations. So, for a while, they circle. "Gentlemen," says Mac, when it comes time by the looks in the eyes of the two men to move from the champagne to a bottle of Chablis, "I appreciate you coming. I need your help."

"I am your humble servant." Archie raises an eyebrow by three or four angstroms, and the wine steward materializes. Mac waits as Archie speaks to him, and then continues.

"Suppose," Mac begins, "there is corruption at the highest level of the United States government—"

"What's to suppose?" Archie says, laughing. "We know that there is corruption in wonderful variety. Keeps gas in the Volvos of you and I."

"Of you and me," Mac, correcting automatically, cuts in. "Suppose, though, we are talking about corruption of a very particular kind. Corruption involving foreign trade. Involving the public officials who deal with tariffs, international trade, that kind of thing."

"Bribe?" Nevins asks.

Mac nods.

"Guns or butter?"

Archie is staring in a distracted manner toward the waiters who congregate at the headwaiter's station, by the front of the restaurant. "I give up," he says. "Can't count them all."

"I, I don't know," says Mac, answering Nevins. "Maybe both."

"Who, then?" Nevins goes on.

"I can't comment," Mac says.

"Ah, this is to be an interview with the oracle at Delphi, Archie," Nevins says to his host.

Archie shrugs. "The oracle's buying. We're talking, I guess."

"Come along, Mac, you can hardly expense a place like this just to talk in riddles. How much money is in this?" Nevins asks.

"When the time comes, you can have this story. You guys can run it first. But you run nothing, you say nothing, until I give the go-ahead. Agreed?"

Nevins runs a pale finger across his cheek. "Very well then, but who *are* we talking about?"

Mac shakes his head. "Whom is the question."

"How many of them, really?" Archie interrupts, still staring at the front of the room. "I count about ten." The other two turn and appraise, reaching no consensus on the number of waiters milling near the head-waiter's station.

"Incredible, the waiters here," Archie goes on. "You want the ones with the black aprons. They outrank the ones in the crimson, who outrank the enlisted men in the white. The guy with the crimson bow tie outranks everybody except God. And God can't get a table here."

"Mac. When does the chap take the bribe?" Nevins asks.

Mac smiles. "Let's say the relevant time period is spring of 1993."

"Spring '93. Hmmm. Well, you've run a Nexis? What do you find your lot up to? Would have been the Uruguay Round, I should think." Nevins rubs a hand up under one of his chins. "Yes. Autumn of '92. Before that, Reykjavik. Three bilateral agreements. TRIPS, TRIMS, '92 . . . and the Pharmaceutical Accord in the spring of '93, wasn't it?" Nevins completes the thought.

Mac shrugs. "I haven't run anything yet."

"Pharms," says Nevins. "Perhaps it is butter, then. Negotiated the thing right here in Paris. You remember it, Arch?"

Pierce shrugs. "Trade agreements, Ian, I, I, what can I tell you. Bores hell out of me."

"But a lot of chaps rushing about in black Mercedes—"

"That I like," Archie agrees.

"What was the pharmaceutical agreement all about?" Mac asks.

"Open up the Yank mouths to more of our pills," Nevins says, leaning back from the table. "Tariff cuts and, more important than that, actually, the mutual recognition agreements. Persuade the Yanks to accept the European government approvals, instead of putting everyone through the purgatory of FDA."

"So," Mac asks, "how much was that worth to somebody?"

"Archie, order up another bottle on the oracle's chit, there's a good lad," Nevins says. He smiles at Mac, and then remembers the question. "All depends. Lot of moving parts. Better start at the other end—from that bribe you don't want to talk about."

A waiter brings the appetizers, exquisite creations, and Nevins studies them a moment before offering this appraisal: "Little chaps, big plates." He looks up. "You know it's three bloody stars when little chaps come on such big plates." Then he looks off again, this time toward the row of other diners. "I think that's Mohammed Al-Khir, the Egyptian flax man. Got a yacht in Monaco the size of a hotel. They say he doesn't go aboard. Suffers terrible seasickness. Fancy a chap with a floating hotel who suffers seasickness."

The men stare at the Egyptian flax merchant with the unfortunate problem.

"One doesn't know a lot about bribes, really." Nevins returns to the subject at hand when the plates have been whisked away. "Few cases here and there, mostly pitifully small things. Bloke done up in the nick for taking a thousand pounds. Bloody silly. Still, one hears rumors, things. Usually laid on by the ones who bid a little less for the bribe, you know?"

A handsome young man arrives with the main course. Archie engages the waiter in polite chat, and the waiter smiles demurely.

"One does like to hear Americans talk frog," Nevins says. Mac doesn't comment.

"You have leave to kiss my colonial ass," says Archie.

"Bollocks," says Nevins.

Mac asks Nevins again, "The pharmaceuticals?"

Nevins has tucked his napkin up into his collar and looks to be absorbed in the veal, his knife and fork poised. He thinks it over for a moment. "Ranitidine hydrochloride. Know what that is?" He smiles at his audience. "Active ingredient in Zantac. Tariff cut on Zantac alone probably worth ten million a year. So what piece of that would you pay in a bribe? Quarter of a million? Half? A million?" He turns his head in that odd way and looks, inquisitively, at Mac for guidance, but there is none. "Rather doubt it."

Mac's lips are pursed, and his lips are working. "Who had the most to gain? Pick one guy, one company, one government, one somebody. Who had the most to gain?"

Nevins answers slowly. "Well, lots of winners. AIDS drugs the big ones. Charge a fortune for them. And ulcer drugs. Sell 'em like bloody Smarties. Endless supply of ulcers in America, you know?"

"It's fifteen of them if it's five. What a place!" Archie is looking again at the headwaiter's station.

"Actually, the veal is rather good," Nevins concedes, filling his mouth.

They eat awhile in silence before Nevins says, "All tucked away in an annex, as I recall."

"What?"

"The ulcer drugs, I think. Last-minute sort of business, tucked into the documents, you know? Annex number three hundred and seventeen sort of thing. Most unusual, really."

The Englishman looks at his wineglass, and in an instant the wine steward materializes and fills it. He takes a mighty gulp, and then goes on as if he has no sense of what he had just said. "The entire U.S. pharms market is . . . well, I don't even think it's measured in the billions anymore. I think it's trillions now. The European share probably went from ten or fifteen billion to three times that. Glaxo and Smith Kline would have had the largest shares. Say they split half of it halvsies. Close to ten or fifteen billion a year in sales for the indefinite, I should say. What's that all worth to the happiest capitalist of the lot? Present-value the income stream, I suppose, if you could predict it, except . . ." He sets his fork down and seems to be lost in thought for a moment, going backward and forward in his mind.

"I see," says Mac. "Thank you." He puts his glass down on the table, and he pauses, his jaw working as only the Mac jaw can. Nevins watches. Something suggests to him that the oracle is actually about to speak.

"Now my question is," Mac says quietly, "could it be worth fifty million?"

Nevins holds his wineglass up to the light, admiring the wine's color. "The true, the blushful Hippocrene, Archie," he says softly.

"Does that fit your pharmaceutical players?"

Nevins swirls the wine in the glass, round and round and round. Then he drinks the wine and sets the glass down. Archie and Mac wait, as Nevins shuts his eyes, his cheeks registering the pleasure.

"With beaded bubbles winking at the brim," he continues, opening his eyes.

"Ian?"

"No," Nevins answers.

"No, it doesn't fit?"

"No, Mac, it doesn't fit."

The sommelier returns, and Nevins smiles to watch the wine cascading into his glass. "Much too much," Nevins says, and the sommelier, misunderstanding, draws the bottle away with a flourish.

"No, no, no," Nevins says to the sommelier, motioning for him to pour away. "Not you."

"Why?" Mac asks.

"Too much money. Far too much."

"No such thing," Archie smiles.

"Oh, no, Archie. There may be no such thing as too much to get. But there is such a thing as too much to pay. And fifty million is far too much to pay for the opportunity to compete. You see, the trade agreement just gets you into the American marketplace. You've still got to elbow aside all the other bloody ulcer drugs. It's too much money. For fifty million dollars, the buyer will hereby be granted a modest Caribbean island, to be held in fee simple absolute by the said buyer and his heirs and assigns forever and ever amen. Fifty million is too much for a bet, Archie. For fifty million, you want certainty."

Mac is the last to leave the restaurant, lingering after the others have gone. He is drunk enough to decree that he has time to finish a cognac, after picking up a tab for the better part of a thousand dollars on the account of Finch-Ephram Media, Inc., the *Herald*'s new masters. There is at least time to finish and savor the digestif before the little buzzers on computers at locations around the world go off and tell the hunters that Mac has come up for air, before the hunters find Lucas Carton on their street maps and hurry toward it. Why is there time? Because Mac decrees it so. Selah! There is time to savor the cognac under the coldly courteous gaze of the ten or fifteen head of waiters, time to smile at each of them before staggering into the Paris night, half drunk, armed only with the sour-smelling clothes he wears, and one quite extraordinary address book.

In a single sitting, Mac has eaten about twice what he usually manages in a day. He has a good sense for timing. And now it is time to go to ground.

CHAPTER 16

I don't feel right about this, telling this story into my little Dicta-phone, when I don't know if the story is even over. I mean, where is Mother? I don't even know if she's alive or dead. Marcy doesn't even know. She said if something bad happened it would be on the news. Which it hasn't been. So I guess I'll keep on with this.

First of all, being in an adventure is not what you imagine. You don't think, "I'm in an adventure," you think, "I'm in this car with these two gross people." I've read about a million adventure books, and the thing they never tell you is how boring it is. I mean, if you're being kidnapped and you're in the back of a car for days and days, I don't care what they say, it's boring. And how do you go to the bathroom? I don't think Miranda Spendlove ever went to the bathroom in seven books. But you do have to go to the bathroom and they made me do it by the side of the road next to a cornfield and you don't even know if someone is going to come along.

There were two of them, like I said before. The Beak, she didn't look like a kidnapper, more like a lady from Chevy Chase late to ballet to pick up a daughter. The Chevy Chase people never smile. They're like, "Get out of the way of my Range Rover!" You know? She was like that. She never smiled. She was all business. And then there was Smokes, and was he gross. He had dark greasy hair and the worst acne, and the main thing about him was, he said the word "fuck" about twice every sentence. He said it so much you couldn't count. About everything, too. Rest stops were fucking rest stops and he might need fucking gas or a fucking ciga-rette and his fucking neck hurt him all the time. He had acne on the back of his neck too. Or, his fucking neck, I should say.

The nights were the best part because when they looked back into the backseat they couldn't see whether I was asleep or awake. I could lie down, almost, across the seat and it would be dark.

Late on the second night I think it was—the second night after they took me—I was half asleep, kind of, when the car shifted and slowed down and I knew they had pulled off the highway. I got my breathing going steadily so that when they stopped the car and turned off the radio and it was quiet in the car they could hear me sleeping. I kept my eyes shut except I would open them a tiny tiny bit. If you've ever tried that you can open your eyelids just a fraction, so that you can still even see the blur of the eyelashes across just a little sliver of light, and if it's dark out grown-ups think your eyes are closed. I've fooled Mother lots of times that way. So I kept my eyes just like that and I breathed steadily and I listened be-tween breaths until I heard the tires crunching over gravel or dirt or some-thing. Then the car was still.

The Beak switched the engine off. Then I could hear some katydids making a racket and the cars going by on the highway in the distance.

"Hey, kid!" I could tell the Beak had turned around in the driver's seat.

I didn't answer, but kept breathing slowly, like I was asleep.

"Kid!" Then her little claw was on my shoulder, shaking me. Yuck. I kind of stirred like a kitten and then scrunched back into the seat and I sort of mumbled a few garbled words like you do when you're talking in your sleep. I've done that to Mother too, and it fooled her every time.

The Beak took her hand off of my shoulder. "She's asleep," she said to Smokes.

"Fuck. So am I," he said. Then they started talking, low, kind of a rumble, and I couldn't make it out, but suddenly I felt the springs give slightly and I heard the front door opening. The door shut again and I could hear the Beak walking away. I kept up the breathing, because I knew Smokes was there. It was quiet for a while longer and then I heard Smokes kind of mumbling to himself, getting impatient. "Come on, dar-ling," I heard him say. Then he sighed, and said it again. Finally he says, "Fuck me," and then, "Hey, kid, you wakey?"

I kept on breathing.

Then I heard him take the keys from the ignition, open his door, and step out. The door shut behind him.

First I thought it was a trick, like, I'd open my eyes and there would be one of Smokes's zits about ten inches away from my nose. So I kept up the breathing for a minute or so before I opened my eyes a crack wider. From where I lay with my head behind the driver's seat I could see out the passenger side. Smokes was having a cigarette, leaning up against the car. Beyond him there was a dirt parking lot, and a streetlight, and beyond that it looked like woods or something, not real woods but junky weedy type

woods like you find by a highway with gross sumac trees and old cigarette
cartons and beer cans and things. Suddenly Smokes turned around, and
jammed his face up against the window, looking in, and I shut my eyes.
When I dared open them again, I could see Smokes sidling off toward the
edge of the lot.

He got to the edge and kind of looked around him and then I could
tell he was going to take a pee. I looked back over my shoulder the other
way and saw this kind of white diner thing in the distance, and before you
got to that a couple of gas pumps in front of a shed. It was bright around
the diner and under the pumps but it was dark between them and me, and
I couldn't see anybody.

First I thought about leaning on the horn, honking the horn and
maybe running for the street, but it was pretty dark and I knew Smokes
would be on me in a second. Maybe that would have been the best thing,
but I was too scared. I looked back at Smokes. He had his back to me and
his arms held in front of him. That's when I reached forward to the front
seat as quick as I could and grabbed the car phone.

You know, if they had kidnapped Mother, she wouldn't have known
what to do, because she never had a car phone and gets all flustered if she
tries to do anything else in a car except drive. She won't have anything to
do with them. But I've used Dad's car phone plenty of times.

Who do you call when you've been kidnapped? I don't know, so I
called 911.

This voice said, "Jackson County 911, this call is being recorded. How
may I help you?"

"This is Isabel Higginson and I'm being kidnapped," I said to the lady.

"Where are you?"

"I'm in a car. They went to the bathroom."

"How old are you, Isabel?" the lady asked, sort of like she didn't believe me.

"I'm twelve."

"Where is the car, Isabel?"

I looked over and could see Smokes doing something with his hands.
He was finishing up.

"Isabel?"

"I'm in a car," I said.

"Where?" the lady said.

"I don't know. It's a diner or something. With gas pumps."

"What is it called? What road are you on?"

"I don't know. Shoot," I said.

"What is it?"

"Smokes is coming back."

"Tell me something about where you are. What can you see?"

I should have been cool but I wasn't. "I don't know, it's all white. It's wood and you can hear the highway and there's a dirt parking lot and, just call my mother, okay? She's Louisa Shidler in Bethesda and her number is 263-3010."

That's pretty much all I got out before I got too scared and snuck my arm back across the armrest to stick the phone in the cradle. But I don't think Smokes knew, because I had my breathing going before he got back to the car.

We sat there quite a while, and I hoped the police might come, somehow. It was a few minutes before the Beak came back, and then we had to wait for Smokes to go off and eat. The Beak never left the car, and I kept pretending to be asleep. We were there for a long time, but the police didn't come.

CHAPTER 17

Just another dull shift on the overnight, that is how the twenty-sixth began for Lonnie Billings. Smoking cigarettes in the dispatch office, she kibitzed with the third shift as they began to drift in around eleven. It was hot in western Missouri, and the report was for more heat on the way. And then the call came in. It found Lonnie kind of sluggish, never in step through the whole conversation.

Now it is early on the morning of the twenty-seventh, and she is going to have to listen to the tape again, with the lieutenant, and Sergeant Peterson, and Debbie Cantalupo all listening, too.

She watches the tape spools on the blue machine whir to a stop and then the machine goes clunk, and they start slowly forward, and the hiss comes, and then her own voice and the child's, coming out over the wall speakers while everyone listens to it yet again.

"This is Isabel Higginson and I'm being kidnapped."

This is awful. Lonnie didn't ask her any of the right questions. What was the model of the car? Old, new? What color was it, for gosh sakes? Lonnie feels their eyes on her, sees it in the way they frown.

"I'm in a car. They went to the bathroom."

She watches the mahogany tape feed slowly from one spool, through the housing of the magnetic head, and over into the other. How many of them? What did they look like? White, black, Hispanic? Old, young? Male, female? Lonnie shuts her eyes. She can tell that the lieutenant is not happy.

"It's a diner or something. With gas pumps."

Val's is like that, out on 24. And the All Night Rest has pumps, doesn't it? There can't be too many like that. The spools whir on a moment longer, and then there is the tone as the line goes dead. Lonnie lets out a long sigh and looks down at her hands.

"Well, we got an Isabel Higginson on the national wire?" the lieutenant asks.

Lonnie has looked. There was no report of a kidnapping.

"We try the mother?"

"No listing like that in Bethesda, Missouri, lieutenant," said Peterson. "No Bethesda in Kansas, Iowa, or Nebraska. Ain't checked Arkansas or Illinois yet."

"Anything on the diner with gas pumps?"

"Hell, lieutenant, where? Could be anywhere outside Kansas City. Could be I-70, 71, 435, 24 . . . ."

"There's Val's," says Lonnie, in a weak sort of voice.

"Val's and two dozen others." They sit in silence for a moment, until the lieutenant speaks again. "She didn't sound like she's from around here," the lieutenant says. "Ya'll tried Bethesda, Maryland?"

They haven't, and Lonnie goes to the phone.

While Lonnie is looking up the area code, Debbie Cantalupo examines the atlas, and says, "You was coming west from Bethesda, Maryland, I-70'd be the way you'd go."

Lonnie interrupts her. "There's a listing for L. Shidler, in Bethesda, Maryland," she says.

Louisa is lying in bed, sleepless in the darkness. She is still dressed. She is trying to envision Toby, to paint his expression on the mind's canvas. She cannot picture him, and that is the frightening thing. The phone rings. She grabs it instantly, before the ring has ended.

"Yes," Louisa says, and then she hears an official voice say that she is Deputy Sheriff Billings from the Jackson County, Missouri, sheriff's department. "Oh, God," Louisa says softly to herself.

"Ma'am?" asks the voice.

"Nothing," Louisa says. "What is it?"

"Is this Louisa Shidler speaking?" the voice asks.

Now Louisa tries to prepare herself. But how do you do it?

"Yes?"

"Do you have a daughter aged twelve named Isabel Higg—"

"Yes!" she blurts out. Yes, yes, oh, yes, what is it, what is it, woman?

"Is she with you?"

Lord. They are listening. *"Is she with you?"* For a moment, Louisa is paralyzed.

"No," she stammers, finally, "She's with her grandparents in North Carolina. Why, ma'am, why do you ask?"

"Ms. Shidler, Jackson County Sheriff's Department received a call at eleven fifty-one P.M. Central Time from a person claiming to be Isabel Higginson and saying she had been kidnapped. She gave us your name and telephone number."

"I see," Louisa says.

"Ma'am," says the voice, a slight exasperation creeping into it, "is your daughter missing?"

"No, no. I'm sorry to bother you. She must have been playing with the phone. I'm sorry." Louisa hangs up.

In the Jackson County dispatch office, Lonnie frowns and shakes her head. "She says she has a daughter Isabel. She says her daughter is with her grandparents, in North Carolina. She says she hasn't been kidnapped at all. Must have been playing with the phone."

But the four law enforcement officials are looking around the room, each with the same thought. You cannot be playing with a phone in North Carolina and place a call to Jackson County, Missouri, 911.

The midnight-blue Cadillac is heading north on Interstate 29 when the car phone rings. The woman Isabel calls the Beak takes the call and grunts a few acknowledgments before her features darken and she hands the telephone to the man Isabel calls Smokes. "You worthless sack of shit," she says. Smokes winces as he listens to the voice on the telephone.

Fifteen minutes later the Cadillac exits the highway, following signs for Route 136 and the Missouri River. The highway is lonely and, passing only here and there a solitary eastbound traveler, they soon reach the Missouri and cross into Nebraska. Three or four miles past the river, they come to a rusted signpost, "Nemaha," and Smokes turns left onto Route 67.

No one else is driving on Route 67. If there were another traveler, twenty minutes later, he might hear, from a distance, the shrieks, and, as he came closer, discern in the shrouded moonlight of that cloudy September night the outline of the Cadillac parked on a dirt road off the highway, alongside a wheatfield. By the rear fender, a man is faintly visible holding something—on closer inspection: a child. A second figure, a woman, can be seen methodically raising the open palm of her right hand and bringing it down sharply on the child's face.

CHAPTER 18

All across Europe, all across Asia, all across the world's stream, are Henry MacPherson's little stepping-stones, mapped out in the dog-eared address book he carries in his jacket pocket, his atlas. To be sure, the stream has washed over many of them, submerged and rolled the stones to God knows where, so that the telephones are disconnected and the addressees unknown and all inquiries will be returned to sender. So many of the old stones have rolled away now. But not all. Not all the pencil marks are historical facts. Mac is old, but the book is thick. He goes to ground.

To Brussels first, and then Antwerp. Old Reuters hands, Unipressers, old stringers from the battlefields of Mac's youth. Two nights in Brussels with an old friend from the AP. But she has a husband now, and Mac makes him uncomfortable, so Mac resorts to the book again.

In Antwerp, a man named Gunnar lives in a bed-sitter. His life proceeds by artificial light, the light of screens and neon. At night he watches dreary pornography on the cable television. In the afternoons he sometimes walks to the town to visit the bars. But there the sights are also television screens, even when the sun is out. He pulls across his head thin strands of hair the color of cigarette ash, and he has grown fat. His face boils with the alcohol that soon will kill him, but there is no other spark in him, no animation.

No one would guess today that once Gunnar was the best freelance photographer in Indochina. He took a thousand riveting photographs: a thousand images of horror and fear and dirt and blood; a thousand chances to be raked or strafed or burned, and his index finger never shook over the camera shutter the way it does now when curling around a glass. No one would guess, watching Gunnar huddled plump and ineffectual over a gin at midday on a barstool in Antwerp, the instinct his lens had for the human face, for the line or grimace or shout that could bring a lump to the throat of a Pentagon bureaucrat.

Amid all the superb work, there was one transcendent exposure: the photograph of the young woman and the child and the boots. One woman, one infant, boots—a photograph that ripped the heart out of 10 million people. She is young, beautiful, her hair lush and dark, but her body too bony, and her cheek grime-streaked. She crouches on her haunches in the ashes of a wasted village, holds at her breast an infant, naked and dead, her infant, your infant, it doesn't matter. The nipple has slipped from the child's helpless mouth. The mouth hangs slack, and one's eyes go in horror to it. Behind her are the boots, the boots of Americans, dark boots of large, unseen Americans towering over and out of sight and oblivious to the dead infant. In the center of the photograph are her eyes, indicting you. You did this to me, say the eyes, to my baby. All of you. And, please, for what?

For what? ask the eyes. They ask it of everyone who sees the photograph, and even today there is no answer. It was a photograph that did more to turn American foreign policy than a thousand Vietcong ambushes. It lives on in the historical record, the archives of the news services, in scrapbooks. Gunnar took the photograph twenty-seven years ago. No one would believe that now. He has lost the negative.

In fact, Gunnar has forgotten what the woman looked like. It was a confusing day. The rain stopped just before sunrise. He was rushing to keep up with the platoon after the dawn attack, and his clothes were soaked through from the rain, and his head lice were bad. He had more hair then, and that is what he remembers on the rare occasions when he tries to summon the day to mind: the head lice. He barely saw her. God took the photograph, used Gunnar's fingers.

For three nights Mac sleeps on Gunnar's couch. While Gunnar drinks, or stares at the television, Mac studies. At least Gunnar turns the sound down. Staged moans, Mac thinks, are even more dispiriting than staged images. In the mornings Mac lies flat on the floor and tries to stretch the kinks out of his back, while Gunnar stares at him mutely. Then Mac goes for walks, to breathe, to think, to rid himself of the stale air and gloom of Gunnar's bed-sitter.

But he also uses the telephone, calling Archie again, with a request. "Can you find me a Frenchman named A. de Soissons?"

"Probably find you three dozen."

"I just want the one who lives in Mr. Racine's file."

"That would be the late Mr. Racine."

In truth, the name had leapt from the page even before Mac left the café in the Place du Bourg-de-Four, although he didn't know quite why. A handwritten name in the Swiss lawyer's close script: A. de Soissons. The contact. The cutout who communicated with Racine.

For his part, Gunnar asks no questions concerning Mac's affairs. He cares nothing for today, and wants only some affirmation of his own yesterday, even at those rare times when an old acquaintance, like Mac, shows up, rank-smelling, on his doorstep and steps into his bed-sitter out of more than twenty years of darkness. At his point in life, the questions are all of yesterday, not today. There is no point to today. He would rather talk of Saigon. There was a woman in Saigon, a time when Gunnar was a superman. Does Mac remember her, Gunnar's woman? Vaguely, he does. A slim young Vietnamese girl in an *ao-dai*. She never smiled. Gunnar talks of her. She was beautiful, wasn't she? Yes.

"We had sex twice a night. And once in the morning, for good measure." He says this blankly, staring at the staged images flickering on the television screen.

Did he, this ineffectual man? It doesn't matter. Mac looks at him, the poor sexagenarian Romeo sitting fat and listless on the couch in his bed-sitter, his face bathed in the blue of pornographic images. Gunnar wants no reality but his memories, and that makes them real enough.

So it goes until October 2. Mac needs the time to let the surf wash over him, and then, frustrated, roll back out to sea. A week when the computer sleuths will be poised in ambush, waiting to swoop in at Mac's first appearance at an ATM or airline counter. The computer sleuths can find the electromagnetic tracers anywhere, and instantly.

But they cannot find Gunnar. And Mac's book is full of Gunnars.

CHAPTER 19

I saw a road sign that said "Welcome to Wyoming, the Cowboy State," with a picture of a big buffalo. But I didn't see any cowboys, or buffaloes either, just wide-open rolling dusty desert with these little sagebrush clumps as far as you could see, and the road a long ribbon away off in the sun, with nothing on it except maybe like a pickup a mile away that was coming toward you, and mountains in the distance, and sometimes a little dirt driveway kind of going off to a little gate with antlers on it. Sometimes you'd see one of those drives and it would go for a mile back from its little antler gate and there at the end of it would be a trailer, just a little trailer home.

The sagebrush was all brown and looked dead, like little brown dead bushes, until you get up close to one, and they have these like pale-silvery-bluish leaves. God, Wyoming went on forever, it seemed like. Then, after a whole day of driving, they put this blindfold on me. It seemed like we went on for a whole day after that.

We got off the highway and onto a road that wound in loops and sometimes would go on for a long straight bit and then turn at an angle. I hardly ever heard another car go by. Then after a while the road turned into a dirt road, gravelly and bumpy, with us bouncing around and a lot of dust coming in through Smokes's window. And finally we turned down a little hill, it felt like, with the car bouncing in and out of ruts, and came to a stop.

I would guess it was about midday. They took the blindfold off and let me out and it took a while for my eyes to adjust. We were in among this group of log cabins, with brown logs and little green roofs and green shutters with the paint all peeling, and behind them was a riding ring made of logs, and beyond that a barn. It seemed like some kind of a summer camp. Nobody was there. The sun was out but it was cool in around the cabins. There were big trees down there in among the cabins, and I could hear a river not far off. In the distance in every direction but the one we had come were mountains, big red and gray pillars of rock rising out of the foothills. I asked the Beak where were we but she just gave me that "Shut up, stupid" look and so I shut up. She scared me more than he did, actually. They led me off down the hill to a big cabin and I thought, this place is like a prison of mountains.

That was the last time I got outside for about two weeks. They had me in this cabin, and they put me in an upstairs room. It had one little window which Smokes nailed shut. Then he went outside and got up on a ladder and nailed two big two-by-fours across the outside. So I got a little light in was all.

Well, I stayed in the room. Smokes told me if I tried anything cute they would kill me, or fucking kill me, actually, and Smokes said he'd fucking just as soon do it. And twice a day they brought me up stuff to eat. Peanut butter or cereal or sometimes canned stuff. Gross franks and beans and ravioli and that kind of thing. And they let me out to go down to the hallway to go to the bathroom, and once every day to take a bath. That was the big moment of my day: bath time. And they let me read books. They were mainly old paperbacks, all brown and crumbly, and pretty boring, except some of them, I have to admit, had sex scenes in them.

There was one thing: the phone. They had figured out how to trick Dad, somehow, and three times they made me talk to him and pretend I was with Papa in North Carolina. This part was confusing. Isn't my dad supposed to know I'm kidnapped? So he'll get a million dollars or something to set me free? But Dad didn't even know I was kidnapped. They sat right next to me and made me tell whatever me and Gammy and Papa had done that day. They said if I let on that I was kidnapped they'd kill him and they'd kill Mother too. So I did as they said. I tried to drop a hint once, but it didn't work out too well.

I'd hear the television a lot. They'd watch the soaps and the talk shows and at night they'd watch television until late. And football games. I'd hear the car, sometimes, when one of them was going off. And then, sometimes the next day, I'd hear it come back. I got to listening for the littlest thing. I knew they slept downstairs because I could hear them walk around and then I could hear the downstairs bathroom. I don't know if they were a boyfriend and girlfriend or not. He was totally gross, I couldn't imagine even the Beak—still, what else was there to think about? I was only curious because there was nothing else to do.

I cried a lot at night, I have to admit it. I'd cry when the sun went down.

CHAPTER 20

Unusual things happen to animals—and humans—in captivity, as biologists and sociologists have long known. They begin to act in ways that cannot be accounted for by the laws of natural selection. Under Louisa's house arrest, she finds strange things happening to her, as well. She paces incessantly, from the living room to the kitchen and back again, over and over and over.

And she begins listening to Birch Thornacre each night when he comes on at 10:00 P.M. She cannot account for why, exactly. She has never had the slightest interest in talk radio and always regarded Thornacre as laughable. But there is something mesmerizing about these programs, and she tunes in. Besides, like everyone else who listens to him, she has insomnia.

"Hello and good evening, Margery," he says. "It's Monday, September thirtieth, and you're on the Birch Thornacre program."

He has an awfully good voice, a resonant bass, reassuring, deep, a voice that suggests Thornacre's physical antithesis—a bearded farmer, or a lumberjack, instead of the pipe-cleaner of a man she knows he is.

"Yes, Birch, hello. I love your show," a woman is saying.

"Thank you, Margery."

"I guess you can say I'm a Reagan Democrat," she begins.

"Well," says Thornacre soothingly, "Ronald Reagan was himself a Democrat once, so you can be forgiven a few errors of youth, too."

They laugh together. Ugh. Why is she listening to this? But she is.

"Only thing of it is, why don't the Democrats understand why people like me have lost patience with them? Giving all the money to the blacks. And that Belakis, sleeping with that girl under his poor wife's own roof!"

"They just don't understand that the American people want leadership, do they, Margery? I really think they just don't get it. They don't understand that ordinary people like you and me and the people who listen to the Birch Thornacre program are looking for a little decency from their leaders. The kind of man who could carry on with a young woman in the den while his poor wife slept upstairs, why that's one thing. . . ."

The story Smaug mined has consumed the tabloid press for a week now. While going through a bitter divorce with his first wife, George Belakis, the Democratic vice-presidential candidate, put up a staffer named Diana Felotti in a nanny suite for two weeks. Some months later she got an apartment and moved out, and they began dating publicly. His wife now says that they began an affair while the staffer slept under her roof. Belakis has denied it, but the denials ring hollow, and Felotti has refused to comment.

". . . But the real message, Margery, the real message is not George Belakis. The real message is Sam Proctor, and the Democratic leadership. Where's their judgment of the American electorate? Where is their respect for the people they would lead, to assume that we are as morally bankrupt as they, that we would not renounce such conduct? That's the real message, Margery. They just don't respect you."

Across the Potomac River, at his home in Alexandria, Virginia, the lawyer Krasnowicz is dressed in his pajamas and sitting up in bed, next to his wife. Zelda Krasnowicz wears her nightgown and leans up against a small mountain of bolsters and pillows. She concentrates on the television. Krasnowicz looks at it too, but his thoughts are far from the program she is watching. He is thinking about Louisa Shidler.

He has been thinking about her ever since morning, when his secretary brought the FedEx package into his office with the rest of the mail. Sent from Paris, sender unidentified, the envelope inside said, "Hand-deliver, personally, to Louisa Shidler. Do not open. Do not discuss by telephone." That made him a little nervous. Do not discuss by telephone?

Krasnowicz didn't open the package, but he ran his fingertips over the envelope, and was pretty sure it contained nothing but paper. For the rest of the day he worried about it. A lawyer who smuggles contraband to a client becomes a criminal himself. But evidence? The envelope came from Paris, where all of this supposedly began. As the day wore on, the lawyer's instinct for self-preservation asserted itself. Whatever the hell this package was, it was now in *his* possession. So he checked the terms of the pretrial detention order, taking some comfort from the fact that it contained no limitation on Louisa's right to receive mail.

At about four o'clock, Krasnowicz parked his car in Louisa's driveway. He stepped nervously from it, looking over his shoulder at the neighbor's house across the street. Just then a child rode by the house on a bicycle, and it spooked him a little, so that he stumbled as he quickened his step to Louisa's front door.

Inside, his client took note of his uneasiness at once. He wonders, now, if somehow she had guessed at the contents of his briefcase before he opened it. The thing that was almost eerie was how smoothly she took charge of the conversation.

"Louisa, I have something for you" was all he managed to get out before she interrupted him.

"Oh, the rest of the Jencks material, yes, thank you Mr. Krasnowicz, I know you wanted to discuss that with me."

Sitting in bed, he replays that strange remark to himself, and all the strange remarks—lines from an improvised play, it seems, now—that followed. He hadn't brought any of the Jencks material—statements of the government's witnesses that it must turn over to the defense. She knew that, and she had never asked to look at it before. But there in the foyer of her home, she was calling it the Jencks material and, before Krasnowicz could correct her, putting two fingers to his lips.

Other than to shake his hand, she had never touched him before.

All during the strange fifteen-minute pretense that followed, she'd discussed imaginary government evidence with him, forcing him to join in as they sat on the couch. Now, lying in bed, he remembers the words she scribbled on his yellow pad while talking to him.

"We'll discuss in court, not here" is what she wrote.

So distracted is Joel Krasnowicz by this, that it is not surprising when the remark tumbles out:

"Zel, I gotta tell you, this Louisa Shidler I cannot figure."

"The bribe one? From the embassy or whatever?"

"U.S. Trade Representative. Yeah. Not that I should care. Meeting with her is a trip to the dentist, I can tell you."

"So she should be different from your other clients?"

He has said too much. He decides to stay away from the package, at least directly. "She is different from them, Zel. Them I'd rather hang around, personally."

"I worry about you, Joel."

"Shidler's a priss," he says. "She just doesn't seem like a criminal. The U.S. Attorney wants her to do a shitload of time, which personally I don't think she'd get even after trial, never mind a plea. And she wants to plead."

"Maybe she's guilty."

"Zel, even guilty people don't sign up for this kind of time."

Zelda answers impatiently. "So she wants to plead already. Hey, did you lock the screen porch?"

He hasn't heard her and is rattling on. "And she doesn't want to talk about information. I got no information, she says."

"You got a thing for her or something? Louise Shidler, Louise Shidler. What about the screen porch, Joel? Did you lock it?"

He laughs.

"What's so funny?"

"Me having a thing for Louisa Shidler."

"The screen porch, Joel. Did you lock it?"

"I think so. Maybe. Stop *tchepping* me, Zel."

She frowns, getting up from the bed to check. From the stairs she says, "Too busy thinking about this Louise to protect your own house. When our house is broken into and all of us are murdered in our beds, remind me to stop *tchepping*. You, with your Louise this and your Louise that, and I should stop *tchepping*."

He chuckles. "Louisa. Zel, you are something, you know that?"

"I heard she's pretty," she says from downstairs.

"Depends what you like."

"What was that?"

There is a tramping downstairs and he notes that she locks the screen-porch door with a dramatic flourish, to ensure that he hears it. It is well and truly locked, that screen porch! And it wasn't locked before! Too busy fantasizing about Louisa Shidler!

Zel can communicate a lot by a slam. She has an entire dialect of them.

Returning, she switches off the television, then insists that he repeat his last remark, and so he obliges.

"What's that supposed to mean?"

She slides under the covers, then rolls to her side, presenting her back. Ah, Zelda has found a way to make this about herself. But Krasnowicz is strangely talkative this evening. Lying in the dimly lit bedroom, he cannot get Shidler out of his mind.

"Zel, she is a serious snob. You and me are the help, maybe."

"So? I'm a *yenta,* and you're into self-loathing."

He laughs out loud. "Zel," he says.

"I don't want to talk about it."

"Zelda, for Pete's sake." He is still laughing.

Zelda sniffs.

"Zel, the case just doesn't make sense. Shidler is too in love with herself to dirty her hands with a bribe. Money, after all, that's so, so common."

"Yeah, right," Zelda says.

"And all of a sudden, plead guilty, I got no information, I don't wanna trade, that wasn't a government of which I was a part, ten years, sure, where do I sign? It is not adding up. It is not adding up."

"I don't want to hear about it."

" 'I got no information,' she says. She's fucking bursting with information. I can tell these things."

"I don't want to hear about it," says Zelda Krasnowicz.

"Well, Lord have mercy, look at this man coming in here half past eight o'clock on a Monday night with his dirty shoes tracking cross my house!"

It happens that on that last evening in September, Louisa Shidler has already been the subject of another couple's conversation. Eugene Phillips and his wife of thirty-one years, Angela, a short, stout whirlwind whom he calls Sissy, have exchanged words on the topic as well. Sissy is one of those people who is not content to live life: it must be narrated.

"And his tie all hanging down, expecting his dinner! Look at him! Does he kiss his poor woman first thing he walks in the door? Does he tell her he loves her? Does he hang his coat up in the hall closet like she asked him a thousand times to do, or does he throw it over a chair?"

He kisses her. "Love you, honey."

She snorts. "You don't look after your clothes, they won't look after you. Look at that coat, wrinkled, dirty. It's shameful, the way you mistreat that coat. Shameful. Now don't give me them choirboy eyes, Mr. Eugene Phillips, and set there not telling me a thing about what you do all day while I got to keep the household together on my own, and half the evening too, without a soul to speak to—"

"What, baby, you didn't talk to Monica today?"

This is part of the ritual, too. Sissy talks on the telephone to her sister Monica, in Spartanburg, every day, seven days a week, fifty-two weeks a year. Talking to Monica is as regular as breathing. Sissy eats, she breathes, she talks to Monica. Gene shakes his head and wonders what-all there is to say to a person that takes *an hour every day of your life.*

"Well, if you was in your own house an hour a day, you might know. You might know a lot of things!" She'd said that once.

"God strike me if the man don't want to take my telephone away too and leave my poor sister in Spartanburg even lonelier than she is—and me with not a soul to speak to, and you showing up here in my kitchen with them choirboy eyes and expecting me to fix your dinner. Mmmm-hmmm." She is, in fact, warming the dinner on the stove. The reading of the indictment continues, as all five feet two of Sissy, scowl on face, works a wooden spoon in Gene Phillips's dinner. "Mr. J. Edgar Hoover, he home for supper every night, with that boyfriend of his . . ."

"What do you know about J. Edgar Hoover?"

"I read it in *Parade*. They was all gay and home for supper, all them white men, running 'round country clubs and putting on their Klan robes and I don't know what-all."

"That what you think?"

"That's what I *know*, Gene. I read it in *Parade,* and you, you out doing who knows what every night with them gay white men in their country clubs." She lets out another snort, and it dissolves into a giggle. "You ain't feelin' a *change* coming on, now are you Gene?"

"Why, I don't know, honey, you keep on with me, might seem kind of attractive."

"Mmm-hmm. Just what I need, a woman my age. A homosexual *white* man." She laughs again, a cheery, snorting sort of laugh.

Long experience has taught Angela Phillips to doubt most things said by most men, and in particular, anything said by the FBI, but Gene's retirement is in sight now, and she looks forward to it as anxiously as he does. For all her fussing and bustling, he has been getting home early lately. And most nights, like this one, her hard eyes will soften at some point, and she'll snuggle up against him, and ask, "You all right, baby?"

Eugene Phillips has long known that he has been shunted to a siding. His office is still in "the Puzzle Palace," the massive block of stone that is FBI headquarters, the J. Edgar Hoover Building on Pennsylvania Avenue. But he cannot help noticing the newer, sleeker, more powerful engines—the Picarros of his world—hurrying past while he watches. He has been aware of this for some time. Maybe it is just that he is getting on. Maybe that agent out in Chicago, the one who brought the race discrimination suit, was right. Phillips has been detailed to administrative assignments with increasing frequency—the Shidler investigation fell to him as something of an accident. It came in quickly, and Robertson and Bergen, who might normally have been called, were on assignment. That's the way Jim Fitch, the FBI deputy director, explained it to him.

When Gene Phillips arrives at the office in the morning, he finds the sport-coat jackets are already on the hooks, and the lights on, and the bright young men and the bright young women well into their second coffee. They nod quickly at him and then return to their phones and their reports. And when he puts on his blue raincoat and pork-pie hat at night, the office lights of the young agents are still burning brightly. On his way to the elevator, young men with sleeves crisply rolled are hurrying to meetings, meetings to which he has not been invited.

He remains philosophical about this. Phillips knows he tires more easily, lacks the stamina for long surveillances and days on end without sleep. More and more his mind dwells on South Carolina, his plans for tomato plants and runner beans and collard greens and muskmelons. In his briefcase he sometimes carries reports, some of them even secret ones. But always he has a copy of his latest 401(k) statement. His pension is vested. In spare moments he recalculates the interest, does budgets.

His briefcase also carries seed catalogues. Sometimes over lunch he studies new varieties of spaghetti squash and his favorite lettuces.

Phillips thinks often about his daughter Barbara, who has been going with a grad student for two years or more. Maybe there will be grandchildren soon. Sissy longs for that, and he thinks he will enjoy it himself. His mind goes to these things, even in the middle of the workday, and he looks at the young men and the young women in a distant way.

"Don't know about this one," he says suddenly.

She can tell by that look that comes across his eyes, that's been coming across his eyes for the last few days, what "one" it is.

"Shidler?"

"Mmmm-hmmm."

"What's the matter?"

The words come slowly, thoughtfully.

"For thirty years, they never let me near a case like this. And now, here's the biggest bribe anybody ever heard of. Bigger than the last ten bribes anybody ever heard of put together. We got money flowing here, there, everywhere all around the world getting into this Swiss bank account with her name not exactly on it but kind of hanging around it. She a housewife, a little suburban white woman who didn't never jaywalk in her life, far as the record show."

"Sometimes you can't tell about people."

"When the last time *you* couldn't tell about a person?"

She laughs again. "Well, that's different."

"Maybe. Maybe not so different. Because I can tell too, usually. And I saw her, Sissy. I saw her twice."

He eats some, letting the remark settle. She studies it. Seeing, for Sissy, is believing.

"You know what else?" he asks. "She want to plead guilty. We ain't traced the money nowhere, and we ain't got a statement from her, we ain't got cooperation, we ain't got nothin' on nobody else in this thing. We ain't got nothin'. She got a lawyer, and he got the Jencks package, and we ain't got nothin', and he know we ain't got nothin', and so she know we ain't got nothin'. And she want to plead guilty."

"What did the SAC say?"

" 'Great work, Gene! You done good. Great investigation. Time for the next one!' " Gene shakes his head, takes a drink. "How stupid them people think I am, baby?"

It is the old subject. The scab has been knocked loose and raw flesh is behind it, she can see that.

"No sense gettin' into it," she answers. "You got three years, and then we going to South Carolina, and we ain't never gonna worry 'bout Mr. J. Edgar Hoover or any of them people no more. We goin' to South Carolina and we gonna build you a smokehouse, and we gonna have a garden thirty feet square, with kale, and asparagus, and Jerusalem artichokes, and every kind of greens, and you gonna bring me turnip greens every day, and mustard greens, and I gonna cook them up with ginger, just like you like, and—"

She is stopped by the look in his eyes, a flash that betrays the depth of the old wound.

"Sissy," he says, "that's what *they're* thinking! Don't you see? 'Ol' Gene got three years before his retirement, and ain't nothin' going on between his ears but the design work for his watermelon patch.' Baby, that's what *they're* thinking."

CHAPTER 21

In covert operations, more violence results from accidents than from malice, and so it is with the death of Amada Montes. Under "cause of death," the coroner's report will later list "internal bleeding: two gunshot wounds to chest," but it might as well have said "Murphy Oil Soap."

On Tuesday, October 1, at 11:15 A.M., Montes is traveling north on Wisconsin Avenue, halfway to her next cleaning job, when she remembers her blue bucket. An hour earlier, she'd put it down inside Henry MacPherson's study door when she began to do the vacuuming. She had forgotten it on her way out. Among its contents were a canister of Ajax, two heavy-bristled scrubbing brushes, her rubber gloves, and a plastic ammonia bottle. All of these she might have done without, for she had another bucket full of cleansers and brushes in the car. But the blue bucket contained her only squeeze bottle of Murphy.

Earlier that morning, it seemed to her as she cleaned the MacPherson townhouse that Mr. MacPherson must not have have been home since her last visit. Certainly he had never left the kitchen that clean before, and there were none of the books, papers, and magazines she usually found spread about the kitchen and the front room. The kitchen and bathrooms were just as she had left them a week before. That's why she didn't need to use the blue bucket. She vacuumed and dusted—you have to do something to be sure you get paid, after all—and while doing this, she turned on the radio, loud. When the time came to go, her head was full of pop music and plans for Friday night with her new boyfriend. Daydreaming, she carried the white bucket to her car and drove off for her next appointment. But she had forgotten the blue bucket, just inside the study door.

Amada is on her way to the Janeses, and Mr. Janes is a very particular client. The desks and tabletops must be polished, the shelves dusted, and, most important, the cherry flooring in the kitchen cleaned with Murphy Oil Soap. Mr. Janes has always been quite emphatic on that point. It must be Murphy.

As she sits in traffic, waiting for the light to change, she curses her luck. Might Mr. Janes overlook a substitute? Amada frowns, realizing that it isn't possible. He will notice. So she turns the car around and heads back toward Georgetown.

Fifteen minutes later, the intruder in MacPherson's townhouse hears the clear, unmistakable report of the door latch, and then rapid steps across the foyer. Unfortunately for Amada Montes, both he and the blue bucket are in the study. There is neither time nor place for him to hide. Amada crosses the entrance hall and turns the corner into the room.

Amada Montes has no time to react, no time to scream, barely time to register the confusing images: the stack of papers on the desk that she had just seen tidy not a half hour before, the dark-haired man standing by it, the gun in his outstretched hand with the odd-looking device attached to its snout.

It is over immediately—perfunctorily, you might say. Other than by falling to the floor, she makes no more sound herself than escapes the gun's silencer.

The killer takes a moment to reflect. Then, standing by Amada's body, he flips open his cell phone and punches in a number. He is thinking that perhaps advantage can be taken from necessity. "We have the file," he says. "But I was interrupted." He turns his gun over in his hand thoughtfully. "We need to arrange for our subject to be the registered owner of a Beretta Model 3000 Series .32 caliber Tomcat."

The voice on the telephone assures him that this will be seen to immediately.

At the moment of Amada Montes's death, Toby Higginson, now unemployed, is only eight blocks away, in his Georgetown apartment, punching in the eleven digits. There follows a brief exchange with John Shidler—sometimes it's Emily, but it hasn't been very comfortable with *either* of them since the separation—and then Isabel gets on the line. She says she's okay. After a few minutes of chatting, he hangs up.

This is carried off so smoothly that he never guesses that he is not actually speaking with John, nor that his daugher is far from Yadkinville, North Carolina. The dialing of the Yadkinville exchange sets off a circuit in Toby's telephone that diverts the call to a small office park in Waldorf, Maryland. There, an operator waits with a digital recorder and a menu of split-second cued responses. Each has been recorded from the actual tap that monitors the Yadkinville phone round the clock. The menu has John saying, "John Shidler," "Hello," "This is John Shidler speaking," "Just a minute, please," "Yessir," "Nosir," and, most important, "I'll get her." The menu of Emily's responses is even wider, although it lacks the last remark. It does contain a handy "Just a minute, please." For tricky situations, the operator can revert to a digital voice synthesizer. Each day the computer downloads recorded conversations to the database and further refines its voiceprint for John Shidler. By speaking into the conversion microphone, the operator activates the software, and the program converts his words. Although there is a slight delay and the quality is imperfect, Toby hears what sounds like his father-in-law.

As the Waldorf operator manipulates the conversation with Toby, a second line is activated. And in a moment or so, Toby really does speak with his daughter. What he doesn't know is that she is not in Yadkinville but sitting between two kidnappers in a cabin in northwest Wyoming, fresh from the warning that if she says or does anything out of line, they will arrange for the execution of both of her parents.

And what if the Shidlers should call their estranged son-in-law? The computer routes the call to a perfect simulation of Toby's voice mail.

CHAPTER 22

October has come: the last month, the home stretch of the Breed–Stillwell campaign, and for Jack as for Jill, each day brings only a firmer conviction that neither will ever again want anything to do with politics. Smaug's swings of temperament, always mercurial, exceed anything even rumored before. She wants the weeklies. She doesn't want them. Bring the coffee now. Take it away. Don't just stand there, you slack-jawed marsupial! Where is so-and-so? (You canceled the meeting, Cynthia.) Canceled the meeting! Get him, get him *now*, for Chrissake! She misses appointments, screams at Jill to reschedule them. What are these fingerprints doing all over my desk?

She consumes Mylanta and Zantac and Tylenol by the bottle; drinks nothing without caffeine. She demands the morning polling data, flies into a rage when she sees the trends.

The trends are flat-lining. Her team is in front, but expiring, gasping. The challengers are churning up ground, and the only question is the length of track to the tape. She knows that there is sufficient time to lose. October can be a long month.

Time already has the election "too close to call." Everybody else puts Proctor within the margin of error. At the rallies, the shouted questions are all about the horse race, for the press has lost interest in the issues. Breed looks indecisive. Smaug and two media assistants have spent many hours in the Oval Office, many more in the private quarters of Air Force One, working on his delivery.

Stillwell is hitting five events a day, and beginning to show the strain. At least the Shidler story seems to have shown no legs. No play on the national news, inside coverage in the newspapers. No second-day stuff, no sidebars, nobody hounding Royall.

Late at night, Smaug sits in her office, surrounded by the day's news, trying again to feel the pulse of Mr. and Mrs. Couch Potato, the faceless Americans, the channel surfers who will decide the election. She used to feel that pulse in her own bloodstream, as if her fingers were pressed firmly on the soft underside of their wrists. Now she has lost the sense for it.

For Jack and Jill, the only respite comes when Smaug boards Air Force One to ride with the President to the next staged rally, testing the media, the crowds. On those trips, she shows the world nothing but her usual confidence. The tantrums, the hysteria, are saved for later.

"Just shut it down," Smaug is shouting into the telephone late in the afternoon on October 2. The Crab is sitting with her, in a chair drawn up before her desk, a file spread before him. Jill has surprised them with the advance on the new Proctor ad series. It looks bad: he's gone positive with a big national buy. "Do what it takes, spend what it takes, use the networks. You have unlimited budget on this. Just shut it the fuck down. Got it?"

Smaug looks up, sees Jill quivering across the carpet. "For Chrissake, don't you ever knock?"

In Georgetown, Toby Higginson, just returned from his squash game, sits in his living room, still in his sweats, and dials his in-laws.

"Hello?" It is John Shidler's voice.

"Hi, John, it's Toby. How's it going?"

"Pretty well, pretty well, thanks."

"And Emily?"

"She's fine, thank you."

"What's new around the farm?"

In Waldorf, the operator switches to manual, since he hasn't a good response here. "Usual stuff, you know," Toby hears.

"Yeah. Well, good to talk to you. May I speak to your granddaughter?"

"I'll get her," the voice says.

Meanwhile, in Valley, Wyoming, Smokes is ready. Isabel, too.

"Hi, Daddy," she says, coming on a moment later.

"Izzy, how are you, baby?"

"Okay."

"How's with the hillbillies?"

"They're okay, Dad."

"You sound a little down, sweetheart."

"No, Dad, I'm having a nice time."

"I miss you."

Isabel looks up at Smokes to stop herself from crying, as she answers, "I miss you too."

"What you been up to?"

"Not too much. I help Papa with the cows."

"Yeah?"

"Yes . . . We had a couple of calves today."

"Really?" her father asks. "How many?"

"Three." She looks down at the table.

"Did you see them born?"

"Mmmm . . . no. Just afterward."

"Are they cute?"

"Very."

"That's nice, baby. Well, I miss you very much."

"Miss you too, Daddy."

"Maybe I'll see if I can come down and visit. Would you like that?"

Isabel's eyes dart up to her captors. The Beak mouths the words.

"Yes, Daddy, that would be very nice."

"All right. Sometime soon."

"Dad?" she asks.

"Yes?"

"How's Mother doing?"

"Oh, she's fine. Don't worry about her. She's going to be all right."

"Okay."

"Love you."

"Love you too, Dad."

Toby Higginson hangs up and trundles off to the shower. At that moment a blow falls roughly on his daughter's cheek, a blow that sends her toppling to the floor of the Wyoming cabin.

"Don't you ever pull a stunt like that again!" the Beak shouts.

Isabel sobs, holding her jaw. Smokes looks at the Beak incredulously.

"Never, you little bitch. You understand me? One more stunt like that and your parents are gone! Gone!"

"The fuck is the matter with you! What is it?" Smokes asks.

"Calves in October! Get up to your room!"

Isabel, sobbing, hurries upstairs.

A minute later, the Beak is asking the operator in Waldorf, "You get that shit about the calves?"

"Yeah."

"Father picked up on it?"

"Don't know. We'll monitor him closely."

"And what about coming down this weekend?"

"Don't worry. He's got a date."

The Beak needn't have worried on either score. Toby isn't planning to go to North Carolina. And Toby has never known, nor cared, when beef cattle have calves, nor any other thing about farming. His daughter's signal goes unheeded.

Stir the coffee in the morning quiet, stir the coffee and think. Watch the liquid swirl around the stick, and wait until it comes to rest. Link your thoughts to it, bring them to rest. Phillips is at his desk early, reviewing the teletype. First he puts in a call to Central Database Section, requesting an all-sources report on Henry MacPherson. Then he walks slowly across the hall, knowing that he'll be lucky to get a prelim out of them by lunch. Phillips has never had any pull with Central Database Section.

That is why he is so surprised, when he returns to his desk ten minutes later, to find the light on his message machine flashing. They have info for him already? He's even more surprised when he hears the message. It is from Fitch himself!

"Yo, Gene, nice coat!"

Phillips looks up from dialing to see young Bobby Picarro walking across the room, chewing gum and grinning at him. A winking, gum-smacking, strutting, cock-of-the-walk damnable wiseass white boy, grinning at him like that. God, but he'll be glad to be out of here. And what the hell's the matter with this coat, anyway?

Phillips turns his attention back to his phone and speaks to Fitch's assistant. "Special Agent Phillips. Is Mr. Fitch available?"

A moment later Fitch comes on the line.

"Gene, how are you?"

Gene? Eugene Phillips has met this man three times.

"Fine, sir."

"Good. Listen, saw your all-source request on Henry MacPherson, and I was just wondering what investigation that's on."

"Louisa Shidler."

"I see. We're looking into MacPherson on this Montes shooting, and we've got that end pretty much covered. If we come up with anything useful, we'll get it to you, okay?"

"Yes sir."

Late last night, Gene Phillips had drifted off in front of the television, his head lolling on the chair. And then, out of the heaviness of fatigue, his mind snapped on again, and it hasn't snapped off since. It was a story on the evening news about the murder of a housemaid in Georgetown, at the townhouse of a man who, District police say, is now missing. A newspaper man named Henry MacPherson.

He hangs up the phone. Yessir. *Yassuh, Boss! Yassuh, Ise gwine wait right heuh fo yo call!*

He stirs the coffee again, takes a sip. Why does the deputy director of the FBI know about a routine homicide? And why *doesn't* he ask me what MacPherson has to do with my Shidler case? Fitch doesn't know that MacPherson was at her arraignment, or that Shidler worked for him years ago.

"Yo, Gene. Can't sleep, or what? You been gettin' in here early."

"Boy, didn't you know that about us? We never sleep. Always wakeful." He looks at Picarro enigmatically.

Stir the coffee, stare at the pool swirling there. Go away like a good little boy, Gene. Do as you're told until you retire. Twirl the plastic stick in the brown liquid as a wry smile forms on your face. Banter with the kids. It will be nice down in South Carolina. Only three years to go. That's a good boy, Gene.

Damn, but I never got that kind of turnaround out of Central Database Section before.

CHAPTER 23

By October 3, Mac has been able to learn from Archie a little about
A. de Soissons in advance of his visit with the old man. For thirty years,
from 1963 until the early nineties, he was aide and constant companion to
a French businessman named Claude Housez. They were together in
Laos, and afterward in Indonesia and Australia. And then for a time in
France. Housez whistles up the yacht for a cruise, and there is faithful
Alain organizing the provisions. A fellow comes to the villa to see Housez,
and, for fifteen years, he meets Alain first. Alain looks him up and down,
decides whether he passes through the screen.

Then there came the day when Alain had some bad luck—popped
into the Frankfurt airport with half a toothpaste tube full of cocaine, and
next thing anyone knows, it's eighteen months in a German jail. He
walked out of the jail in 1995 and into obscurity. But not complete obscurity; not an obscurity that Archie couldn't penetrate to find the old
man living in an absolute shack of a bungalow on the outskirts of a village
in the Auvergne, smelling of cowshit and fertilizer, the housefront wind-
blown with highway litter.

He smells bad himself, garlicky and of old sweat.

"Alors, vous êtes Monsieur Pierce?" the old man demands, squinting
at the light as he stands in the open door. Mac leans against the door frame,
catching his breath. He has walked a mile and a half from the village.

"Oui, monsieur," he answers. Since Archie made the arrangements,
Mac has borrowed his name.

"Qu'est-ce que vous voulez?" The old man motions him in.

Even before they are seated, the old man has said it: What does Mac
want? He wants Housez, of course, and perhaps de Soissons has guessed
this. But first: "I have brought a bottle of wine. The least I can do," Mac
says, in French.

This will help. But still, it will be difficult. The old man has thick lips, and a large nose exploded by years of drink. He stares at Archie's card through the explanation, which didn't sound very credible to Mac as he practiced it on the train. Mac's biggest fear is that somehow he met the man once in a Saigon bar. He pulls an enormous sheaf of notes from his briefcase and fumbles through them. The table wobbles a little when he puts the papers down.

So, de Soissons thinks, as his suspicious eye looks his guest up and down. Perhaps the American *is* writing a book about the end of the French presence in Indochina. He eyes the papers on his table and their custodian warily, the way men of action eye men of papers.

But Mac's is a special skill, and without quite knowing how he was induced to it, de Soissons finds himself talking. He talks first of Laos, where he met Housez. After a while, Laos melds into Housez, for the Laotian opium fields were the beginning of Housez—of what he became. They were indistinguishable to de Soissons. Not that he says this directly. But somehow the name comes out.

"Agence France Presse, was he?" Mac asks.

De Soissons smiles and fills his glass. "Of course."

"And then, later, he became a businessman?"

"You might say. In Laos, everyone was a businessman."

"Tell me about that."

Alain de Soissons drinks, shuffles off to the lavatory, returns, drinks some more. A little ring of purple appears beneath his glass, begins to smear the table. De Soissons speaks of Vientiane, of Saigon and Phnom Penh before the Khmer Rouge; of soldiers and smugglers, rogues and technocrats. He mentions many women. Evening comes. No one ever talks to Alain anymore, and so now Alain cannot stop. Without hurrying him, Mac circles back to it.

"Now, that Hougais fellow, tell me—"

"Housez."

"Oh yes, sorry. Became a businessman, did he?

"You have not heard of Claude Housez?"

Mac frowns. "No, I'm sorry."

"One of the richest men in the world."

"Really?"

"Certainly. I worked for him for many years."

"Yes?"

"Yes. Many years. Now I am retired, with my sister Gabrielle. At my age, it is good to live with a sister. You have a woman around to look after things. But it is not necessary to look at her naked. You want one for that, you go to the town, find a younger one. Better this way. You think so?"

It is not clear whether Mac agrees or disagrees.

"And, was he rich in Laos, when you knew him?"

"I have known him many years, but he was not rich in Laos at first. That is where he had, shall we say, his apprenticeship."

"What was his field?"

De Soissons laughs. "Tell me, this book you are researching, you will write in it, Alain de Soissons tells me these things?"

"Ah, yes, of course. One has to document . . ."

"Then you must ask Claude Housez in what is his apprenticeship."

"I see," says Mac. There is silence at the table, and he empties the last of the bottle into de Soissons's glass.

"Too bad, monsieur le professeur."

"I have another." Mac reaches for the new bottle.

"I'll tell you this about Housez," the old man continues, his eye brightening. " 'Alain,' he says to me, 'when you go to a strange place, what is the first thing you must have? The most important thing?' "

"And I guess. I say, 'The tickets?' Or, 'The passports?' Something like that. He scoffs and we play the game again. And perhaps once I say, 'A hotel, a good hotel.' And then he smiles. I have been a good student for a change. 'This is closer, Alain,' he says. 'But what is a hotel?'

"I don't like these games. Old Alain is not so clever as Housez, so I don't like the games as much, but Housez, he must play a game. What is a hotel? A great big building with rooms and beds and a restaurant."

" 'Almost, Alain,' he says. 'Almost. Everything but the most important thing. That is the difference between us,' he says. 'You see almost everything, I see almost nothing, and yet you miss the thing I see, the important thing.' So he says."

De Soissons puts his glass down on the table, staring hard at it, as though he does not trust its bottom to make contact with the tabletop until he can feel it. "Pah!"

The French is too fast; Mac hasn't gotten all of it. He tries to sort through the words, while the old man stares into his glass. Sometimes with French the words come later out of the redivided sounds, like a good anagram.

"But what does this have to do with the professor's study of Indochina?"

"He was a player on that stage," Mac answers. "It was a small stage, you know. I must get to know them all."

De Soissons is unsatisfied. There is a moment of tension. But then he feels the wave of alcohol and shrugs. Who cares? Did Claude Housez help him in Frankfurt? Besides, it is not important. The American has brought good wine, not the vinegar Gabrielle buys from the shop. De Soissons wants to talk more about the collapse of the Diem government, the destruction of the old Saigon. And the women. The women in the bars on the Rue Catinat, more beautiful than the women in Paris, he says. More loving. Desire and fear, sex and war, those are his memories, and how each was made more vivid by the other. In this he is no different from Gunnar, no different from all the others who left the Land of Tigers and Elephants in their youth but could not quit its ghosts.

Gabrielle, a short, stout woman in a floral print dress, returns from the market, her string bag bulging as she bangs through the door. Her legs are wrapped in bandages. She frowns, nods perfunctorily, and goes into the kitchen, breathing heavily. De Soissons says nothing to her.

"She rattles all the pans now, you will see," de Soissons says when she is gone.

Sure enough, the sound of banging pots and crockery is heard.

"She doesn't like me to drink too much before dinner." The eyes are full of laughter, but they are hard eyes nonetheless.

"I see."

The interview winds to its end. "Oh yes," says Mac, as though the thought has come late to him, as he is gathering his papers. "I forgot one thing. Have you any photos from that time? I always make it a point to ask."

Later, when Mac takes his leave, de Soissons has consumed almost two bottles of the wine, and is a little wobbly. He comes too close and showers Mac with a blast of garlicky breath.

"Thanks for taking the time."

"It was nothing," says the old Frenchman.

Mac takes a step toward the road, and then turns in the darkness. "Monsieur de Soissons, what *was* the most important thing in a strange place?"

"Pardon?"

"That most important thing that Housez quizzed you on."

"It is the one thing that finds all the other things," Alain de Soissons answers. "So you don't have to find them for yourself. It is the concierge."

"This was Housez's practice? He had a concierge in each place?"

"Certainly."

"How interesting. Bon soir!"

"Bon soir, monsieur le professeur."

CHAPTER 24

Why is he smiling at me that way? Mac wonders. It is Friday, October 4, and night has fallen in Paris. The lights burn late in the seventh-floor window of a building along the Boulevard Haussmann. The desks overflow with news clippings, computer printouts, magazines, but the offices of *The Economist* are deserted, save for Mac and Nevins, who is twirling a fountain pen in his fingers and smiling in his detached and rather annoying way at the American.

"What is it tonight, Mac, Taillevent? Or did we hop the overnight from D.C. for another round of three-star blindman's buff?"

Mac is too tired to pick up on the banter, and if Nevins doesn't know that Mac hasn't left Europe, it's just as well. "Archie has found something," he answers. "A man named Alain de Soissons. Lives in the Auvergne with his sister. Something of an alcoholic."

"Well done him."

"His name was in the Swiss lawyer's file. In 1995, he finished up a hitch in a German prison for smuggling a small amount of cocaine, and now he gives out that he's retired. What's interesting about him is what he did before that."

"Which was?"

"Apparently, he spent most of his adult life working for Claude Housez."

"Claude Housez?" Nevins removes his glasses, sounding perplexed.

"You know him?"

"One doesn't *know* Claude. But one most certainly knows *of* him."

One also has a file on him. The news of a link to Housez in this curious matter seems to confuse Nevins, but there is no doubt of his sudden and remarkable elevation of interest.

"He's a sort of a French Howard Hughes," Nevins explains.

"Met him?"

"Once. Brief interview outside the viewing circle at the Hippodrome. Bois de Boulogne. He was the silvery chap in the morning coat, fresh white carnation, striped trousers creased down the front, lemony plaything alongside. We were the ink-strained wretch in a rather old macintosh, none of whose many creases was imparted by design."

"Hippodrome?"

"Likes his steeplechase. Sport o' kings. Photographs round the horseflesh, word or two for the press, tip o' the topper, gone upstairs."

"Is he in pharmaceuticals?"

"Not that I know of. Not particularly, anyway. Probably owns a little bit of many things."

Mac is picking through the scraps on Housez, odd photographs, news clips. "What about the pharmaceutical deal?" he asks.

But Nevins doesn't hear the question, for he's trying to fit things into the wrong pigeon holes. Some fit, some don't, and it's the leftover ones that puzzle him. The fountain pen twirls back and forth in his fingers.

"Sorry?" he asks, at length.

"The pharmaceuticals, Ian."

"Don't know. Can't work the bits together, can't see my way round it just at the minute. May have some holdings."

What is it about the photograph Mac has pulled out of the file? Mac lights a cigarette, stares at it. There is something odd about the man, a feline quality. "Tell me about Housez. What does he do?" he asks.

Nevins smiles. "Oh, they say he'll do about bloody anything, as long as the margins are good. He's a Venetian, that's what he said. I doubt the bloke has spent much time in Venice. Views himself as stateless, a mercantilist of the seven seas.

"More guns than butter for Claude. Claude's a middleman, a broker. As he waited there outside the paddock in his morning coat and striped trousers, I asked him, 'What's your secret, Mr. Housez? King of the deal, they say. How d'you manage?' Know what he says? 'Monsieur, there's always a Jew with a daughter, and a Gentile with a son. And no one but me arranging for them to be married.' That's it: starter's orders. Interview over, plaything tugging on the arm, so sorry, must be off to the race. But rather a nice metaphor, I thought. So Housez goes about the world rounding up the Jews and Gentiles, performing the benedictions, and quietly collecting the fee."

Mac listens as he leafs through the file. An article from an Italian furnishings magazine on Housez's ranch in Montana and his chalet near Geneva. A picture of him in a hotel lobby. In black tie at the Cannes Film

Festival, a woman on his arm young enough, but far too attractive, to be his daughter. Another black-tie. An opera house? Another attractive girl.

"He's made a success?" Mac asks.

"Made a success? Rather! And old grandfather Rothschild was a nice little trader who made a few bob in his odd-lot house. Yes, you could say he's made a success."

Outside, the engines roar as the evening traffic races by. Mac continues to pick through the file. More photographs of Claude with horses—must have been taken at the Montana ranch. The caption is in Dutch, and Mac can't read it. More photos and articles. Housez photographed on a viewing stand at the 1993 Frankfurt Air Show. More horses.

"Problem is, mostly the money's been in guns," Nevins goes on. "You lot built the greatest weapons factory the world has ever seen, and then you declared peace. Left a bloody great supply looking for a new demand. Housez's been one of the world's biggest arms players."

Mac sighs, closes the file. He goes to the window and looks down at the street. He knows that he cannot long remain hidden. They say a computer can beat a grandmaster at chess now. Certainly the computers can find one old man in a sour suit.

"How do you know?"

His back to Nevins, he stares out at the Paris evening. His sacroiliac aches fiercely: too many nights on couches.

"Mac, one knows because it's all *legal* now. The governments are all in the market. They don't even have to lie about it anymore. President Breed set up an 'Advocacy Center' in your Commerce Department, a bloody trade show for the arms merchants. They say that CIA is basically an industry consultant, now. Don't you write about this?"

Mac shakes his head.

"It's the best business story of our decade, right under your nose. Example: Under your Arms Export Control Act, Bell can't sell Cobras—that's an attack helicopter—to the Pakistanis. Poor sods not in good graces, you know—we imperialists being rather down on brown chaps building the bomb. So, Bell sell Islamabad the helicopter stripped, then Giat, the frog arms conglomerate, do them a nifty kit to fix it up with all the stingers and smart bombs and radar jammers and the thermal imaging units and all the other toys. And the wonder is that everybody knows this. It's not just not illegal—it's not even bad form anymore. You'd have a job finding someone to be *embarrassed* about it. In the States, Commerce is bloody cheerleading."

"And Housez?"

"Housez pronounces them man and wife. He makes the deals go. Lines up the Pakis, or the Indos, or the Montenegrins, or the Saudis, or the defenseless American ally of the month. This week it's Cobras. Next it might be two dozen Chris-Craft, along with the telephone number of the gent in the Bahamas who'll fit you up with the latest antisubmarine weaponry. And then next month something else. Who knows, plutonium from the Chinese, nuclear triggers from the French, package the lot in Amman, FedEx it to Baghdad. Might be some real money in that."

Mac returns to the desk and reopens the file. For a few minutes neither man speaks, as they page through different parts of Nevins's Housez file.

"Snappy dresser," says Mac, squinting at a photograph of Housez looking dapper in white tie, escorting a woman of painful thinness into a ball of some kind.

"Oh, yes. Likes the fruits of success, does our Claude. Cars, boats, villas, suits, women. Long ones. Long and thin. Women, I mean, not suits."

Mac tosses the photograph back into the file. "Ian, how does this all work? Suppose I'm the government of India, and I want a missile launcher, who can get that for me?"

"Damn few people, actually."

Nevins settles back in his chair, adopting the manner of the don in tutorial. "Minister of Indian defense rings up the chaps at McDonnell Douglas and Aeropa and one or two others and says, we need a telecommunications satellite, care to bid? Mind you, that's a big bid, and everybody wants it. Need the rocket ship, the computers, the satellite, the lot, probably need to hire a launch from the frogs or from Ivan or your chaps. McDonnell Douglas draw up a bid. They know Aeropa's bidding, a few others. Then they go to their Washington solicitors. The whole thing has to be licensed, you see—advanced technology, weapons-related equipment, that sort of thing. The solicitors draw up the licenses and one of the senior ones rings up the chief counsel to your secretaries of commerce, defense, state. Our client is in a bid for a billion-dollar contract with the Indians, he tells them. 'We'll be sending along the papers. Would you mind having a word with the secretary?' Because, you see, when the deal is done, your government will control the terms, tell McDonnell Douglas whether we like the Indians this week, whether we can do the deal, what the price is, what color to paint the fins on the bloody rocket ship. If the government like the deal, the next step is for your secretary of commerce to go round to see the Indian defense minister. 'My chaps would rather like that contract,' he'll say. Then, the usual. The minister will tell him that of course he'd like to oblige the Americans, but dear oh dear, Aeropa has presented such an attractive bid. They may negotiate some terms. Becomes rather Moroccan at times, actually. Or your chaps do a boorish one, threaten to add a runway to the local American air base and have the brass bloody Marine band play 'God Bless America' during the hols. You know?"

"But it gets done at that level? The secretary?" Mac asks.

"Billion-dollar contracts, weapons of war, yes, that's the level. So the question is, Mac, is that our level?"

Again the curious smile. Mac hesitates, his jaw working.

"Mac, it's material to the inquiry," Nevins says, gently. "What can your chap get done? Can he do a deal to sell twenty fighter jets? How high is he? Let's say I *am* the government of India, and I want a communications satellite. Can your chap sell me the launcher? Or I'm the Israelis, and I need a Cray supercomputer. Get my drift, old lad? Whom do we have here? Do we have Doris, who smiles sweetly, and hands out pocket calculators at the trade fair, or do we have a chap who can sell me a ballistic missile guidance system?"

"Who else is at that level?"

"Bloody cipher you are," Nevins says, shaking his head. "As I said, not too many. Secretary of commerce. Perhaps an undersecretary. Three or four of them, I think. The vice president. Secretary of defense, perhaps his undersecretaries. That's it, really. State and Defense get to bless the arms ones, but they don't manage the deals the way Commerce does. These days there's so much that involves high tech that your lot have become more and more like the Russians used to be."

Nevins gets to his feet and expels an impatient breath. "Right, form, end of lesson. Let's all turn over our exam papers, then. Question number one. Fifty million—guns, butter, or drugs?"

Mac is puzzled. He doesn't answer.

Nevins the schoolmaster: "Can't be butter. Too much. Therefore guns or drugs. Correct?"

Nevins plays the form too: "Sir, that's correct, sir."

"Right," the schoolmaster answers. "Question number two. Name of suspect. It wouldn't actually happen to be *be* Doris, would it?"

"Excuse me?" Mac looks up.

"Mac, even poor we have our little white Nexis boxes. Punch in the search, out pops latest from the Yank broadsheets. Now, what *about* this Louisa Shidler person who's been bidding for Great Bribes of Western History? Eh? Assistant to the Trade Rep, isn't she?"

"Yes."

A silence then, as each waits for the other to go on.

"What do *you* make of that, Ian?" Mac asks, finally.

Nevins sits back down, the demonstration over. He sounds weary when, at last, he answers. "Can't make aught of the bloody thing. Stumped. Too much money for butter. Leaves guns or drugs. Along comes Mac with Claude's fingerprint. Claude does guns; used to do drugs, so they say. But why muck about with drugs if you're Claude? Messy things, get you left off guest lists. Don't need the money anymore. Leaves guns, doesn't it? What about Doris, then? Guns? The United States Trade Representative doesn't actually do guns. Doesn't do them at all, not legal ones. Illegal ones, d'you suppose? Chap on the national ticket a gun runner? Would be rather a scandal, don't you think?"

CHAPTER 25

As Mac's interview with Nevins proceeds in Paris, in Washington, D.C., Louisa has come to the courthouse to plead guilty. She barely reacted when Krasnowicz telephoned a week ago to advise her about the prosecution's unreasonable demand. She sounded indifferent.

But she is not indifferent when the time comes, even Joel Krasnowicz can see that. Krasnowicz has worries of his own, and he is late getting to Courtroom 3: just the right sort of late, so that a large crowd can see him march in just minutes before two to join his client at the defense table. Louisa sits there alone. She cannot bear to look behind her at the rows of filled seats, so she hunches over and keeps her gaze resolutely forward.

Across from the defense, at the prosecutor's table, sits Mark Roth with a young assistant. Next to them is the U.S. Attorney, Hanscom French himself. He has come to the dock so that, when it is all over, he can hold the trophy fish for the photographs.

"Hi, Louisa, sorry I'm a little late. Traffic was terrible," Krasnowicz says, extending his hand to her as he hurries up. "I need to talk to you about . . . What's this?"

The package lies on the defense table. As he takes his seat, she leans toward him and whispers, "I want you to take it back, keep this for me."

Krasnowicz looks down at the package, then picks it up and examines it hurriedly, noting that it has been torn open and is now stapled closed. The idea, he recalls, was to get it *out* of his own possession, whatever it is. He is frowning as he leans toward her to whisper. "We were supposed to talk about this in court, remember?"

She shakes her head.

"Louisa, you mind telling me what's going on?"

She can smell garlic on his breath. "Yes, Mr. Krasnowicz. I mind. Please just store this for me, at your office, okay?"

"I can't do my job if I don't know what the hell is going on." Krasnowicz snaps his briefcase open and hunts through a jumble of yellow pads and photocopies, at last pulling a sheet of fax paper from the stack. "This just came in this morning. Who's Mac?"

The prosecutors have now taken an interest in the conversation and are looking over at the defense table. Louisa holds the fax close to her. The legend indicates a Paris, France, exchange.

"He the guy who sent you the package?"

She reads:

> Louisa—
> Delay the plea hearing. New information. I will get it to you soon.
>
> —Mac

"Parties ready?" Louisa and Krasnowicz look up. The clerk is beckoning from the door to the judge's lobby.

"I need a minute," she whispers to Krasnowicz.

But judges are contrary that way. When you are pressed for time—when your client is impatient, or when you just absolutely have to get such and such a witness on this afternoon—that's when a judge takes a call from someone at the American Bar Association, or turns a five-minute recess into an hour to receive a visit from Senior Judge McGillicuddy. But when *you* want a minute—always, when you want a minute—a court officer is shouting "All rise!" and someone in a robe is striding toward the bench.

The someone striding toward the bench now is United States District Judge Helen Freegard. Louisa asked about her a week before, and Krasnowicz simply shrugged his shoulders and said, "Unpredictable." Now the judge bustles into the room and takes her seat. She nods—a little frostily, it seems to Louisa—at the U.S. Attorney. "Good afternoon, Mr. French," she says.

"Good afternoon, Your Honor," he beams, bouncing to his feet. He is a florid, summer-stock actor sort of a man; he'd make a good Polonius.

"Mr. Krasnowicz."

"Good afternoon, Your Honor."

"Will you be representing the government this afternoon, Mr. French?"

"No, Your Honor, I'll leave that in Mr. Roth's capable hands."

The judge smiles too, but briefly, and cryptically. "Parties ready?" she asks.

"Ah, Your Honor, if I could have just a minute," Krasnowicz says.

He leans down to Louisa's side. Their heads are together, and the eyes of the room are upon them.

"What is it? Who is Mac?"

She shakes her head silently, closing her eyes. New information, what could that be? But she thinks again of Isabel. "Mr. Krasnowicz . . ."

"Look, if you want me to, I can tell 'em we've had a change of heart. We might—"

"Keep the package, Joel. Keep it in your file for me. Please."

"Mr. Krasnowicz?" It is Judge Freegard again. "Do we need to take a recess?"

Louisa looks up at Krasnowicz. "No," she says. "I'm ready."

It is High-Church Episcopal, the courtroom, big as a church, and high-ceilinged as a church, with freshly painted, cream-colored walls; the bench might be an altar, with swaths of red velvet behind it, and a thick maroon carpet. Judge Freegard looks like an Episcopal minister, and there is a choir of good Episcopal clerks and probation officers, and a well-dressed congregation—none of your slovenly municipal court rabble—and everything except organ pipes and a placard on the wall to identify the hymns. Missing is the hurly-burly of the courthouse Louisa would have hoped for, the anonymous confusion, the distraction.

"I understand we're here this afternoon on your client's change of plea, Mr. Krasnowicz?"

"That is correct, Your Honor."

"Ms. Shidler, will you please rise?"

Judge Freegard has a kindly aspect. She is an attractive woman, about fifty, prematurely white-haired but young-looking and bright and quick about the eyes. She looks like your favorite aunt, the quirky one who goes on vacation to exotic places and gives you the cleverest Christmas gifts, the one who rattles with laughter over off-color jokes at Thanksgiving while your father frowns. She stares inquisitively at Louisa, and Louisa realizes that this is not going to be easy. Instinctively, Louisa likes her.

There are people all around her, but Louisa feels very much alone, standing beside Joel Krasnowicz in the center of this vast courtroom. A painful dialogue ensues. In a federal plea hearing, there is no hiding behind legal obscurity. Nothing in government is plainer. By God, they are going to drag guilt out of your soul, make you stare at it, embrace it, affirm it in a dozen ways. They are going to beg you to contest it before they let you out of there.

"Have you taken anything this afternoon which might impair your judgment?"

"No, Your Honor."

"And you freely and willingly wish to plead guilty this afternoon?"

"Yes."

"You understand the nature of the charges in the complaint?"

"Yes, Your Honor."

"And that by pleading guilty you subject yourself to possible imprisonment and fines?"

"Yes, Your Honor."

"Do you understand that you have a constitutional right to be tried by a jury on each of these charges?"

"Yes, Your Honor."

"And that you have no obligation to testify, or to prove anything, in such a trial?"

"Yes."

"And you wish to give up your right to have that trial?"

"Yes, Your Honor."

Judge Freegard rubs her chin, frowns.

"Ms. Shidler, do you understand that in such a trial, the government would carry the burden to prove your guilt beyond a reasonable doubt, and that if it did not do so, you would be entitled to an acquittal?"

"Yes, Your Honor."

And on it goes. The Constitution of the United States provides her with enormous safeguards, the court is committed to protecting her rights—and Louisa Shidler wants to throw all of this away and plead? That is the effect of questioning. It can be a little vexing in the regular run of case, after the prosecutor has pummeled the defense into a plea, this ruse that but for the defendant's headstrong insistence on throwing away her rights, the government would just as soon convene a jury to ensure that those rights be protected. That is not the case for Louisa—she just wants it over. Yes to the questions, yes, yes, yes! Enough!

"Count one of the complaint alleges violation of Section—"

God, Louisa thinks, she is going to recite the elements of each count. And Judge Freegard does. She goes element by element. Does Louisa understand that the first element of Count 1 is thus and such, and that the government has the burden to prove that element by proof beyond a reasonable doubt, and that she, Louisa, has no obligation to prove anything, and that if the government fails to carry the burden of proof on any element of the charge, that she is entitled to an acquittal?

She understands. On to Count 2 for the same drill. Does she understand? She understands. Still on her feet, she punctuates the questions with the rote answers. Yes, Your Honor. Yes, Your Honor. Her leg begins to itch beneath the collar and her hose, and she wants to lift a toe to try to scratch it, but she daren't. You can't get under the thing anyway. Louisa is in the church service from hell, chanting the solitary responsive to an endless psalm. And then the last question comes.

"Ms. Shidler, are you guilty of these charges?"

She had been staring at the table, and she looks up quickly and with an expression of surprise. Judge Freegard peers down from the bench, seems to peer right through her, and Louisa reddens, hesitates, as she can see that the only thing written on the judge's face is curiosity. Is this really necessary?

"Yes, Your Honor," she says, looking down again, her voice catching slightly.

But Judge Freegard has seen something. Something about the initial hesitancy, something else about the way the defendant avoided her eyes. She stands, walks to the corner of the bench, puts one hand on her hip. "Ms. Shidler, come up here, please. Mr. Roth, Mr. Krasnowicz? Yes, you too, Mr. French."

What now? Dutifully, Louisa follows Krasnowicz to the sidebar, and they huddle there before the bench. The judge leans down from above, her face kindly. "Mr. Krasnowicz," she whispers, "I've got some problems with this one."

"Your Honor," he answers. But his voice trails off as he gives her a kind of a shrug. What do you want me to do, Judge? My gal wants to plead.

You can't say this kind of thing in words, but lawyers say it with gestures, and Judge Freegard understands. She nods, and goes on. "A bad feeling. Hasn't this happened kind of quickly, Mr. Roth?"

"The case *has* moved quickly, Your Honor," French chimes in. The poor fellow doesn't understand. "I think the government and Mr. Krasnowicz have acted—"

She cuts him off. "I'll say. Complaint, plea, wham, bang, thank you, ma'am! Is this about money?"

"Your Honor," Krasnowicz says, "I don't believe so."

"Some fear on her part of the not inconsiderable expense of your fees?"

Krasnowicz colors a little.

"Your Honor, that is not the situation here," Louisa interrupts.

Surprised, Judge Freegard smiles at her. "No, I'm sure it isn't. That was inappropriate and I apologize, Mr. Krasnowicz. It is only that I am puzzled. In fact, your being here is somewhat reassuring. The court knows that you are a conscientious attorney. Sometimes, shall we say, a feisty one. I'm sure you wouldn't counsel your client to plead guilty if she weren't guilty."

"Your Honor, I never counsel a client to plead guilty. That is the client's decision."

"I see, Mr. Krasnowicz." She turns, and looks in a kindly way at Louisa. "Ms. Shidler, this pile of charges comes out of the blue in your thirty-seventh year. I'm told from the pretrial detention memorandum that after a blameless, a faultless, career, one day you decided to take the biggest bribe in history."

She pauses, and Louisa thinks, We could have used her at USTR. She has that knack of using silence to make you speak. Louisa has to check herself.

The judge continues, "I've seen a lot of defendants. Usually I can figure out why. You don't fit the greed profile very well. So I have a little problem understanding why. Are you guilty? I can't accept your plea unless I believe you are guilty."

Louisa is frozen for a moment. This judge is kindly; could she somehow put an end to all of this? She is only a foot and a half away, and once again she is leaning down and looking right through her. Louisa's eyes dart to the stenographer, and she is reminded that what she says is being taken down.

"May I have a moment, Your Honor?" she asks.

"Of course."

Louisa turns and whispers to Krasnowicz. He shakes his head.

"What is it?" asks the judge.

"Ah, Your Honor, the privilege."

"Fiddle the privilege, Mr. Krasnowicz. What does she want?"

Krasnowicz frowns. "Well, Your Honor, would the court be willing to meet with Ms. Shidler?"

"Certainly. That is what—"

"Alone?" Krasnowicz continues.

"Alone?"

"Yes, Your Honor. Without a record. Without counsel. Without me, or Mr. Roth? Or Mr. French, either." He smiles, as if to say, "Intending no offense to the United States Attorney for the Eastern District of Virginia."

Now Judge Freegard is taken aback. She stops, pondering, her face screwed up into a frown. "Never been asked that one before," she says. "Mr. French?"

But it is Roth, not French, who tries cases and who argues for sentences. He gets his bearings quickly. It is time to put an end to this female bonding and get on with the plea hearing. "Ah, the government would have to object, Your Honor. I mean, the court will have to sentence the defendant, and—"

"Yes, you're quite right, Mr. Roth. What was I thinking? I suppose I could meet with the defendant without counsel if both parties consent. I don't mind telling you I'd be a little uncomfortable with that. But not without a record. I wouldn't do it without a record. And the government would be entitled to that record prior to sentencing." Judge Freegard shakes her head. "Sorry."

Louisa nods. There is a brief silence then, with Judge Freegard seemingly even more perplexed. And then she remembers her question.

"It is important that I act publicly, I'm sure you understand that, Ms. Shidler."

Louisa nods.

For one last time, Judge Freegard is turning herself into Aunt Helen, and in a half whisper, she leans down and says, "But why don't you tell me what's on your mind? If there is some question in your mind about this, I want to know. You can talk to the court."

Louisa looks up at her and asks, "I can talk to the court?"

"Yes, yes," says Judge Freegard.

But Louisa stops herself. She knows it was foolish even to have risked this. It's just that there was something about the judge that . . . Then it is there again. Isabel's face.

"Ms. Shidler?"

"Yes, Your Honor. I am guilty of these charges," says Louisa.

Helen Freegard sees that only Louisa's mouth is saying it. She is still troubled by the request to speak to her alone. But the defendant's eyes are blank, and her face is a mask. The judge nods. She knows now that she has done what she can. A federal judge has a lot of cases. You do what you can in each one, and then move on.

When the lawyers have resumed their places at counsel table, Judge Freegard takes her seat and makes the finding. "Ms. Shidler, the court finds that your plea is freely and voluntarily made, and it accepts that plea, and finds you guilty as charged in the indictment. Terms of pretrial detention to remain in effect. Mr. Looney, let's set this down for sentencing."

There is some palaver as they schedule the sentencing hearing, and then Judge Freegard stands again. She looks unhappy, uncertain, as she begins to leave the bench. "Ms. Shidler," she says, "this is a very sad day. We will see you at the sentencing hearing." She shakes her head and walks off the bench. At last, Louisa thinks, it is over.

CHAPTER 26

It is past 11 P.M. on Friday night. At the *Washington Herald,* Suse is in the slot, tonight's traffic cop for the paper. She has a phone cradled on her shoulder as she coaxes another quote from a reporter covering a story in Chicago. Across the newsroom, someone is yelling something at her. Someone else is yelling something at him. Her monitor is blinking. Another reporter is on hold. In short, a typical night at the *Herald.*

She finishes with the man in Chicago and somebody yells, "Suse, pick up two!"

"D'Agostino."

"Suse."

"Mac?"

"Yeah. How are you?"

"Mac? Jesus Christ, Mac? That's not as pertinent a question as how and where the hell you are! Where the hell are you?" Suse looks over her shoulder, lowers her voice.

"I've been out of town for a while, Suse, I need—"

"Mac, have you talked to the police?"

Now there is a silence at his end.

"Christ, Mac, your cleaning woman, what happened."

"My cleaning woman? What do you mean, my cleaning woman?"

"Your cleaning woman, Mac, your dead—"

"What?"

"Jesus, Mac—"

Voices are yelling for her. "What? Wait a minute, just hold it!" she hollers back at them. "Mac, we're closing the first edition and it's pretty crazy around here."

"Suse, I don't have any idea what you're talking about."

"Mac, your cleaning woman was murdered, and the police are looking for you. You haven't talked to them?"

"My cleaning woman was murdered?"

"Yes. You haven't heard?"

"Jesus Christ."

"Where are—"

"Where?"

"What?"

"Where was she murdered?"

"In your house, for Christ's sake! Mac, everybody on earth is looking for you! Where have you been? We've had cops and the fucking publisher every half hour and—"

"Amada was murdered in my *house*?"

"Yes, yes. Your house. You're missing, wanted for questioning."

"Someone thinks I murdered Amada? When did this happen?"

"Last weekend, I think. Mac, where the hell *are* you, anyway? Hold on a minute." She puts her hand over the mouthpiece, and he waits, listening to the muffled sound of her hollering into another phone about needing six more inches on the ways and means vote. It gives him a moment to think. Voulke, the publisher, has been in the newsroom, looking for him? The publisher never comes to the newsroom.

"Suse?"

"Christ, Mac, we're closing the paper—"

"Suse, do me a favor."

"Oh, yeah, sure."

"Get me a fax number for an FBI agent named Eugene Phillips."

"Sure, Mac, anything else while I'm closing the first—"

"What's happened on Shidler?"

"Shidler? She pled."

"Shit. When?"

"Today."

"All right. Get me that number, will you Suse?"

So it is that when he returns to his desk on Monday morning, October 7, Special Agent Eugene Phillips will be looking at a telefax of a passport and plane ticket, showing Henry Stevens MacPherson entering Switzerland at Genève-Cointrin on September 25, 1996. Also faxed are the blank passport pages, devoid of a reentry stamp. The fax legend turns out to be that of a copy center in Paris. Well, it could easily be a fake, Phillips thinks. Still, he folds the paper and puts it in his desk drawer.

Whatever Louisa imagined in court on October 4, it is not over. A change of plea hearing is relatively straightforward, but sentencing takes time. The system remains true to its ponderous past. You cannot even concede defeat with anything like efficiency. As Krasnowicz explains to Louisa, it may be months before sentencing. Probation—their old friend Mr. Ferraro and his colleagues—will have to prepare a presentence report, and, as everyone knows, Mr. Ferraro cannot be rushed. And so, an excruciating exile sets in at Louisa's Bethesda gulag, a waiting for the system to catch up.

Krasnowicz comes to the Bethesda house several times. He arranges for meetings and tries to start conversations about the plea, the length of sentence, the particular correctional institution, and so on. Once, he tries to ask her about the package—now restored to his office—but she cuts him off quickly. He sits on her living-room couch trying to engage her, trying to discover any human contact. Another time, he tries a joke, and the air seems palpably to cool in the silence that follows his punch line. Louisa has no interest in any of that, and mainly, she wants the man out of her house. Each time, as Krasnowicz leaves, pausing at the stoop, he looks around at the quiet neighborhood, and shudders, reminding himself that there is nothing about this case he likes.

Nothing—there is nothing to do. Louisa receives Krasnowicz when he comes. She sits in silence and wonders why Toby does not visit, not once. There is a boy who arrives to deliver the groceries, and she tries to talk to him, but he is all monosyllables and in a hurry to get out of there.

Days creep, hour by painful hour. A cold foggy chill is felt in the night air. Nights are the worst. The Renoir woman sits in the living room with her tangled hair falling uncombed around her shoulders, and her hands folded in her lap, and wonders when she will function again. Louisa has begun to slip into the catatonia of depression, and she can remain on her couch for hours, motionless, as though in a trance.

One or two minutes a day can be put behind her through ritual. She reads the personals every day. Then on Wednesday, October 9, turning first to the *Herald*'s personals section, studying it on the kitchen table as she drinks a cup of coffee, she finds another message.

> **Old Newshound seeks Latin companion for epic adventure. You read, I sing, and together we find the truth in first impressions. Ref: 9024.**

Louisa puzzles over the message all morning, but it is as though her mind's threads are stripped, and whenever she tries to tighten the screw, it simply slips. She turns and turns and the screw stays in the same place.

CHAPTER 27

At the bottom of the gut of the foreign correspondent, beneath the layers of stomach acid and stale coffee and nicotine, is a geographical pathology. When something happens, he has to go there. Phone lines and fax lines and e-mails and video uplinks are all very interesting, but there is, for him, no substitute for personal presence. Whether it be a hurricane, or a plane crash, or a drought, or a war, Mac's hands go to the airline schedules, and his mind to the name of the first stringer he can remember living within three hundred miles of ground zero. Often, in his life, he has arrived where something—storm debris, bullets—was flying dangerously close. But he has always had to go to the place, to see it for himself. This is a chronic condition; even ten years as an editor has not purged it.

This time the impetus comes from Archie. For he has done some snooping too, and it is a triumphant Archie who proclaims the news: "Know where he's going to be tomorrow night?"

The annual meeting of something called the World Institute for International Trade is the answer, where, on October 11, M. Claude Housez is to be a speaker. The Sorbonne, of all places! The arms man—merchant of death—in former times a pariah, is now an emblem of the promised land of international trade. Legitimate business will troop to a lecture hall in the Sorbonne to hear what he has to say. Reception to follow, at the Musée d'Orsay.

Getting a pass to the speech cost Archie exactly two phone calls and something less than four minutes. It was harder to obtain the other pass— much harder: AP's was already allotted, and Archie couldn't work a trade with any of the other hacks in town. In the end, it helped that he had an old friend in the information office of the American consulate. Even so, the best Archie could do on such short notice was an invitation in his own name.

"They've got the whole goddamn building. Jesus, *that's* a party. The Orsay is the size of a train station." Archie shakes his head. "It *was* a train station, once. And they've got the whole thing. Open bar. Open bar, Mac, for a *museum*! Sure you don't want me to go?"

"He'll be there?"

"Special guest star. Yeah, he'll be there. Along with three dozen other tycoons and seven head-of-state wannabes." Archie types instructions into his computer. "Nosy security types in your shorts. 'Les papiers, ou sont les papiers?' And don't spill your drinks on the Gauguins, or it's the garrote, pal. Hey, Mac, what's your height?"

When Archie finishes typing, he goes into the closet. "Come in here," he hollers.

Well, not a closet exactly. Under the rubric "office equipment," Archie long ago caused the Associated Press to invest in a used laminator and a Polaroid camera that he stored on top of a toilet in what served as the bureau's darkroom, next to a narrow metal table cluttered with the bottles of fixer, the paper cutter, and the developing tray. From time to time, a reporter wants admittance to places where he is not particularly wanted. Archie has learned the virtues of self-help.

And so, about fifteen minutes after snapping the photo, smiling like a proud papa emerging from the delivery room, Archie Pierce hands Mac a card, still warm from the laminator, with photograph and suitably fictional personal detail, identifying the bearer as one Archibald Pierce. They inspect it together under the desk lamp.

"This how you did that other card, the one I showed de Soissons?" Mac asks.

"Yeah, but that was just a card. This is a work of art."

"Where'd you come up with this, what the hell is it?"

"Carte d'identité. All you need are a darkroom, paper cutter, scanner, and Microsoft Publisher. Best thing since movable type." He frowns, however—something bothering him. "Here, let me have it for a sec. Give me that cup." With a pair of tweezers, Archie prizes the newly laminated plastic apart, and carefully pours in three drops of coffee.

"What are you doing?"

"Instant aging." Pierce waves the card back and forth. Finally he smiles and drops it on the table. "You need a tux."

Mac shakes his head. He's never needed a tux before. A few minutes later, the card still in hand, he is leaving. He looks at it doubtfully. "Archie, is this goddamn thing going to get me into trouble?"

"Mac, you already *are* into trouble. This just gets you into a museum."

The skies have lowered throughout the afternoon, and the rain starts almost at the moment Mac steps out of the cab. When the rain finally comes, it is as though all the water in heaven has waited, as patient as a Swiss engineer, for the precise moment of his arrival. Suddenly it is pouring down in sheets, walls of water pounding the pavement. The rain soaks Mac through in the thirty seconds it takes to hurry from the street up the museum steps.

Somehow the other guests have managed to stay dry. And none of them has left his finery in cold storage. So Mac, bursting into the museum lobby, soaked from the neck up and from the thighs down, looks about as inconspicuous as a panhandler at a state dinner. Archie was right. In the lobby are enough men in black tie to form a large symphony orchestra, not a few dozen head of them with wires trailing from earpieces into their suit jackets.

At the tail end of a troop of jostling Italians, his press badge around his neck, invitation and phony identity card in hand, the American in the wet suit presents himself to the scrutiny of the woman at the door. She frowns a little, perhaps at Mac's party clothes, and sniffs at the card. He's in.

It *is* huge. The Musée d'Orsay houses the largest collection of Impressionist paintings in the world. Light, airy, its curved roof arching far overhead, its galleries stretch off into the distance before him, one after the other. Beyond, above, everywhere, room after room of paintings. I'll never find anyone in this goddamn place, Mac thinks.

At one end, on an elevated dais, before a canvas by David, a jazz band is playing "Begin the Beguine." A vast ice sculpture shaped like a globe dominates tables piled with hors d'oeuvres in the center of the ground-floor gallery. Beyond it a crowd is milling. The bar, evidently. Off to one side is another group. Cameras are flashing. That will be the trade ministers and their spouses.

Around Mac is the low roar of a party gathering momentum, but not yet in full swing. He hasn't spoken a word since he left the taxicab. He begins to scan what he can see of the central gallery. Hundreds of guests are present, throngs of black dinner jackets and gowns, but no Housez. So Mac begins a circumnavigation, ambling through room after room of Seurats, Cézannes, Matisses, Manets, Monets.

He lingers in the Renoir room. Louisa. Well, not really Louisa. But the woman in *Le Déjeuner des Canotiers,* the one in the background who leans against the banister rail observing the party with a smile, reminds him of Louisa in better times.

On his second tour he finds Housez standing before a sad Millet that depicts a forlorn reaper under a grim autumn sky. Housez is a little different than Mac expected, a little slighter. Silver-haired, impeccably turned out in a white dinner jacket, he is encircled by at least a dozen guests.

Mac sidles off to the next room, then takes a post by a bar from which he can watch the entrance to Housez's gallery. He orders a scotch and water and settles in. Soon the party moves into the main gallery, Housez remaining the nucleus in an amoeba of partygoers. Though the cell shrinks and grows by turns as the party swells, there will be no bumping into him in this group. He is closely surrounded by a number of admirers, not to mention the bodyguards—"guests" who are too young and beefy to be anything else, and have the look of thugs who have been scrubbed behind the ears for the occasion.

The taller one wears a dirty-blond ponytail and an earring, and scrutinizes each person who approaches Housez. His companion is not quite so tall, but looks like a block of granite wrapped in fabric. There is also a woman in the party, visible now and again through the crowd. Dark, lean, her gown seems in dramatic peril of dropping off at any moment. She stands at Housez's side. This core group moves slowly across the room, meeting successive delegations that arrive, apparently, to do homage and then depart.

Housez? Seeing him in person, with his bodyguards, crystallizes the thought Mac's drink has helped him grope for. The watchful look on Housez's face, the deep, blank eyes, with perhaps the merest suggestion in them of something between mischief and predation. No, it is the cheeks and the eyes. He wants only whiskers and headgear, and he'd be the Cat in the Hat. The Cat in the Hat, attended by two very well-fed bodyguards. Thing One and Thing Two.

What could be so bad about this pleasant fellow with his two amiable Things? As Mac considers this, there is the slightest envy in him, as sometimes is the case when lifetime Fourth-Estaters contemplate their former peers who have moved on to positions of power or wealth in government or business. We were both kids in Vietnam, Mac thinks. Now he's in a dinner jacket in Paris, attended by bodyguards, holding forth in a goddamn art museum on his views on macroeconomics. There used to be something vaguely suspicious about making piles of money in international transactions. In 1996, it is esteemed, whatever the industry. He's a goddamned merchant of death, Mac thinks. But he's also the toast of the party. This is 1996, after all.

Opportunity arrives about a half hour later. The Housez cell seems to be splitting up. Housez and Thing One begin to move toward the lobby, leaving the woman and Thing Two behind with the others.

Mac has an idea where they are going. Once in youth, during one of his rare Washington tours, Mac was dispatched to the Capitol to cover a Senate hearing. In the Senate bathroom, where he had trespassed to take a leak, he met the Hon. Montgomery Basbas himself, senior senator from Tennessee. Basbas! *Ursus americanus*—a bear of a man with a ponderous head, everything about him outsized, shoulders and arms and hands, legs and face and belly and, no doubt, bladder, big and broad. His laughter rumbled the earth. His eyebrows were massive, bushy things, his hair thick and white. As Mac stood at the urinal, there came Monty across the tiles to rain down his mighty cataract on the adjacent porcelain. The young reporter had summoned up his courage; the vote was to be the next day, and Monty was thought to be the swing man. There was wide speculation about what he was going to do, but no one knew.

They stood shoulder to shoulder, or shoulder to elbow, anyway. "How you?" Basbas asked, and then sighed, as his waters began to flow.

"So, Senator," Mac asked, "which way are you leaning on this one?"

What the issue was, what the vote, why Basbas was the key man, all these things Mac has long forgotten. What he remembers is the massive senator at the neighboring urinal who never looked at Mac as the smile broke across his face and his shoulders began to go up and down.

"Boy," he rumbled, "if I were leaning any fu'ther back, I'd be peein' on my shoes!" And how the laughter spilled out then! Even when Monty had finished and zipped and washed, he was still shaking with it. It was as though the urinals themselves were haw-hawing with Basbas as he left the men's room. So, Mac thought, watching the door swing shut behind the senator, this technique needs a little refinement.

But that was a long time ago.

When MacPherson reaches the men's room off the Orsay's lobby, he finds Thing One combing his hair, staring into the mirror, while Housez unzips at a urinal by the far wall. Providence: the urinal next to Housez is free. Senator Basbas, permit me to try again.

"Monsieur Housez, how are things in the Old Town?"

Housez turns to appraise the tousle-headed man who has addressed him. No dinner jacket, a suit rumpled and soaked below the knees, his white hair a little wild. I saw him—where?—in the galleries? All of these thoughts flash through Housez's mind. "Do I know you?"

Housez's English is soft, and only faintly accented. Hearing it, Mac realizes that Housez's voice betrays not where he is from, but only that he is from somewhere else.

"Not unless we met a long time ago, in the Land of Tigers and Elephants," Mac answers.

The expression—one Claude Housez has not heard in a long time—brings him up short. The catlike eyes open a little wider. At the end of the room, Thing One has taken notice.

"You remember the Land of Tigers and Elephants," Mac continues.

"No one forgets it," Housez answers, softly. "And you are . . . ?"

"I am a friend of a senior American official. He is very concerned."

"Is he? And who might this official be, Monsieur . . . ?"

When there is no answer, the Cat in the Hat's eyes betray, just for a moment, an uncharacteristic vexation. He is a man accustomed to having questions answered. And now Mac has ignored two in one sentence. Housez remains at the urinal, although he has finished.

Mac has too. "We need to talk," he says. "I'm partial to Renoir, myself." He turns and heads for the door, nodding politely to Thing One on his way out.

"And what concern has the mysterious American official with me, Monsieur Silence?"

It is a delegation. Housez, with Things One and Two in formation, the woman behind, has come calling from across the gallery, finding Mac in the Renoir room. The band is playing a medley of Fats Waller numbers, the party reaching its crescendo. Yet another retainer has joined Housez and his Things, a nervous man with glasses and a briefcase. Housez waves off his party. It waits at a short but anxious remove.

In the corner of the room is a bench that faces a painting of a couple dancing outdoors. Side by side, Mac and Housez sit across from the painting. It depicts a man with red hair and a goatee; in his arms, a young woman with a glow in her cheek and a smile of pure joy.

"She's beautiful," says Mac.

"Aline Charigot," says the Cat in the Hat. "Renoir's wife." He adds, dismissively, "A bourgeoise."

"Looks like fun, being a bourgeoise," Mac says.

"It is a matter of taste."

"And what is your taste?"

Housez turns from the painting to face Mac. "Perhaps someday we will discuss that interesting subject," he answers, in a voice that suggests the day will be a long time coming. He folds his hands in his lap, then nods, watching. Behind him, the Things seem poised to act.

"Mr. Stillwell is very concerned," Mac says.

"Ah, Monsieur Stillwell." The Cat in the Hat shows nothing now, no twinkle, no anger. He pronounces the name carefully.

"Your Geneva seems to have become a very unsafe place." Mac goes on. He used to teach his reporters that information is like a dog. You want to catch a dog, you don't run after it. You open a door and stand away, wait for the dog to come in. Or the Cat, as the case may be.

Housez studies his interlocutor closely. Such an odd way his mouth has of puckering as though it were grimacing around a word. He tries to remember when he has seen that before. His voice retaining a perfect formality, he asks, "Who are you, monsieur?"

"Why don't we leave it at Mr. Silence?"

"He sent you?"

Mac nods. "In a manner of speaking."

"You are a confidant?"

Now it is Mac who looks again at the painting of the dancers. Questions are good. Questions before answers. "Confidants are a luxury, Mr. Housez. Let's say that like you, Mr. Stillwell has intermediaries. A concierge, is that the right word?"

"You know the Concierge too?"

"Yes," Mac lies. "Him too."

Another flicker passes across Housez's eyes, and is gone. With it, his face seems to darken, but then that passes too, and Housez's expression returns to its inscrutable evenness. From outside the room there is a sudden lull in the noise of the central gallery as the bandleader announces a break. The Cat in the Hat falls silent. He has regained his subtle smile.

Something is wrong. Mac was making progress. Now he's not. No more questions. No answers, either, and the Cat seems to be indifferent to the open door.

He presses ahead. "Mr. Stillwell is concerned about the security of the Swiss banking system. It seems—"

At this moment, an interruption. A party of Koreans has somehow breached the security fence erected by Things One and Two and the nervous man with the briefcase. "Monsieur Housez, Monsieur Housez!" The Koreans surround him, bowing and offering hands, popping up and down like pistons.

Mac puts another question, as Housez rises to meet them. "Can you give him any assurance regarding the files of the unfortunate lawyer? It would be a shame if you were to be associated with any of that unpleasantness."

Housez doesn't seem to notice. Or, more particularly, to care. He is greeting the Koreans.

"Claude!"

Mac's voice surprises not only the Cat's party but Mac himself, for he doesn't know what to say next. Housez turns and waits, and the Koreans hesitate. "The painting," Mac says, gesturing at it. "Would you say she is beautiful, la bourgeoise? Tell me what you think."

The Koreans look back at Housez, wait for his answer.

"I would say, rather, that she is necessary, Monsieur Silence. A man wants to dance, he takes the girl. Now, will you excuse me with these gentlemen? I return in a short while to talk." With Old World gentility, the Cat in the Hat takes his leave. His flotilla now having taken aboard the gentlemen from Seoul, he sets a course back to the main gallery.

The room empties. At length, Mac rises and takes another tour of the galleries to try to find them again. But they are all gone. The Cat in the Hat. The Things. The woman. Perhaps she's hunting for safety pins. Gone, all gone. Even the briefcase, and the man it was attached to. Had enough fun for one night? Another party to get to? Or was it my after-shave? If I were wearing any goddamn aftershave . . .

He returns to the bar at the front of the museum, orders another drink. Count them, MacPherson. This one makes three. You don't do three so well any more.

What was it about his eyes? It was when Mac said he knew the Concierge, wasn't it? He tries to replay the conversation, can't, and so sips the drink. Looking up again at the central gallery, he flatters himself that there must be someone in the goddamn room he knows. But he can't recognize anyone except the Koreans.

Christ, MacPherson, you drunken sot! Forget three, you can't do *two* scotches any more. The Koreans are here, and the Cat in the Hat is gone. With all his Things. They haven't gone off to do business. They have gone to check.

Outside the museum, the rain is still driving down in sheets, and two doormen, the tails of their coats flapping, struggle heroically to hold the umbrellas over the guests surging for taxis and limos. Women in heels are stumbling, stout men in long coats hurl themselves into cabs like basket-ball players diving for a loose ball. The street is a black sea of driving rain and headlights.

Mac turns and looks at the queue behind him. From a distance of about ten feet he receives a nod, then a chilly smile. He turns quickly to face the front.

"Hello, old Thing," he sighs. Next to him, a well-bosomed, blue-haired lady looks up and flutters her eyelashes.

Behind him the door is a bottleneck, and the doormen slowly open the spigot to issue partygoers into the rainy night. In the jostling of men and women, the laughter, the gentle pushing of the crowd struggling to reach the door, Thing One remains about ten feet back.

Suddenly Mac has reached the front of the queue, and one of the doormen is holding open the door of a cab. As Mac goes to it, Thing One slips out behind him and jogs for a Mercedes waiting twenty yards up the street, his right hand shielding his forehead against the rain. Mac hesitates on the pavement, the rain crashing down off the awning.

Mac is frozen there, the door of his cab held open, as he watches Thing One get into the front seat of the car.

"Monsieur?"

It is the doorman, impatient. "Monsieur?" he demands again.

"Sorry," says Mac. "Forgot something inside!" He returns to the lobby.

But he cannot long avoid the ubiquitous Things. Soon the two of them have rejoined the guests thronging the lobby. It might as well be twenty. When Mac turns for an exit, or a telephone, or the main gallery, or the elevator, there is one or the other, arms crossed, nodding at him. "Christ," Mac repeats, this time to no one in particular, and finally he accosts Thing One, his nose at about sternum height.

"I'm going to have a goddamn drink," he says.

What follows is rather comical. The glass of scotch stands on the bar, and the white-haired man stands by the glass, and the Things stand next to the man. For an hour. Mac is wobbling a little bit. Call the police? The doormen? Archie? Once I'm found, I'm found. Amada was murdered, Suse said. Christ, I definitely need a better plan.

"What about you?" Mac demands, suddenly, jabbing a finger at Thing One. "You prefer Degas's dancers, or Van Gogh? Or are you a Millet man? Well?"

No answer. Mac might as well have demanded to know the cube root of 511.

"Beauty," Mac says, carrying on. "Beauty, Thing One! Know what that is?"

The man stares at Mac mutely, then pulls a finger through his ponytail, still with the blank, disinterested expression of a man who is in no particular hurry to kill you but will get to it as soon as it is convenient and the crowd has thinned a little.

"Ah, for Chrissake." Mac looks back at the scotch, checks his watch, frowns, his mouth muscles doing overtime. "Where the hell is Housez, anyway?"

And then, a life raft. A big life raft with oars and provisions, and the sinner Henry Stevens MacPherson vows to his Grandfather Ebenezer and every pinched Presbyterian in the family Bible that henceforth he will sin no more. "Ned?" he calls to the chargé passing through the gallery. "Christ, is that you, Ned?"

It is indeed Ned Davidoff and party who pass by. He's gray now, not the blond-headed sport Mac remembers from a Middle East post long ago. "Henry MacPherson," Mac hails, rushing at him with hand outstretched, and a little too much scotch on his breath. The Things rise behind him, but hesitate, uncertain how to handle this development.

"Mac? Good Lord, Henry?" a surprised Davidoff answers. And then, hurried conversation. Inquiries after the wife, the kids. Or is it grandkids? Jesus! I remember scraping you off the paving stones in Tel Aviv, or wherever the hell it was! MacPherson works the diplomat. The latest post, let's talk of the latest post. Has he time for a drink? He hasn't. Just one, for Chrissake! (Just one, with your security team nearby, on full Thing alert.)

Afraid not. In fact, Davidoff has to get back to the embassy for a briefing tonight. In all this mess. The chargé shrugs. They wanted him here tonight to shake hands; they want him in Zurich tomorrow for an afternoon meeting. "I'm afraid that's the life for we foreign servants," he explains.

Us foreign servants, Mac thinks, but keeps it to himself. For Henry MacPherson, sent a life raft in the midst of a pitching sea, will not correct the oarsman's grammar. He will shin aboard.

"Ned," Mac finally says, "my goddamn raincoat is soaked through, and I'm out of francs."

So it is that ten minutes later, without quite knowing how or even why, Ned Davidoff has agreed to give old MacPherson a lift across town in the diplomatic limousine. A big black Cadillac it is, incongruous in Paris, with obnoxious diplomatic flags on the fenders, soaked by the rain. When it pulls away from the curb, a Thing in a Mercedes parked a block away reaches for the gear shift.

The next morning, a bleary-eyed Ned Davidoff is puzzling over the e-mail. Henry MacPherson wanted in connection with a murder investigation? Dangerous? Local authorities not to be contacted but report immediately to Washington by secure transmission? How did anyone know he'd seen him?

Davidoff sighs. Oh yes, he saw him. But not just that: he gave him a *lift* on the United States of America, walked him right into the embassy, smoked a cigar with him, and called him another car to take him to his hotel. An hour ago, after getting the e-mail, Davidoff checked with the driver, who was ready to sign an affidavit that he'd taken MacPherson to the Hotel Crillon and watched him go inside. Maybe he had. But it wasn't Mac's hotel, not his hotel at all. They had no record of him. Henry MacPherson had not been a guest there. Or anywhere else.

The aide is at the door. They will be late for the Zurich train. Davidoff switches off the computer, deciding he will finish the report later.

Although Ned Davidoff has no way of knowing it, the driver was right. MacPherson did make a pit stop at the Crillon. He scuttled through the lobby into the restaurant, waving off the headwaiter, and then continued into the kitchen. There he nodded at the chef, his jaw working, and smiled politely at the sous-chef, who watched him hurry out the rear door and into the alley. He disappeared then, the odd man in the raincoat, lost in the darkness up along the alley toward the Place de la Concorde. The sous-chef shrugged at the chef, and went back to his sauces.

Mac looked both ways before crossing the boulevard, but there was not a Thing in sight.

CHAPTER 28

On Sunday, October 13, at about noon, Isabel hears from downstairs in the cabin the low rumble of their voices. Something about the Beak going to town. She lifts the curtain and watches through the gaps between the two-by-fours as the Beak gets into the Cadillac, listens as the engine roars and settles to a hum. The car bobs slowly out of view and then can be heard heading for the road.

The day passes, and the car does not return.

As night is falling, downstairs she hears the television come on, what sounds like a football game.

She glances at the knapsack on her bed, containing Buster and her sweatshirt, then pounds on the door.

"What do you want?" Smokes hollers from downstairs.

"Can I take my bath now, please?"

Smokes trudges up the stairs. The key jiggles in the lock. He grunts and stands sentry as she shuffles meekly into the bathroom. She hears him behind her turn back for the stairs as she passes. She does not hear the sound of the key in the bedroom-door lock.

Isabel hates the way he looks at her.

Downstairs again, Smokes frowns at the television picture, then begins fiddling with the cable-box control, muttering to himself. The box contains a switch that governs the electric motor mounted on the stanchion that supports a rusting satellite dish outdoors behind the cabin. When it was new, the dish must have swiveled on the switch's command, but when Smokes flicks it up and down, nothing happens.

"Fuck!" he says, going to the kitchen. In among the bales of twine and glue and the lightbulbs, the packets of thumbtacks and the broken cabinet knobs, the papers and the old maps in the kitchen drawer, Smokes finds the two incorrect tools all Americans rely on in moments of frustration like this one: a crescent wrench and a pair of pliers. Then he checks the padlock on the backdoor, realizing that the Beak has the key.

Upstairs, he hears the roar as Isabel opens the bath faucets.

At the front door once again, Smokes pauses, listening for a moment to the sound of the bath water running. He can see, in the snowy television picture, the orange jerseys of the football team. "Shit," he says, thinking of the two-fifty his bookie has placed on the over for the Broncos game. He hurries through the door and locks it behind him. Then he sets off with his flashlight and crescent wrench to deal, again, with the satellite dish.

The dish is about twenty yards behind the cabin, and the grass needs mowing, now that the dude ranch is no longer used. He wades through the tall grass until he reaches the dish. It is pointed too far toward the east. He has to angle it back toward the north. Shining a flashlight on the mounting assembly, he realizes he forgot the Phillips-head screwdriver he needs to get the box open.

"The fucking thing," he mutters.

Back he goes to the cabin. Rounding the front porch, he unlocks the door. Upstairs, the bath water is still running. He goes into the kitchen. He hunts through the drawer again and finds the screwdriver, then heads back outside.

Smokes has to wrestle with the dish for several minutes before he can get it to point the right way. Returning to the cabin, he examines the picture critically, and then settles into his chair, resigned to the snowy field of orange jerseys he will have to follow. Some minutes go by before the thought occurs to him.

"That's enough water!" he yells.

There is no answer. The roar from the faucets continues.

"Turn the fucking water off!"

This too goes unanswered. And now the combination of the lousy television reception, the stinking baby-sitting assignment in this godforsaken desert, and the smart-ass kid combine to send him over the top, and he runs furiously up the stairs, ready to pound hell out of the door and, if necessary, take a strap to Isabel.

But the door needs no pounding. It yields to a gentle push. And what Smokes sees through the steam is no adolescent, no sprawl of clothes, nothing at all save the lapping of the bath water near the rim of the tub.

Later, after he has let loose with a stream of cursing that puts to shame anything Isabel heard on the ride west, he finds the open window in the kitchen bathroom and realizes that she was probably in there when he returned for the screwdriver. And that leads him to another round.

Just under a mile to the northeast, on the west side of the road and across a dry field, with wind-blown tumbleweeds piled up against its sides, stands a yellowing mobile home in a small yard surrounded by a barbed-wire fence. A rust-red Dodge Dakota pickup is parked outside, next to a satellite dish. A diamond-shaped clothes-drying frame leans crazily from the dirt. But inside there is a light, and Isabel makes for it.

An old man in a dirty vest T-shirt, with rubbery lips and streaks of tobacco stain in his beard, answers the door. It swings open too quickly, the lightweight, dented aluminum crashing against the trailer wall and frightening Isabel as she looks up from the step.

"Well, I'll be damned," he says.

On the East Coast, Louisa Shidler is holding a can of Progresso vegetable soup to the electric can opener; she stares woodenly at her reflection in the window above the kitchen sink. Her mind has wandered, and at first, she does not notice the ringing of the telephone. With a sigh she lets it into her consciousness and lifts the receiver, wondering what bothersome detail Krasnowicz is calling to vex her with.

"Mother?"

She is unprepared for the sound, and it stuns her like an electric shock. Even before the second syllable has come faintly through the earpiece, even before Louisa can answer she is crying and exulting, all at once. They have let her hear her daughter's voice.

"Isabel? Oh, Isabel, where are you?"

"I'm okay, Mother—"

"Are you all right?"

"I'm okay, I'm okay. I'm in Wyoming, Mother, near a town called Valley, Wyoming. It's up near Yellowstone Park, sort of. I'm all right. A nice man named Mister Johnston has let me use his phone."

"Isabel, are you all right?"

"Yes, Mother, yes. I got away from them. I'm all right."

And in that moment Louisa plummets from utter joy to despair, realizing that she has betrayed her.

"Isabel, oh my darling don't say anything else! Nothing else! They are listening, they are listening to this call! I didn't realize, I should have stopped you. Don't say another thing. Oh my darling, get away, get away! They are listening to this call, they will be trying to find you! Isabel, you've got to hang up and get away. Don't call me, because they will find you. Don't trust anyone! Don't call the police. Please! You have to get away. I'll find you somehow."

"How, Mother?" comes the muffled voice.

Louisa knows that she must hang up the phone: she must disconnect it. Her mind races. Up near Yellowstone Park.

"Isabel, wait!" she says. "You remember Erin's postcard?"

"Erin's postcard?"

"Yes. Do not say the name. But remember where Erin's postcard, what it showed, what the card was of?"

"The place, you mean? Yes, I think so."

"Don't say it on the phone. But do you remember the place?"

"Yes."

"That's all right. You must find it. You can find it, I think. Ask some-one—not the people you are with, because they will come and find them and then they will find you again. You must ask someone else, and go there."

"But, Mother, how—"

"I know you don't know where it is. You must find it. You must find it and go there. Isabel, I love you. I love you so much. Now go! Go quickly!"

Louisa breaks down then, for it is too much, and she can hear Isabel sob, too.

In the kitchenette of the Wyoming trailer home, the old man leans up against the sink, nursing his can of Coors, and looks with kindness at this strange apparition, this little girl with the braces on her teeth and the tan-gled brown hair whose eyes were filled with such terror, who had replaced the telephone in its cradle. "My mother says I have to go," she says, the tears still in her eyes. "But do you have a map of Wyoming?"

"Honey," he says, after he has fished a coffee-stained Mobil Oil state highway map from the kitchen drawer. "Why don't we just call the sher-iff's office? They can help you."

But now there is the sound of an engine. Johnston looks up at the window and sees the headlights bouncing fiercely as a car races up the dirt track from the road.

"Who in the hell is that?" he is asking as, behind him, the aluminum door rattles against the frame. He looks back and the little girl is gone.

"There!" The Beak shouts to Smokes, as she sees the dark shape flit under the pale door light of the trailer home. The Cadillac bottoms out, lurches, slams its fender into the potholes of Johnston's track.

Off to her left, Isabel sees the crazy headlights leaping from the earth to the sky. She races for the fence gate, clambers over it, and is in the darkened field. She has put perhaps seventy-five yards between herself and the gate when the Cadillac slams to a halt outside Johnston's trailer.

"I'll take the inside. You get the girl," says the Beak. Grabbing a flashlight, Smokes runs for the gate.

CHAPTER 29

Louisa's mind races as the receiver clatters into its cradle. They are coming. They are coming for her, they are coming for Isabel. Men are on telephones, radios, men in automobiles, men with walkie-talkies and hoods and guns and worse, undoubtedly worse. It will happen with ferocious speed. She looks down at the collar on her ankle, and when she looks up again, she has the beginnings of a plan.

It takes Louisa less than a minute to race to the basement and return with Toby's backpack. She pounds up the stairs, and then down. No time, she is thinking, there is no time at all. Into the pack she throws a down jacket, a sweater, a toothbrush, some scissors, a pair of socks. She pulls a pair of blue jeans over the collar and puts on hiking boots, which jams the collar up on her calf. It bites into the leg and she feels a stabbing pain. The boot won't lace over it properly. She grabs her watch, the money on the bureau, her wallet, and races downstairs.

She pauses at the front door to catch her breath. "Think, think," she tells herself. Haste makes waste. But there is no time! Think! The Honda? No, they took the keys, and besides, even if she finds a way to get it started, every police officer in America will be looking for it in ten minutes. The collar sends a shooting pain up her leg. She thinks further. Toby has a pair of bolt cutters, somewhere. Where? Has he taken them? Are they in the garage? If they're in the garage, she will set off the alarm merely by going to look for them. Maybe the basement.

She is in luck, finding them behind the power drill and the circular saw he kept under the workbench, each as brand-spanking-new as the day Toby, in a sudden and passing fit of home-improvement enthusiasm, dropped six hundred dollars on the lot; none of which, as far as Louisa has ever observed, has seen action. She hauls the bolt cutters back upstairs, to just inside the front door; tampering with the collar will activate the alarm, and she has not a moment to waste. All is quiet. She struggles to resume control of her breathing, listening for a moment. Outside she can hear nothing. From upstairs comes the gentle melody of a Chopin etude, playing softly on the radio. Toby's backpack leans against the door, and the bolt cutter is in her left hand.

She works the cutter's blade around the thick plastic of the collar, and jams the handle down. The plastic device bends, then pops apart, and clatters to the ground. Hyperventilating, Louisa hurries through the door, then freezes for a moment, and races back into the house for the road atlas. A moment later, with the pack on her back, she crosses from the yard to the sidewalk. Just then she thinks she can hear her telephone ringing. She hurries up the street.

At 10:51 P.M., October 13, 1996, the FBI's National Computer Information Center issues a nationwide bulletin to FBI field bureaus and local law enforcement offices.

> WANTED. Louisa Catherine Shidler, 37, of 27 Drew Lane, Bethesda, Md., SS no. 363-80-7244, 5′ 5″, 125 lb. wf, brn hair, brn eyes. Confined to Bethesda, Md., home on electronic monitor per order U.S.D.C.—E.D.Va. 9/23/96 pending sentencing for federal bribery and money-laundering charges. Escaped from home at approximately 9:58 P.M., October 13, 1996. Subj phgrph posted www.ncic.gov. Subj believed alone and on foot. Not known to be armed. Subj. husb Tobias G. Higginson, 210 34th St. NW, Washington, D.C., daughter Isabel Higginson, d/o/b 4/17/84. Parents John and Emily Shidler, Reynolda Road, Yadkinville, N.C.

Louisa watches from the corner of Thirty-fourth Street, up the hill toward the university from his town house, since she knows he doesn't come that way. He will come from Wisconsin Avenue, walk up the right side of the street, and cross under the streetlight. If he comes home at all. She waits, hoping he will come, hoping his feet will shamble a little in the pale street light, that shamble she knows that tells her he will soon be fast asleep.

It is about ten-thirty when she sees him two blocks away. He is walking along the right-hand side of the street, as she expected, and he crosses under the streetlight, as she expected. It is just that Louisa has not expected the most obvious thing. His companion.

She feels a little sick to her stomach watching them, and retreats into the shadow. But she needn't trouble, for the pair are oblivious to their surroundings. The woman giggles a little, leans against Toby at the door, snuggles into his chest. She's a little tipsy, maybe, or maybe just a little excited. Her hair shines like caramel under the streetlight, and she wears an olive raincoat, long: Louisa cannot make her out, but the shape looks familiar. Someone, no doubt, whom Louisa has met at a political function. Then the door opens and the pair tumble into the town house. The door shuts behind them.

God, she thinks, now it is just, just naturalism. She might be a little old lady in a coppice wearing a straw hat and looking through oversized binoculars. Here we observe the mating patterns of *Cad higginsonus*. Louisa watches the bow window and counts, one, two, three. At seven the light has not come on. Did we stop for a grope on the stairs? The least you could do is get upstairs first! Now it is on, the light in his front room. It is the room where Louisa goes for the Isabel hand-offs, and where, looking about, she has to stop herself from picking up. A bachelor's living room: furniture that does not belong there, or together, no curtains, windows like scars on the empty walls. A television, of course, a huge black thing with a gazillion channels—which she can tell he *dusts*! Pacing from foot to foot, there in the darkness on Thirty-fourth Street, Louisa is distracted for a moment, thinking about Toby dusting his absurd television with five hundred channels. Stereos and televisions: they are a male thing. Why does anyone want five hundred choices of anything? Of programs, of compact discs? Of mates? At any hour, Toby's television can find a basketball game between two unknown junior colleges in a gym so empty you can hear all the shoes squeak. Next to the television is the stereo, with its lacquered stand of compact discs up to the ceiling. Toby is a musical snob—he listens to a superior sort of jazz, the kind without melody.

In her mind's eye, the room inventory proceeds. At its back, away from the window, is the kitchenette, the counter stacked with magazines and newspapers and the unwashed scrambled-egg pan, no doubt still on the stove, and a dish-rack pad that teems like a tidal pool, and the fridge with beer and Gatorade and six old jars of mustard in it and, like as not, not a piece of fresh fruit in the entire place. And—she is still cataloguing the room, its contents, when the light goes off.

Louisa feels sick again, snapped back to another confrontation with Toby's infidelity. For a few moments it hurts, and then she thinks, no, this is probably better, since she hasn't much time.

It is 11:45 P.M. The key slides noiselessly into the lock, and Louisa pushes the door open softly, then sets the backpack down and eases the door closed behind her. She waits at the base of the steps, waits to assure herself that she can hear nothing from upstairs. All is quiet. First she runs her fingers over the table in the foyer, hopefully. But she knows it will not be that easy. Then she is on the staircase, avoiding the fourth step, the loose one that squeaks, stealing softly up to the landing. At the top of the stairs she listens, hears nothing at first, but then notes the low rumble she knows so well, as she comes to the threshold of the darkened front room. She remembers *Macbeth*'s drunken porter. Drink, which provokes the desire, but takes away the performance. An old memory surfaces: *What* performance? she had asked her ninth-grade English teacher, as the other children snickered. Now alcohol is Louisa's friend, for whatever performance she missed was brief, and Toby has fallen fast asleep.

They have left the bedroom door open.

Again she stops to listen. Toby's gentle snoring is the only sound, and the buzz of the refrigerator. All is dark. Even the kitchen light is off. He didn't wait to finish a drink, she thinks, or even to start one. Why waste time breaking the ice when you can just copulate! With a twenty-two-year-old, a twenty-two-year-old who, in twenty minutes, is ready to copulate again! Louisa waits a moment at the entrance there, waits for her eyes to adjust and her mood to calm again, until she can see the shapes in his living room: the back of the couch, the bookshelf, the lamp, the chair, the coffee table, the sloppy stack of magazines on it, the television. As her pupils grow, she takes note of more detail: a set of keys that just catches the soft yellow light of the street from where he dropped them on the table, the olive raincoat on the couch, a purse next to it, his Harris tweed jacket, lying across the armchair. It is his heather one.

Louisa steps into the center of the room and rests her hand on the chair back, looking past the kitchenette to the bedroom door. It is halfway open, and within there is a deeper darkness. She listens to the rumble of his snoring for another moment, listening for another sound too. But his companion sleeps silently. Louisa turns to the heather jacket.

Her fingers rifle through the pockets, but it is not there. Nor is it on the counter, nor on the coffee table. Nor in the kitchen drawers, nor in his overcoat pocket in the hall. No, she knows it will not be in those places. So, this will be a fair trade. he will finance her escape, but she will be forced to confront the face of his infidelity. She creeps to the bedroom door. A coldness has come over her, a coldness that will permit her to do what she must do next without emotion.

A pale light from the garden behind the town house falls across the bed. They are naked there, he flat on his back in a happy oblivion, the woman curled into a ball, her back to him, the sheet pulled across her middle. The object of all my desire, Louisa thinks. He is, well, he is such a handsome man when dressed, but not at his best in sleep, the way his jaw hangs open stupidly. She turns, curiously, to look more closely at the young woman, for the light from the window falls across her face.

Louisa ought to be terrified, but other emotions have supplanted fear. Twenty-two was not a bad guess. Louisa wonders about her. At that age, can she talk? Other than to punctuate his talk with "Cool," "Wow," and the like? It was so long ago, twenty-two; barely out of college. Maybe she is older than that. Has she had an idea recently? Or ever? Other than adultery, anyway?

Again Louisa catches herself—she hasn't the leisure to think of these things. His trousers, where are his trousers? She moves cautiously toward the foot of the bed, and sees them, in a heap by the far side between the bed and the radiator, scattered among the rest of his things, and hers. A floorboard groans. Louisa freezes. The girl sighs, mumbles something, and burrows into the pillow. Toby snores on. Still frozen, Louisa looks again at the clothing scattered around the floor. God, she thinks, looking at the happy abandon, the last time we made love, we disrobed as though for a doctor's physical.

Louisa gains the side of the bed between the girl and the window, less than thirty inches from where the girl sleeps, and crouches down to the trousers. In a moment her fingers have retrieved it; she should go. But she must just look at the girl for a moment. Louisa can hear her soft breathing now, can see the faint rise and fall of her breast. Couched in the shadow, with the pale light from the garden coming in from over her left shoulder, Louisa finds that she must study the girl's face. It is so soft, so free of—of geography—of ridges and valleys and wandering watercourses. She must consider, for a moment, the voluptuousness of that waterfall of hair, full as Louisa's own, as it sweeps over the girl's shoulder. The woman—girl? woman? who can tell?—she is so young, so young. There isn't a single gray outrider in that dark wave of hair. As Louisa rises from the floor with the wallet in her hand, trembling just a little, she whispers, all but inaudibly, so softly that the sound remains half imagined.

"I am his wife."

Toby snores rapturously. The girl remains asleep, her breathing child-like.

"His wife," Louisa whispers again, and then she slips out.

Louisa is in luck, if that word can be used to describe anything that has happened to her tonight. In Toby's wallet she finds $124, his MoneyOne card, and Visa, Mastercard, and American Express cards. She liberates the MoneyOne card, knowing, as she does, that he is forever removing it from his wallet to put it in his running shorts or gym bag or something, and then losing it. She also takes $104, before leaving the wallet on the kitchenette counter. The morning after such an evening, Toby's memory will be, at best, imperfect. And then Louisa has a thought, and a faint smile traces across her face, as she looks across the darkened living room to the couch. My dear girl, there is, after all, a price for sleeping with my husband. Inside the purse she finds the wallet, bulging with credit cards. Perhaps she will not miss one. Louisa looks through the AmEx, the Discovery, MasterCard, and Visa, and decides that the MasterCard bears the fewest scars of use. She removes it.

The girl's name is Samantha Snow. Louisa peers at the Virginia driver's license for the date of birth: August 3, 1973.

The purse contains one more thing: a Day-Timer notebook. She hunts through the Day-Timer by the light filtering from the front room window. She tries C for Card, B for Bank, finds nothing. She tries P for personal. S for Snow. Still nothing. Think! What do we have here, twenty-three? Go for obvious. How about N for "number"? And there it is: a list of otherwise unidentified numbers. Some are frequent flyer numbers: OnePass, Worldperks, and the others. And then there is an unidentified four-digit number. Louisa smiles and commits to memory Samantha Snow's address, age—and, of course, the four digits.

CHAPTER 30

There were two times that Sunday night when I thought I was going to die. The first was when Smokes came back to the house and I was hiding in the kitchen bathroom. The door was only a flimsy pine-plank door, and I held my breath in there, listening to him rattle around in a drawer, looking for something, saying "fucking this" and "fucking that." But he didn't hear me, and I got out the window a minute later, after he'd gone out the house around the other side.

I was barely half a mile up the road, I'd say, when I saw the headlights and realized the Cadillac was coming back from town. I hid by the side of the road as it went by, saw the Beak's profile, just as stony as a Russian statue in there. Then I went as fast as I could to the nearest house, which was a trailer home, actually, where this man Mr. Johnston lived.

Well, it didn't take them long. When I looked up through his window and saw those headlights bouncing and stabbing the air, I knew they were coming to kill me for sure. I just ran. It's a good thing my pack was on and the map was in my hand when I saw the lights because I like panicked and I wouldn't have even thought to pick them up. I was out that door and across his yard for the fence in a second and before I got over that gate I could see the headlights coming for me out of the corner of my eye. And then I ran and ran through this field full of sagebrush, big bushes of it scratching my arms and face cause it was so dark I couldn't see anything. I was lucky it was dark or I'm sure they would have got me easy.

When I stopped to look back, I saw the little spot of a flashlight and I could tell one of them had come over the gate after me. I crouched down. There was a lot of sagebrush in the field and I could hide pretty well behind a bush—they're about three feet tall. I could hear him breathing and kind of scrabbling around through the brush. I looked up a little and he was sort of coming my way, but he was going to miss me by a little ways if he went straight. So I decided not to run, but to kind of watch that flashlight and move slowly away from it, slipping as quietly as I could from bush to bush. I knew I was dead if he heard me.

He came pretty close, though. I'll bet he was thirty feet away and I held my breath when that flashlight swung around. He stopped for a minute and I had my face jammed against the dirt behind that brush.

And then he went on a few feet.

I wasn't going to move for anything. He went off past me and I turned to watch the little bouncing light of his flashlight.

Then I heard the shots. They were over by the trailer—two of them. I never heard a gun go off before, except on TV or in the movies and once when Papa took me clay pigeon shooting with Uncle Will. It was a horrible loud explosion of a sound, echoing all around, and then I knew that they had killed that man Mr. Johnston. The flashlight whirled back toward the trailer, and I could tell he was running then. Straight for me. I was between him and the trailer. I started crying. I tried my best to stop myself and to keep thinking straight, but I was just so sure they were going to kill me too that I was almost, like, frozen. Its hard to explain now, as I'm sitting here with this Dictaphone, but I almost called out, "Here I am, I give up," and stood up in the beam of that flashlight. I was just so scared. I was the scaredest I've ever been right then.

But what happened next was that he stumbled or tripped or something. I heard a scuffling noise and a "Goddammit!" and that shook me loose. I raced along in that field and I don't think he ever heard it or anything, he was so intent on getting back toward the house. In a minute I could hear their voices back at the trailer, but I didn't stop to listen. That field started to head uphill, and I headed uphill with it, and then I came up to a rock wall and I started to climb that too. That's when I heard him yell.

"Isabel!" he was yelling. "Isabel!" His voice was away off down at the house, but it echoed all around. He yelled my name a few more times and I stopped, hanging on this rock wall and panting and trying to stop panting so hard. I listened, and he yelled, "Isabel, there's only one way out of this valley! You can't get down the river, it's in a canyon, and on either side are mountains too steep to climb and nothing beyond them but wilderness. The only way out of this valley is up the road thirty-five miles! When morning comes, I'm sure to find you. You best come on out now. You come on out and I'll go easy on you. You make me find you in the morning and I swear I'll fucking kill you!"

He had a real way with women, Smokes. I'll be nice to you or I'll fucking kill you. He yelled a little more like that. He'd cajole and then he'd threaten. I clung to that rock wall and never said a word, even though a little part of me still wanted to give up. I think I would have given up except for that night when the Beak beat me by that wheatfield. After a while I turned and started climbing. I climbed and climbed, as far as I could. The rock was a little crumbly and sometimes a bit would break off in my hand, or my feet would slip a little and kick up the stones. The moon and stars weren't out, and it was so dark. I stumbled once and I scratched my right hand on a rock. I felt like I was climbing for hours. Finally I stopped and kind of collapsed down on this ledge behind some sagebrush and just lay there, with the sound of my breath in my ears. It was cold and the ground was rocky and hard. I must have lay there a long time before I fell asleep.

CHAPTER 31

A pair of headlights flashes on among the darkened, silent huddle of the big trucks at the rest stop, as a tractor-trailer seems to awaken, and Louisa, shivering, hears the diesel throb to life. The truck pulls out and begins to roll toward her. Out goes her thumb. The driver eases on the accelerator, and the truck slows and comes to the shoulder.

It sits there, a great, gleaming dragon of throbbing chrome and steel, towering over her, noisy and huge in the darkness. On the passenger door is the name "Sugaree." Louisa bites her lip as the door opens. Out of the darkness of the cab pokes a great head of iron-gray hair. She sees hair in the darkness—hair pulled back from the forehead in a ponytail, a long, thick beard cascading onto his flannel shirt. Its owner is broad-shouldered and so large he seems to have to curl even within the truck's expansive cab as he ducks his head out the passenger door to look down at her. He looks like the sort of man who is accustomed to stooping in doorways and turning sideways in corridors. In the dim light of the parking lot, his dark eyes seem kind, although that could just be wishful thinking.

He shouts over the noise of the engine, "Where you headed?"

"West!" she shouts back.

"That's cool. I'm Bear." He extends a hand down, fingers like sausages, and she stretches up over the truck's front tire and watches as her hand disappears in his. But his grasp surprises her with its gentleness. "Climb on up," he says, then ducks into the darkness.

This is precisely the kind of offer that she has trained her daughter never to accept. Taking a breath, she mumbles thanks, hands him her pack, and then hoists herself up the aluminum steps and clambers into the darkened cab.

At first, edging primly toward the door on an oversized passenger seat, she simply watches the driver with nervous fascination, as he works his truck through the gears. Louisa has never ridden in one of these things before. She studies the controls, looks at the big knob on the gear shift, the switches overhead, the car phone.

"I thought that truck drivers used CB radios," she ventures.

"CB radios! You must be older 'n you look," he laughs. "We're like everybody else, now."

The road seems far below from up there, and it is a marvel to her how many gears the driver puts the truck through in maneuvering it out from behind the restaurant and back onto the highway.

"What's your name?"

"Louisa," she answers. And then, to herself, "Idiot."

She changes the subject. "So, what do you have back there?"

"In the trailer?"

"Yeah."

"Dryers. Eighty-six of 'em."

"Clothes dryers?"

"Yup."

The subject is exhausted a little too quickly. How exactly do you chat about clothes dryers? She frowns, drops it.

"How far west you headed, Louisa?" He has a gentle voice, deep and soothing and a little country.

"Wyoming."

He nods. "Long trip." The truck joins the traffic on I-70. For a moment Bear concentrates on his gearshift and his rearview mirror. When they have settled in at about sixty-five miles per hour, he asks, "You from out there?"

"No."

He nods his head again, to signal that he understands that she prefers silence. "Well, I can take you most of the way. I'll be heading through Denver on I-70."

"When will you get there?"

"Tomorrow night or day after, most likely."

Outside the cab, the tiny cars zip skittishly across lanes. From where Louisa sits, their headlights look puny, and their cones of light illuminate a layer of darkness below her level. Bear's truck never seems to change speed, or even direction. It rolls majestically along the highway, a great shark accompanied by a train of darting pilot fish.

"Want to find something on the radio?"

She flips the dial, finding nothing agreeable. Then this: "When we return to the final hour of tonight's Birch Thornacre program, an hour with Ambassador and vice-presidential candidate Royall Stillwell . . ."

"Oh, my God," Louisa says.

Bear reaches across to change the station. She stops his hand.

"You don't listen to this stuff?"

"I don't," she answers, "but would it be okay if I listened to this? For a little bit, anyway?"

And then there it is: his voice, right next to her in the cab, billing and cooing with Birch. The talk-show host croons, he gushes—he invites the candidate to bash his opponents, which, of course, Royall declines to do with statesmanlike self-control. But what does the candidate think of this or that Proctor outrage? It will be for the American people to say.

"What does he know about the American people?" Bear asks.

Birch turns to the Breed administration's agenda for the next four years. Then Royall is quoting statistics about emerging world markets in Europe, the Far East. "Government," he says to Birch, "needs to be a hauler . . ."

"Beautiful. Neither of them guys every been in a truck, and government needs to be a hauler."

Louisa interrupts the radio voice. "We need to help get American business to market," she says, just as Royall says it himself.

"How'd you do that?" Bear asks.

"I've heard it before."

That is when Louisa's eyes stray to the car phone.

"Bear, can I borrow that phone?"

For fifteen minutes, Birch's line is busy. She punches in the numbers and it is busy. She does it again and again. Busy. Again and again and again. But she continues undaunted, punching in the numbers time after time after time.

Until at last the telephone rings. She feels her pulse quicken. Now will it simply ring off the hook?

"Birch Thornacre Program, what is your name and where are you calling from, please?"

"Louisa. And I'm on a car phone in . . . Tallahassee."

"What do you want to talk about?"

"I want to ask the ambassador about foreign trade. I don't think it's been brought out how successfully he has represented American business at the foreign trading table, how important he's been for American business. I wanted to ask what plans a second Breed term would have for aerospace, semiconductors, and textiles. How that would help American business."

Louisa holds her breath during the pause.

"Okay," says the voice, "hold on. We're going to commercial and then we'll come back to you." The doubts begin to come then, as she waits in the darkened cab. Bear says nothing, but shakes his head once.

"Louisa, in Tallahassee, hello and welcome to the Birch Thornacre program."

In the cab, Louisa motions Bear to turn the radio down. "Hello, Birch," she says, "I love your program. Hello, Ambassador Stillwell."

Over in the driver's seat, Bear's grimace comes clear through his beard.

"What's on your mind?" says Birch.

"Birch, I just wanted to say that I think the ambassador deserves recognition for all that he has done for foreign trade," she begins. Sugaree begins a climb, and Louisa has to raise her voice over the roar as Bear guns the engine.

"Who is this?" Stillwell asks. He knows, but cannot yet believe.

"He has been our leader in hammering out the EU accords, and he deserves a lot of credit for that."

"Well, I agree," says Birch.

"I—" Stillwell tries to interject, but Louisa carries on.

"But I think the ambassador should share for us why he took a fifty-million-dollar bribe and deposited it in a numbered Swiss bank account at Duclos and Bernard—"

"Who is—"

"And what he and his people have done with Isabel Higginson, a twelve—"

"Louisa?" Stillwell asks.

Thornacre cuts her off. "I'm sorry, Ambassador, sometimes these calls get through."

Before Birch's finger gets to the switch to end the call, Louisa asks, "Where is she, Royall? What have you done with Isabel Higginson?"

And then the line is dead, the Birch Thornacre program goes to commercial, and four million or more Americans begin to put the conversation out of mind. Sugaree crests the hill and they roll westward in silence for a moment.

"What was all that about?" Bear asks.

"I'd, I'd rather not go into it. But thank you. Thank you for the phone. I'll pay you whatever it costs."

"Do you know him? Stillwell?"

"Yes."

"And is all that, all that about the bribe and—"

"Bear, I'm sorry, I can't talk about it."

The exchange takes forty-six seconds. After Birch cuts her off by going to commercial, he rolls a few more spots to bury it. And then come a series of other callers, so that the exchange makes no lasting impression on millions of Americans, most of whom later recall only that a woman began ranting about bribes and a girl named Isabel—or something. But there are many ears tuned to Birch Thornacre's program.

Hundreds of miles to the south, Lloyd Esterhaze, a reporter for the *Winston-Salem Journal,* has also been listening as he drives back to the office from a late-night planning-board meeting. He calls his city editor from his car phone.

"Bert," he says, "you closed the paper yet?"

"Yeah, few minutes ago. Board do something tonight?"

"Naw. But I got a question for you about Louisa Shidler."

Shidler has been a fairly big story in the *Journal,* given the local angle. "Yeah. What you got, Lloyd?"

"What was that bank account she put the money in?"

"Swiss bank, they said."

"No, I mean which bank?"

"Hold on."

Davies waits while Bert runs a key word search to pull up the story. "Something called Duclos and Bernard."

"I'll be goddamned," says Davies.

"Why?"

"That's what she was saying."

"Who?"

"Woman who called Birch Thornacre on the radio just now. She said she was Louisa from Tallahassee and wanted to know why Stillwell had taken a bribe. That was the bank she said: Duclos and something. Sounded like a car phone she was on. Isn't she under house arrest?"

"Think so. Hold on." He yells to someone in the newsroom. "We got anything on Shidler tonight? Anything on the wires?"

Bert comes back to the phone. "Shit, man, there is something on the damn wire. Moved a half hour ago. She escaped tonight. Car phone, you say? Sure it was her?"

"Damned if I know. Said she was Louisa."

"Hmmm."

"There was something else, too, about Isabel. I didn't hear it right. Wasn't that her daughter, Isabel?"

"Yeah. Look, we'll talk in the morning. Hell, I don't know. A loony-tunes calling Thornacre—I'm not sure it's a story. Know what I mean?"

She seems shaken to him, after she has replaced the telephone in the cradle. She stares at the road in silence. It makes him a little nervous. "Want to get some music going?" Bear asks. "Tapes are back there in that box."

It is a crate, not a box, which he indicates behind the passenger seat, and it contains too many cassette tapes to count—upwards of a hundred, Louisa guesses, each marked, as she sees when she holds them up to the highway light, in a lazy felt-tip script, with only a few words, and a date: "San Antonio, '69," one reads; "Filmore East, '72," says another; "Altamont, '73," a third.

After a moment she asks him, "Are these Grateful Dead tapes?" She looks up and sees that he is lighting a joint.

Even in the darkness she can see him smile. "Pretty much."

Louisa fishes out one that says "Ann Arbor, '70," and in a moment, through a somewhat tinny-sounding recording, comes the gentle, melancholy tenor of Jerry Garcia.

"Jerry Garcia, didn't he die?"

"Not dead," Bear answers. "Immortal. You want some?" He reaches toward her with the joint.

"No," she answers, too quickly, and then, "Thank you," in a tone that is anything but grateful. She retreats to the far side of the seat, as though there she might avoid the acrid smoke.

Perhaps it is the smell of marijuana. Even with Isabel's image before her, the gentle insistence of the melody begins to take her on a trip back through time, to a place Louisa never really inhabited so much as observed. She remembers the Deadheads passing the afternoons hanging out by the wall along one side of the parking lot at the high school. She would walk briskly past, her books folded up against her chest, keeping her eyes forward. Odd, how gentle the melodies sound now. Then they were threatening to her.

Time passes, and Louisa's mind wanders. She is figuring, figuring. It will take about three days to get to northwest Wyoming. Three days.

Where is Isabel? Can she make her way, alone, for three days, her daughter from the Maryland suburbs? Will she have found help?

The music goes on and on, songs that veer into long acoustic excursions before circling back to an odd lyric or phrase that, for a moment, summons her mind out of the present. When one tape is done, he asks for another. As they roll out westward through that long night, the melodies lull and transport her. She fades off into reverie, bouncing in and out of consciousness, and a sort of fitful sleep.

In the deepest hour of the morning, when even on the interstate only sporadically does a set of headlights round a distant bend to break the darkness, Louisa wakens as a gentle rain begins to fall, her gaze mesmerized by the sweep of the wiper blades. She blinks away the sleep.

"This is the best time to drive." His voice surprises her, coming suddenly out of the darkness. "Just me and Sugaree and the windshield wipers, and my headlights poking a hole in the darkness for us to slip through before it closes up behind. It's nice, man, this time of night, nice and peaceful, just before the dawn comes up in your mirror. Got some coffee back there in the condo. Think you could make some?"

Still drowsy, Louisa picks her way back between the seats.

"Switch is above you," he says.

She finds it and then a light fixture illuminates the "condo": a cozy kitchenette with a pallet at the rear. Bear has caulked in a dry sink, and rigged a clever feed tube from a ten-gallon water bottle. She takes the feed hose and fills the coffee maker. It runs off his on-board generator, along with the coffee grinder and the little half-fridge beneath the counter, where he keeps a bag of coffee beans. A moment later Louisa leans against the counter, listening to the rasp and burble of the coffee maker, over the whine of the engine. She has the sense of being below decks in a galley in a small power boat. After that, still half asleep, she is enveloped by a delicious warmth as the scent of the coffee fills the cab. She looks at her watch. Quarter to five.

A memory stirs within her, but she cannot place it. It comes of preparing something warm in half somnolence, in the darkness, a man nearby: some long-forgotten sensation from the early days of her motherhood. It feels good to hand him the mug. She has poured herself a cup, and resumes the passenger seat.

CHAPTER 32

In her Washington office, Smaug rereads the report under the soft light of the table lamp. It alone lights the great office, whose walls and corners fade into shadow. At this hour, even Jack and Jill have gone. Only Smaug's nocturnal retainer remains, sitting silently at the table. *Of all things.* They have kept this story as quiet as an acolyte, an inside story, nine-point type, and now Shidler has escaped. And now there's this, this phone call! Smaug leaves the report on the table and steps to the window. She looks out at the Capitol dome, lighting the Washington darkness. This has been her city for a long time now, and she means to keep it that way. The end of Smaug's cigarette glows red in the darkness as she smokes by the window.

"Play this out for me, Ken. Go straight to the end game."

"He goes down," the Crab answers.

"Such the optimist."

"You don't pay my kind of money for optimism."

"True. But this is noise. It's noise. A phone call from a kook, in the middle of the night, on fucking Thornacre, of all things. We'll squash it like a bug. Who cares?"

The Crab's gravelly burble sounds in the darkness, methodically carrying on, as though he had not heard. "Four million insomniacs heard it. Ten percent remember it. One percent of those matter. One percent of those do something about it. That's still"—he does the math—"four people. Four people who know, and matter, and do something about it, turns back into four hundred thousand pretty quick. And then four million. And then forty. They all get to play, 'Was it a kook, or was it Louisa?' Nice story." He smiles in the darkness, thinking about it. "He goes down, Cynthia."

Every successful organization has someone like the Crab in it, some-one who is not well liked, someone who seems to enjoy bad news. He will always speak the hard cynical words to which no one else wants to give voice. One truth speaker, with no more sentiment in him than a light switch, and no more discernment of gray than the switch has. A person who sees everyone else as up, or down.

Smaug exhales more cigarette smoke, and more, staring through the glass.

"Play it. Play out the hand."

The Crab says: "A few hours from now, some kid with Pulitzers in his eyes is browbeating the managing editor of *The New York Times,* or the L.A. *Times,* or one of a hundred other papers. 'Boss,' he's saying, 'listen to this. A felon flees in the middle of the night. A call to Thornacre. She says Stillwell was in it too!' And so the M.E. gets to thinking. It *was* fifty million, wasn't it? That's a shitload of money. Fifty million isn't a bribe, it's the earnings line on a decent-sized financial statement. And then he's shouting, where the hell have we been on this? Why haven't we been all over this story? The guy's thinking, this is my chance to be Ben fucking Bradlee. Next thing you know, Freedom of Information requests every-where, everybody interviewed, agents, district attorneys, family, friends; microphones in the face of Shidler's attorney, her husband, her parents, her friends, her secretary. And Stillwell? The complete proctology exam."

She remains by the window, her back to him, cigarette in hand.

"For weeks. Every photo op, every interview, every debate. Mr. Am-bassador, what about this Shidler thing? Can you comment on the allega-tions of bribery? Where is Shidler? Where is her daughter? Questions screamed at airports, in streets. For three weeks, Cynthia. You've got the lead in every nightly news report for three weeks. Want to hear it?"

"No, I think I can guess."

"New information today in the swirl of charges and countercharges surrounding Royall Stillwell . . ."

Her voice comes softly and deliberately. "We have to silence it."

"You can't silence it. America doesn't know what silence sounds like. Besides, we haven't even mentioned Proctor. He will turn loose every Democrat in the country. You'll have fifteen thousand amateur sleuths out there." Is it a sigh, or is she merely exhaling? The Crab is not sure. "He goes down," he concludes.

"And we go down."

"No Republicans in the White House, Barnett and Associates goes down too," says the Crab. "That's if it stops there."

She turns, fixes him with an angry look, and somehow her eyes are visible, luminous, in the darkness. "It had better stop there."

The Crab shrugs.

"All right," she announces, "we run hard on Felotti." Smaug begins to pace. The Crab watches as the red glow of the cigarette traces the outline of the dark corners of the room, as she moves, begins to build the case, begins to sketch in the packaging, the leaking, the key media outlets, the setup.

"Chickenshit," comes the gravelly voice, after a time.

"He fucked the woman under his wife's own roof!"

"Cynthia, this is 1996, okay? It's chickenshit. Belakis fucked a woman. So what. His wife was a drunk, anyway."

"No." She paces up to the window. "We go hard with Felotti. We leak the tape to the *Union Leader.* National press has it on day two, we run it hard, ads, everything."

The Crab thinks it over. "Nah, too late."

"Ken, Belakis—"

"So Belakis fucked a woman. But people will be saying Stillwell fucked a country. Fucking a country still counts. I don't know, I think it does, anyway. Besides, he resigns? Remember Eagleton? He resigns, and ten thousand media are all over this, and the best you can say for our luffing sail of a president is that he doesn't know what's going on around him. Again."

"Well, fix this for me."

The Crab has no answer. "Hard one," he says. "It's a problem."

But she has gone from the room, left one French door standing open like an ambiguous invitation. He hesitates, then accepts, following her to the balcony. Outside, it is cold. Smaug leans against the wall over in the corner, looking southeast at Justice, smoking her cigarette. No moon or star is visible, there is too much ambient light for that. Still, it is a cold darkness, a predawn cold that clenches arms across chests. And quiet— hardly a car horn is heard in the street twelve floors below. Across Pennsylvania Avenue, Justice and the IRS stand mute and dark. Closer by, lights dot the windows of the FBI building, but even there, almost all the offices are empty.

The Crab shivers a little. He could go on with his monologue, but senses that she has gotten the point.

"You know, Ken, our lease is up next year."

He fidgets, tries to think of something that might need doing in his own office, some excuse to escape. Her back remains to him, as she goes on. "Brokers say we could save ten dollars a foot three blocks from here."

Does she want conversation? Did she pick *now* to talk about the lease? He decides that it is better to wait.

She holds the cigarette aloft, its ash a red pinpoint in the darkness. At length, he ventures, "So what did you tell them?"

When she turns, he feels suddenly colder than before, even less clothed. "I told them to negotiate an extension."

Then she walks briskly back toward the doors. "This is my street, Ken. You say we can't silence the noise. But this is my street, and I'm not moving for ten dollars a foot, not for fifty, and I'm certainly not moving for *noise*. You say you can't stop it. But there's one thing you can do about noise."

Responding, at this point, would be rather like stepping in front of a train. So he waits for her to identify the one thing you can do about noise.

"Remember the kid in college with the loud stereo?" she goes on. "You couldn't get him to turn it down?"

He nods.

"But you could drown it the fuck out. With a louder noise. A much louder noise. A noise that brought the sonofabitch to his knees."

The Crab knows this inflection, knows and fears its certainty. But you can't offer to engage a speeding train in debate.

"When does Mr. Couch Potato rally round his president?" she demands, stabbing the air with the cigarette. "When were Bush's seventy-seven favorables? During the Gulf War."

Smaug's soliloquy has brought her face-to-face with her deputy, so that the cigarette's red ash lies close to his hand, and he looks nervously down toward it. He can smell her scent now. He turns his eye down, avoiding her, feeling the cold, feeling the power of her resolve, and mostly, feeling extremely nervous.

"Under attack from foreign devils," she continues. "Barbarians. That's when we rally. Pull together."

"I don't follow you," he replies softly.

"That's all right, because you don't want to. You just execute, Ken. You just execute. And you execute faster and cleaner than you've ever executed in your life."

CHAPTER 33

"Where are we?"

"Maryland, coming up to Keysers Ridge."

"Maryland!"

"Goes farther west than you think. Be in Morgantown in a little bit."

The news depresses her. She has ridden half the night and hasn't even left Maryland. "I didn't see any milk, so . . ."

"Yeah, take it black, thanks." And then it is quiet again.

After a long period of silence—Bear seems like the kind of man who is not afraid of silence—he speaks again. "So, Louisa, where are you headed in such a hurry? You don't seem like the hitchhiking kind."

Louisa wonders, for a moment, the question bringing her back to a colder reality, to her guileless confession of her name earlier that night. Could he, too, be one of them? Be wired for sound and armed and ready to call the whole thing to a halt with a badge and a pair of handcuffs? Louisa looks at the dark silhouette, and then smiles at her paranoia, thinking of the box of Dead concert tapes, a collection she doubts even the Department of Justice could assemble.

"To my daughter."

At that moment the sweetest lyric is playing softly on the tape player, to a gentle bass accompaniment. Bear is singing softly with the band.

If my words did glow
With the warmth of sunshine
And my tunes were played on the harp unstrung,
Would you hear my voice
Come through the music,
Would you hold it near as it were your own?

"That's pretty," she says. "What is it?"

"It's called 'Ripple.' "

The song reaches its plaintive chorus, and the delicate strum of a mandolin is at once sad and optimistic, come from a disappointing yesterday, bound for a better tomorrow.

Ripple in still water,
Where there is no pebble tossed,
Nor wind to blow.

"Where you going to find her?"

There is a road,

the song is saying,

No simple highway
Between the dawn
And the dark of night.

"She's in Wyoming, I think," Louisa answers. "She's only twelve."

"She with your old man?"

Louisa wipes away the tear that has formed in the corner of her eye despite resolute efforts to banish it. "No," she says.

"Runaway?"

"No." Bear looks across at her for just a moment, and then he leaves it. The song is coming to a close.

And if you go
No one may follow,
That path is for your steps alone.

They sit quietly, and the song's gentle rhythm rocks Louisa as though she were a baby.

If you should stand
Then who's to guide you?
If I knew the way, I would take you home.

It is still dark, and she wants to change the subject. "Tell me something about yourself, please."

The big man with the gentle voice talks to her, as the rig rolls down the empty highway, and the Grateful Dead songs play on the tape deck. He worked in a paper mill in Wisconsin, like his father had done, "but that didn't turn out so good." So he hit on the idea of driving a truck as a way of making a few dollars between Dead concerts, and, he tells her with modest pride, there were five years in the mid-seventies when he missed only one concert "on the continent." She asks him if he ever married, ever settled somewhere.

"Oh, yeah, I got me an old lady, Becky, and a son, Travis. That's their pictures up there."

The Polaroid snapshots are rubber-banded to the overhead visor. She pulls them down and looks at them. In the older photograph, which is cracked along one side and curls with age, a big, round-faced girl with thin blond hair, parted in the middle, smiles broadly from a crowd. She wears a T-shirt over a peasant dress. The second photograph is more recent: a chubby boy with a big cowboy hat and an intense expression of concentration.

"But my old lady likes me better in small doses, you know?"

He met her at a Dead concert. (Louisa wonders if there is a cassette in the crate: "Cleveland, '74—Becky.") They traipsed around after the band together for a year or so, but she got older, tired of the life, even lost interest in the music.

"Now, she never listens to the Dead anymore. You got one of your daughter?"

Louisa fishes it out of the wallet, noting with black humor that she still has in there the card Frank Ianella gave her that night at the Willard, with his fancy new promotion noted for posterity.

Bear squints at the photograph under the overhead light, his eyes darting back and forth between the photograph and the road. The big friendly lines in his brow deepen.

"She's awful pretty."

He puts the photograph on the dash and tells her about his Earthship. That's what he calls his home outside Carter, New Mexico. He is proud of its construction. It is built of old automobile tires covered over with adobe. The Earthship backs into a hillside, and its one, broad window faces south. It is heated almost entirely by the sun. The adobe has magic powers, he tells her with an excited edge to his voice. Something about the way it holds the heat, warming the house at night, in the summer tempering the desert sun. In the coldest winter evenings, sometimes Bear will light a small wood fire is all.

She isn't listening very closely. She has retrieved Isabel's photograph. Whenever a pair of headlights flash across the cabin, she holds it up to the light, to see her daughter's mugging smile.

"Got a solar toilet, too," he says.

He looks over, can tell she hasn't heard him.

"You take your dump into this glassed-in box. The sun bakes the moisture right out of it. Shit's mostly water, you know."

"Uh-huh." She punctuates the end of his remark, but still does not appear to have heard.

"All's that's left is a little dust. Sprinkle it on your garden. Peppers like it."

Silence as she stares at the photograph. The sky is gradually lightening from black to blue. After a while, she looks over at him.

"I'm sorry, Bear, what were you saying?"

"Oh, never mind," he says. "Not important."

CHAPTER 34

On October 14, Isabel awakens cold and stiff. A cold rime coats the pale blue and brown of the sagebrush fronds above her head. When she reaches consciousness, she falls into little sniffles. From her hiding place the predawn light shows the road running below her in plain view. Even Mr. Johnston's trailer home is close by to the southeast, a scruffy, yellowing Monopoly piece far below amid the tufts of sagebrush, just a little way back from the road. She climbed over a mile the previous night, up the steep slope through the sagebrush to the base of the red rocks, and then, up their steep and fluted face to the tiny outcropping where she stopped. A faded blue-and-white pickup makes its way northwest along the lonely ribbon of highway, and she can even make out the arm of the passenger, propped on the window frame, as the truck creeps past.

Erin's postcard. It was from the Buffalo Bill Museum. Somewhere in Wyoming, the Buffalo Bill Museum, from which Erin had sent her a postcard over the summer during her vacation. Isabel remembers that.

She looks down at the map. Although it is only a road map, she can tell Smokes wasn't lying. There is only one road out of Valley, and she can see that it splits the mountains as it tracks northeast toward Cody. Isabel knows she would be found along that road. Behind her, to the north on the map, is a wavy line called Ishawooa Creek, and beyond that something called Wapiti Ridge. There isn't another town shown for twenty-five miles.

Above her, all she can see is a steep rock face. She studies the map some more. If she makes her way across country due north, crossing the wavy blue line and the ridge, she should pick up Highway 14, coming east out of Yellowstone.

She looks again at the slope above her. For a moment the girl wants to give in. Where can she go? She ought to return to the highway and surrender—Mother cried on the telephone and said they were listening. They are sure to find her and punish her. At the thought of punishment, Isabel's left hand strays to her cheekbone, and she once again remembers the horrific night beside the lonely Nebraska road, and the second long, hard slapping she got when she tried to give her father a signal. She turns and begins to climb.

The problem is not an absence of handholds and footholds, but that the rock is friable, and bits of it come away in her hand. She starts up a column that looks likely, but backs down after twenty feet when it grows too steep. She scrambles to her right and starts up again. Her climbing moves by fits and starts, but she makes her way up another quarter of a mile until the steep slope gives way to a scree field. The road has now disappeared from view, and her breath begins to labor as she makes her way up another half mile of steep pitches and difficult walking. At length she comes to the base of a cliff. She is only several hundred feet from the summit of the ridge, but this cliff is too steep for her, so she traverses the scree for another mile or so before finding a way up.

At about nine A.M. she reaches the top of the ridge, tired, hungry, thirsty. The sun is up and warm, and if she knew the country better, she would be grateful for that. A dude on a pack trip would be in raptures over the vista to the north, a stunning array of mountains and valleys, of cliffs and gorges and a winding stream. It is vast, fathomless, empty, this land. To the right lies what the map calls a ridge, but "ridge" seems a tame word to Isabel as she contemplates the size of the columns rising like red bones from the land's thin flesh. To the west, wave upon wave of mountains. The country calls to her mind the shape she saw on the license plates. Isabel imagines a slumbering bison with a rough mane of lodgepole pines at its vast hump and a brown expanse at its flank and hip, lying there upon the earth, at any moment ready to stretch and shake mountains of scree from itself.

She looks at her map again. It gives her no sign to tie to the view before her. No sign of the road from Yellowstone is visible before her now. Keeping the sun on her right shoulder, she begins to walk.

She walks in fear, almost with the certainty of immediate capture. For the land is open, and she can see for miles in every direction. Underfoot is the rubble of the earth's great kiln, and as the morning hours slowly progress, the scattered slates begin to shine like ceramic in the hot sun, shards left over from the making of these mountains. Crickets pop up in the dust as she walks by. They sparkle and crackle as though the yellow under their wings is electrified. She sees no other movement, no life.

Far in the distance to the northwest lies what must be a river bottom, green with grasses, the cottonwoods already bare of leaves. Above the gorge, the patchwork green strand quickly gives way to the browns of baked earth and fading goldenrod. And everywhere are the little tufts of the powdery sagebrush. Underfoot, it is an expanse of dust and rocks, with here and there a clump of purple asters or the whitened stumps of sage like driftwood on a dry sea.

Resolve, spunk, fear, they carried her out of the bathroom the night before, up the darkened road to the Johnston trailer, out into the field— even up the red cliffs. But they will not sustain Isabel much longer, not in the face of the vast wilderness that seems to lie before her to the north. Her steps quickly take her downhill, however. In this, as in the weather, Isabel is in luck.

On Monday, October 14, at shortly before six A.M., Gene Phillips is the one turning on the lights in his little nook of "the Puzzle Palace."

He had a call last night and was up half the night piecing together the account. Shidler has escaped, on foot. That is all that is really known. First MacPherson, now Shidler. Local airports, bus stations, and railroads have been canvassed, and so far have come up with nothing. They've checked her outgoing phone calls and found nothing. Later today, the FBI will begin getting responses from the taxicab dispatchers. Meanwhile, to trace the money, Phillips has resorted to a chart. A neat rectangle contains the Liechtenstein corporation. With a plastic rule, he draws the links to the British Virgin Islands Trusts, lines thence to the Isle of Man Merchant Bank. Then still more boxes, more lines. Partnerships in Curaçao, trusts in the Caymans. His diagram becomes a maze. He studies the documents, looking for the path in and out of Acct. 6614723-456 at Duclos & Bernard. Demand deposit accounts, standby letters of credit, powers of attorney. The documents are as confusing as the diagram.

Phillips is making a list of Louisa's relatives to contact when the call comes in.

"Special Agent Phillips?"

"Speaking."

"Agent Phillips, this is Deputy Lonnie Billings, from the Jackson County, Missouri, Sheriff's Department. I saw the teletype last night and was referred to you regarding the Louisa Shidler investigation."

"Yeah?"

"Well, we had a strange call about two, two and a half weeks ago, which you may be interested in. I was the dispatch officer that night, and near the start of my shift, 911 call comes in. Little girl says, 'This is Isabel Higginson and I've been kidnapped.' "

"Yeah?"

"Yeah. She says, Please call my mother, in Bethesda. She's Louisa Shidler. And she gave us a phone number, 263-3010."

That is, indeed, Shidler's home telephone number, as Phillips knows.

"When did you say this was?"

"September twenty-sixth, just after midnight, just at the start of my shift."

He looks at his desk calendar. That was three days after the arraignment. "Do you have the tape of this?"

"Yes. Do you want me to send it to you?"

"Yeah. Definitely." He gives her the particulars. "Did the caller describe the kidnappers, anything like that?"

"No, I'm afraid not. I think it's a car phone, and the girl sounds startled toward the end of the message. We think she saw someone returning to the car."

"Say where she was?"

"No."

September 26, Phillips is thinking, September 26, Louisa Shidler was at home, still on the collar. There is electronic proof of that.

"Did you call the mother?"

"Yes. Yes. She identified herself as Louisa Shidler, then denied her daughter was missing. Said her daughter was with grandparents in North Carolina. So we kind of let it go. But, like I said, I saw the teletype, and the thing seemed weird, so I thought—"

"She said North Carolina?"

"Yes sir."

"I'm glad you called. Send me the tape as quick as you can." Before hanging up, he asks her to confirm what he thought he heard at the outset.

"This was a 911 call, right?"

"Oh, yes sir, absolutely."

It is a long time before Phillips picks up the pencil again. She denied her daughter was missing. The daughter called from the Kansas City area, and the mother denied she was missing.

"Well, boy, the guests are a little antsy."

"Usually the way it goes, ain't it? Up late, in a hurry," says sixteen-year-old Johnny Trapp.

"I'll have to git 'em out to the road. Looks like you got to break camp and clean up. I'll have to take the guests. Yep," Trapp's Uncle Frank goes on, sounding, as he so often does, as though he were having a conversation with both himself and whomever he was addressing.

"Ain't that a surprise, Uncle Frank!" Johnny looks up and winks at his uncle, who always finds a way to stick him with the clean-up on the last day of a pack trip, always with a big smile across his baby face as he bustles through the camp. Johnny calculates that he will have the dutch oven and the griddle to wash up, the coffeepots and the hot-water pots. He looks around the camp at the three canvas sleep tents and the cook tents he'll be striking. F&B Outfitters usually uses this campsite for its last night on a pack trip. It backs against the trees and looks out over a mountain meadow. To one side, Two Elk Brook flows gently. It almost always yields a trout or two, even to the dudes, and this morning one of them caught his limit.

"You gonna leave me Maxine and Rhonda?"

Uncle Frank is working his first chaw of the day around into his left cheek. "I'll have to take Maxine," he says, looking over to where the big bay nibbles at the sparse meadow grass with the other horses. "Have to take Maxine and the mules, yep. Leave you Rhonda, though."

"Well, ya'll better take the tents, then," Johnny says.

They strike the camp and Johnny Trapp chats with the dudes, a bachelor party. They were pretty good company, and they had good fly rods, but only one of the four could fish as well as he could drink. This morning they've been keeping their voices down, their heads pounding from too much bourbon the night before.

He shakes each one's hand as they mount up and wishes them well. His mind is already figuring as he watches them disappear into the trees. He'll get through the cook stuff in a half hour, and then take Rhonda back a half mile to where he knows a good trout pool—one he doesn't share with the guests. The sooner he gets back to the stables, the sooner they'll set him to airing out tents and grooming the horses, and the sooner his mother will want to know if his homework is done. One more day of Columbus Day weekend, he thinks. No sense rushing it.

The truth is in the first impression.

It pops into Louisa's head early in the morning, the meaning of Mac's last message. It comes to her the way the answer to a clue in the Sunday crossword sometimes comes on a Wednesday at lunchtime, three days after the moment when her mind finally conceded defeat. Suddenly the word seems to appear before her, for no apparent reason.

She is staring out at the highway traffic, which has thickened with the morning commute, as the meaning comes to her. "Latin companion," Mac's message said, "epic adventure." Virgil is a Latin companion; his *Aeneid* is an epic adventure, and the truth is in the impression. The first words of the poem come back to her from high-school Latin, the fragment of hexameter verse every schoolgirl takes with her: *Arma virumque cano.* "I sing of arms and a man." "You read, I sing"—isn't that what he wrote?

She stares out at the highway, turning it over. Arms and a man? Arms? Is this about arms trading? Is Mac talking about illegal arms deals? Royall Stillwell? Round and round her mind races. Could he have set up something through his international contacts?

She shakes her head as if to clear it. It is not possible.

Louisa Shidler has slightly missed the mark, just as Nevins missed it, just as Mac missed it. Or she might have quickly seen how very possible it is. For she has been thinking, naturally, of illegal arms sales. In 1996 there is far more money to be made legally.

She has missed the mark. But she has taken the first step toward understanding, toward knowing, her enemy.

"Coming up to I-77," says Bear, and Louisa, registering the voice over the hum of the engine, realizes she has drowsed. "Think I'll find us some breakfast, maybe take a little nap."

"Can we press on a little bit first?"

He smiles. "Louisa, I've got to rest now and then, you know. It's almost eleven."

"Just for an hour or so? Out to Columbus at least?"

"We'll see," he says. "I'll go along a little ways, until I get too sleepy."

They sit in silence for a moment. "So where's your home?" he asks.

"Well, I . . ." she hesitates. "Sort of Maryland, I guess. Sort of North Carolina. I'm not really sure."

"Sort of?" he asks.

"Well, I suppose it depends what you mean."

"I guess I mean the place where, when you have to go there, they have to take you in."

"Who said that?"

Bear smiles. "Robert Frost. 'Home is the place where, when you have to go there, they have to take you in.' I think that's right."

"I guess I might be homeless, then," she says, half smiling in reply. "At least for a little while."

The road passes through the flat farmlands of Ohio, and she looks at the landscape without seeing it. Her eyes stray to Isabel's photograph on the dashboard. I have no idea what I'm doing, she thinks.

"So, Louisa, what kind of music do you like?" he interrupts.

The question stumps her.

"Do you listen to music?"

"Well, sure, I, when I can. I—"

"What kind?"

"Whatever. It's not, it's not that important."

"It *is* that important."

"Fine."

His eyes crease up when he speaks, but he doesn't take them off the road. He's gentle that way, nervous, almost, as though he doesn't want to inflict his size on her even by looking at her too closely. His manner is an odd combination of tentative and persistent. He has a way of circling back to a thing.

"No, it is," he goes on pleasantly. "What do you do for fun, Louisa?"

"Fun?"

"Yeah, fun."

She is punctuating the conversation with sighs of exasperation, but he shows no sign of understanding.

"Lots of things," she says.

"Like what?"

"Lots of things," she repeats, to put an end to this ridiculous subject.

But he sounds as though he really doesn't get it. There's plenty of time to kill on the way west. "Like *what*?"

"Look, I'm not in a mood to call them all to mind right now, okay?"

"Okay." It is quiet for a while after that. Then he says, gently. "You shouldn't get an attitude because I ask you what you do for fun. I'm just trying to make conversation. Hitchhikers are supposed to make conversation." He sounds a little hurt.

"I'm sorry. Really, I am."

"I'm sorry too." He sounds it, but as she looks again, his eyes are creased, and she can see the smile. "So tell me something you like to do for fun."

"Frankly, I haven't had much fun, recently."

"Well, how about before recently?"

"Look . . . Bear, can we talk about something else?"

"Well," he says, with just a little mischief in his eyes, "I'd rather talk about this."

She sighs. "I'm sorry. This is like, this is like talking to *Isabel*. 'What music do you listen to? What do you do for fun?' As though life was just music and fun! As though we're put on this earth just, just to listen to music and have fun, and we should all be measured by our CD collections and which brand of mountain bike we have. That is *not* what life is about."

Where did that come from? She feels a little embarrassed, as they drive on in silence.

"So what *is* life about?" he asks.

God, the persistence of this man, she thinks. Is he foolish, or condescending? She looks over at his shaggy beard and remembers Rufus, an old golden retriever Toby's parents had. After the hundred and fiftieth time you had thrown the sodden tennis ball, Rufus would bring it to you for the hundred and fifty-first. Foolish, she decides.

"Excuse me?"

"What is life about, then?"

She sighs. "What is life about? Life is about getting to Wyoming."

"No, I'm serious—"

"And I'm serious too, Bear."

The silence grows painful in the cab again, and she realizes that she no longer cares if she is not carrying her end of the bargain. She stares at the long line of eastbound traffic.

"Maybe we should stop for breakfast."

CHAPTER 35

There is a noise in the brush. Johnny Trapp looks up, but he doesn't see anything. Just a critter waiting to inspect the camp for the leavings, probably. Grimacing, he turns back to the blackened cookware.

Above the campsite, Isabel creeps down the slope, as if the scent of blueberry pancakes and coffee on the morning breeze had hooked into her nostrils and was slowly reeling her in. She stumbles and kicks a stone, and then ducks behind a rock, from where she can see the camp. She sees only one person, a big, rangy boy in blue jeans and a gray T-shirt. He has a black cowboy hat worn low over his brow, obscuring his face. She watches as he gathers up a mass of pots and pans and walks off down the slope toward the stream in an easy, loping stride.

It seems like a long time before he returns, although probably it is only a quarter of an hour. But then she sees his long stride loping back up the path, and decides to take her chances.

Johnny Trapp watches a skinny dark-haired girl with a backpack in a dirty pair of blue jeans and a sweatshirt making her way down into the camp. She picks her way slowly down through the rocks. He looks at her and, for a moment, figures her for a dude's daughter. But it's a little late in the season for that. Besides, the dudes usually wear brand-spanking new boots. They always have catalogue-fresh fleece tops. He can't recollect any of the other outfitters coming on this trail this week.

"Hello," she says.

"Mornin'."

She stands uncomfortably, casting furtive glances around the camp, uncertain what to say next.

"You lost?" he asks.

"Yes," she says again, and a sort of nervous laugh escapes her.

"Well, you're found now. Name's Johnny Trapp. F&B Outfitters."

"My name is Isabel. Isabel Higginson."

"What party you with?" he asks.

"Excuse me?"

"What outfitter? You with Tom Percy's? Red Ashton's?"

She looks confused.

"Ah, have you got lost from a pack trip, is what I mean?"

"No. I escaped."

"You escaped. Well, that's how most of 'em feel about Ashton's."

She looks up and sees that his eyes are merry. "No, sorry, I mean, I've been kidnapped, and escaped."

"You've been kidnapped and escaped." Johnny Trapp chews that one over, working his jaw with one hand. "Damn," he says, kind of grinning at her with his eyes. "Nice of 'em to let you pack."

"I grabbed my pack and ran. You don't believe me?"

He mulls it over. "Tell me something. You git breakfast before you escaped from the kidnappers?"

"No," she says. "I haven't eaten since yesterday."

"In that case," he says, "why don't you have some pancakes?" He's smiling gently, as he adds, "They're cold, but even cold, they're better than Red Ashton's."

They sit on the folded cook tent, and Isabel tears through the blueberry pancakes. Between mouthfuls the story pours from her like torrents of water, leaving Johnny Trapp in a bewilderment of kidnappers and car rides, of mothers from Bethesda and vice-presidential nominees and beatings in wheatfields and men down the valley. Johnny doesn't know what to believe, except the unmistakable evidence of his own eyes that this slip of a girl hasn't eaten in a while.

"Have you ever heard of the Buffalo Bill Museum?" she asks him.

"Historical Center, you mean. Sure. Biggest thing in Cody."

The girl seems relieved at this. "Good," she says, "Cody's not too far, right?"

"Depends."

"It depends?"

"Well, I'd say it's pretty close if you're settin' on the highway in Uncle Frank's new Ford 150. I'd say it's farther'n that in Dad's pickup. And if you're walking, it's a long damn way."

She is looking at the map. "It looks like if I can get up to Highway 14, that would take me right into town."

"Oh, yeah, click your slippers, and you'll be back home in Kansas, Dorothy." He smiles at her. "Is that all you have, a road map? Won't do you much good out here."

"I'm sure it will be adequate. I'd be grateful if you would start me off in the right direction."

He gives a little laugh. "The right direction? The right direction is back down this trail here, with me, to the road you came from, and back to your folks."

"No, I'm afraid not."

It is silent for a moment. Johnny Trapp is mulling this over, rubbing the back of his neck. A lost girl came through his camp, and he didn't stop her, is the way it will sound. This isn't looking so good.

"Look. You need to come back with me," he says.

"I'm sorry, Johnny Trapp, but I have to go north. If you won't help me, I'll—I'll be on my way."

"You can't do that."

"I'm afraid I have to."

The crickets are popping up all around the campsite now. It is an unseasonably warm day, or morning at least, in October. Trapp sighs, and kicks at a stone.

"For a kid, you talk awful formal," he says.

"Thank you."

"I didn't mean it as a compliment."

"Oh. I'm sorry, then. It's the way I was raised."

"Look, don't take this wrong, but you wasn't raised to be out here in the mountains on your own. You can't just wander off into the Absarokas with a road map, okay? I'm sorry about the kidnappers and all, but you just come with me, and we'll get ahold of your folks, and you'll be okay."

"I'm sorry."

"I'm trying to help you."

"Thank you very much for the pancakes."

Isabel rises and picks her way a few steps down the path from the campsite. Then she stops and looks back at him. "You could help me, actually."

"How's that?"

"If a man comes after me, or a woman, please don't tell them you've seen me. He has short black hair and bad acne and kind of a flabby face and he smokes all the time. And she has blond-colored hair in a page boy and thin little lips and a sort of a hook nose, and she never ever smiles."

He smiles. "Your folks?"

"Hardly." The snobbery is delicious. "Please. Don't tell them you've seen me. They'll kill me."

The matter-of-fact way she says it sends a little chill over him, and he offers no reply as she goes off down the trail. Johnny Trapp follows her with his eyes, sure that she's bluffing, that she'll stop and turn. He stretches his legs, puts his arms behind his head, puts on a big grin. She'll stop and turn, he thinks, adjusting his hat, reinforcing his grin.

But she doesn't. She disappears into the trees along the streambed. He waits a little longer, and after five minutes or so, looking down the slope, he sees her emerge onto the opposite hillside, tracking north.

"Goddammit." This is not good. There is a lost kid about to become a really lost kid, a lost, delusional kid. It's not even his party, and all of a sudden it's going to be his job to do something about it.

"Rhonda, come on." Trapp sets the blanket and saddle on her, cinches the saddle down, and mounts the horse.

A few moments later, Isabel hears the hoofbeats coming up the rise behind her and turns quickly, in fear, then just as quickly turns back. Johnny spurs the horse up alongside her.

"Now, come on now, little girl, you can't do this."

"That is *so* lame." She scrunches her face into its most fearsome look of disgust and strides with purpose, not looking to her left at the grinning rider.

"You can't walk twenty-five miles through this country in Redball Jets, with a damn road map. Okay?"

"They're Reeboks. And why can't I?"

"Because you ain't even smart enough to know why you can't. If you knew why you can't, then maybe you could. Except, you wouldn't."

"Well, that makes a lot of sense."

The horse walks patiently beside her, her shoes clinking on stones and kicking up dust.

"Do you even have any water?"

"I'll get some."

"Where you gonna do that?"

"I'll find a stream."

"And you'll get giardia."

She bites her lip, determined not to ask him the question.

Johnny Trapp leans over the pommel. "What's giardia, Isabella, do you know?"

"Isabel. And it's none of your business."

"That's why you can't do this! You don't know what giardia is! You don't know anything, girl!"

"Then I don't want to be any further trouble to you. Thank you for breakfast."

"Isabel, you are *already* further trouble to me. You'll get lost. Or it will snow. Or the temperature will drop to ten below and a forty-mile-an-hour wind will come up. Or you'll get blisters all over your feet. Or you'll drink bad water and catch giardia. Or all them things will happen to you at once. And then your parents will show up and want to know what in the hell I was thinking, letting you do it. You got nothing to eat. You are bear chow out here, girl."

"I'll be fine, thank you very much. I have a map."

"Well, the first thing you oughta do is chuck that map. Alls *it* is is extra weight!"

The horse strides lazily, its hooves kicking up little puffs of dust from the rocky trail. Isabel juts out her lower lip and quickens her pace.

"What do you mean, bears?" she asks after a while, in a tone that attempts to convey a purely intellectual curiosity.

"I mean a thousand pounds of hairy-assed monster that hasn't eaten in weeks, and would just as soon have a little girl for breakfast, and her Reeboks too. This is grizzly-bear country."

"Yeah, right."

"Isabel, this is the grizzly-bear capital of North America, right here. Didn't you see the sign at the trailhead?"

"No."

"That billboard, warning about bears? You must have seen it."

"I didn't come up by the trailhead."

"Oh, you didn't. Well how did you come? By parachute?"

"No. I climbed up the cliff."

"Sure you did."

"I did."

"Look, hold on," he says. "Stop. Stop! Just talk to me for a minute, okay! I'm trying to help you!"

Isabel slows, and then stops. She looks up at him, squinting in the sun. It is getting hot. The grin seems to have gone from his face, replaced by a vexed look.

"I'm sorry I laughed at you," he says.

She tosses her hair back. "That's quite all right."

"But this is crazy."

She tosses her hair again.

"Look," he says, "what are you gonna eat?"

"I'll walk to the road, and then I'll, I'll think of something."

"The road's twenty-five miles."

"I've walked nine miles before. When I wasn't really trying."

"And when you wasn't really in Wyoming, I'll bet. You'll be lucky to walk nine if you walk all day. And you'll probably walk nine in a circle and end up right here."

The horse whinnies a little, frustrated by the delay. She stamps a fore-leg.

"You've been very helpful, Mr. Johnny Trapp, but I'm afraid I have to be going."

Isabel turns once again and begins to walk up the trail. He sits the horse, watching the little figure, thinking about the trout in the grotto pool, thinking about having to get back to town, thinking about this wasted morning. He wonders, for a moment, if he ought to stop her physically, try to drag her back. No, her father's probably a lawyer from New York or somewhere.

"Dammit," he shouts, "you ain't even going the right way!"

"I am too!"

"Ain't neither!"

She doesn't answer, continues to stride away from him.

"Jesus H. Christ," he says, spurring the horse again.

"Look here," he says, coming alongside of her a second time, and pulling something from his saddlebag. "Just hold on. Stop just a minute."

She doesn't.

"Goddammit, Isabel. Stop!"

She comes to a halt, staring straight forward.

"This is harassment, Mr. Johnny Trapp."

"Know how to read a topo map?" he asks.

"I am familiar with harassment. You will find that I am aware of my rights."

"Well, that's great, but I don't see too many lawyers around here right now, so can we at least make you aware of a topo map?"

She colors a little. "I know how to read a map," she says.

"How about a compass?"

"Of course. It points north."

"Yeah, it does. And E equals MC squared, too, but knowing that didn't never make me Einstein or get me an A in physics. Now hold on a minute." Johnny Trapp climbs down from the horse and begins a lesson in orienteering.

Sugaree's cab is quiet. After the breakfast stop they travel without conversation, a silence punctuated only by requests for a new tape. A black mood has fallen on Louisa as the day progresses. Something is bubbling up inside her. At length she lowers the volume on the tape player.

"I'm sorry about before," she says.

"It's okay."

"I'm under a little strain, is all."

"It's okay."

More cornfields, more Indiana countryside passes by outside Suga-ree's cab. The speed seems slow to her, ponderous. And then, suddenly, Indiana has melted away, and she is telling him about Morocco. Is it to rebuild a bridge? Or is it that the pace seems so slow, as did that of the Land Rovers on their way to Marrakesh? She is speaking slowly, in a di-dactic sort of way, not speaking it so much as being its mouthpiece, as though the story tells itself, as though the story itself says, "Listen. This is how it is." Bear's iron-gray beard is motionless, his eyes gentle and re-ceptive.

"We went to a town called Rabat. A lot of diplomats and so on from our side, and a great tiled chamber full of ambassadors and chargés and cousins and courtiers of the king. Lots of bowing and formal speeches, and then more formal speeches around a long table, with all of the Mo-roccans on one side, and all of us on the other.

"It was a happy meeting. Their head and our head shook hands, and the agreement was made. When the ceremony was over, the Moroccans said, You must come on a visit to Marrakesh. Everyone must go to Mar-rakesh, they said. So our delegation was fitted up in Land Rovers and the drivers took us through Rabat and out into the desert and we drove to Marrakesh. You should see it someday. Big orange walls leaping up like a miracle in the sand. And date palms. It was beautiful.

"The king's people took us into the souk, and it was just as you might imagine, with vendors and charmers and hawkers and goods of every de-scription, crowds and noise and copper pans full of grains, and stacks of cloth in stalls, and strange smells and sights, and long narrow corridors with crowds of little boys grabbing your hand to take you somewhere. 'Come, come pretty lady! Come see pretty things!' It was exotic and ex-citing and dirty and beautiful.

"A Moroccan boy took our group and led us through the maze of stalls until we ended up in a quiet little square. There were two white-washed buildings, one on each side, and in between them the square, with a sort of tunnel leading in from the stalls the way we came, and another across the square, and a tiny fountain where water dripped into a basin. The boy pointed out the fountain triumphantly, and then held out his hand for a few piastres.

"The fountain was a disappointment. I noticed two dogs in the square. A white one was a powerful animal, quite robust-looking, sort of like a bulldog in breadth and strength. The other was gray and scrawny and pitiful and ugly to look at. It held its tail between its legs and cringed and its fur had fallen out in patches. Now, our guide had a salami with him. He cut a hunk off and threw it. It came to the little dog, but the bigger one pounced and snatched it away. He swallowed it down in a single gulp—I don't think he even tasted it. And then his tail wagged once, but in an expectant, not a deferential, way. It was a wag of entitlement. He waited for more. And the skinny dog, his tail kind of half wagged a little too, but it was a craven sort of wag.

"I felt pity for him. So I asked the guide for the meat, and I cut two hunks with his knife. I cut a little one, and a bigger one. And then I tossed the little one to the powerful white dog. As he went for it, I tossed the bigger hunk of meat to the skinny one, feeling, I must say, rather proud of myself for this stratagem.

"Well, the big dog figured it out instantly, *instantly.* He dropped the little piece, and leaped for the throat of the little one. The yelp it made! A terrifying sound, it made me cringe. It dropped its hunk of meat, and the stronger one snatched it up. So the big dog got both. He gulped down the big piece, and then he returned to the little piece, and ate that too. And when he was done, the little one half crawled toward the spot, and licked the dirt where the piece had fallen. That's what the little one got, the greasy dust where the meat had fallen.

"That's my clearest memory of Marrakesh, more than of the walls in the desert and the dates and the piles of brass in the souk. I remember the big dog snatching both pieces of meat, and the little one licking the greasy dust."

Her voice falls silent, and there is only the hum of the diesel in the cabin. Bear glances over at her. "Yeah?" he asks.

A moment passes, and she says, "You asked this morning what life is about."

It is silent in the cab for quite a while after that, and a gloom seems to have fallen even over Bear. After a time Louisa rises and goes back to the condo. "I'll get some coffee," she says quietly.

"I don't think you need any."

"Whatever you say."

He drives a while, but she doesn't reemerge. "All right," he hollers, "you're right. Life is about all the bad shit. The big dogs getting everything. And us little dogs getting nothing. Were you a big dog, too?"

She doesn't answer. He goes on. "Maybe if you were a big dog, you think about the meat all the time. About people screwing you and all, taking your meat. But you know, Louisa, if you're only a little dog, that's why you got to make life about something else. Like music. Hey, damn, look at that!"

"What?"

"Volkswagen convertible. Haven't seen one of those for a while! A little dog's car, ain't it?"

It is half past eleven, and Johnny Trapp is back in camp, cinching Rhonda's pack. He feels uneasy about this, although, when finally they parted, he did leave her with a full canteen, a rain slicker, some more cold pancakes, and the compass and map. Maybe the weather will hold. Maybe she will make it to Highway 14. The horse protests, and Johnny realizes he has cinched the strap too tight. He's rushing a little. He's going to have to get to a phone and call Mountain Rescue.

"And they're going to ask me, 'Well, boy, why didn't you stop her?' That's what they're going to say, Rhonda. And what do I say?"

The horse stares blankly at him while he pulls on the straps.

" 'I tried to stop her, honest, but she wouldn't listen. No sir, she wouldn't.'

" 'Why the hell didn't you just *stop* her, boy? She's all of twelve!' "

Trapp looks up at Rhonda. The horse seems rather uninterested in the cross-examination. He carries on.

" 'Well, I didn't think I could do that. I mean. Think how that could be told, her being a girl and all.'

" 'Oh, use your head, boy.'

" 'I gave her a map and compass.'

" 'If you could give her a map and compass, why couldn't you stop her?'

" 'Well, think how it could be told.'

" 'How it could be told ain't any worse than how it *will* be told, now is it?' "

Trapp comes out of his mock interrogation. It keeps returning to that line, that's the problem.

Rhonda's ears twitch a little, and she turns her head, lifts her nostrils to the breeze, and whinnies, stamping her forelegs impatiently.

Johnny knows that stamp, and he looks up at the ridgeline. A half mile above the camp, he sees the silhouette of a rider's head and shoulders, and then another. Good, he thinks, this'll be the folks looking for the girl. He can point them the right way and get her off his conscience. He sees a flash of light. A pair of binoculars is trained on the camp.

He doesn't have long to wait. Only ten minutes later, three horses, ridden by two men and a woman, emerge from the tree cover on the rocky hillside. The trail winds down from the hillside and, just before the camp, passes beneath a loblolly pine. A low branch cuts across the trail.

Trapp studies them as they come down toward the camp. The lead rider leans forward as he comes under the branch, but the two riders in the rear both lean back, the way a novice does, and they don't sit their horses very comfortable. Maybe that's the mother and father. Trapp looks back at the lead rider. He holds his reins with two hands.

Johnny Trapp is a little puzzled. He doesn't recognize any of them, and Trapp knows everyone who regularly ventures into this corner of the wilderness, certainly every outfitter and everyone on the Mountain Rescue teams, all the sheriff's deputies, all the Forest Service people, most all the park rangers. The woman has a narrow, pinched face. The second man's face is acne-scarred. He fingers a cigarette nervously. Johnny Trapp remembers what Isabel said, and realizes he doesn't like the looks of any of them. And the lead guy, Trapp thinks again, as the horses come to a halt, he holds his reins with two hands.

"Mornin'," says Johnny.

"Mornin'," says the leader, a gray-eyed man who wears a green Gore-Tex anorak and a dark blue baseball cap. In fact, all three of them do. Around the leader's neck is a pair of binoculars. He has packed a rifle in a scabbard. Johnny's eyes roam lazily over the man's companions. Two more scabbards are visible. Why? They aren't dressed for hunting. Why do their parkas match? He thinks again about what the girl said.

The quiet is broken by the crackle of a walkie-talkie, and the lead man pulls a receiver out of his anorak and says something inaudible.

"I'm Johnny Trapp," Johnny says, putting out his hand and looking up at the leader, who leans across the pommel and smiles, taking Johnny's hand. Johnny waits for the man to introduce himself.

"We're lookin' for a lost little girl," the lead rider says. He walks the horse up to Rhonda. It is a hard face, deeply lined and organized around a frown, its sandy hair flecked with gray.

Johnny Trapp hesitates briefly, but the bad signs have made his choice for him: the unfamiliar faces, the poor horsemanship, the scabbards, the parkas, the fact that they haven't given their names, and probably most of all, the way the leader holds his reins—with two hands, like someone from out East.

"Ain't we all?" Johnny Trapp answers, turning away to fish something out of his pack.

The man with the acne scars chuckles, but not the leader.

"Wonder if you'd seen her," the leader carries on.

"How little?" Johnny asks, after a moment.

"About twelve."

Johnny turns back toward the group and asks the leader what outfit she has got lost out of.

"She wasn't on a pack trip," the leader says. "Was with her folks down the valley and run away."

"Y'all her folks?"

The man with the acne nods. "Yeah."

"You know," Johnny says, after a moment, "I did see someone. What's she look like?"

"Five feet tall, white, dark hair down to her shoulders, with a gray sweatshirt on last time she was seen. Braces. About ninety-five pounds."

"Yeah. Well, I ain't sure. But earlier this morning, I was fixing breakfast, and I looked up and seen someone up yonder on the ridge."

"Up there?" The leader turns to look back the way he came.

"Yeah. Pretty much where you come. Person was walking east along the ridge."

"Girl?"

"I dunno. Couldn't really tell from here. Looked like a kid."

"Where'd she go?"

"Well, I didn't really pay attention. I was fixing up breakfast for our guests, and just looked up and seen someone. Wearing something light-colored, white, gray, yellow, I don't know. And the person was going east along that ridge. I remember thinking maybe some other outfitter was camped around here, wonderin' where. And I looked up again and didn't see the person up there anymore."

The group is staring up toward the summit.

"She may have got turned around and headed back for the road along the Ishawooa drainage," the leader says.

"Could be," says Trapp. "What's her name, anyway?"

"Isabel. Isabel Higginson."

The horses fidget some more. Johnny looks up from his pack and says, "I'm heading for the road myself in an hour or so. Who should I call if I find her?"

The leader smiles. "Don't worry about it. We'll go on down and take a look. Thanks, appreciate your help." He gives him a perfunctory smile, a cold smile, and Johnny Trapp knows that he has done the right thing, the way the man smiles. The leader reins his horse around and walks her back to the edge of the camp, where the three gather in a knot and talk for a moment.

"We'll be along, then," the leader sings out after a moment. Johnny watches the horses pick their way down to the stream and into the meadow. Two of them aren't riders at all, and none of them's from around here, he thinks. And they never told me their names.

Johnny Trapp hadn't planned on this. Now it is he who has no map or compass. He knows every acre of that country, but the clouds are thickening. He spurs Rhonda as high up the ridge as she will go, and then dismounts and walks her the last way. Dark afternoon storm clouds are boiling up from the west. The far peaks of the Absarokas are already covered. It will rain soon, if it doesn't snow.

At the crest he looks through the binoculars in every direction. Nothing. "Damn," he says, and leads the horse down the slope, and on to the north.

"I do believe we're going to catch it now, Rhonda," he says.

CHAPTER 36

The highway landscape is unlovely; it is all man's misfeasance, his utility poles and road signs and billboards advertising radio stations or truck stops, all dented guardrails, and green paint peeling off the steel beams beneath the overpasses. It is all roadside rubbish and low squat buildings, heaps of breeze block choked with grime. Sometimes there are the flat brown fields stretching off to another distant line of utility poles, but mostly she sees dreary buildings, tumbledown shacks. Man's architecture has overtaken God's, and it is puny and dispiriting. Even in the cornfields, the uneven stubble of the hewn cornstalks is graceless now, as if God Himself needed a shave—as if He, too, had drunk too much and lay unshaven and snoring in stubble long after sunrise, after the weeds grew up and infested His creation.

For He has not been much in evidence, Louisa thinks. Not when Toby wandered; not when these people, whoever they are, destroyed her career, certainly not when the men in headlamps hauled Isabel out to their car. She blames Him, too, as the dusk comes on.

With the darkness comes Doolie. Wrestling with Mac's snippet from Virgil, Louisa's mind has gone back to Royall, and thence, inevitably, to Doolie. Doolie who knows everybody and who is so frank and profane and refreshingly candid and who confides in you and makes you her friend. Until you begin to trust her. And then she is on your telephone with phony small talk, reading your voice and reporting the results to Royall. Louisa stares into the dusky landscape and remembers Doolie and the night at the Groveberry Inn last summer.

The campaign had booked rooms for Royall at the Marriott in Roanoke, but it was the Fourth of July weekend, and rooms were scarce, and someone had made a grave error. Doolie was scheduled to travel south to Charlotte, North Carolina, to stump for her husband, and some anonymous, and doomed, assistant had neglected to arrange accommodation for her in Charlotte, if such a thing can be imagined. The assistant had assumed, apparently, that she would be staying with Royall in Roanoke. By the time the mistake was noticed, it was too late. And so, on the Fourth of July, there was not, in all of Charlotte, a room available for Mrs. Royall Stillwell.

It fell to Louisa to repair the shambles. She was dispatched to ferry the candidate's wife from Charlotte to an inn off the Blue Ridge Parkway. Doolie sat in the passenger seat of Louisa's Honda, glaring fire at the countryside.

The mood, having begun badly, did not improve. It was not precisely the right moment to shower Royall with praise, although Louisa did. "Royall was really good, today," she said. "I can't believe how good he was with that crowd in Roanoke."

Doolie grimaced. "I can believe almost anything except the fact that I am sitting here in this car," she said.

"I'm sorry about the arrangements," Louisa repeated. She had been apologizing for two days. Outside the car, each twist and turn of the parkway revealed another scene from an eclogue of Virgil: cattle lowing on hillsides behind ancient rail fences, the sky coloring in the soft pinks of summer as the sun set away to the west.

"God," Doolie said, "it's the Fourth of July weekend, and look at this!"

"Yes," Louisa answered, "beautiful, isn't it?"

"Louisa, honey, will you please stop making this worse? No, *this* is not beautiful. It is midsummer and where am I? Am I with my *people*? Did I even make the guest list at the Marriott Hotel in Charlotte? No. I'm in the front seat of a Honda being driven to a tent site in some backward pioneer village that time never remembered, much less forgot."

"It's an inn," Louisa said, after a respectful pause.

"An inn?" Doolie snapped. "Oh, it's an inn we're going to up in Possum Holler, Louisa? Excuse me. That's reassuring. We can all have an extra helping of dumplings and dance a jig in our union suits! How silly of me not to look it up in Michelin."

"Doolie, I—"

A speech of the careworn interrupted her. "Louisa! Please. Please do not prolong the torture of this evening by attempting conversation. Let's just go to the . . . whatever it is."

A half hour later, Louisa pulled the Honda off the parkway and followed a gravel road a half mile to the Groveberry Inn. On the right side of the road, just beyond a cemetery, she saw the gray-shingled walls of the main building, with two low-roofed shed structures visible behind. "Groveberry Inn," the sign read. "Fine Dining."

The car came to rest. Louisa unbuckled her seat belt and opened the door, almost saying something cheery as she swung her legs to the ground but, fortunately, checking herself when she noticed that her passenger was frozen, absolutely stock-still. "You're not serious," Doolie said, her voice grim with outrage as she stared out at the main building.

"Perhaps I can take a look for you—"

"It's a motel!" she hissed. "You've brought me to a motel in Deliverance, Virginia!"

"Well," Louisa answered, trying to retain her equanimity, "the brochure said it's an inn. Renowned for its fine dining—"

"Fine dining! Oh, for heaven's sake, Louisa!" Doolie lit a cigarette, her hands fidgety with rage. "All right, it is clear that I am stranded here." She smoked for a moment, and then waved Louisa off. "Run along in there and get my key, please!"

The Groveberry Inn boasted not only fine dining, the lady at the registration desk assured Louisa, but also a pond groaning with bluegills and catfish. Would the ladies be fishing?

Louisa looked out at the unmoving silhouette in the passenger seat of her car. "No," she said, "my guess is we won't be fishing."

"Well, if you change your mind, you let us know. We've got rods and reels, and Herman can fix you up with crawlers. If y'all will be eating with us tonight, we'll be serving until nine."

Doolie's room abutted the Groveberry Inn's two-story satellite dish and looked out over the fishpond. She stood under the yellow light of the porch and muttered under her breath as Louisa jiggled the key.

Some fifteen minutes later, Doolie and Louisa were greeted at the door to the dining room by a somewhat puffy youth with bright-red acne scars. He wore a rayon shirt with a frilled placket and wing collar. He did not seem to recognize Doolie, but smiled broadly. "Good evening, mah name is Roy, and Ah'll be your server this evening."

Doolie looked once at the unblinking face and then looked away. "Of course you will," she answered. "Who else *could* be?" She smiled a wicked smile, and Roy smiled back, sensing, somehow, that some meaning was intended by the remark that he could not quite catch. He turned and smiled at Louisa, who smiled back—altogether a lot of smiling there on the threshold of the dining room. As they walked in Doolie said, "This is too much. All of this, this place, now, now . . . can you believe this? Could you write this?"

"And if there's any refreshment I could git for y'all before—" Roy asked after they had been seated.

"Get me a double vodka gimlet, please," Doolie said.

"Ma'am?" Roy's chubby, inquiring expression testified to his unfamiliarity with the drink.

"Oh, Lord, a vodka. With lime juice. It doesn't matter, Jethro. Just get me the vodka, dear."

"Name's Roy, ma'am."

"Of course it is, honey."

Roy's evening did not improve; indeed, his career as a waiter did not long survive Doolie's visit to the Groveberry. It began when the young man ventured a recommendation that the ladies try the steak. A world-weary sigh escaped from Doolie then, and Roy's eyes went blank as he stood watching his party in evident pain. At last she waved him away with instructions to bring a salad. Then Louisa made the mistake of ordering wine.

Roy's face was the problem. It stared out at Louisa as though she were speaking in Hindustani when she asked for the Pouilly Fuissé, and then Louisa had gently to spell it out, and point to it on the wine list, and a moment later Roy shuffled back and reported that they were out. So Louisa ordered the Pouilly Fumé, and a minute or so after that Roy shuffled back once more to report that he was wrong before, he "didn't exactly hear you right, ma'am, and Ah thought you was ordering the Foomay when you ordered the Foosay." They did have the Fuissé; they didn't have the Fumé. What would she like?

"She ordered the Fuissé first. She wants the Fuissé," Doolie drawled quietly. "This isn't cold fusion, honey. Bring us the fuckin' Fuissé, would you please?"

Heads turned in the dining room of the Groveberry Inn—including Louisa's, for she had never heard Doolie use profanity in public. She noticed a pair of diners in earnest conversation, and began to wonder whether the incident would make tomorrow's papers.

The end came about fifteen minutes later, just after their dinners arrived. Doolie's salad made it to the table with bread rolls and without incident. The problem was the butter. On Louisa's request, Roy returned with three foil packets of it—in his hand. For a moment, there was the dead calm before a horrendous storm—the gold foil of the butter packets, the pudgy fingers, the anxious, guileless servility in Roy's eyes, the silence. Roy's fingers extended toward the table, naked before Doolie, and then for Louisa came the slow horror of watching Roy's pudgy hand clutching the butter packets, reaching across Doolie, attempting to make a landing on Louisa's plate.

Roy's hand never got there, of course, for Doolie, with regal ire, called a halt. She rose, brushed the arm away, and said, "That will be quite enough, Louisa. Not one minute longer in this . . . place . . . which Royall and his people have so graciously recommended to his wife. Not another minute." She turned and glided from the room.

Alas, there was to be one more difficulty. Earlier that evening, when Louisa went to find her room, she had noticed fish rising in the pond. Perhaps their liveliness was accounted for by the prodigious hatch on that evening. The air was thick with flies. Now, as Louisa escorted Doolie to her room, a dark swarm of mayflies settled on Doolie's dress, attracted by its pale color. When Louisa and Doolie reached the porch light outside her room, the ambassador's wife looked down and noticed the dark mass. It was at that point that an angry shriek was heard from the Room 101 end of the complex to the Room 348 end, and the lady from the registration desk came bounding out the front door to see what was wrong.

Doolie mastered herself quickly but nevertheless was quite as short as Louisa had ever heard her. "Louisa!" she said. "You have taken me to this place, you have submitted me to that, that waiter in there, and food quite unfit for zoo animals, and now I am covered in . . . bugs! We are going to leave this place in ten minutes. You will cancel whatever fool thing I have scheduled for tomorrow, and get the car. We're going back to McLean."

And then the door slammed, leaving Louisa swatting at mayflies under the porch light.

Louisa drifts in and out of sleep, or some other nonconscious state. It is dark outside, and yet another endless Grateful Dead tape is playing.

I sing of arms and a man, she remembers. She wonders what Mac is doing. *Arma virumque cano.* She may be dreaming, or maybe she is remembering an old professor, Fitzgerald his name, whose course on ancient epic poetry she took at Duke. They read the *Aeneid*, the *Iliad*, the *Odyssey.* He was a small, bashful man with bushy eyebrows, who wore a beret to class and carried his notes in a green shoulder bag. But when he lectured on the *Odyssey* he became mesmerizing, and even the fraternity boys in the lecture hall sat spellbound. She is remembering one lecture in particular.

"How," Fitzgerald asked, "how shall we meet Homer's hero, the master mariner and warrior? In command of armies, a spear in his hand, or at the helm of a warship? No. No armies, no ship, no companions at all. The household on Ithaka long taken; the wife almost taken but soon to succumb, and everything else, the storehouses of grape and grain, all but exhausted. A dog on the steps, too old and far gone even to scratch at fleas."

And here he turned a fiery look, a possessed look, on the class. "We meet him naked," he said.

"The gods take his ship, take even his clothing, and cast him into the sea. And before washing him ashore on Scheria, the poet scrapes the hero's body itself"—here the professor's voice rose slightly, almost a desperation in it—"along the cliffs of the rugged island. So that, ladies and gentlemen, when we meet the hero, even his *skin* has been taken from him. There is nothing to distract you, nothing to gape at, no finery, no crowds of admirers, almost no man at all. Just a life force, washed ashore on a strange island, covered in leaves, because there are no clothes. A life force. Nothing left, except wit, and heart."

She remembers Homer's description of Odysseus, Fitzgerald's favorite passage. Odysseus pulls his naked and nearly lifeless body from the ocean. He covers himself in leaves, "as a shepherd, far from any neighbor's fire, buries a glowing ember in the ash, saving it for another day."

"That, I think, is the poet's message," Fitzgerald had said. "Lose everything, but not that; save wit, save heart, save for another day that essence of yourself, and you will reach home. He will."

Fitzgerald's face drifts away from her, and she comes back to the darkening cab of the eighteen-wheeler. Outside, another cornfield goes by. For a few minutes she studies the man behind the wheel: the way that Brillo-thick ticking of beard disguises but does not mask altogether a smile, a contentment; the well-muscled definition of the forearm that angles up to the top of the steering wheel; the happy roundness, the almost pregnant sphericality of the belly that massages the bottom of the wheel. He is a man of muscle and belly in equal measure, she thinks. He is a measured man, a man who has reached home.

The previous evening, another listener picked up on the call to the Birch Thornacre show, a sixty-eight-year-old retired FBI field agent and Birch devotee named Pete Rankin. Now living in Eugene, Oregon, Rankin never fails to tune in to Birch, whom he regards as the only clear-thinking voice in the mass media. And that will prove to be a lucky thing, for he picks up more details from the Louisa-Royall exchange than anyone else.

The next morning, he telephones FBI headquarters in Washington and inquires about the Shidler investigation. His call is shuttled to various extensions, and at last is routed to Gene Phillips, who is sipping coffee and staring at the wire stories and the FBI telex as Rankin's call comes in.

"I think I heard Louisa Shidler telephone the Thornacre show. Anyway, that's what she said. She accused him of taking a bribe, and of kidnapping somebody named Isabel Higginson."

"That's her daughter. She accused him of kidnapping her daughter?"

"Well, words to that effect. Something like 'What have you done with her?' "

Phillips thinks about this for a moment.

"Listen, Pete, thanks for the call."

"There was one other thing."

"Yeah?"

"Whoever it was called him Royall. And he called her Louisa. Sounded like they knew each other."

From his desk in Washington, Phillips works the case. A taciturn John Shidler, reached in Yadkinville, says he won't talk to anyone on the telephone. If they want to talk to him, they should send an agent to meet him personally. It takes Phillips an hour to find one and put him in motion.

At least a half dozen calls are spent in persuading the Birch Thornacre producers to cough up the tape without a subpoena. "I thought he's supposed to be a law-and-order guy," Phillips shouts into the phone at one point, to a difficult assistant. Finally they relent and agree to turn it over to an FBI courier in New York, who will bring it to the forensics lab in Quantico that night.

Later in the afternoon, a field agent from Greensboro, North Carolina, calls in from a rest area on Interstate 40.

"I just went up to the farm to meet Shidler," he says to Phillips. "And he told me he hasn't seen his granddaughter since last summer. She hasn't been down here."

CHAPTER 37

High up on Wapiti Ridge, southwest of Citadel Mountain, Johnny Trapp slides off Rhonda gratefully and tumbles to the ground. "Damn, Isabella, you are one difficult child."

"Isabel," says the girl, who is huddled next to the bole of a gnarled stump. "And I'm not a child. And why do you keep following me?"

"Because I ain't the only one."

It is late in the aftrernoon, and growing colder by the hour. The temperature will plunge below freezing well before the sun sets. The girl is shivering. Her sweatshirt and his jacket provide little protection. She has come to rest on the north side of a bald ridge, sheltered in a circle of rocks and the tree stump.

Johnny Trapp clambers back up to the ridge and trains his binoculars on the river valley to the south, moving them from left to right, then back to left again, panning slowly over the vast, empty countryside, much of which has now fallen into shadow.

"C'mon up here," he says after a few minutes.

Isabel turns and looks up at Johnny's silhouette and sees by his manner that he is serious, and so she joins him. The outcropping affords a view back south and west over the meadow they traversed that morning, and then down into Ishawooa Creek. At first she can see nothing in particular except the pale-green grasses stretching out below the tarn, dotted here and there with stands of forest-green lodgepole pines out into the distance. She is trying to catch her breath and says, "What?"

"There," says Johnny, "by the base of that cliff over yonder, coming off of Clouds Home Peak, see the one with those kinda reddish stripes along in the pale stone?"

She looks back to the southwest, following the line of his arm. Squinting, she catches sight of a distant rock outcropping, about three miles away.

"Now look down from that, a little to the left, just where the trees start," he says.

She stares at the spot; at first, even when directed toward it, she sees nothing. But then, gradually, a shape, a tiny speck moves against the backdrop, darker than it, and as her eyes adjust to it, another emerges, and a third.

"That's the way we both come," says Johnny.

"How many are there?"

"Three, looks like," he says.

"Are you sure?" Isabel can't remember the cliff, but in truth, she has not been a terrifically good observer.

"That's the way I come," he repeats. "You, too, I expect." In a broad panorama of hundreds of square miles, encompassing more than 180 degrees of arc from the rocky post, only three human beings are visible. And they ride where Johnny rode but two hours before. "If they come out a half hour ago, they might a seen me," he says.

He stares for another few minutes through the binoculars, then says, "It's them, all right. Looks like they got a . . . I can't tell for sure . . . yeah, dammit. Isabel, why are them people chasing you?"

"I don't know. I was kidnapped from my house in Maryland. They took me away and didn't tell me anything and they held me in a house back in that valley down there until I got away. That's all I know."

"A house in the valley?"

"It was like an old summer camp or something."

"Valley Ranch, maybe. Hmmm. Old dude ranch, hasn't been used in quite a few years. Well, you are about to get found, girl. We got to go." Johnny Trapp scrambles to his feet, and in a minute, leading the horse, the two are plunging down the hillside.

"How can they follow us?" Isabel asks.

"Because they got a dog."

Now the trail climbs more steeply and the grasses and the sagebrush fall away. The chalk and khaki colors of the rock begin to harden into grays, and above them and stretching away to the northwest are the summits of the Absaroka Range, many now snow-covered.

"They like to know we're headed this way," Johnny says, "but if we get up into that scree and head off the trail, maybe . . ." Isabel looks up and sees, high above them, the boulder field lying between two granite horns.

"We got to get through the saddle soon or they'll catch sight of us when they come up the ridge. And this is too steep to double up on Rhonda. You've got to move fast."

Isabel fights her panic and feels the soreness again in her legs. Johnny bounds up the trail ahead of her, leading Rhonda by her halter. Isabel waits for a moment, listening to her own breathing. They are just above ten thousand feet, and she finds herself out of breath even at the slightest activity. Biting her lip, she strikes out after him.

The trail is steep, and Isabel looks up at the saddle after what seems an eternity, only to find it no closer. Johnny begins to slip ahead of her.

"Can we stop?"

"Not till we're over the saddle," he says, and as he turns she sees the fear in his eyes. If their pursuers reach the base of the saddle with them still visible on it, he doubts they will make it through the night.

"C'mon, Isabel," he says once, "you got to go faster than that."

"All right," she says. "All right."

The wind picks up, and beneath their feet there is nothing except the rock and the pale-green lichens that cling to life in the granite cracks. There are no flowers, no grasses. Isabel struggles up the slope until the saddle is in view, and at last the pitch eases, and then levels off. Gasping, she looks up at the two peaks that throw their position into shadow.

"Don't stop now, Isabel. Let's get down out of sight," he says, and they spring eastward, down the slope. A hundred yards or so off the spur, he pauses and looks off to one flank and then the next.

"I reckon they know we're making for Cody. That's to the north. So maybe we oughta fool 'em and go west?"

"No. I have to go to Cody. My mother's meeting me there."

"There's more cover to the north, anyway." A mile or so away, they can see that the trees poke up almost to their altitude. "We need the cover."

She watches him leap nimbly back up the slope to the saddle and waits, nervously, for him to return.

It takes a few minutes, but he comes back in a hurry. "They're headed up the saddle," he says, seizing Rhonda's halter. "And they do have that damn dog." Rhonda whinnies in protest, but Johnny is bounding from rock to rock, leading the mare. Isabel brushes the hair from her forehead and sets out after him.

In a mile they get down from the scree to where they can ride, and soon after that they are into the trees, a lovely mountainside glade of lodgepole pines. It starts to rain. They ride on as darkness falls, and the girl slumps against the pommel. Johnny knows that, with the dog, they will easily be followed, and so he calculates to get the pursuers into tight trees, where they won't want to carry on past dark. The wet pine twigs and saplings lash their faces as he urges Rhonda on through the woods. Rhonda labors, and Johnny starts to feel dizzy himself. But he has at least another six miles to go. The rain continues, cold and hard against their faces.

With one hand, Johnny Trapp holds the reins, and with the other, the sleeping girl, as he presses on toward the northeast along the flank of the mountainside.

Then they hear it, and the horse quickens her pace. "Easy, girl," Trapp says. The horse's nostrils flare as she smells what she cannot see. He spurs her on to the creek.

They sit by the bank in the darkness while Rhonda drinks. Johnny knows they have another two or three miles left to do before they can rest, really rest, that night, but he's smiling. They're going to be all right, he's thinking.

In a few moments he and Isabel take the halter and begin walking Rhonda downstream in the bitter cold water of Pagoda Creek. A quarter mile downstream they pick up the trail to the highway.

In Washington that night, Phillips at last gets through to Toby Higginson.

"Mr. Higginson?"

"Yes."

"This is Special Agent Phillips of the FBI."

Toby has already been interviewed twice. He is frightened and gun-shy about the sudden notoriety of the case. "What is it now?" he asks, querulously.

"There's been a report that your wife, Louisa Shidler, called a national radio talk show last night, while Ambassador Stillwell was on the show. I'm calling you to follow up on that."

"Well, I don't know anything about that. And I don't know where she is."

"I understand. Mr. Higginson, someone called in, saying it was Louisa Shidler. And the caller claimed that your daughter, Isabel, has been kidnapped."

"What?"

"Mr. Higginson, where is your daughter?"

"She—she's with her grandparents, in North Carolina. Isn't she?"

Late in the evening, at the FBI crime laboratory in Quantico, Virginia, a team has gathered. The forensic audio technicians begin to replay, for the first of many times that night, the taped Louisa-Royall conversation, studying every sound on the recording. Over the course of many hours, the information will begin to be digested. The name Duclos & Bernard is familiar, of course; it is the bank into which the bribe was placed. Isabel Higginson is the news here now.

Phillips is drumming the tabletop with his pencil. "Shidler's smart," he says. "She's escaped, she knows she's hot. This might create a pretty good diversion. You think she's trying to distract us?"

"Maybe," one of the agents agrees. "If Isabel is kidnapped, why not give us this stuff while Louisa's under house arrest?"

"Don't know. We do know that Shidler got a call from the Jackson County sheriff's office on September twenty-sixth and *denied* Isabel was kidnapped. But the girl appears to have been in the Kansas City area when she called 911."

"Any family out there?"

"No."

"So why is Shidler accusing Stillwell of a kidnapping now, if she denied one two weeks ago? What the hell is going on here?"

They are interrupted by a phone call. "Fitch is on his way out," someone says.

"Fitch?" Phillips is incredulous. The deputy director? Coming out here tonight?

"Why?"

"He's curious, I guess."

Great, Phillips thinks, now we need a fucking political baby-sitter in the middle of the night. The conversation returns to the talk-show tape itself. "What do we know about it?" he asks.

"Not too much yet," answers Special Agent Feinberg, "except that she's calling from a car phone on what I'd say is a late-model diesel tractor-trailer, maybe a White."

"Large one?"

"Eighteen-wheeler, my guess."

"So, we think she's hitchhiking?"

"Maybe. Now listen to this."

He cues the tape and replays it. There is a roar of noise behind her voice as she says,

". . . *ambassador deserves recognition for all that he has done for foreign trade . . .*"

"Hear that?"

They shake their heads. He replays the tape.

"Listen," he says, "that's the sound of an eighteen-wheeler down-shifting. They were going uphill when she called. What the hell, we've just ruled out Kansas and Rhode Island!"

The two men look at each other without comprehension. "Just kidding," Feinberg says.

A young agent pokes his head around the door. "Agent Phillips? You've got a call."

"I'll take it on two," he says, and steps out of the room to take it. "Phillips here."

"This is Frank Ianella," a voice says. "Returning your office's call from earlier today. What can I do for you?"

"Yes, Mr. Ianella, I'm following up on the escape of Louisa Shidler."

"Who?"

"Special Agent Phill—"

"No, who are you following up on?"

"Louisa Shidler. She used to work for the ambassador, didn't she?"

"Oh, yeah. Sure. I remember now."

"I wanted to ask the ambassador about the call that was made to the Birch Thornacre show last night."

There is a brief pause, as though Ianella is momentarily off the beat of the music. Then he says, "Ah, jeez, Agent Phillips, I haven't had a chance to catch up with him today. He's at a dinner, and then he's got a senior staff meeting. I can't get to him right now."

"Maybe tomorrow then. The caller called the Birch Thornacre show last night when the ambassador was a guest, and she accused the ambassador of taking a bribe and putting the money in a Swiss bank account, and kidnapping her daughter. I'm wondering—"

"I understand it was a crank call, you know, that's what I heard. I haven't talked to the ambassador myself."

"It was a crank call?"

"Afraid so, Agent Phillips. You get a lot of nuts dogging a candidate. You should hear some of the calls I get."

"Yes, well, I guess so. Still, the allegations—"

"The allegations? Christ, a nut called! Do we need to respond to the allegations of every crackpot who gets through on a radio talk show? The allegations are false." Ianella sounds a little defensive to Phillips.

"Okay," says Phillips. "Fine. Well, I have one other thing, I guess. The ambassador knows Shidler, right, knows her pretty well?"

"Sure. She worked for him for years, as you know."

"Right. So, can he confirm whether it was her or not?"

"Excuse me?"

"The caller. Was it Louisa Shidler? Did he recognize her voice?"

There is a pause, then, before Ianella says, "I, uh, I need to check for you on that. He's on his way to that meeting, and, you know how it is. Let me check for you on that and get back to you."

"Thought he was at a dinner."

"He is. He's leaving the dinner shortly, on his way to the meeting," says Ianella impatiently.

"Sure," says Gene Phillips, replacing the telephone receiver. Sure. Only, how did Ianella know about it being a crank call? How did he know about the call at all, if he hadn't caught up with Stillwell today?

There is a knock on the door of the little office, and a young agent's head pokes around again. "Mr. Fitch is here," he says. "He wants to see everybody."

What a damn nuisance, Phillips is thinking as, at last, he points his Buick northward on I-95 at ten minutes past one. Fitch wants to see every report on this investigation. Daily briefings. This is going to be a *sensitive* case. Now that Stillwell's been dragged into it, Fitch is going to be in charge of massaging any kinks out of the politics. So much for a law enforcement investigation. Still, why should Phillips care, at this point? Three more years and he's done.

At last, he pulls the car into the driveway in front of his darkened split-level, switching off the headlights so as not to wake Angela, who will wake anyway and say, as she has for thirty-one years, "Lord have mercy, Gene, do you know what *time* it is?"

The house is dark. He sits for a moment in the car, thinking. This is a white case. This is a paper case about a white woman in a white agency taking white money, white money that flowed through Luxembourg partnerships and Isle of Man merchant banks and Barbados corporations into a Swiss bank in Geneva. This is the kind of case that for thirty years goes to a white boy while Gene is doing coke heads and loan sharks, standing on the street corners in Anacostia wondering whether his backup is there. "Agent needs to improve organization of his reports" is what the performance evaluations have said for years. Translation: keep the black man on the streets of Anacostia with his brothers, and give the paper cases to the white boys.

He looks up at the darkened windows and sighs. No sense worrying about it. So what if that's what they're thinking. It won't be long now. Three years until his pension. Why should he lose sleep over it? Sell this place, and move to South Carolina. It's not his problem anymore.

CHAPTER 38

Well, I was cold and scared and hungry when I woke up on that cliff. You couldn't believe how close I still was to the road, that's what scared me the most. I climbed up to the top of that ridge. The rock was steep and reddish, and kind of crumbly, and I was crying and crying. I climbed up the cliff and when I got to the other side I felt a little better. I had looked at the map I had and I thought if I just went north I would find the highway. Even if I didn't go straight north, I knew I would hit it. Except, which way was north?

Pretty soon I was in luck, though it didn't seem like it at first. I met Johnny Trapp. He was one of those boys who are extremely arrogant. He was some kind of guide, and with his uncle he would take people out on pack trips to camp and hunt and fish and whatever, and I found him on the other side of the ridge clearing up a camp. He was tall and kind of skinny and he had a big black cowboy hat and cowboy boots and he wore the hat pulled down over his eyes. He was very tan and he winked at me like he didn't really take me seriously. He was extremely arrogant. He was about sixteen and thought that he was cute, I could tell. I guess he probably was kind of cute, but he was too arrogant for me.

I was starved and he gave me lots of pancakes, but when I told him what had happened to me he didn't believe me and was, like, come on little girl with me back to find your momma and poppa. Like I was some kind of child. He was extremely condescending.

Well, I thanked him very politely and said I had to be going north, and I hiked off. And then he kept coming after me on Rhonda—that's his horse—and telling me I couldn't possibly walk north to the highway, it was too far and I was just a little girl and didn't know anything about the outdoors. In a way, he was right, but I found it extremely irritating and arrogant. He kept riding up next to me. Finally he gave up and went back to his campsite.

Now, he was actually a very kind person, although, as I say, arrogant. I have often found that is true of boys. Before he left, he lent me his map and compass, which was extremely generous of him. I had a road map, which probably would have worked out all right, on account of the country being so open, but the map he gave me was better. And he taught me about contour lines—they show the steepness of a slope. It's really quite remarkable how they can show you where you are. He also gave me some water and food and a rain jacket. And then he left me and I carried on walking.

I spent a whole day walking north, but by four-thirty it was getting cold and it seemed like a storm was coming, and I have to admit I was pretty frightened. I sure couldn't see any road. And I was awfully glad when Johnny Trapp showed up again.

He was nervous, not like before. He looked out from the top of this mountain and he could see them riding after us. Smokes and the Beak and another man, and they had a dog. We rode Rhonda some and we walked some and rode some all day and all into the night. Round about then it started raining, and I got cold. Then he made Rhonda walk through this stream for a while. The water was like ice. It wasn't until two A.M. that we got to the highway. I was so tired I couldn't even keep my eyes open.

He hitched us a ride into town in this pickup. And pretty soon we got into Cody, where everything was dark and quiet, and there was no one around, not a soul. He showed me the Buffalo Bill Museum. Across from it was a high-school football field. He said I could come to his house or go to the police, but I told him no. Mother had said no. So he grumbled a little, and the driver was getting impatient, and then he gave me a sleeping bag from his pack, and ten dollars. I gave him his compass back, and he said if I wouldn't go to the police I should try to go sleep under the bleachers. He didn't have to tell me twice. It was pretty wet under there, but I didn't care.

CHAPTER 39

At Paris-Orly on Tuesday morning, October 15, the passengers mill around in front of the embarcation clerks, tickets in hand, hurrying forward when the green lights invite them to submit themselves. The clerks lean up against the little podiums, eyeing the passengers with a bored expression as they present their tickets and passports.

"Votre passeport, monsieur?"

Henry MacPherson hands his airline ticket and passport to the young man and waits. A frown builds upon the clerk's face as he flips back and forth between the ticket and the passport.

"Is there a problem?"

"Ce n'est pas juste," the man says. He is shaking his head.

Mac plays his part. Exasperation, impatience. He looks at his watch. He is a businessman, a tired one. He has a plane to catch. He plays the part below the level of a scene; just the level of discomfort for the young man.

"What is the problem?"

"It is not permitted that the ticket should vary from the passport, monsieur. You are Monsieur MacPherson?" The young man enunciates the first syllable carefully.

"Yes, of course."

"This ticket is not your name, monsieur."

"Of course it is."

"No. This is—"

"Jesus Christ, it's a misprint. A computer error. Look, 'H. M. Stevens'—travel agent got the names backwards. MacPherson's my last name, Stevens my middle name. See that?"

From the overhead speakers comes a reminder that Flight 710 to Boston is boarding.

"That's my flight," Mac says.

The man shrugs. Around him the passengers are shuffling through. The offending ticket remains on the podium, and Mac points at the letters of the name again. The young man nods, uncertainly, squints at the documents. Young men look at documents; older ones at people.

It is not permitted. An abstract rule: it is not permitted that the ticket should vary from the passport. But that is all right. Half of Mac's life has been what is not permitted.

There is a dance, a rhythm to these things, and they dance it, the two of them twined around the little podium, the young embarcation clerk on his stool with his nose pointed down into the documents, Mac leaning and fidgeting on the other side, as all around them the passengers filter through to the flight for Boston.

It is the province of the good embarcation clerk to observe the rules as to what is permitted and what is not. But it is the province of the duty officer to be a man of the world. Mac recognizes him—not personally, of course, but he recognizes the type, for he has met this type so often before—when, after some minutes, he is summoned to the desk: the mustache, the fat contented cheeks, the convex throat pouch that looks for all the world as though it might contain something saved for digestion later, and, most of all, the way the man has, the way all such men have, of training a hard stare at one, a stare with a practiced, if affected, firmness to it, a stare rehearsed in mirrors, as if to say, with all sophistication and savvy and experience, that this man of the world can rely on his powerful gaze alone to root out fraud. Who could stand against it! And so the man stares, as they all do. Mac looks at his watch again.

And then, of course, they are brothers. Of course it is a typographical error. Computers, pah! And the embarcation clerk—an idiot! But we understand this. Without rules, we should have to rely on idiots for judgment, you and I. So say the gesticulations of the duty officer. At this point in the dance, it is important to join in fellowship with the bureaucrat, to commiserate with him. Mac does this too.

And so Mr. Henry MacPherson, carrying the seat stub that was ticketed to "Stevens, H. M.," goes along the jetway to board his plane. In four days, from a different source, Mac's pursuers will find the evidence of his walking through passport control at Boston's Logan International Airport.

But their computers missed the ticket. Artificial intelligence is blindingly fast and has about it the thoroughness of divinity. And yet, in so many simple ways, it's just . . . artificial.

The tractor-trailer is parked in a rest stop near Independence, Missouri. In the blackness of predawn Louisa starts from sleep suddenly, in fright. It must have been a dream, but she cannot recall it. Her back and neck are sore. She looks at her watch in the half light, listening to Bear snoring on the pallet. Five forty-five, Eastern Time, four forty-five in Missouri. She knows she will not sleep again, so she pulls out the map to memorize the names of the towns, and once more note the distances between them.

A thousand miles to the east, in McLean, Virginia, Special Agent Tom Molloy of the Secret Service is wiping sleep from his eyes. It is 5:45 A.M. as he unlatches the gate to the pool area and pushes it open. How long, he wonders in his morning fog, will it be before I get used to Stillwell's predawn routine? It seems damned late in the year to be swimming outside: Molloy's freezing, and he's dressed. Briefly he looks up and down the pool deck, seeing nothing unusual. The lap pool, shaped like a lower-case *b*, is ringed by the slate deck, which is fringed by a lawn. Along its border are Doolie's plantings, backed by a high hedge on the house side, with a gray pool shed and wooden fence at the pool's shallow end. Few things are as peaceful as the sight of mist rising off the perfect glass of a swimming pool in the early morning. The Secret Service agent assigned to a vice-presidential contender should be conscious of the scene's lulling effect on him. But Molloy is not quite as alert to his surroundings as his more experienced colleagues would be. Another politician who can't sleep, and I'm going to be his bodyguard, is all he is thinking. The calmness of the scene has begun to betray him.

Molloy crosses the grass border to the deck, with no thought in his head except that the deck chair will be cold and damp with dew. Were his vision exceptional, were he a more experienced, a more cautious, man, the light from one small corner in the pool shed's window might tell him that something was wrong. One of the panes reflects the predawn light at a slightly different angle. Hardly anyone would notice such a thing, and Molloy doesn't. He might also have noticed, but does not, that his customary deck chair, by the table, is arranged with its back to the pool shed, and that the three companion chairs are on the other side of the pool. There is nothing unusual about this either, and he has not been at this job long enough to absorb the routine. Predawn lap swimming is still new to Tommy Molloy. Nothing occurs to him, as, still somewhat groggy, he takes a seat, and eases his body against the dampened chair back to watch the candidate.

Royall Stillwell, clad in his white swim trunks, stands at the deep end, breathing slowly, clearing his mind. He shakes his arms, loosening the triceps, as he exhales. His routine calls for one hundred laps: sixty freestyle, ten breaststroke, ten backstroke, and then twenty freestyle to finish. His swim is almost the only time in the day he has to himself. This is why he swims when he does: it is his time in the day when there can be no disturbance of any kind. He looks down to the end of the pool, across the motionless plane of its surface, noting little drifts of morning mist, toward the dark pool shed in the shade of the overhanging cedar. He adjusts his goggles and dives.

Stillwell's is a lazy but powerful freestyle stroke. His arms revolve unhurriedly, his legs fluttering without commotion beneath the surface, his body moving purposefully up and down the length of the pool, stroke, stroke, lazy stroke, glide, the elegant, split-second commotion of the flip turn, and then the body gliding back the other way, the arm rising powerfully from beneath the surface, the swimmer stroking again up the length of the pool, stroke, stroke, lazy stroke. It is hypnotic. Molloy watches for a few minutes as his charge moves up and down the pool with the regularity of a metronome, and then his mind begins to wander. His chin slips onto his hand. He looks at his watch. Ten minutes to six. Jesus.

For about five minutes more, the candidate for the vice presidency swims his laps. As he comes abreast of the deck chair, the gentle splash of his stroke will mask any stray sound Tommy Molloy might otherwise hear. Stillwell breathes regularly to his left, only occasionally to the right. As he swims away from the shed toward the deep end, his head turns away from the Secret Service agent to breathe, and as he returns to the shallow end, each breath gives him a view of the agent's poolside chair.

The candidate has covered sixteen laps, and the agent, motionless, has settled into the chair, his chin remaining on his hand. The sky is growing lighter. Behind the glass in the pool shed, a third man, who has watched thus far in silence, decides that it is time.

As Stillwell, swimming up the pool, reaches its center, a gloved hand inside the shed removes the loosened pane and lays it on the sill. Without rushing, the assassin takes aim and squeezes the trigger, and a single shot, making through the Glock's silencer a muffled sound no louder than the punch of an office stapler, strikes the back of Agent Molloy's skull squarely in the center. Molloy slumps forward, dead but still seated. Even as the shot is fired, the assassin turns to look at the swimmer. Stillwell has not heard. He carries on up the pool, stroke, stroke, lazy stroke. Now the assassin moves quickly, for he has timed the swimmer's pace and knows that he has approximately twelve seconds. Darting from the shed and across the deck with swift but unhurried economy of motion, the assassin reaches the slumping agent in the deck chair before Stillwell has finished a flip turn at the far side of the pool.

Stroke, stroke: the arms lazily ply the water as Stillwell approaches the pool's midpoint. Breathing to his left, he notices through the goggles' bubbles a glimpse of an unexpected figure in a wide stance near the table. He has no time to think about it, for as his mind registers the unfamiliar form, his left arm comes across his field of vision. But it never takes the stroke. A second, perfectly aimed shot strikes him in the left temple. Ambassador Royall Stillwell dies instantly, at 5:56 A.M., October 15, 1996.

Never hurry; listen always. The assassin is experienced, is a man who has studied his craft. He stands silently by the poolside, ears tuned to every sound. To his left is Agent Molloy, still slumped in the chair, his head forward, a dark mat of blood dripping from his hair down to his collar. The body of the ambassador floats in the pool, back up. Little wavelets lap gently against the gutter as the reddening water falls still. Across the fence toward the house there is no unusual sound.

Now he moves, still quietly and with deliberation. He stows the Glock in his backpack, returns quickly to the shed, and looks briefly at the shelf where he lined up the first shot. He pulls the door to, and slips through the plantings to the yard at the rear. He pauses for yet another moment, listening, but still there is no sound other than birdsong. A moment later there is only a slight brushing noise, as he pulls himself over the fence and slips into the woods. Five minutes after that, he has stuffed his rubber gloves in the pocket of his track suit and gained the footpath in Pimmit Run Park, and is to all appearances simply another morning jogger.

Special Agent Gigliotti, posted at the front door, looks at his watch again and sighs. It is 6:27. Stillwell, a man of routines, is five minutes late. A busy day of meetings lies ahead. The candidate will be late to the 7:00 A.M. breakfast. Switching on the walkie-talkie, he asks, "Four-Two?" There is no answer. "Tom?"

The jogger in the blue track suit and the backpack slows to a walk as he nears his pale blue Olds Cutlass Ciera, parked on Brookhaven Drive at the edge of the park. He stops when he reaches the car, leaning on the trunk, then stretching lazily. A young woman in a blue Lycra jogging suit comes up the street, her blond ponytail bouncing from side to side. He waves to her, and she smiles as she goes by.

"Jesus Christ," says Gigliotti, pushing open the pool gate. "Oh, Jesus. Oh, Jesus Lord!" as he reaches frantically for his two-way radio. It is precisely 6:30 A.M.

At 6:39, three police cruisers screech to a halt almost in unison in the Stillwell mansion's driveway. The wail of an ambulance is by now audible in the distance. Andrew Edelstone, Stillwell's neighbor for six years, looks out a window in his breakfast nook at the commotion as the cars roar past up the lane. "What on earth?" he wonders, as the ambulance roars up behind the cruisers, gravel spraying against the oaks. Upstairs in Stillwell's house, the curtain in a window of the master bedroom falls as an ashen Doolie rushes for the stairs.

At that moment, an unmarked car with a portable siren slapped on its roof screams across the Key Bridge onto the George Washington Memorial Parkway, carrying two Secret Service agents. The tires squeal as the car weaves through the rush-hour traffic. As they exit onto Chain Bridge Road, they pass the Olds Cutlass Ciera in the line of commuter traffic heading in the opposite direction, toward the District.

"You awake?"

"Yes," Louisa says. The barren fields, shorn of their crop of winter wheat, have fallen away now, and the buildings and billboards appear more frequently. They are approaching Kansas City. She looks at her watch, which she has not adjusted for the time zone. It is 7:40 A.M. on the East Coast.

"Truck stop in about ten miles," he says. "Think I'm about ready for breakfast."

Fifteen minutes later, Sugaree comes to rest in a dirt parking lot behind a truck stop called Francine's, on an access road just east of Independence. Louisa says she'll wait in the truck.

"Suit yourself." He shrugs and hoists himself down to the ground, stretching for a moment by the fender. He yawns and then ambles into the diner. She watches him go, thinking that she ought to eat. It's just that she isn't hungry.

The door rattles shut behind Bear and he stands at the threshold, uncertainly. About a dozen people are crowded behind the far end of the counter along with two waitresses in blue-and-white T-shirts and the cook, spatula in hand. No one is talking. The only sound in the place comes from a radio. No one looks up when he comes in.

"We don't know, Peter," a voice is saying on the radio, as Bear approaches. "Moments ago hospital staff confirmed he is here, but they will give no further details." The broadcast is live from somewhere, and there is background noise, confusion, shouts, a clatter of equipment, noise from a loudspeaker, more voices. Next, the familiar voice of a news anchor is questioning the reporter, asking him if anyone else has been hurt. There is some more confusion and then the reporter says something inaudible. "The President was not involved," the anchor is saying. "We repeat, the President was not involved. The White House has confirmed that President Breed is safe. He plans to make a statement from the Oval Office at eight-thirty A.M. Eastern Time."

"What's going on?" Bear asks a man in green overalls, wearing a dirty white trucker's cap.

"Stillwell," the man says, "the one running for vice president. He's been shot."

"Here," says Bear, climbing back into the cab a few minutes later. "Brought you a muffin and coffee."

"Thanks."

"You want to use the ladies' or anything?"

"No, thank you. I went back at the rest stop. Can we carry on soon?"

Bear smiles at her. "Sure," he says.

When Sugaree is back on I-70 westbound, Bear flips on the radio. "The radio said somebody shot Stillwell this morning."

The radio cuts in before Louisa can respond: "—minutes ago released a statement. Peter, it contains almost no detail, but it does confirm that Royall Stillwell, who joined President Breed's reelection ticket three months ago, was assassinated this morning sometime before seven A.M. Eastern Time, at his home in McLean, Virginia. The statement, in its entirety, reads as follows:

" 'The President and Mrs. Breed are deeply saddened to report that vice-presidential candidate Ambassador Royall Stillwell, and Special Agent Thomas Molloy, of the United States Secret Service, died early this morning in McLean, Virginia. The ambassador and Agent Molloy, who was part of the Secret Service detail assigned to the candidate, were assassinated early this morning at Royall Stillwell's home. The Federal Bureau of Investigation, working together with the Secret Service and other federal and state law enforcement agencies, is conducting a joint investigation. The President and Mrs. Breed have expressed their profound shock and sense of loss to Mrs. Stillwell, Mrs. Molloy, and the Stillwell and Molloy families, and they call upon all Americans to join with them in expressing their sorrow and condolences in this time of national tragedy.'

"And that's the end of the statement, Peter."

"Oh, my God," says Louisa, listening to the radio broadcast over the roar of Sugaree's diesel. "I just talked to him—when was it?—yesterday."

"Peter," says the voice of the reporter again, "at this time federal officials will release no information about the suspects or any alleged motive here."

"Has there been anything on the murder weapon, any information like that?'

Again, the reporter cuts in from the hospital, shouting to be heard over the background commotion. "There is no official statement as to what happened. Unofficial sources, speaking on background, said that the ambassador was shot while doing his morning swimming laps."

For two hours that morning Louisa remains in shock. She sits rigidly in the passenger seat as Bear fiddles the dial to try to obtain more news.

Eugene Phillips has resolved his internal debate before the call comes in, and so it does not surprise him. For all his anger about the FBI's treatment of him, Phillips has remained with the bureau for so long because he is, at heart, a loyal man. He has always believed in the mission of law enforcement. It is hardly surprising that the deputy director has assembled a special investigative team, now that the Shidler investigation has apparently expanded from public corruption to escape to assassination. Fitch calls him into his office at 9:30 A.M. to tell him that information indicates that there is no link among the series of events. Nevertheless, this has to be handled delicately. Phillips should not take this the wrong way. He's done a good job.

Phillips nods. Sure. He feels a little defensive, and has since his phone rang at 6:55 that morning: his own investigation has turned up nothing that would have suggested Shidler could be involved in anything like the Stillwell murder. He understands that there is an election on, and everyone in the agency is in a panic. This has to be the A Team. And so he understands. It is the natural order of things. It had to happen this way.

Halfway down the corridor toward the elevator, he stops—he is on the point of returning to raise a fuss. He wants someone to explain the daughter's kidnapping to him. He wants a better understanding of the source of the 1993 wire transfers. He wants to know why Stillwell called her by her first name, and why Stillwell's man, Ianella, lied to him. He wants to know why the girl was somewhere near Kansas City when she called 911, and why the mother lied to the Jackson County Sheriff's Department.

But he doesn't turn around. He goes back to his desk. To hell with it, let the young fellows work it out. Phillips feels a sense of relief and then, amid all the confusion and noise, all the panic of the bureau, withdraws into himself. He withdraws into thoughts of the bulbs he needs to get in before a hard frost. He planted daffodils last fall, almost put his back out doing it, and some infernal kind of new beetle got into them and wiped most of them out. That's why he has to replant. He spends the morning trying to put Shidler and Stillwell out of his mind, surreptitiously reading up on ways to tackle those bugs. Bugs—how he hates them, how he lies awake at nights thinking of ways to thwart white flies, Japanese borers, weevils . . .

Suddenly Phillips emerges from his withdrawal with the obvious idea. He grabs his coat and heads out, looking around somewhat nervously. He needn't have worried, for on October 15, 1996, no one is paying attention to Eugene Phillips.

CHAPTER 40

At about nine o'clock A.M., October 15, in northwest Wyoming, the leader activates his cell phone and places the call.

"Give me the situation," a voice says.

The man in Wyoming begins to talk. "The girl went overland out of the river valley of the south fork of the Shoshone River. There's nothing to the west but fifty miles of the Absaroka range, and Yellowstone Park. Nothing at all to the south or east but wilderness. Twenty-five miles to the north, Route 14 runs east–west from the park to Cody. Thirty miles to the northeast is a reservoir. Cody, Wyoming, is to the east of that."

"So where do you get a postcard from? Where is Higginson going?" the voice demands.

"Most likely would be Yellowstone itself. Old Faithful, maybe. The girl may have gone north to the highway, and then planned to hitchhike into the park."

"Anywhere else?"

"Only other thing nearby is Cody. If she hitched in the other direction."

"Anything in Cody you'd get a postcard from?"

"There's not much in Cody. It's a small town. Three most likely possibilities are: one, the Irma Hotel. Center of town, founded at the turn of the century by Buffalo Bill himself. Named after his daughter. It has an old Victorian bar in it and attracts a lot of tourists. The second is the rodeo. One of the biggest in the state, apparently. Tourist would likely go there."

"The third?"

"The Buffalo Bill Historical Center. Old West museum on the western side of town."

"Nothing else?"

"Nothing obvious. Plenty of motels, trading posts, and so on. But we're talking a postcard picture here. Shidler clearly saw this as a meeting place. We'd better go with those three."

In Wyoming, the leader unrolls a map, and his companions stare at it as he talks and points. "The hotel and the museum are close, only about four blocks apart. The rodeo is another mile or so west. Each one is easy to scout. Museum has one entrance, plain from all angles of the parking lot. Hotel, here, is in the center of town. Pretty easy to monitor who comes and goes."

"And the rodeo?"

"Manageable parking lot, and one entrance. Cody's doable."

"Assuming the girl moved at a good speed overland, when did you put her on Route 14?"

"We think she had help, a local kid with a horse. So we figure yesterday."

"And what are we doing to locate her?"

"We had a team back there tracking her. It's difficult, because the dog picks up a lot of outfitters."

The voice pauses, digesting. The Wyoming team waits. "All right. Proposal?"

"It's either Cody or the park. But Yellowstone Park is damn difficult. Lots of cars with youngsters entering the park, even this time of year. On the other hand, we are monitoring both for mother and daughter. We put a team at the eastern park entrance, and a second team at the geyser; high-powered scopes, night vision. Cody, we'll have to make do with one team."

"Three teams . . . with helicopter backup?" asks the voice on the telephone.

"Sure."

"You people think that's enough manpower to find a twelve-year-old?"

There is no answer. The Wyoming group scowls at the phone—all except the leader, who shows no emotion. In a moment, the voice goes on. "Remember, you can key off the mother. Do it."

The leader switches off the phone. "Well?" he asks the others.

"Fuck the Concierge," mutters the man Isabel Higginson called "Smokes."

"Steeves," says the leader, "you are the fuckee in that relationship. Best to keep that in mind. Particularly in light of your good work so far.

All right. Four in the park, two cruising the town. No more fuckups, please."

Sugaree skirts the metropolis of Kansas City, passes west into the suburbs, and then out into the Kansas wheatfields. Neither Bear nor Louisa speaks much. She reaches down for the box of cassettes, rattling through it, her hands shaking. She feels Bear's intermittent stares as he turns his eyes from the road.

"Let's get a tape going," she says.

"Sure, Louisa."

She finds one, a bootleg tape of a Syracuse New York concert, but the music, or at any rate the sounds that come from the cassette player, are such an exotic Dead space jam that it provides none of the necessary distraction.

She fishes through the box for another one, her fingers shaking, rattling against the cassettes. One slips from her hand.

"Louisa," Bear says, his throat dry and his voice on edge, "who are you?" She notices that he is breathing as hard as she is.

"I . . . Let's just leave it at Louisa."

"What was all that on the phone about Isabel and Royall Stillwell and a bribe and all?"

She doesn't answer.

Sitting silently, biting her lip, she stares forward through the windshield at the highway. He looks at her, then back to the road, and then at her again, and then back to the road. She reaches down to switch the radio on. Another news bulletin. There is nothing on the radio but this story, but the networks are beginning to catch up with the breaking news, and there is some organization to the reports, teasers that in five minutes we will go to so-and-so at the State Department, and then to so-and-so at the Capitol; and they have had a chance to plug in commentators. She listens, intently.

"Louisa," he begins, his eyes still bouncing from the road to the passenger seat.

"Look, do you want me to get out? You want to leave me here?"

He thinks it over in silence. Outside, the road is almost empty now, stretching straight as far as the eye can see, past mown fields. Bear is breathing hard, actually hyperventilating, and he pulls the truck into the breakdown lane and stops.

It is a lonely spot. A stiff wind comes out of the field on the highway's north side and rattles the cab. But Louisa doesn't notice this. Her eyes have gone wide watching the big man shaking in the driver's seat. Bear has turned pale, a dead-perch-floating-under-the-swamp-alders-along-the-Yadkin kind of pale, and a line of sweat rims his forehead. In a moment he is hyperventilating wildly, loudly, with a rasp to it, like an asthmatic, and his hands and his fingers shake crazily as they reach for his shirt pocket. In the close confines of the cab, the man's size is a danger in itself—the shaking seems like it might throw him in any direction. There is a wild, trapped look in his eyes as his head thrashes back hard against the seat. The pill bottle falls, and it rolls under the clutch pedal.

"What is it, what is it?" Louisa shouts.

He doesn't answer, doesn't even turn. His hand is grasping for the bottle.

Louisa shinnies across his feet and retrieves the bottle, helps him get it open, ducking stray blows like a wrangler dodging a bucking horse. He gulps two of the brown-colored pills. He gasps and wheezes. Then Bear lurches from the seat and stumbles behind to the condo. He curls on the mattress and lies there shaking.

Outside the truck, a car goes by. She looks off to the west and sees another in the distance. "Bear, my God, what is it? What should I, should I . . . ?" Her voice trails off. She stands between the seats, helpless as she watches the big man quaking on the mattress. His breathing begins to quiet, and then it comes more steadily.

My God, Louisa thinks, at any moment a state police car will stop to investigate.

"Bear," she says, "I'm going to have to drive."

It takes a minute just to figure out how to move the seat. Even then she has trouble pushing the pedals all the way to the floor. She has almost to stand on the clutch to engage it, and Sugaree stalls as Louisa wrestles with the gears, trying to find the right one. She starts the truck again. The transmission whines and the truck lurches, but she finds the right low gear this time, and eases Sugaree forward along the breakdown lane, only then realizing that the side mirror is angled incorrectly. With the engine racing in neutral, she gets the window down and pulls on the mirror. A minute later, one of her jams on the knob of the shift gives her enough power to get the big rig up to forty miles per hour. She eases the wheel left, and the eighteen-wheeler crawls back onto the highway.

In Bethesda, Phillips pulls his Buick up to the curb by the Shidler house. A patrolman is posted at the door, and an FBI sedan is parked in the drive.

He flashes his badge at the young patrolman, who lets him in. "Your buddy got here a little while back," the patrolman says.

The first floor of the house is empty and quiet. Phillips's hello receives no response. He goes first to the kitchen, there observes the telephone. Nothing is obviously wrong. He lifts the receiver and notices faint scratch marks on the side of the handset, where it appears someone may have used a screwdriver to pry open the housing. With a pocketknife he pries it open himself. The inside looks unremarkable. Then he hears a noise, apparently from the basement.

As Phillips trots down the basement steps, a man is moving quickly away from the far corner. In his hand is a screwdriver.

"Phillips, FBI," Phillips says, flashing his badge.

"Gaines, also with the agency," the man answers. He is older, too old to be a new recruit. Phillips doesn't recognize him, but he does have a badge.

"Don't recognize you," says Phillips, "you in the field?"

"Yeah, just reassigned. They've got me on this."

"Uh-huh, who you working with?"

"Not supposed to say."

"What you got there?"

"Nothing," says Gaines.

"I came by to look for bugs," Phillips says. "Didn't find any upstairs in the phone. Thought there might be a transmitter down here."

Gaines looks at him coldly. "That's what I was looking for," he says. "But I didn't find anything. Excuse me, I need to get back downtown." As Gaines squeezes past Phillips on his way up the basement stairs, Phillips notices the box of circuit breakers in the far corner of the basement.

And so, again, nothing. When Gaines has gone, Phillips inspects the upstairs, finds nothing. I've never seen that sonofabitch before, he is thinking.

But later, something. Returning to his office, Agent Phillips finds the brown-paper package from the Jackson County, Missouri, Sheriff's Department. He smiles, opening it: inside is Lonnie Billings's spool of brown magnetic tape and a note. Phillips thinks, for a moment, about giving it to Fitch. While he is turning the matter over in his mind, he pulls the latest FBI directory and looks for Gaines's name. It's not there. Then he heads off to Supply section to use a tape player. He returns about a half hour later, opens a desk drawer, and nonchalantly slides the tape into the back. Fitch's new people can order another copy for themselves, if they're interested, he thinks. Hell, I'm off the case.

As the long Kansas afternoon wears on, the sun comes into view and begins to slip down into the west, glaring off the remorseless baked-white expanse of highway ahead. Louisa has no sunglasses and squints against the glare. She sticks grimly to the right-hand lane, at a steady fifty-five miles per hour, hands clutching the wheel. Outside, an occasional automobile darts past and fades into the distance.

Moving gently and slowly, Bear's bulk appears between the seats. He settles into the passenger seat. She glances to her right and he seems calmed.

"Are you all right?"

"Yeah, thanks."

"What happened to you?"

"That was a bad one."

"It was *horrible*. Are you sure you're okay?"

"It was a panic attack. Worst I've had in a long time."

"Bear, I'm sorry."

"Oh, don't be. I'm sorry, I must have scared you. It's a thing I've had, ever since I was gassed in that mill. Louisa, I'm all right now. But you'd better pull it over. I'm not supposed to let anyone drive. Could get into a lot of trouble with the company."

He tells her the story, slowly at first, but then talking in long unbroken intervals as they travel through the fields of central Kansas. It happened years ago. As an eighteen-year-old out of high school, Bear followed his father to the brick towers that loomed over the small Wisconsin town where he grew up. He went to work in the Kaukauna paper mill as a welder's apprentice, joining his father, who was a millwright and a respected man there. They drove to work together in the mornings; they laughed at the foolishness of one of the foremen. Bear worked there for a year and a half, clambering with his welding rig along the catwalks and through the forest of vessels and piping that filled the rambling brick edifice by the Fox River.

The inside of the Kaukauna mill was a Dickensian maze of water-stained piping, brick, and concrete walls filthy with the grime of years, vessels and boilers clogged with the dreadful by-products of paper manufacture. There was always, in the mill, a faint hiss from somewhere, the sound of something escaping to where it didn't belong.

Making paper is a deadly business. Bear explains to Louisa how the giant kettles—kettles as big as the bungalow where Bear was raised—

cooked the wood chips down to a slurry, in the processing giving off methyl mercaptin, hydrogen sulfide, and other foul gases. In the early years of the century, when the oldest part of the mill was erected, these gases were vented to the atmosphere. Even now a fair volume escapes, giving the mill town its remarkable pungency—you can smell the Kaukauna mill before you can see it, and you can see it a long way off. In the late 1960s, piping was installed so that the deadly gases—noncondensables, they are called, or NCGs—could be collected and piped to a kiln for burning. In the Kaukauna mill, on April 22, 1968, there was an NCG line running just above the catwalk to the number 4 effect evaporator.

People in Kaukauna talked about the accident for years after. There had been men hurt in the mill, lots of times, men who'd hurt their backs, or fallen, or got a little gas from a hot well and had to go up to have Dr. Forsgard look them over and sign for them and say they were all right. But no one had ever died up in the mill, as far as anyone could remember, not before April 22, 1968.

It happened on the first shift, during a semiannual maintenance shutdown. Bear Samuelson and Ricky Beaulieu were repairing cracks in the hatch to the number 4 effect evaporator vessel, which stood amid the dark tangle of piping like a four-story milk bottle. Bear had been sent to help Ricky there, while Happy Vance was running a crew nearby at the strong black liquor tank. That's what they told him later, in the hospital, although one of the funny things—everyone seemed to say so—was how Bear didn't care to find out what happened to him—not at the time, anyway, how he didn't want to talk about it. He lost his memory of the day in the gassing, at least the kind of memory you can summon up—and so you'd think he'd want to know. But he didn't ask questions until long after.

From the outset Bear knew the memory was there, but it would come only at the times and in the manner of its own choosing. Mostly it would come in the night, the darkness bringing it on, and suddenly Bear would see that steamlike gas pouring out of the damper, and the flashing red light, and hear the sound of the men below screaming, "Gas! Gas!" and then feel the gagging and then pain like a stiletto in his chest.

Sometimes the bugs would come back: horrible insects, man-sized crawling things coming out of the steam for him. Bear talked for years about the insects, and people would just shake their heads about it, saying, Wasn't it a shame, what the gas done to his mind, until Kenny Keohane figured it out. He was down at the union hall, and the men were talking, and Kenny, who had worked at the mill for more than a decade, he said, you know, the kid was having convulsions when they come for him on that catwalk, and with their masks and respirators, maybe he thought they was bugs, in that state that he was in, with his head banging against the railing, and Timmy Perrault and them others in the dark with their masks on and hoses coming out of the masks, trying to get the oxygen mask on him. And the men in the hall nodded, and it got around, generally, in Kaukauna, where Bear's memory of the bugs came from. So Bear understands this now, too, but when the panic attacks come, he still sees them, and they don't look like men. He sees bugs.

Much later, as many as ten years after he was gassed, Bear went back to the mill town and talked to the men, every one of them he could find who had been on the shift that day. He didn't learn much from most of them. It is that way with accidents. The few that really were involved, that saw and heard and smelled it, they most often don't say much. The ones that talk about it are the ones who weren't a part of it, who got there late, and like to speculate and gossip. But he also talked to Sam Norton, Kaukauna's director of safety in the 1960s, who was retired and gone to the Upper Peninsula. He found Norton living alone in a fishing camp near Bergland. His wife had died a few years before, and he was living year-round in the camp. It was the kind of place that made you think, "Damn, but it must be a long winter up here." On a cold September afternoon, they sat by the wood stove talking until there were tears in both their eyes, and Norton, who Bear always thought was hard as a crowbar, asked for Bear's forgiveness.

Louisa sits in her seat quietly, staring out at the empty road as he talks. For this strange interlude the unreality of the news about Royall has been, for a moment, pushed to one side.

Bear is talking, but it is as though she too is in the fishing camp. Norton said he was ashamed, still full of shame about what had happened, and though he wouldn't look at Bear, he sat staring at the fire and it all tumbled out like a pile of tools jammed into a shed and just waiting for you to open the door. The story just tumbled and clattered out until it sat in an ugly heap there in the fishing camp, Bear sitting in silence and listening and the old man Norton who had held on to this, not caring anymore and, no, more than not caring, realizing that he wanted more than anything to do this. To lay his own sin out before the young man and beg for his forgiveness.

He couldn't look at Bear. Instead, except for a couple of points where he had to stop, he told that story just as a matter of fact, like an adjuster who last week has completed his investigation and is reporting to the insurance company. Two oversights had caused it. First, Norton said, the foreman didn't follow the lockout procedures right, and so when they did a digester blow that morning, it pressurized the NCG lines in the evaporator mill. The lines are supposed to be blocked off during mill repair work, and the foreman is supposed to check the locks, but when the lockout started a compressor had crapped out, and the foreman had to run his pickup across the river to get another one, and by the time he got back he just forgot the lockout procedures. And Norton went off on every detail of the lockout, and the compressor, and the foreman who forgot, and he clung to those details long after Bear had digested that first point.

Norton took a poker and stabbed at a log and little jets of flame jumped out. Then he got up and went hunting for something from a kitchen cabinet and was fussing in there until Bear had to prod him just a little. "You said there was two oversights caused it," he said, gently. The old man didn't answer, at first. He came back to the fire with a bottle and two glasses.

"You want some?" he asked.

Bear shook his head. "I can't anymore. You go ahead."

The old man took a drink, and then he told the rest of it.

The day before the accident, Manny Green in instrumentation had taken out a defective flow switch from the NCG line running by the number 4 effect evaporator, and got to joking with the boys in the control room, or some foolishness, and he'd forgotten to replace it, and nobody'd checked the log that day. That was Norton's fault—the failure to check the log. His voice cracked and quavered when he told Bear how that afternoon, after the ambulance had taken Ricky and Bear off to Good Sam and they didn't know if they was alive or dead, Norton pulled the log, and saw MEG initialed where the flow switch had been removed, and nobody had written that they put one back in, and he, Sam Norton, hadn't checked.

"I don't know why I didn't check it that day. I've asked myself many a time. I just don't know why," he said. He did some more stirring up of the fire at that point in the telling, but the fire didn't need it, and Bear could see he wasn't able to go on right away.

"It's all right."

"Joanie got to be an alcoholic, you know."

"Well, don't think on that. She might have tended that way, Sam."

"I just don't understand why I didn't check it that day."

And the old man looked desperately at him and said, "I checked that log almost every day for forty years, Bear. Why did I have to miss that day? I don't understand it."

"It's all right."

It seemed awful lonely to Bear then, this old man living alone in his fishing camp up north of Ironwood on the Peninsula with his fireplace and bottles of cheap whiskey and, out at the little strip of beach, his fishing house leaning kind of crazily toward the lake, waiting for the long white season in the ice. After a time, Norton finished the story, but Bear could probably have told the rest himself. Without a flow switch, it wasn't too hard to figure. The blanks weren't in the line to block the gases, because of the foreman's failure to oversee the lockout. When the mill discharged gases to the line from a digester blow, the gases pressurized the line in the evaporator building, and when the gases reached the Jamesbury valve, the flow switch wasn't there to tell the valve to close. The valve was open, and Bear and Ricky Beaulieu were sprayed with hydrogen sulfide gas.

They are halfway across Kansas as Bear returns to the accident itself. "Ricky died. When the gas knocked him out, he rolled off the catwalk and fell two stories and broke his neck, and he was dead when they found him there, lying across a steam duct. They got me out first 'cause I was still on the catwalk. Then they got him out, and just as they was taking him out the number 3 gate in the ambulance, in roars the Ford Fairlane with Joanie, his wife, who'd got word somehow that there was men hurt down at the mill, and she had a premonition. So there was the ambulance on its way out and her in that old light-blue Fairlane with rust up to the windows on her way in, and them two reaching the gate at exactly the same moment. And she couldn't see nothing and had no way of knowing who was in the ambulance, but people say she turned that car right around and never got out of it or stopped or even rolled down the window to ask anybody what happened or nothing. She just turned that car around in a spray of gravel and followed that ambulance up to the Good Samaritan Hospital, and she followed them right in to the emergency bay and watched them take her husband out the back. And she knew right then he was dead. It was eerie. People talked about it for years, how Joanie knew Ricky died without anyone telling her.

"That's what happened to Ricky. I was luckier. They got me out from that catwalk where I passed out. But I was in a coma for two days up at Good Sam, and I guess they took me to Appleton and then to Madison up to the university."

"I'm so sorry," Louisa says.

He asks for the box, and she holds it, numbly, in her lap, watching the thick fingers fumble for a tape. And in a few minutes they are listening to "Uncle John's Band," turned down low. With the Grateful Dead and the hum of the big diesel engine, Bear seems to relax, just a little. Outside, Louisa sees the sign for Salina.

"Why don't I make you some coffee?" she asks.

She has not pressed him, but she knows the story is not over, and he needs to tell it through. "What the gas does is kind of peculiar. The doctors don't really understand it. But it kind of scrambles the part of your brain that keeps the emotions in check. You know? Anyway, ever since that day," Bear says quietly, "well, my mind isn't right. I look in the mirror, and I see the same man. But inside, I know I'm different." His lip quivers a little, and he pauses, steadies himself, measures his breathing.

"It's okay," Louisa says. "You don't need to talk about it."

"No. It's good to talk about it. Good for my coping. You see, I can't ever beat it, but I can cope with it. I can manage it. If I'm careful. It's just that I get nervous sometimes. I have trouble . . . I've had trouble with Becky. Being a man for her, if you know what I mean."

She doesn't know what to say, so she reaches over and holds his forearm. He doesn't seem to notice.

"I'm, I'm delicate, is what it is. I get these attacks. Not so much anymore, but once in a while. My pills help," Bear says.

"You don't look delicate."

He smiles. "Well, looks are only looks. You don't look like someone who . . ."

"What?"

"Who's done whatever you've done. With all them Washington people and all."

She lets it go, and later he talks about the accident some more. This is therapy for him. At first the attacks came all the time. Bear couldn't work, couldn't do anything but lie in his bed at home and smoke grass and listen to music. The worker's compensation people told him there was nothing wrong with him they could find on the tests, but he knew he could never go back to the mill. He couldn't be in and among those pipes, the darkness, those sounds and that sickly sweet smell.

After two years the voc rehab people suggested he try for tractor-trailer school. He found that the long hauls along the highways suited him. There's a little stress, sometimes, when you get on a tight schedule. But if you're not in a big hurry, you can manage it. Now, he tells her, the attacks only come once in a while, and he manages them better, and before they come, he gets a little warning. Enough to pull the truck off the highway and settle in, to get his pills.

"The attacks," she asks cautiously, "what do they feel like?"

He smiles wanly. "It's hard to describe. The panic attacks, it's, it's kind of like being in a movie theater, at first, watching a nice happy movie, a comedy, or a love story, and all of a sudden the movie starts to run a little fast, and then faster, faster and jerky, and the screen gets bigger and bigger and is all around me and then is kind of closing down on me, and the sound is louder and louder, and the movie itself, the images have all changed, and it's awful, horrible now, with blood and people screaming, and flashes, explosions. Or sometimes the bugs again. It comes closer and closer and louder and louder on me, and meanwhile, I can just kind of glimpse the real world behind it, the highway or my room or Becky or whatnot, but I know that I can't cope with it, can barely even see it."

There is hardly any traffic now, just the noise of wind against the cab, and the hum of the diesel engine.

"But, you know, everybody's got his own thing to deal with. I've had this a lot of years, and I get along." He sighs, stretches one hand toward the cab's roof, and fishes on the dash for his sunglasses. The sun burns directly into the windshield. "Afternoons in Kansas, sometimes they go on forever. Better to be headed east, I'd say."

CHAPTER 41

Kansas does seem to go on forever. Louisa's mind cannot fix on anything. It bounces from one unexpected place to another, from glimpses of Toby, to Isabel, Isabel as an infant, Isabel getting on the school bus in grade school, Royall Stillwell when they signed the first accords with the Chinese on CDs and film piracy. When a life is devoted to things that disappear, what remains of the life? When your man leaves you, when they take your child and your career, what remains of you? If they take them all away, have they cut out your heart any less surely than if they had done so on the operating table, with a knife?

Once again she hears Professor Fitzgerald, talking of Odysseus. Well, Odysseus was left for dead, too, but he kept his wits. Those they could not take from him.

She just cannot see her way through this. The thing that has kept her alive until today is her knowledge, the power she had to disrupt Royall. This must be the reason for the elaborate plan: the kidnapping of Isabel, the fact that she herself was still alive. She assumed Royall was behind it. And now he is dead. Outside, the fields in the late-afternoon light look bleak. The road vanishes at the horizon, no end in sight.

"Bear," she says, "you asked me before who I was."

"Yeah."

"I used to work for Royall Stillwell. In the government. I discovered something—something I wasn't supposed to find."

"So what was all that about your daughter?"

"They took her to buy my silence. Through the election."

He sighs. "Seriously?"

"But she escaped. I'm trying to find her."

He doesn't answer.

The calculator in her returns to the crucial fact. Louisa was Royall's cover, but in a very real sense he was hers, too, at least until the election. Now that has changed. Now there is no cover at all, no reason left to keep Isabel alive. Or her.

It is an hour or so later, in a roadside rest area, that she realizes that her mind has begun to grope toward a plan. She is standing behind the rest rooms, looking out at the prairie. The internal voices are quiet now, the memories no longer battling for her consciousness. She looks out at a brown field beyond the hog-wire fence, her face turned into a steady wind. The plan emerges painfully from an internal dialogue. Louisa the planner, the calculator, gropes toward ideas. But her other self is full of reservations.

Her eyes are searching the field when she is startled by a blue uniform. A state police trooper walks by, tips his cap at her. Nervously, she smiles back, then turns and hurries for the truck, feeling her heart pounding.

It will not be me, she thinks, not what I am good at. The closest she has been to acting a part was when she was in the chorus in the eighth-grade production of *Annie Get Your Gun,* which filled her with dread at the time. She will have to learn to act.

She looks down at the map, and then out of the cab at the road sign, and then says, "Let's try Wakeeney. They've got to have a Wal-Mart or something, right?"

He shrugs, and pulls the truck off the highway and follows route 283 to town. "I need diesel, anyway."

There isn't a Wal-Mart, but there is a JCPenney. In the parking lot, she gives him the list of items. He asks, "What color?" when she gets to the lipstick.

"Try . . . coral," she answers.

"That's a color?"

"More of an attitude."

And so Bear, sheepishly displaying his purchases beside the JCPenney register, pays for the items on the list: the sunglasses, the bandanna, the Revlon coral lipstick. Later, inside Sugaree, Louisa sits cross-legged on the pallet and applies the lipstick and then, pinning her hair up, ties on the bandanna. "Now Samantha's ready," she says.

"Ready for what?"

"For a makeover."

Bear waits twenty minutes in the truck until she returns, carrying two JCPenney shopping bags. She disappears for another fifteen minutes in the condo. When she emerges, his face registers a reassuring surprise. The makeup lies thick on her face: a pancake base, too-heavy rouge beneath the cheekbones, mascara, eye liner. She is wearing tight white jeans and a pink mohair sweater that exposes her navel. Her figure seems somehow changed. On her feet are platform mules.

"What do you think?" she asks.

"Liked you better before."

"Good. Let's go."

"Back to the highway?"

"No, not yet. I made an appointment. It won't take long, but I need to do it."

"An appointment?"

"Yes. With the hairdresser. We need to get over there before she closes."

Barbara's Beauty and St. Tropez Tanning Salon is on the outskirts of Wakeeney, in a little strip mall next to a liquor store and a pharmacy. It is, by the look of it, a salon into which Louisa Shidler would never go, and is therefore perfect. A smiling dumpling of a woman rises to greet her as Louisa enters.

"Honey, I *like* that sweater."

"Thanks," says Louisa, "my boyfriend gave it to me."

"Nice. You the one just called?"

Louisa nods.

"So how are you today?" the dumpling asks.

"Good, thanks. You?"

"Just fine. What can we do you for?"

"I want you to do something with this hair. I want, like, dramatic, something special. Tired of this old dark hair."

Together they look through the magazines. Louisa hits on a photograph of Charlene Taylor, the country-western singer. In the photograph, she has a pouty "come hither" look. But Louisa is more interested in the hair.

"That," says Louisa, "that's what I want. Can you do that?"

"Red, huh?"

"Fire-engine red, honey. I want you to light me up!"

The dumpling giggles. "Yeah, we can fix up this old hair of yours," she says. "What's the occasion?"

"Oh, me and Brian are celebrating our one-week anniversary to-night," says Louisa, and the dumpling giggles again.

Louisa has her head back in the sink, and the dumpling is rinsing her hair, when, glancing up at the news report on the television, she says, "Terrible about the ambassador."

"What?"

"Didn't you hear?"

"No. I been up with Brian all day."

"You didn't hear? It's been on the TV all day how he was shot this morning."

"Shot?"

"And killed too. Yes. A-rabs done it."

"What?"

"Yeah, that's what the TV said. They already caught some guy at an airport in Mexico City, or something. Sit up now, hon."

The dumpling begins to apply the curlers, rolling up the newly red hair in tiny ringlets, one after the next. The dumpling pauses, looking up at the television.

"A-rabs, in Mexico City?"

"He was a fox," the hairdresser goes on, watching Royall's face on the television screen. "A silver fox."

"Yeah," says Louisa. "But what were they doing in Mexico City?"

"Runnin' away."

"I see. What kind of A-rabs, exactly?"

"Oh, A-rabs is A-rabs, I guess, honey. Iraqis, or maybe Iranians. Can't remember. It's pretty much the same thing, isn't it?"

"Not sure they look at it that way," Louisa says.

"What?"

"Nothing."

"The CIA caught them. Or the FBI or somebody. Here. Lean over this way." She goes to work with a new set of curlers. "They got 'em, anyway."

"They killed them?"

"That's what the TV said. Terrorists."

"That's convenient."

The dumpling isn't listening, her attention split between the television and her customer. "There's a woman, too," she goes on, "some woman who took a bribe and escaped from jail, and used to work for him, or something. They're looking for her too, the TV said."

"What's her name?"

"I don't remember. Louise something."

"Huh."

"What's she look like?"

The dumpling squints up at the television. "She's a suit. You know. They had her picture on before. She looked kind of frumpy to me."

"Frumpy?"

"Yeah. I didn't like her hair at all."

CHAPTER 42

Mac stands tired and blinking by the bank of telephones in the international arrivals lounge at Boston's Logan Airport. Like everyone else in the airport, he had debarked to the stunning news of the assassination and stared, bewildered, at a television screen in an airport bar for twenty minutes before doing anything else. He is on the point of telephoning the office when he remembers that Duncan, his son, is only eight miles away in Cambridge, at Harvard.

Mac confronts an old problem. Mac's fondness for Duncan, his eagerness to see his son, varies inversely with the distance between them, and now the telephone looks forbidding to him, and it is forcing him to remember. He stares at the panel of buttons, which becomes the face of the child psychiatrist. Of all things—that fucking little man.

Once, long ago, Alice took Duncan to the child psychiatrist. He had a soft voice and soft eyes and a weak handshake and a way of saying your first name as though he had a right to, as though he had looked at your medical chart and that gave him dominion over your name. He wore a cable-knit sweater. He didn't sit behind his desk as he ought. He came around it and sat in a chair, next to Mac, their legs too close, almost touching.

We had a good talk, Henry, a good talk. He's a brilliant boy—an extraordinary mathematician, you know. Just a little troubled.

Oh, yes, a clever dig. You astound me with your powers, Mr. Holmes! I did actually know about my son's gift for numbers, thank you very much. And thank you for your insight. A forty-minute talk with an adolescent, and now you understand a problem I have wrestled with constantly for twelve years.

Well, all right, maybe not constantly. Mac can hear Alice. "Constantly? You were constantly *gone*, that was your constancy!" Off and on then. He'd done what he could.

I asked him what he likes to do with his mother.

Mac relives it, remembers a sudden self-awareness of his own sullen, guilty expression, remembers the way the soft man saw it and noted it for his chart. And then the doctor discoursed on Duncan's list of what he liked to do with his mother. There was no end of the things. He liked it when she let him cook with her. He made the pesto, pounding the pine nuts with the mortar and pestle, mixing in the oil. She made the pasta. Liked it when she quizzed him about girls and embarrassed him and then gave him hints about how to act around them. Liked to sit in the kitchen late at night when she drank her tea—the kitchen where she was and where Mac wasn't because Mac was God knows where. Liked the way she was with his buddies, how cool she was, how she knew the rock-and-roll groups, the football teams, the cool movies. He liked to go for walks with her in Virginia. He liked her politics. Politics! They talked about politics, Alice and the boy!

Mac has never had politics of his own. Politics are growing crops: healthy crops, diseased ones, crops starved, crops for harvest, but always other people's crops. He never chose. All crops are equal. He takes their measure, observes them all, harvests none.

Would you like some coffee?

Save the coffee, save the bullshit. Let's get to the point. It's not like I have all afternoon for this. But there is no businesslike nature about the child psychiatrist. Mac grows impatient, and the cable-knit sweater makes a note of the impatience in his chart, and that makes Mac more impatient.

In the arrivals lounge, Mac stares at the digits on the pay phone, snapping out of it for a moment. But the cable-knit man returns.

I asked him what he likes to do with his dad, Henry.

Mac is willing himself out of this now, pulling himself out of the quicksand. He is staring at the digits on the buttons, at the telephone receiver. He is listening, trying to listen, and there is a voice on a loudspeaker, something about British Airways. A black phone, a metal box, blue letters spelling NYNEX. He thinks of the oddly complected man Racine, the way his fingers went for the breast pocket, the rain outside the window as he looked across at the crooked smoke deflectors on the Geneva rooftops, of Gunnar, of the stupid embarcation clerk, the file, Louisa Shidler.

He thought about it for a long time.

The Hotel Bernini, the men at Racine's office, Nevins, de Soissons's garlic breath, Racine's secretary. And maybe they know Duncan is at Harvard. Maybe they have tapped his phone, too. Yes, the last last thing I should do, the most foolish thing I could do, would be to telephone him now. That would only put him at risk. I will see him again soon, some other time. Yes, that is it.

But he couldn't think of anything.

Fuck it, fuck it, fuck it. Fuck the child psychiatrist. Who in the fuck is he to sit with my son for forty minutes and ask him asinine questions and draw conclusions in his fucking little medical chart from a twelve-year-old's reticence? Who? I wouldn't talk to the narrow-chested son of a bitch, either. Duncan has come out all right in the end. It's the way we are, we MacPhersons, the way Duncan is too. He's fine. He's an admirable young man.

Not anything at all, Henry.

Mac takes refuge, at last, in the television. The candidate has been murdered, Jim Breed's unofficial vice president, Patrick Finneran's successor. A new thought comes, as Mac stares at the buttons on the telephone. Patrick Finneran, Mac remembers, retired to somewhere on Cape Cod.

Mac reaches for the telephone and goes to work.

It has that special awkwardness of an end-of-journey parting—when you have too long to prepare for it, staring at the shrinking mileage on the highway signs, groping for something meaningful to say. And then suddenly the car is idling by a roadside, and a head is ducking uncomfortably through the window. There is no time for the prepared words, and the extemporaneous things come out badly; indeed, often nothing at all comes out right and the moment is confused and frustrating. So it is at the I-25 interchange in Denver, where night has fallen when Louisa parts from Bear. The headlights race by with the roar of the trucks, and Louisa fumbles her prepared speech and so hurries down the steps from Sugaree's cab. The backpack follows her, in his big, gentle hands, and the whole thing looks incongruous now, given her makeover. The roar of passing trucks makes it hard to hear.

"Good luck, Louisa!"

She shouts back from the roadside, things she should have said from the cab. "Bear, thank you so much for everything!"

"You going to be all right now?"

"Yes, thank you. Well, no. You know."

"Listen, little dogs gonna have their day, too." She can make out a smile in the Brillo, and his eyes are twinkling. "You ever, you know, you ever come through Carter, New Mexico, you call me. You come and stay. We'll listen to some Dead! Smoke a few!"

The trucks are roaring past on the highway. She clambers back up the steps and plants a kiss on the big iron-gray thatch over his cheek and throws her arm across his shoulder.

"You keep that medicine handy."

"Oh, sure."

"You're a good man, Bear."

He turns just a little red, but she presses ahead.

"I think your Becky must be very lucky." And then Louisa hurries back down and up along the roadside, without waving. She mustn't let him see her face.

"Hey, Louisa?" he hollers after her. "Smoke a joint with me next time I see you?"

She stops and turns, despite herself. Is he winking at her? She can't tell for sure, but she has to smile. "Maybe," she hollers back. "Maybe I will."

When Bear has driven five miles to his exit and come to a stop at a red light off the exit ramp, something on the dashboard catches his eye. It is a photograph. Louisa forgot to take the photograph of Isabel with her.

CHAPTER 43

It is a half-mile walk from the bus stop in Cotuit village on Cape Cod out to Atlantic Avenue. Mac's back has started to flare up—nothing is harder on it than a bus. He's tired and jet-lagged, he's footsore, he's confused, and in the late afternoon he has pretty much lost track of time. But, by one miracle, Patrick Finneran was at home; by a second, he took Mac's call from the airport, and by a third, Mac is soon walking past the big Victorian summer houses that line the avenue as it proceeds out toward the harbor, and beyond to Nantucket Sound. The houses are mostly closed up for the season, some of them shuttered, the yards full of leaves. He squints up at them until, reaching a corner, he sees a number 47 next to the letter box on a house with peeling gray paint.

The house wears a pleasant aspect, not grand, but roomy and comfortable; it has detail enough for charm without gingerbread self-consciousness. It sits easily on the corner lot, not far off the road, and has a faded gray wraparound porch and an oval window in the front door. Around the yard is a high white fence, the paint peeling here and there, which seems to hold back from the road exuberant masses of rosebushes and lilacs. The rose canes look withered by October wind, and the ranks of lilac have taken on the raggedness that marks autumn and the approach of winter. This yard needs raking too.

Mac peers for a few minutes through a gap in the shrubs. The porch swing holds the remains of a newspaper catching a gentle breeze. On the south side of the house is a maple, fire-engine red. The leaves on the oak behind are yellow.

When he comes to the door, Patrick Finneran looks older than Mac expected, less substantial, a little thinner. Finneran stands in the shadows of the foyer for an uncomfortable moment before saying anything at all, and then speaks over his shoulder.

"Maggie, he's here." Mac hears some sort of muffled response from the back of the house.

"Let's sit on the porch," says Finneran, coming out slowly. He stoops to clear away the *Boston Globe* to make a space for Mac on the porch swing. "Can I get you something?"

"Thank you. Whatever you're having," Mac answers. "A beer would be great."

"How about an iced tea?" asks Finneran.

"That'll be fine."

The former vice president disappears for a moment, then returns. There is a silence, which he seems in no hurry to fill.

"Mr. MacPherson," he says, at length, "what can I do for you?"

"Sir," Mac answers, "this isn't an interview."

"It isn't?"

"No. Not the usual kind. This isn't on the record. I'm not writing a story. In fact, I've probably lost my job by now."

"Have you, then? Join the club."

"I thought you resigned, Mr. Finneran."

"Yes, yes of course. The unemployed club, I meant. I resigned." Finneran allows himself a smile at this, his private joke.

Patrick Finneran's resignation had come as a shock to everyone. He had been one of the few Boston Irish to break ranks with the Democratic party. Finneran's tireless brand of street-corner politics—heel-cap politics, he called it, for the wear and tear it put on his shoes—had yielded a city council seat and, after long years, the mayor's office in Boston. As mayor, Finneran had excelled. Even the most partisan of his Democratic opponents had to admit that the city had never functioned better. The subways ran more cleanly and more promptly; public school enrollment rose for the first time since the sixties, the streets were tidy, the city worked. At some point during the Reagan years, the national press discovered in Finneran the antidote to one of its periodic handwringings about the collapse of the American metropolis. All of a sudden, Patrick Finneran was on panels; he was a guest on the Sunday talk shows; reporters from the national press arrived to spend days following him around.

He is a hard man to pigeonhole: the first ever Boston Irish *Republican* mayor. And he was the first ever self-effacing one. "I get things done," he would shrug. "I give a mediocre speech, but run a good city."

Patrick Finneran had served three terms when the wise men of the party, deciding that Breed needed a boost in the Northeast and an image as a can-do man on the domestic front, tapped Finneran for the vice presidency.

Maggie Finneran brings the iced tea, and they talk for a little while of Stillwell.

"Did you know him, Mr. MacPherson?" she asks.

"Yes."

"We didn't know him very well, did we, Patrick?" Her husband shakes his head. She goes on, anxious to talk. "But it's a terrible thing."

Mac is studying Finneran as Maggie talks about the years in Washington. The former vice president of the United States stares out at the lilac bushes along the fence, nodding now and again to punctuate Maggie's chatter. There is something about her monologue that takes hold of Mac's attention, and then all of a sudden it is clear, and just in the moment that it is clear, he catches Finneran's eye, and there is a brief signal. The signs are subtle, but once identified, the slight slurring, the manner she has of speaking a fraction too loudly, are unmistakable.

"Well, Mr. MacPherson, I'm afraid I have to leave you two gentlemen and start on supper."

"Thank you, love," says Finneran, getting to his feet. He smiles after her as she goes.

Finneran spent just over three years as vice president. They were undistinguished. It was not, in truth, the right job for him, being as far removed from hands-on administration as any post in Washington. So when it was announced without warning, in July of 1996, that he would not run again as the President's running mate, Washington chalked it up to some combination of an unnamed financial scandal and disaffection with the job.

Mac has set his glass on the porch rail. "Mr. Finneran, you and I are about the same age, so maybe I should just come right to the point. No one just resigns from the vice presidency. No one except you. Not unless there's a hell of a scandal. And with you, there were leaks, suggestions, but nothing that ever amounted, in my judgment, to a goddamn."

"Well, that's very interesting, Mr. MacPherson."

"Did you go willingly?"

He chuckles. "I resigned, as you know."

"And the answer to my question?"

"The answer is that I have no further comment, Mr. MacPherson."

"I'm too old and you're too old for that. Call me Mac, please." Mac sighs. "I'm sorry, I've had a long flight."

"All right, then, Mac. This seems an odd time to rush up to talk to me about it."

"Is it?"

The former vice president examines Mac quizzically, then looks away at the leaves strewn across the yard.

"One day in July, it is very quickly very necessary that you should decide to resign. One day in October, it is very necessary that your putative successor should be executed. Mr. Finneran, I'm wondering what is going on here. Why did they need to get rid of you?" Mac asks. "Was it to bring him in?" He senses it is best to be direct with this man.

"You recall that I resigned," Finneran says. He places a certain ironic emphasis on the word. "As for Mr. Stillwell, he was a pretty impressive *package*. He had the war record; he looked about right. His past was un-, shall we say, uncomplicated."

The inflection of the word "package" is not lost on Mac. "And so what happened to you?"

"It's like the newspapers said, isn't it?"

"I don't believe it. I'm wondering why this president can't seem to hold on to a vice president."

"If your conspiracy theories were justified by facts, given what's happened to my successor, do you suppose I'd tell you?"

But Mac advances now, going on as though he has not heard. "Who's behind it?

"Mr. MacPherson, I don't know what to say. This is a sad time."

"Mac," he reminds his host.

They go in to watch the television. It is the story again, of course. Television is doing what television does worst: jumping skittishly between the studio and a dozen field reporters, pursuing gossip, guesswork, drawing conclusions before there are facts.

"Twelve-alarm fire," Finneran says.

"Sorry?"

"Chaos," he explains. "Like a twelve-alarm fire."

"I see." Mac nods, and they continue to watch the program for a few minutes.

"You know, mayors know fires," Finneran says. "I got to be pretty good at them. I've never seen television capture anything like the feeling of being at a fire. You've got flames, people dead and dying, neighbors watching behind the police line. You've got a mother sobbing on the sidewalk, you've got a young fellow, a carpenter or a bricklayer, who's lost everything. You've got noise and hoses all over the road and light in your eyes, law enforcement tripping over itself and the press in the way everywhere. It's chaos." He pauses a moment before adding, "I loved it."

"Sir?"

Finneran looks at his guest. "Mac," he says, "you see a great big bear of a firefighter come out of a second-story window onto a ladder with a baby cradled in his arm, and right in that moment you know you're alive. And an hour later, when the baby, black with soot, is breathing again, and that fireman is sitting on the back of the fire truck, next to the oxygen tank, sobbing like a baby himself, his beard soaked in his own tears, why, you come upon that, witness that with your own eyes and ears, you witness the Almighty Himself."

Mac can say nothing. Finneran looks back at the television critically. "Poor Jim Breed. Fires aren't his specialty."

The two men return to the porch. Mac hasn't much time before he must leave to catch the only bus back to Boston. But Finneran seems not quite ready to let him go. In the gathering darkness he studies MacPherson, almost as though it were he conducting the interview. He begins to speak very softly.

"When I was mayor, we had media people. We'd say, We're doing such and such—get the word out. Or we'd have a problem with something, and we'd tell them to get the word out. But we didn't work for them. They worked for us.

"We didn't ask them what we could say, what we could vote for, what we could believe in, what we could stand for. In Washington, it was backwards. We worked for them. They set the fires, it seemed like, told us which ones to put out, which ones to turn our backs on, which ones to drench in gasoline. It was like a big game. They were the coaches. We were just players. Good players are kept. Bad ones, traded down."

Now is the time for Mac to wait, wait for more. When a man wants to say something, sometimes the art is in the waiting. It is Mac's special skill.

"Execute the plays, and we'll get you elected. Don't design the plays, execute them." He looks up. "Mr. MacPherson, I have nothing to say to you for the record, do you understand that?"

"Yes, sir."

"But there were things about that life that I no longer wanted any part of."

More waiting, more silence. Mac's jaw works slowly, and Finneran spends a few minutes sizing up his man. And then, in a faraway voice, he says, "I told them I didn't like . . . things. I was uncomfortable with the influence of . . . well, I told them I was uncomfortable. Pretty naïve of me, wouldn't you say?"

Mac doesn't answer.

"I've never been a sophisticated thinker, you see. I just told them what I thought. And so they came to me. Very quickly, too."

"Who?"

Finneran catches himself, stares very hard at Mac. He looks over his shoulder toward the house. "I love her," he explains. "Do you know what that means?"

"I, I . . ." Mac, who is never at a loss for words, cannot finish the thought. He is looking at his hands when he answers. "Sir, you have shown me."

The two men sit together in silence, Finneran rocking slowly on the porch swing. Evening has fallen. Finneran does not engage Mac's eyes now. He carries on in that detached way, as though he is talking to himself.

"It's a disease, you know, like any other. Might as well blame someone for getting cancer."

Mac listens raptly to this man. How is it, he wonders, that he was in Washington three years and I never had an inkling of his depth?

Finneran goes on: "They said they could have her picture on the front page of the next morning's *Star*. They said they had quotes from a house-maid, and a bartender. And photographs from the ladies' room in a restaurant. Bloodshot eyes, or something, a bottle in her hand in the ladies' room. Can you imagine the human being who would take such a photograph, Mr. MacPherson? They said they could do it anytime they liked."

The porch swing creaks as the man who was the mayor of Boston and then the vice president of the United States rocks slowly in the fading light. Mac can no longer see his face clearly.

"Funny. Thing like that, if it happened to me, might help me. I'd have said, bring it on! Bring it on, damn you! I'd have held the damn photograph up to the cameras myself. Imagine the scum who took this, I'd say. I've never pretended to be more than a man. Scratch me and I bleed. You see, people understand when you fight back against these things. But that's me, Mr. MacPherson, not Maggie. It would have destroyed her."

When it is time to leave, Patrick Finneran leads Mac to the road, holding open the gate as Mac goes through it. For a moment they stand in the darkness, on opposite sides. That is when it occurs to Mac that he received, in just a few minutes with this man, much more than mere information.

"Mr. Finneran, it has been an honor to meet you."

Patrick Finneran's hand extends across the fence.

"Go cautiously, Mr. MacPherson."

It has been too many nights in the condo, so Bear finds a motel. But he doesn't sleep very well. It is one of those nights where to lie still is a penance, and a man watches the clock to find out when he has paid enough. At five A.M. he rises, restlessly, and flips on the television to yet another news report about the assassination.

"Even as the CIA reported that two terrorists were killed in a dramatic gun battle twenty miles outside of Mexico City, an Islamic fringe group, Guardians of Allah, has claimed responsibility for the assassination of Ambassador Royall Stillwell," the newscaster is saying, "according to the Jordanian news agency Al Kumrah, which says a note from the shadowy and little-known organization was faxed to its offices this morning. Meanwhile, Arab leaders scrambled to distance themselves from events Tuesday. Syrian president Hafez Al-Assad expressed his nation's 'shock and outrage for this despicable act,' a sentiment echoed by Palestinian and Iranian leaders."

The story cuts to an Iranian diplomat at the United Nations, expressing his country's revulsion for this "evil and cowardly act."

The newscaster continues: "CIA sources have not named the alleged terrorists, but an agency spokesman said today that three men were intercepted in Mexico City as they attempted to escape to Africa. In the ensuing gun battle, all three were killed.

"According to State Department sources speaking on background, Guardians of Allah is a splinter group of Shiite fundamentalists that several years ago left Hamas. The note, they say, is a rambling proclamation that the Islamic Revolution must 'cut off the serpent at the head,' and vows more acts of terror.

"The State Department and the Secret Service announced that they have increased details assigned to the presidential candidates. President Breed has vowed to carry on with his campaign."

The story cuts to Breed, speaking at the White House. "The American people will not permit their political process, the most open in the world, to be held hostage by terrorists and cowards. My good friend Royall would not want it any other way. Tomorrow morning, we will be back in the streets, in the towns, on the country roads, in the cities, with the people. We will not be intimidated."

The newscast switches back to the talking head. "State Department sources said travelers, particularly at airports, should expect increased delays."

Bear switches off the television, pulls the curtain aside. It is still dark outside Denver. A few minutes later, Sugaree is idling placidly in the darkness as Bear sips a cup of coffee in the driver's seat. It's quiet in the cab. What a long, strange trip this one has been, for sure. Best just to deliver the dryers and head home to Carter. Still . . .

When he's finished his coffee, the old hippie guides his truck slowly along the empty streets toward Interstate 25. At the interchange, the signs point north for Cheyenne and south for Colorado Springs and New Mexico. He hesitates, rubbing the back of his neck for a moment, before steering the truck onto the ramp.

CHAPTER 44

At ten past three in the afternoon, Louisa approaches the Buffalo Bill Historical Center on foot, self-conscious in her pancake makeup as she crosses the parking lot. For three days she has bent all her energy, her ingenuity, toward reaching this spot. But what now? She crosses a small, sunny plaza before the great stone façade and walks slowly up the steps. Inside, she buys a ticket. It is, in fact, a large museum, with whole wings devoted to the art of the American West, Native American art, and, of course, Buffalo Bill. Even at a brisk walk, it takes Louisa the best part of half an hour to walk through all of the galleries. She does not find Isabel.

Three blocks east, a dark-blue Cadillac, mud up to the fenders, moves slowly along the westbound lane of Sheridan Avenue. The woman Isabel calls the Beak, in the passenger seat, catches sight of someone up ahead, darting over the avenue from the high-school football field across the road. "There," she says to the man Isabel calls Smokes, and Smokes accelerates. She activates the cellular phone. "Scout Two," she says, "we've got a package."

Now what, Louisa is still wondering. She stares through the museum's plate-glass window, across the parking lot, but there she can see nothing except the occasional tourist's arrival or departure. She returns to the main hall, walking over to the yellow mail stage in the lobby. But her pulse is racing and she cannot focus. And then, with her back to the entrance, she hears the woman at the ticket desk say, "You coming back again today, honey?" A small voice says yes, and Louisa whirls. There at the desk, her hair in tangles and streaks of dirt on her face, is Isabel.

Both are in tears when they embrace, and even a few are shed by the ticket taker, who, although not comprehending precisely what she is seeing, knows that it is a special reunion. For her part, Louisa feels the tension in her own back begin to melt at the touch of her daughter's hands. Isabel sobs, softly.

Outside, the Cadillac eases to a stop in a parking space about fifty yards from the entrance to the museum. The Beak hops out and then into the backseat. She slides across to the driver's side, propping herself up against the door. "Okay," she says, "lower the window."

Smokes presses the button and the passenger-side rear window lowers halfway.

"That's enough," she says, removing the scope from its case and fitting it to her semiautomatic rifle. *Kachick.* The silencer snaps into its mount. Now, with scope and silencer fitted, she jerks the stock to her shoulder and measures the shot through the scope, noting with satisfaction how steadily the cross-hairs hold on the point six feet from the doors.

Smokes looks up at the reflective glass on the museum. "How's the shot look?"

"Good. You've signaled the bird?"

"Six miles north on 120," he answers. "It's moving to position now. Okay, as soon as they exit and get clear of the doors, take them down. Take out the mother first."

"No problem with the shot. This *is* an awfully public place. You'd better get us out of here in a hurry." She is rolling cotton wool into two little balls. She places one in each ear.

"What are you doing?"

"You should try it. This silencer isn't very effective. Shooting one of these off in a car is a good way to go deaf."

Inside the museum, Isabel's eyes are closed as she yields to her mother's embrace, both of them still sobbing.

"My darling, God, I thought I wouldn't see you again."

"I was so scared, Mother."

"I was scared too, sweetheart. But it's okay now, the worst part is over. Let's go into town and—"

But Isabel's eyes are open, and she is not listening to her mother, for her gaze is riveted elsewhere. Through the lobby's plate-glass window, she sees the car.

"Oh my God, Mother, it's them!"

"What?"

"Them! Look!" And Louisa does look out, now. She sees the dark Cadillac parked in the lot in front of the museum, and looks again at her daughter's expression, which tells her more than words can. Louisa turns to the woman at the desk, still wiping tears from her eyes, but suddenly all business. "Please call the police. At once!"

"Cody Police emergency, this call is being recorded."

"Please listen very carefully. This is Louisa Shidler speaking. I am with my daughter, Isabel, at the Buffalo Bill Historical Center on Sheridan Avenue. I wish to turn myself in to the police, but we are in danger. We have been followed here and—"

"Ma'am?"

"Just send the police to the museum, *at once*. Louisa C. Shidler. I am wanted by the FBI. Please check it out, but hurry!"

"Come on, come on!" Smokes is saying, his fingers drumming against the dashboard.

"Be cool."

"The fuck are they doing?"

"It's her daughter. It's an emotional scene in there. She's probably going to use the bathroom to wash her up. Be patient."

The noise of Smokes's drumming fingers fills the cabin. Otherwise it is quiet. "Let's go in," he says.

"Be cool."

"I'll go in. I'll do it with a fuckin' pistol. You—"

"Quiet. What is that?" she interrupts, listening.

"Shit!"

To the south, the sound of a siren grows, and then is joined by the sound of a second siren.

In the rearview mirror, the Beak catches the flash of the blue lights. Instantly, she stows the rifle in the case.

"Something's wrong," she says. "Let's move away from here. Nice and gentle."

"Goddammit!"

"Nice and gentle. Pull down the road a bit and watch."

Three Cody police cruisers idle in front of the historical center, their blue lights flashing. A knot of tourists and staff is on the front steps, trying to see through the glass doors, which have been cordoned off. It has been quite an afternoon for Mrs. Kindle, who had looked on in shock when Patrolman Scott Pates burst in to the museum with his gun drawn. Then the woman at the desk identified herself as Louisa Shidler and asked him calmly to put his gun away, as she presented her wrists for handcuffs.

"This is my daughter, Isabel," she had said. "She must come with us."

By the time the two are led from the museum, the news has gotten around, and in minutes it will be all over the small town. Louisa Shidler, wanted by the FBI! Up in the Buffalo Bill!

At just past four o'clock, Louisa, handcuffed in front, and Isabel, close behind her, are led to one of the police cruisers. The convoy quickly pulls away.

The car phone in the Cadillac beeps, and Smokes answers.

"Go ahead."

"Scout One, you are blown. Unhitch yourself."

"Two, are you monitoring Cody PD?" Smokes asks.

"That's affirmative."

"Do they have the plate?"

"Negative. They have make and model and victor alpha, but no tag number."

"Fuck. Do they have Scout Two?"

"Negative."

"What are they doing?"

"They are transporting the packages to Cody PD. Unhitch and sign off. We'll be back to you."

It is only a short ride to the Cody Law Enforcement Center, a low-slung brick building on the corner of Beck Avenue and Eleventh. They have put Louisa in the back of the Ford Crown Victoria patrol car, next to Isabel. Pates drives, Detective Lifton next to him. Isabel's backpack sits in her lap. After a careful inspection, the police have satisfied themselves that its contents are innocuous: a sweatshirt, a pair of pants, a teddy bear. Louisa smiles to see Buster's nose pop out of the sack.

The patrol car heads east, toward the center of town.

"Officer, are your people searching for that Cadillac?"

"Excuse me?"

"The Cadillac. You need to find that."

"Lady, I'd advise you to keep silent," Lifton says.

The police lieutenant looks up to see the burly visitor with the long gray beard who stands at the counter.

"Can I help you, sir?"

The man has a little trouble getting the words out. He looks nervous. "Excuse me, ma'am, this is the police station, right?"

"Yes sir."

"Okay. They sent me here from the museum. I was wondering if you have Louisa Shidler here?"

"Sir?"

"I'd like to see her, if that's all right?"

"Are you an attorney, sir?"

"Me?" Bear has to smile at that one. "No. A friend."

"Then it's not allowed. I'm afraid I can't help you."

"Okay," Bear nods. "Well, can I, like, talk to one of the cops?"

"I'm afraid not at the moment, sir. Maybe later, if you want to leave your name and wait. You can sit over there." She indicates a chair and returns to a stack of forms at her desk. With a shrug, Bear writes his name on a slip of paper, sits down, and begins to wait.

The Land Rover is parked on the side of a switchback on a dirt road high up on the east ridge of Rattlesnake Mountain, west of the town. From this vantage, it looks down over the guardrail into Shoshone Canyon and, off to the east, Cody. The town is fading from view as evening comes on. To the west, the clouds are dark and thickening, and the temperature has dropped in the last hour. It looks as if it will snow in the mountains tonight.

Two twelve-foot antennae extend upward from the rear bumper, and to one side of the car, a twenty-four-inch white dish rests on a small aluminum tripod, angled toward the east. Inside the car, Steeves— "Smokes"—adjusts the dials on a black module, listening through headphones.

"I got it."

"Talk to me." Peter Loggia leans in the driver's-side window.

"Hold it," Steeves interrupts, his hand in the air. A minute or so goes by. "Sounds like FBI's flying a Gulfstream 3 up from Salt Lake," he says finally. "They're going to meet them at Yellowstone Regional."

"What time?"

"ETA nineteen forty-two. They're in the air."

Loggia looks at his watch. "Gives us just under an hour. Here, let me have that." It is a small Nokia cellular phone, normal to all appearances. It is, however, loaded with a special signal encryption device that scrambles the conversation to any other phone lacking the same device. Steeves hands the phone to him, and Loggia punches in speed-dial 1.

"Homepage, this is Scout Two. Radio traffic indicates handoff in five zero minutes, Yellowstone Regional Airport."

Loggia pauses, listening to a series of instructions. "That operation is not feasible," he answers, somewhat hesitantly, into the phone.

Steeves looks up, and notes the doubt.

"That airport is only one mile out of town," Loggia is saying. Then he listens awhile, and answers, "Understood," before switching the phone off.

"Well, Concierge's orders are to take them out."

"Concierge?"

"That's affirmative."

"Concierge wants us to take out the whole fuckin' Cody Police Department, or the FBI, or both?"

Loggia turns, kicks at the dirt, and sends a shower of pebbles raining down into the canyon below.

"Concierge doesn't care. Concierge notes for future reference that so far we have been bitch-slapped by two females, one of whom has not yet reached puberty. Fuckers." He climbs back into the Land Rover and spreads the map across the rear seat. He studies it, and makes notes in a little notebook.

"All right," he says, ten minutes later, "They want an old-fashioned shoot-out, they'll get one. Get on the hooter to Scout Three and ready the bird to move in fifteen. And call Scout One. We rendezvous with the bird here"—he indicates—"and then we take them out."

"Where?"

The stubby finger jabs down at the map. "Right here."

"Damn. How we gonna do that?"

"We'll show up to the party a little early. And try to keep the other guest away. You on the unicom?"

"Yeah."

"Good. Monitor the approach. When they're about fifteen miles out, jam the shit out of the FBO, and advise our good friends from the agency to circle and hold."

Inside the police station, Bear sits quietly, realizing by now that no one is going to speak to him, but uncertain what else to do. There is noise in the back, the sound of men hurrying this way and that. Telephones ring; voices are heard, curt and urgent. The dispatcher fields call after call. The cops are two-deep around the counter. After a few minutes an older cop in a white shirt hurries in the front door.

Bear's mind wanders, and out of boredom he begins to study the large street map of Cody on the wall. He listens to the conversation of the police officers. At one point the dispatcher says, "That's affirmative, Captain, three units. The lieutenant said to transport at nineteen-twenty. The FBI will land at Yellowstone Regional at nineteen forty-two." Bear continues to study the map, pretending not to eavesdrop. His eyes fall upon the diagram showing one long runway and the service buildings of a community airport, just east of the city center. Yellowstone Regional Airport.

At a quarter past seven, Bear quietly slips out. From Sugaree's cab he watches the police station through the rearview mirror. A few minutes later, three police cruisers exit the lot. As they pass his truck on Beck Avenue, heading east, Bear recognizes a flash of red hair in the back of the second vehicle, Cody Police cruiser 472. He starts up Sugaree and eases her into the line of traffic heading the same direction.

The three brown-and-white Cody police cruisers wind slowly through the little town, their blue lights flashing as though it were the Fourth of July. Bear's truck follows them from a couple of blocks behind. On Highway 14, the McDonald's and the Burger Kings and the Taco Bells fall away, and at half past seven exactly, the three cruisers begin to proceed down a long, empty straightaway flanked by a chain-link fence on the left side marking the airport perimeter. Across the road to the south is a small reservoir. Only a few cars pass in the opposite lane.

The police convoy makes the left turn into the airport, passing through the small lot with its small rank of Hertz rental cars. Bear pulls to the roadside and watches as the police cruisers are flagged along the terminal to a gate and then admitted to the runway side of the airfield. Once through the gate, the cars disappear from view. In a moment, they reemerge to the east side of the terminal, heading slowly to the end of the runway, their blue lights still flashing. They reach the runway's end and come to a stop. Bear watches for a moment. Without quite knowing why, he puts Sugaree in gear and nudges her back onto the highway.

"Hey, Charlie, what do you reckon's going on?"

Nineteen-year-old Charlie McAuliffe turns from the counter at Spirit Aviation to answer Danny Naris, who is taking a break from this evening's task: pulling a Lycoming engine from a Cessna 172. A socket wrench in one hand, a rag in another, Naris is staring out the bay doors toward the runway, where the three police cruisers proceed with their lights flashing.

"Cody PD got some big deal going on. The FBI is flying in from Salt Lake to pick up a prisoner."

"No shit!"

"Yeah, I heard it over the scanner," McAuliffe says. He gets up from the counter and joins Naris in the hangar bay to watch the sets of police lights recede into the darkness.

Just as cruiser 472 stops at the far end of the runway, there comes a sudden drumming across the roof and windshield. The occupants are startled for a brief moment at the rain's sudden intensity. "Oh, my God," Louisa whispers softly a few minutes later from the rear seat.

"What?" Isabel asks.

"Nothing," her mother answers. "Just the rain." She tries not to look out past the perimeter fence to the big silver tractor-trailer that has pulled off the road and parked by the side of the highway.

In the front of cruiser 472, neither Lieutenant Pete Snyder, the driver, nor Patrolman Pates says anything.

Twenty-two miles to the southwest, the FBI Gulfstream 3 banks gently to the left. Air National Guard captain Philip Kemp, the pilot pressed into service on one hour's notice, is scanning his altimeter, turn-and-bank, and artificial horizon gauges. With the increased cloud cover and rising winds that have moved in from the northwest, he is most intent on the artificial horizon. He notes air speed of 250 knots.

The Shoshone River valley, ten thousand feet below, is invisible, as is the Absaroka range to the west. In the strong westerly winds the jet bobs like driftwood in heavy surf. "Which way to the beach?" asks copilot Hal LoPresti.

"That'll be about two thousand miles on your six," Kemp answers. "Thousand-foot ceiling from Denver to Coeur d'Alene. Let's ready the VOR approach. What's the unicom for Yellowstone Regional?"

LoPresti flips through his Jeppesen manual. "One twenty-two eight," he says. He sets the radio to frequency 122.8 and depresses the TRANSMIT switch on the yoke.

"Yellowstone Regional, this is Gulfstream November Nine Seven Four Romeo, twenty-one miles out and southwest of the field for landing, request advisories."

By activating the unicom, LoPresti has posted a message on the universal radio frequency for Yellowstone Regional. The system is used by pilots flying in and out of the smaller airports, which, like Yellowstone Regional, have no tower. Instead of relying on an air traffic controller, pilots rely on one another to monitor the unicom frequency and stay out of one another's way. In a few minutes, Kemp expects to advise all traffic that he is commencing his approach to Runway 2-2.

Unicom messages also squawk over the black, Diet Pepsi–stained two-way radio receiver at Spirit Mountain Aviation, the sole fixed-base operator at Yellowstone Regional. Spirit runs a refueling and mechanic's service, and always has its two-way radio turned to the unicom frequency. But when the Gulfstream's call comes in, Charlie McAuliffe is sixty feet away from the counter, looking out the hangar bay through what is now a driving rainstorm at the obscured blue lights of three police cruisers. So he misses that message, and the reply that Kemp hears.

"Seven Four Romeo," a voice answers the Gulfstream. "This is Spirit Aviation. Yellowstone Regional Runway Two-Two currently unavailable due to vehicle blocking runway. Suggest you divert to alternate."

McAuliffe, hearing the distant sound of radio traffic on the unicom frequency, turns and heads back from the hangar bay.

In the air, Kemp's displeasure is obvious. "Jesus Christ," he mutters. "Vehicle blocking the runway?" He activates the transmission control on his own yoke and says, "Spirit, this is Seven Four Romeo, that is negative, repeat negative. Unable to divert to alternate. Please advise nature of problem."

Now McAuliffe, returning to the Spirit Aviation counter, hears the response clearly. "Seven Four Romeo, this is Spirit Aviation, we've got a problem down here. We've got a motor vehicle accident and a serious fuel leak on Runway Two-Two. Cody Fire Department is en route."

McAuliffe stares at the radio transmitter on the counter. *I'm* Spirit Aviation, he thinks. Who the hell are you?

He listens to the pilot answer the message. "Spirit Aviation, this is Seven Four Romeo. How long estimate expected hold?"

"Seven Four Romeo, unknown. We're doing the best we can with a bad situation down here."

"Roger, Spirit. Seven Four Romeo will hold. Please advise when runway clear." Kemp releases the switch, and sighs. "Better tell the boys back there we got a little delay," he says. He banks the jet toward the east, to begin circling counterclockwise in a long holding pattern.

On the ground, behind the counter at Spirit Mountain Aviation, Charlie McAuliffe continues to stare at the radio set. "Hey, Danny," he yells, "we got a vehicle accident out on Two-Two or something?"

They hear the *whomp-whomp* of the chopper's rotors before they see the shape of the helicopter itself, and then, through the rain, the Bell 1H-UH drops from the darkened northwest sky and approaches the runway. Inside Spirit Aviation's hangar bay, McAuliffe and Danny Naris hear it too.

"Who's that?" McAuliffe asks, jogging up to the perplexed mechanic, who stares out northwest across the airfield toward the helicopter approaching through the rain.

"Don't know. Can't see any markings in this shit."

"He sure as hell didn't call in on the unicom."

The helo grows in size as it approaches the airfield.

"Old Bell Huey," says Naris.

"Yeah, looks like," McAuliffe answers. "Damn, Danny, we got one guy on the unicom, who don't ought to be, and says there's an accident, which there ain't, and here we got another guy, who ought to be on it, and he ain't. This is one weird night."

Danny doesn't say anything.

It is about to get weirder.

"Thought they was comin' by plane," says Pete Snyder, squinting through the sweep of the wiper blades at the helicopter. It hovers toward the middle of the airfield, where the runways intersect. "Don't look like he sees our blue lights in this mess."

"I'll get some flares going," Pates answers. He leaves the car, throws on his slicker, and opens the trunk, crouching over it in the rain as he removes two flares from the emergency pack stowed there. Stepping off about fifteen yards from the rear of the vehicle, he plants the first flare, a ten-inch cylinder set atop a spike, into the wet grass, then ignites it by twisting off the cap. He is walking past the cruiser to the front of the car when he sees that the helicopter has apparently caught sight of the flare, and is moving toward it.

Captain Fred Quartarone and Patrolman Tim Dacey step out of the lead vehicle and don orange slickers. Pates looks over his shoulder and sees

Patrolmen Larry Steiner and Tom Dinolfio getting out of the third cruiser, throwing the slickers over themselves and striding up to Quartarone.

In cruiser 472, Captain Snyder remains with the prisoner and Isabel.

Now the helicopter approaches, and a powerful searchlight stabs through the driving rain to find the three patrol cars lined up in the rain by the edge of the field. Pates, his second flare still unlit, is just out of the circle of illumination.

Inside the second cruiser, Louisa listens to the *whomp* of the rotors, watching the helicopter approach. The cruiser windows are spattered with raindrops and obscured by fog. In the darkness and the rain Louisa cannot see much at all.

Isabel reaches across Louisa's arm and squeezes her mother's hand.

"Seven Four Romeo, this is—" McAuliffe begins, and then he is cut off by a screech of static as his signal is jammed. He jiggles the microphone switch and tries again. "Seven Four—" The same thing happens. He tries it again. And again.

"Yellowstone traffic, this is Seven Four Romeo, you're breaking up."

"Damn!" mutters McAuliffe. "Somebody's jamming me!"

Then the strange voice comes up again. "Seven Four Romeo, be advised we've had a problem with a ham radio hacker. Runway Two-Two remains down."

McAuliffe feels the blood pounding in his throat. "Danny," he shouts, "get on the phone to Cody PD. We got something seriously wrong here!"

As Danny Naris picks up the phone, McAuliffe hits the switch, and manages to blurt out eight words before the jam hits.

"Two-Two is open! Two-Two is open!"

When the message comes over the radio, the Gulfstream is at thirteen thousand feet, eight miles east of the field, set on a course to the north-northwest. Kemp looks across at his copilot. "What do you make of this circus, Hal?"

Shrugging, the copilot unbelts. "Sure don't like it. Let's fill them in back there," he says.

A moment later FBI Special Agent Stan Griffin is leaning over the copilot's seat as Kemp finishes briefing him on the radio traffic.

"This is a small airport," says Kemp, "out in the middle of nowhere. They might do a dozen flights a day. Blocked runway be kind of unusual. And I've never run into a hacker on the unicom before."

"Maybe somebody doesn't want us around," says Griffin. "I think we better get down there in a hurry."

"How are the minimums?" Kemp asks.

"Six hundred feet," LoPresti answers. "We got at least ten or fifteen feet to spare."

The joke gets no response out of Kemp. "Let's go in for a look."

He pushes the TRANSMIT button as he begins a bank to a westerly bearing. "Yellowstone traffic, this is Gulfstream Seven Four Romeo, eight miles east of the field. We are commencing approach for a visual monitor, and will be entering a right downwind for Runway Two-Two." He flicks off the switch and says, to nobody in particular, "I don't know what the hell we can see in this mess, anyway."

Eight miles to the west of the Gulfstream, at the same moment the call goes out from the plane, the helo hovers before the little convoy of police cruisers, an olive-colored hymenopteran scrutinizing a potential meal. Its rotors beat the rain-filled air above the tar macadam, thirty feet from the three vehicles. Then the helicopter settles to the tarmac.

On its right side, the slide door opens and a man emerges. He is wearing a blue windbreaker with the letters "FBI" across the back. He jogs up to the four Cody police officers in rain slickers, shakes their hands, flashes something at them. A second man remains in the helicopter's bay.

Louisa glances over and sees that Isabel is dumbstruck, staring through the windshield at the man who remains inside the helicopter.

"What is it? What is it, hon?"

"Mother, it's them, it's him—inside the helicopter!"

"Who? Honey?"

No answer—or rather, the most eloquent of answers, as the eyes of the girl go wide. Isabel, paralyzed, dumb with fear, can only nod.

"Lieutenant," Louisa is shouting, "Lieutenant, this is not the FBI! This is a trap! These are the people who—"

"Lady, shut up!" Snyder shouts.

Before she can respond, Lieutenant Snyder's radio crackles. "Base to Four-Four. Cody to Four-Four, captain, do you have anything out there on the airfield?"

On the runway the little group is breaking up, and Snyder sees the man in the FBI jacket head back to the helicopter, as Quartarone turns to motion toward Snyder. Snyder picks up the microphone. "Four Seven Two to base. That's affirmative. We have the FBI."

"Helicopter? Are they in a helicopter, Pete?"

"That's affirmative."

"Well, Pete, can you get a positive read on identification? We've had a report from Spirit Aviation that FBI is inbound on a Gulfstream 3, and this helicopter appar—"

That is as far as the transmission proceeds. Unbeknownst to Snyder or his base, it is also being monitored aboard the helicopter itself. At a command delivered via headset, the apparent FBI agent drops to the ground, and a broadside of automatic weapons fire-sprays the four Cody police officers. It happens instantly, a dreadful, split-second burst of murderous gunfire from the bay of the helicopter, and almost immediately, four of them—Fred Quartarone, Tim Dacey, Larry Steiner, and Tom Dinolfio—are dead.

The next seconds are a blur. "This is not the FBI! This is not the FBI!" Louisa screams. Snyder slams his car into drive and spins out away from the helicopter, across the field. Shots rake the vehicle, and Snyder takes three rounds in the arm. The windshield explodes in their faces; glass and wind and rain are flying everywhere. Fifteen yards from where cruiser 472 was just parked, Pates, still standing in the field with the remaining flare, drops to the grass and pulls his sidearm, firing at the man on the runway, missing him as he sprints the last steps toward the Huey. The man dives into the bay just as the helicopter lurches into the sky.

Tears of anger mixing with the rain and blurring his vision, Pates looks back toward the two empty Cody cruisers and sees that four police officers in orange slickers lie outside them, motionless on the wet tar macadam. He hears the crackle of the radios, but realizes that his set remains where he left it, on the seat in 472.

The three occupants of 472 are all still alive, and Pete Snyder, his foot jamming the gas pedal to the floor, tears through the field. But the chopper swerves in behind and swiftly makes up the ground. Inside the cruiser, all is a bloody chaos of glass, metal, Plexiglas, torn seats, and blood. The window glass has been blown out, and the cruiser's metal surfaces ripped as though by a giant claw.

Now the helo rises again and suddenly is in front of the cruiser. Snyder swerves back toward the runway, and the chase continues. The car darts and skids crazily now, with the thump of the rotor blades directly above, or dancing in front. Panicked, Snyder is swerving across the wet grass beyond the airstrip, dodging fire from continuously changing directions as the helicopter, hovering and swooping and diving, attempts to corner it as a cat corners a wounded mouse. Riddled with holes, the cruiser's gas tank is pouring fuel out on the slick grass.

"Isabel! Isabel!"

Beneath a blanket of broken glass, Isabel cringes in the rear passenger-side foot well. She hears the angry pursuit of the rotor blades. There is a fusillade, and another, and yet a third. And then they hear the screams, as the third blast finds home, and another police officer is dead. Snyder slumps to the right, pulling the wheel with his lifeless hand. His boot remains jammed on the accelerator pedal, and the car begins to careen in a circle. Louisa clambers feetfirst through the gaping hole where the Plexiglas divider was, over the seat and the dead man's slumped body. With her manacled hands she takes the wheel, and she slides her foot next to that of the dead police officer.

"Not much time," yells Loggia from the pilot's seat of the helicopter. "Get a shot on this bastard and finish this!" Below him the police car has pulled out of its circle and is again dodging and swerving forward and back. He maneuvers over it, trying to get in position for a shot.

Now the wounded police cruiser is skidding back toward Pates, and as the helicopter races in behind it, six rounds from the AK-47 go astray and catch him: three in the left arm, a fourth and fifth that slice his left leg to tatters, and a sixth which punctures the iliac artery. Pates remains conscious, but he is losing blood fast.

CHAPTER 45

It is a giant bug, hovering and dancing and dealing death.

Sugaree is parked, idling, three hundred yards away at the perimeter fence. The corners of Bear's mouth quiver ever so slightly. His vision begins to cloud, the images enlarging and coming too fast. He feels himself helpless, just as though he were in the dream, the dream where your legs are in oatmeal and you cannot push them through to get to that refuge which is within sight, the dream where your body becomes stone and you cannot fight your way to that place. He is frozen, his hands frozen on the steering wheel, and he feels it deep within his nervous system, coming now, the anxiety attack. No, he thinks, not now, don't come now. But it wants to come. It wants to come very badly.

One and one half miles to the east, the Gulfstream 3 descends through seven hundred feet. A scene of darkened confusion, one that includes the unmistakable profile of a hovering Bell Huey helicopter, comes into view. "What in the hell is that?" Kemp asks.

There is an explosion as something hits the police cruiser's engine, and the car swerves to rest. Louisa presses the pedal to the floor. "Please, oh please, God!" she screams. Nothing happens. She tries to start the car. Again, nothing.

"Isabel, get out of the car! Get out of the car!" But Isabel is stone-stiff with panic, motionless in the rear foot well, too frightened even to shake the glass from her shoulders.

Overhead, Louisa now hears, feels, the pulsing of the rotors. With both manacled hands she clutches the microphone on the police radio, but to no purpose, for an earlier round has already disabled it. The pulsing comes nearer; the wind from the rotors whips rain through the cabin.

"Isabel!" she screams. "Isabel!" She scrambles over the seat back to cover the girl.

The helicopter settles toward the earth, searching this last cruiser with its bug eyes, hovering before it, looking for any lingering sign of life. Its rotors beat the air even more closely as it drops to face the blown-out windscreen of the vehicle. Turning its flank, the copter unleashes a murderous blast from the AK-47 in the side bay. Louisa and Isabel are crouching in the foot well, and the cruiser's V-8 engine lies in the line of fire; although the fusillade rips obscene gashes in the vehicle, neither is struck.

He is not gasping, not yet, but the breaths are shallow, loud, and they come more quickly. He hears it, the grating, the rasping in his own throat. Don't come now. Don't come now. Out on the airfield, the bug is hovering in the rain, lowering for the kill. The flashes start to swirl through his mind, the images, and the fear, and the darkness closing in, and steam is coming from the valve, and he feels the trembling, as he leans against the window of the driver's door, with the rainfall beating against it, and his heartbeat pounding like a jackhammer in his ears.

Don't come now.

Bear hears the words far away, maybe even says them aloud. He hears them again, louder now, and then he knows his lips are moving around them, stating the words, not begging with them, not pleading with them. He is stating them. As an equal. It wants to come, but it hears the words, and hesitates. It has never heard them except in a plea, and it has contempt for a plea. There in the cab, inches away, it hesitates. Bear says the words again, and now they sound almost like a command. *Don't come now.* He feels the dark presence, his other self, staring at him in the cab. He turns from it. Rain drives against the window. Outside, lowering in the sky through the rainstorm, a bug. No, a helicopter.

My breathing, Bear thinks, my breathing. He hears it now, and it has slowed some. It is calmer. *Don't come now.* There in the cab, still uncertain, still nonplussed by words that sounded like command, is the presence. Bear's eyes are open, and his breathing has settled. The rain pounds down against the cab. He hears the rain and the sound of his breathing. But he can no longer hear his heart. It's not a bug. It's not a bug at all.

Don't come now. His hand shakes as it moves. It still shakes. But its grasp on the gear knob is firm.

Come later. Not now.

Scott Pates struggles through the wet grass, his leg leaving a greasy smear behind him. They are all dead, he is thinking, all dead. We are all dead. I am dead. He pulls himself along by his arms and right leg, the mangled left leg dragging behind. The rain beats down on him, half blinding him. His ammunition is gone, his sight is failing, his life spilling into his abdomen from the punctured iliac artery, and out behind, his destroyed leg. Still he drags himself through the dark, sodden grass. In his right hand he clutches the cylinder, which he is still holding from that innocent errand a mere ninety seconds earlier when he went to stake out the flare.

He is twenty-three years old, engaged to be married, and about to die.

Pates was born and raised in Cody. It has been a good life. He got his first elk at thirteen; five years later, he graduated from high school, and three years after that from the police academy. He eats dinner with his mother and father every week, and hunts with his father and brothers, Butch and Adam, at least twice a season.

It has been a good life, if a short one. He is one of the best-loved young men in the town. He had been the star of a good basketball team, a team that won its division twice in his career and, in his senior year, went to the state semifinals. Pates was a point guard, a playmaker, a clever passer, and a reliable outside shot. As a senior, he was the captain and led the team in both assists and points. He was named honorable-mention all-Wyoming, and he and his family attended a dinner in Cheyenne. High-school basketball is popular in Cody, almost as popular as rodeo. Pates's skill as a basketball player made him something of a local celebrity. His handsome baby face was often in the newspaper.

It has been a good life. Dragging, dragging, he inches through the long grass toward the bug-eyed helicopter, pulling his leg along like a heavy sled over broken ground. Fifty feet, forty feet: he comes closer, leaving himself in a trail behind him, but knowing, with an odd certainty, that he will reach the helicopter before the last blood drains from him to be drunk down by the field grass. He is within thirty feet, twenty-five. The noise deafens him and the rain and wind pound his bleeding body.

The helicopter jerks upward and maneuvers to the side of the stricken police vehicle, shifting in the air so that its tail is toward Pates. It begins to settle down so that the man in the bay can see down into the foot wells of 472. The tail is toward Pates, the wind from the rotors buffets him, and neither the pilot nor the men in the helicopter can see him in the rainstorm, an orange shape moving forward through the wet grass.

The Huey now hovers directly above his head and starts to settle. As it approaches to within ten feet of the ground, no wind from its rotors can be felt directly beneath it. When Pates, his hand shaking, unwraps the flare, it sparks into life, and the little flame is not extinguished. The red sparkles burst out hungrily, hot sparks flying into his face. But he does not flinch.

Downward comes the Huey. As the chopper settles toward the earth, the gap left by the smashed windshield opens up to view before the man in the open bay. He brings his weapon to his shoulder. Louisa Shidler is centered in the focus of the killer's squinting eye.

In the minutes before his own death, Patrolman Pates fires a murderous shot of his own, with his last weapon, the sparkling flare. His wounded left hand, shrieking with pain, grabs for the strut, and the right comes over the helicopter floor with the flare. It flies unimpeded over the bulkhead, bouncing to the floor. In an instant the cockpit is filling with smoke and sparks.

"Fire!" someone screams, as Pates tumbles back over the strut to the grass.

Loggia freezes, panicking, and then, misunderstanding the shout to mean that his helicopter has come under fire, he jams the yoke back to gain altitude. Smoke begins to billow through the cockpit. Coughing, cursing, he screams for his men to find the source of the smoke. Steeves stumbles and falls to the floor, bruising his hip on something hard. Smoke billows from the flare.

The men in the helicopter are choking and blinded, and the flare's smoke and bright hot sparks are thick in the cabin before they find it and manage to kick it toward the earth. The helicopter climbs steeply, and then, gasping and coughing, Loggia turns the nose earthward and dives, knowing that putting the helicopter's nose down will release smoke aft. In the confusion and the smoke, as the helicopter lurches and rolls toward the earth, no one notices the small black object that also skitters out of the cabin and falls. Loggia performs this strange maneuver three times, each time clearing the cabin of more smoke. But the process takes longer than a minute.

Just then, the Gulfstream thunders by on its first pass. Kemp pulls the aircraft up and out of it into a steeply banked climb. "The runway's clear, anyway," he says. "We'd better get down there."

LoPresti activates the unicom. Getting down there will take only another ninety seconds, but five Cody police officers are already dead, and the sixth will be by the time the plane lands.

A half mile away, several cars have pulled to the side of Highway 14. In moments the number will swell to a dozen. The occupants peer through the rainstorm at the incomprehensible show at the airport: the diving and hovering helicopter shooting at the police cars. Now the radio waves around Cody, Wyoming, are alive with strange reports. Every police car, every sheriff's vehicle, every fire engine, is rushing toward the airfield. In two minutes the first of them will arrive, too late to see the helicopter racing toward the west. And too late, by almost thirty seconds, to see the other remarkable thing that has happened this evening.

All through the night the Cody Police and the FBI will take statements, as the drivers wait in the rain by the highway shoulder to explain what they saw. It will become more, not less, chaotic at the airport: police cruisers, sheriff's deputies, ambulances, fire trucks, media remote trucks. Highway 14 comes literally to a standstill as people from miles around converge on the airport to rubberneck and speculate. All they can see is flashing lights and rain.

Only by early in the morning of October 17 does a coherent account begin to take shape. The helicopter seemed to set down by the side of that last police cruiser; some say on the ground, some say not. Someone clambered aboard, that is the consensus among the witnesses. The woman from Idaho says it was definitely a man, but two other witnesses say, yes, it might have been a woman. No one can remember seeing a child climb up with her, but it might have happened. It was hard to make it out with the rain driving down, and the helicopter being on the far side of the police car. Rich O'Leary, an electrician who was heading home to Emblem at the time, thinks it was a policeman who clambered aboard. He was wearing a policeman's rain slicker: O'Leary is adamant about it. But the cheerleader says she didn't think it was a policeman's slicker. It didn't look the right color to her. And besides, the investigators sadly note, all of the police officers were accounted for on the ground. Jody Alfred, who was driving in to begin her evening bartending shift at the Eagle, thinks the person didn't actually make it into the helicopter. When it is pointed out to her that five other witnesses think the person did get aboard, she reconsiders. It was hard to see through the rain. Maybe she saw it wrong.

Smoke billowed from the helicopter: they all agree on that point. It flew erratically and smoke poured from it. Their accounts differ after that point of consensus. Was the smoke black, or white, or, as the schoolteacher insisted, red? Did it issue from the cabin, or the tail, or the rotor cogs, or, as the electrician maintained, was there actually a fire in the cabin? The investigators cannot square the accounts. They theorize that shots returned by Snyder or Pates, before they died, must have caused some kind of electrical fire.

The strangest part of the account was what happened next: the vehicle. Most agree that the vehicle that smashed through the airport's perimeter fence and raced toward the police cruiser was a tractor-trailer. This was after the helicopter seemed to catch fire and to start flying crazily up and down. The electrician thinks it was an emergency vehicle, but everyone else disagrees. There is no consensus on the color: white, gray, and silver receive the most votes. The schoolteacher thinks someone from a mile down the highway crashed through the airport fence to go to the aid of the policemen trapped in the car. The truck stopped, briefly, by the side of the cruiser with the passenger's side in view. But no one could see what happened next. No one saw the driver. No one could tell what was going on right then. The truck stopped by the side of the vehicle for less than a minute, the schoolteacher said, and then it roared off, returning through the gap in the fence to the highway.

And what happened then? The paralysis of the unexpected. Everyone was stunned. No one followed it. No one saw the license plate.

By early morning, when the Cody police have written down the statements and digested them, and put out the APB, Sugaree has put more than 150 miles between itself and the airport and rain is still falling hard.

CHAPTER 46

It was the afternoon, and I went back to the Buffalo Bill Museum to see if she was there. I had gone in the morning, and again at lunchtime, but no luck. And I began to wonder, was that what the postcard was of, the museum? Or was it something else? You know how it is when you go to meet someone and they aren't there, and you start to wonder, was it four o'clock, or three? Was it on New Jersey Avenue? She did say New Jersey Avenue, didn't she, or was it New York? That kind of thing. And so by that third time I walked in I was really worried that I was in the wrong town or something.

But the lady at the desk recognized me again and then, in the next second, there was Mother. I started crying. I had a little trouble recognizing her at first, because of the way she had her hair and her clothes. First, she had dyed her hair red, and she had had it permed in like the grossest perm you can imagine. It was so big it looked like a big shrub on her head. She was like one of those women who you want to go up to in the mall and say, "Excuse me, but your hair is too big." You know? It was very trailer park.

And so were her clothes. They were very trashy and made her look like, well, let's say like somebody's mother trying a little too hard. She definitely didn't look like Mother.

But I didn't care. There was this big, open lobby in the front of the museum, and the windows were floor-to-ceiling plate glass, and you could look out at the parking lot and across the street to the high-school football field where I'd spent most of two days hanging out. I was standing there just hugging Mother and crying. I felt so safe again—for, like, two minutes. And I looked up beyond her at the parking lot and there it was. The blue Cadillac. Oh my God, I think my heart just stopped.

So Mother had them call the police and the police came, and then they put Mother in handcuffs and they put us in the police car and drove us to the police station. I didn't see the Cadillac when they took us out of the museum.

When we got to the police station, there was a crowd of these cops just standing there gaping at us like we were rock-and-roll stars, or murderers. Then they took us in the back and they had us in a little room by ourselves. There was nothing in it but a table and four orange chairs. Four orange plastic chairs and me and Mother and for a while this Cody policeman. Mother kept saying, "I want to give a statement," and they kept going, "Ma'am, you can give your statement to the FBI." And I was like, "Mother, wait for the FBI." But she kept going, "No, I want to give a statement." And they wouldn't write it down. Now, I've seen the shows. They're supposed to want you to give a statement, and you're supposed to go, "No, I'm not saying anything without my lawyer." But with Mother, just the opposite. She wants to give a statement and they won't let her. That's Mother. She's kind of contrary.

Not that they weren't polite or anything. This Cody policeman who was with us, he had a bolo tie on instead of a real tie and he was extremely handsome and also extremely serious. Then he left and this woman police officer came. She took me into the ladies' room and then I saw myself in a mirror for the first time in, I don't know, however long it had been since I got out of that camp. I was a mess. Have you ever seen a sheep that's been out in the fields for a while, and it's all gray and all kind of matted with grass and little flowers and whatnot in its wool? That's what I looked like. I had stuff in my hair, and I was just gray with dirt. So I washed up and that felt a little better.

She was very nice. Her name was Doris Irma Kipler. She was a patrolwoman, Patrolwoman Doris Kipler. She was very proud of her middle name because she said there was a hotel in that town that was famous called the Irma, which Buffalo Bill himself built and named for his daughter. And it has all kinds of I don't know what in it, she was telling me, a big bar or something that the Queen of England gave because she liked the Wild West Show so much. It sounded very interesting but I never got to see it. But she was very nice. She got me a sandwich and three bags of potato chips and a Coke and I pigged out.

They took us in a police car, me and Mother, to the airport. They walked us out of the police station and they held Mother's head as she ducked into the back of one of the police cars. She had on handcuffs. It seemed colder, and it was dark by then, and I should have known things were going to get worse. They had two more police cars, one in front of us, and one behind, and they put on their police lights. I asked Mother what's going on and she said the FBI was coming to get us and they would fly into the airport. And I was like, "The FBI?" And she was like, "Yes."

So we got out of the town and then drove into the airport and through this gate and out on the runway. It was the tiniest airport you've ever seen and we just drove right out onto the runway, and then right to the end of it. It started raining, and by the time we got there it was raining hard. The policemen sat around, not quite sure what to do next. And then Mother was saying, "What's that noise?"

It was a thumping sound. And then there was this helicopter away at the end of the airport. One of the policemen—it was the handsome one, who had come in our car—he said he was going to get a flare. He did light a flare, I think, and after that the helicopter came toward us. Then me and Mother and the other policeman, we were all staring out the car at the helicopter, and then it dropped right from the sky next to the cars, right across from us in the rain, a big ugly helicopter with a rotor making a horrible beating racket. It had a sliding door like a minivan. The door opened, and a man got out, and behind him, there he was. Smokes. With a gun in his hand.

My memory's a mess about what happened next. Mother was screaming at the policeman, and then everyone was shooting and I was just screaming and screaming. There was cursing and windows and things were being blown right out of the car and the driver let out this long curse. And then the car was racing along through a field, and Mother was screaming at me to keep down, and then she was gone—at first I thought she was gone and I screamed again, but she was driving. She had climbed across the seat through where the Plexiglas had been, and I guess she was driving, somehow. God, my mother panics when she has to make a left turn into the mall. But give her a helicopter to shoot at you and a rain like Noah's flood and your windshield blown out and people being killed and handcuffs on, and she drives.

The policeman, Mother told me later, he was already dead. But I could only hear the pounding of those helicopter blades above the car.

We bounced and rattled over that field, and Mother wrenched the wheel and we'd skid around, and you could hear the blasts through the rain as the helicopter shot at us. And then the car just stopped, and I heard that *whomp* sound coming closer, and Mother was screaming for me to stay down.

There was so much noise, that was the thing about it. And it was raining right in the car, and I remember rain falling on my face and I was crying and screaming. And glass. There was glass all over me. They'd killed the policeman in the front seat, and all the other ones too. There was just blood and metal and glass everywhere and I thought I would go deaf with the noise. I didn't really know what was happening, even later, when the big man with the beard was there, carrying me away, and I remember thinking, just for a minute, and I know this is totally weird, but I looked up at this man with a big gray beard coming out of the rain, and I wondered whether he was God.

He wasn't God, but it was a miracle. We didn't get killed, or even shot, Mother and me. That is the miracle of it. Everyone else did but us. You know what, even Buster got shot. He had a big hole in his belly but the bullet wasn't there. I found him later in the backpack with the bullet hole in it and his stuffing leaking out.

CHAPTER 47

A wrathful rain pounds Sugaree's cab, but it is not enough, Louisa thinks. It is not enough to wash away the blood, no not enough to begin to clean the soil of blood, to rinse away the blood from the police cruiser. It is not enough to drown that hellish noise, to put out the fire and smoke, to wash the blood from the faces of the men.

Louisa sits on the pallet, rocking in the darkness and holding Isabel, hearing the drumming of the rain. Wracking sobs keep coming and coming and they will not stop. All of those men killed—all of that blood and destruction. The brutishness of it! The beating of the rotors and the gunfire ripping gashes through the police cars, the explosions and the broken bodies and the welts in the earth itself, and the empty look in the eyes of the man in the helicopter—the rain cannot wash it away.

And when Bear had thrown her bodily into the cab and the truck was racing for the fence, she could see in the rush of his headlights across the field a man, a young policeman in a rain slicker, lying in the wet grass. She could see him there clearly in one moment, and then the headlights swung past, and he was gone. Now, as she sits on the pallet, she keeps seeing that policeman lying in the grass, and the sobs keep coming and coming.

At last her chest stops quivering. She listens to the sound of her breathing, and of Isabel's, to the roar of the rain on the windshield and on the roof of the truck, to the diesel rumble beneath her. She listens, and tries to calm herself. Her cheek nuzzles Isabel's shoulder—with her hands manacled, she cannot hold the girl. Isabel shivers a little.

Images come on her, one upon the last. The policeman in the field. The man with the machine gun in the helicopter bay. Clambering over the heavy bulk of the dead policeman—feeling the seat wet and sticky with his blood. Then an old memory comes to the surface, of Emily Shidler in hysterics over a foreclosure notice, sobbing up in the bedroom. It is Louisa's mental picture of despair.

They are going to find us and kill us. She reaches the conclusion in the darkness, listening to the rain on Sugaree's roof. In a minute, in ten minutes, in an hour, another helicopter, another car, another airplane. And then the fire and machine guns and Bear bursting apart like a pumpkin in the cab. You can't stop them in their remorselessness, and once they have set upon you, it is only a matter of time before they have finished devouring your career, your loved ones, your life, and you. They are going to keep destroying, keep shattering and wrecking and ruining until Isabel and I lie among the broken bodies of the dead.

Even before October 15 has come to an end, Smaug hears the first trickle of it from the campaign. The trickle fast becomes a brook—a babbling one. Newsweek has called them, and not long after that the San Francisco Chronicle, and then NBC. Everyone wants a comment on Louisa Shidler. The terrorist theory of the assassination has held up so far, but the media are looking for linkage to Louisa Shidler. And the rumor is that Newsweek will go with a cover story. Smaug stands by the window, looking out at the city spread before her.

The phone rings again, but she ignores it, lost in thought.

We are about to lose control of this, she realizes. A week for the allegations to boil up, and then two more weeks until the election. By then, will she be able to contain it, to distance the President from it? There is still plenty of time to lose. There is a noise by the door and she turns around.

"You look terrible," she says to Jill.

Jill, eyes downcast, stands in the doorway and stammers something.

"What? What is it?"

"The White House. It's the President."

She looks at the girl as though she were an idiot. "I don't have time for him now. Tell him . . . tell him I'm out, and get me Sauer."

She flips on the television.

"A new and bloody twist in the national manhunt for fugitive Louisa Shidler," says the newscaster, interrupting the late-night programming on the East Coast. "Law enforcement sources told NBC News tonight that a rural airfield near Wyoming's Yellowstone National Park was the scene of a murderous gunfight that left six policemen dead and Louisa Catherine Shidler once again at large. We go now to Jim Pearson, of affiliate KFCS in Cody, Wyoming. Jim?"

A storm-soaked TV news reporter stands outside the Cody Law Enforcement Center. "Tom, details are still uncertain, but this Wyoming town has suffered its bloodiest night in decades. It began earlier this afternoon. According to a statement released just minutes ago by the FBI, a Cody patrolman spotted Louisa Shidler in an Old West museum here in Cody this afternoon. The thirty-seven-year-old ex–trade deputy, who pled guilty to bribery charges, escaped from house arrest in Maryland last Sunday.

"Cody law enforcement officials made arrangements to hand her over to FBI agents flying in from Salt Lake City at the Yellowstone Regional Airport, east of Cody. A convoy of police cruisers waiting at the airport then apparently came under attack from a helicopter. Six men were killed, and Shidler escaped."

The newscaster interrupts. "Shidler formerly was Royall Stillwell's deputy, is that right, Jim?"

"That's right, Tom. Although an FBI spokesman said the events are coincidental, Shidler had been Royall Stillwell's deputy in the office of the U.S. Trade Representative. There is widespread speculation linking her escape to Tuesday's assassination of the ambassador and vice-presidential candidate."

"Jim, is there any word of where Shidler is now?"

"Tom, it's too early, and too confused out here to say much of anything for sure. There are all kinds of unsubstantiated rumors flying around. KFCS has learned, for example, that there may have been a truck involved in the attack, and fifteen minutes ago, the Cody Police Department issued an all-points bulletin for a tractor-trailer, white or silver in color, make and model unknown, tag unknown, thought to have left the airport at approximately eight P.M. Also, according to some accounts, which the police have not yet confirmed, Shidler may have been traveling with her daughter, twelve-year-old Isabel Higginson.

"Tom, all we know for certain is this: Six Wyoming police officers are dead tonight, and Louisa Shidler is gone again."

At this point the anchorman switches to one of his Washington correspondents for the White House reaction to these events.

The little girl has heard the muffled sounds, sounds familiar to her since the earliest days of childhood. When she hears the muffled sounds, she waits until dark and then slips softly down the stairs, clinging to the banister, pausing on the last tread to peer around the corner and across the room at the man who sits by himself at the kitchen table, one hand rubbing his temple. The little girl has learned to do this when Emily Shidler is sobbing in the bedroom. When Emily despairs, the girl goes to examine her father, to see if the hopelessness is there, too. She has never known what she will do if she sees it written there, on his face as well. She watches him as he sits at the kitchen table, serious but stoic, his brow furrowed. The vision fades.

Another. Professor Fitzgerald again, the bushy eyebrows going up and down, a look somewhere between exultation and frenzy on his face. *Lose everything, but not that; save wit, save heart, and you will reach home. He will.*

But you will not reach home. The rain will not wash out the blood; it will not wash out the tracks. The sun will rise and then the men in machines will come to finish their work. She is without cover; even darkness is not cover, and the darkness will fade.

Louisa's arms are draped across the log by the roadside, her body thrown forward like that of a supplicant, and the big man towers above her in the darkness. She sees the ax swing through the rain, and then watches it fall toward her. She flinches, her eyes squeezing shut. There is an explosion as the chain is severed.

Back in the cab, he roots through his toolbox and produces a hacksaw, then roots some more. "Pack of spare blades." He smiles with that look of a man finding something he only hoped would be in his toolbox. "You want to try, so I can drive? Or should I do it? You don't look so good."

Still shaking with the fear of that ax head, she cannot answer him. There has been altogether too much violence. Then there is a small hand in the darkness, reaching for the saw blades.

"I can do it." It is Isabel.

Sugaree heads south once more.

He coughs, once. She looks over at him, through the haze, unable to make out the road ahead. That pungency she smells is marijuana.

"Are you all right?"

"Yeah. Stoned is all."

"Can you drive?"

"Yeah."

She has been stroking his hand. She slips her fingers from it and brushes the hair away from his forehead.

"Why did you do it?"

"I was worried about you."

"I wish you hadn't."

He pulls on the joint. The smoke in the cab makes her eyes water. "They would have killed the two of us," she says. "Now it will be three they kill."

"Maybe not."

"Three dead, Bear. It would only have been two. Two is better than three."

"Depends which two," he says.

"No," she corrects. "Two is always better than three."

He tries to reassure her. "Things will look different in the morning."

"Will they?"

"They always do."

She takes his hand again, staring through the rain-splashed windshield into the darkness, wondering when they will come again. She cannot thank him, not after her mind's eye has placed him bleeding in the cab.

She is still awake, has been most of the night. He hands her the joint and she brings it to her mouth, pulls on it, watching its ash flare red in the darkness, and then fade. There is no talking between them, as they smoke the marijuana together. Then Louisa returns to Isabel on the pallet.

Better images come, gentler ones. John Shidler turns to look at his daughter peeking round the stair rail. "Your mother dwells on all we have lost," he says. "She counts up the things, one by one. That makes it harder. In the bad times, you have to remember what you have left. The things you have left are what will see you through."

Another image. She is standing by her father's side on the bluff by the river field. "Can't be in a hurry if you're going to farm," he says. "Can't think about where you'd rather be. Where you are takes all the concentration a person has." He turns and walks up the track toward the barn, little clouds of red dust rising around his boots.

Again in the kitchen. Her father's steadying gaze returns to the column of figures on the table, and little Louisa is climbing the stairs to her bedroom, because she knows that she can sleep now. Soft footsteps, climbing or descending? There is a sound, a comforting sound, like a child's soft footfalls on the treads. But it is a guitar, not a child, a guitar descending through the familiar chords of one of Bear's old chestnuts. "I lit out from Reno, I was trailed by forty hounds," the gentle voice sings. The tenor sings on, a song she recognizes: "Friend of the Devil." She looks in silence around her at the darkened shapes of the dry sink, the counter, the shelving, the piles of Bear's clothing. In the crook of her own arm, she strokes her child's silky hair. "I just might get some sleep, tonight . . ."

The Renoir woman pushes a lock of hair back from her forehead. In her mind, she spreads a clean sheet of paper on the table, and begins, slowly, deliberately, to sharpen the pencils, one by one. When that is finished, she brushes the little wooden shavings into a pile.

The light grows, away out over the plains in the east. John Shidler's daughter is imagining the little pile of shavings, and thinking of the things she has left. The rain has stopped falling. She sees a sign for I-25. The interchange is forty miles away.

"Bear, those dryers you have back in the trailer. They're in boxes, aren't they?"

CHAPTER 48

On October 17, Mac chooses his man with care. He needs a young businessman—someone on the make, someone looking for bragging rights, a score. He needs someone who buys trinkets from the Sharper Image and has the wheels on his BMW waxed.

It doesn't take long to find his mark, seated by the window in the departure lounge at Logan Airport, awaiting with the other passengers the boarding call for Flight 1215 to Los Angeles. His man wears an impeccable blue suit, tassle loafers, wire-rim glasses, a perfectly knotted tie. He's reading *Sports Illustrated*. He might be a young investment banker.

"Excuse me, friend, I've got a problem."

The young man's first look is defensive, of course. This is a man who learned at an even younger age to avoid panhandlers. Especially panhandlers in airports. But Mac is in gear, and the young man will be no match for him.

"I've got a first-class ticket on this flight, but I've just learned that my client is on his way to the airport to join me, and the dumb sonofabitch insists I take a seat next to him. In the back. Damned airline won't give me a refund, and the flight's been booked. So, anyway, if you've got a coach ticket, and fifty bucks, you can drink your way to California on me."

The young man, unable to believe his good fortune, stares up at the white-headed apparition. Mac's jaw works up and down. He shows the man his boarding pass. Sure enough, it is for seat 3B on American Airlines Flight 1215 to L.A., in the name of H. MacPherson.

The young man is smiling when he hands Mac his own boarding pass, for seat 20A, and then counts out fifty dollars.

In a few minutes they begin boarding the flight. As first class is called, the young man looks around, once, for MacPherson, to thank him. But he can't see him anywhere in the crush of passengers. He hands the attendant the pass and boards.

He needn't have troubled. MacPherson is already in the next terminal waiting by another gate, for Continental Flight 73. There he is in luck. They issue him a replacement ticket, and no one asks for identification. After a few minutes he boards.

An hour and a half later the passenger manifest is input into the American Airlines national database, and within two and a half hours of that, in a small office in suburban Maryland, a computer monitor is flashing.

"Looks like MacPherson's back," says a man in that office. "He bought a ticket this morning."

"Where to?" his companion asks.

"L.A. From Boston."

"Did he board?"

"That's affirmative. Henry MacPherson. Flying first-class, too."

Well, not quite. In fact, at that moment Henry MacPherson is sipping a bourbon in seat 14D of Continental Flight 73 to Salt Lake City.

Although it is early in the morning, the rank of tractor-trailer trucks is already long, and growing longer. Trucks roll to stop at the tail more rapidly than their predecessors head back toward the highway from the head. The men in the mirrored sunglasses and the shiny black boots flag them from the highway, one after the next. They come to rest and then the boots crunch across the road grit on the breakdown lane and the men in the mirrored sunglasses look up at the men in caps who roll down the driver's windows and who, most often, don't ask why, because they already know. They've all heard it on the radio.

Little knots of them gather by the throbbing fenders of the trucks, men with skinny butts and long narrow legs, and big bellies hanging over their jeans, wearing baseball caps and hunting vests and flannel shirts, looking over their shoulders to see how far up the line the state police troopers are.

"Sir, may I see your license and registration, please."

Seeing himself reflected in the sunglasses, Bear mutters something. He hands over the license, the other papers. The young trooper looks through them, hands them back.

"What you hauling?"

"Dryers."

"Got a waybill?"

Bear reaches into the little satchel he uses for the paperwork, produces the waybill, hands it down. The trooper—his name is Rivera—squints at the faint reproduction.

"Baltimore? Come from Baltimore?"

"Yeah."

"Going to Denver?"

"Yeah."

The mirrors face him again. "So what you doing up here?"

The nerves: Bear has absolutely no face for concealing them. "I came the northern way. Route 90." He tries to hold the face steady, but cannot. He sees it quiver in the mirrors, looks away.

"Step out of the truck, please, sir." Rivera climbs up and glances through the cab first, then has Bear go back and open up the trailer.

It is hot back there. Trooper Rivera looks at the cartons of clothes dryers stacked three high, three wide, and too many deep to count. He heaves a sigh and hauls himself up. He removes his hat and sunglasses, then takes an Exacto knife to the first carton, pulls a square of cardboard away, bangs his fist against the metal surface. He moves to the second box. He does the same. On to the third. The fourth.

Bear watches from the ground for as long as he can manage.

"You know," he says finally, "I'm going to have a little problem explaining all these ripped boxes to the company."

The trooper looks down from the darkness and says, "Tell them six police officers were murdered, in case they hadn't noticed."

Bear walks back to the side of the cab and leans up against the steps. He reaches into his breast pocket for his pill bottle.

Rivera paces down one side of the cargo, returns, goes along the other. Beads of sweat form on the end of his nose, drop plinking onto the aluminum floor of the airless cargo space. His palms grow wet; the sweat gets onto the Exacto knife. Damn, but that guy was nervous, he thinks. Nothing in here but clothes dryers? Why's he falling apart on me?

Rivera climbs to the top of the stack, shins around there and lies on his stomach, reaching down alongside the top rank of boxes. It's even hotter up there. He reaches down awkwardly, jams the knife in the cardboard. The blade has dulled a little. The knife slips, rakes across the back of his left hand.

"Son of a—"

A thin red line traces the path from between thumb and forefinger to the back of his wrist. A surface cut only. He climbs down. Holding his hand, he leaves the truck, goes back into the sunshine to find a cruiser with a first-aid kit.

The captain finds him as one of his companions finishes taping a bandage.

"What happened to you?"

"Dull blade is all."

The captain looks at the bandage. "You finished with that truck yet?"

"Almost."

"Hell, boy, this line ain't getting any shorter. Come on over here and look at this."

Three state troopers stand over Bear, their hands folded.

"What the hell's the matter with him?"

"One nervous truck driver, is alls I can say," the captain answers.

Bear is quivering. He looks like a man with a really bad flu, a man with the shakes. The worst of the attack has passed. He got his pills down all right and he's calmed himself, but he still looks terrible. He leans up against the truck.

"White as Casper the fucking ghost," says Rivera.

"Sir, are you all right?"

"Yeah," says Bear. "Yeah, I'm better. I have a nervous condition." He holds out the pill bottle.

Sure, Rivera thinks. Nervous condition. He changes the blade on his Exacto knife. "So what you got in the truck, Mr. Samuelson? You want to save us some time?"

Bear looks up at him, startled. Then he looks away.

"Suit yourself."

"Rivera," says the captain, "check the cab again."

The cab and condo are empty, but the two men search them carefully: the condo, the cupboards, the shelves. They poke through the ashtray and the pouches on the doors; they get on their knees and search under the seats and in the crate of Grateful Dead tapes, but they can find nothing. They do not find the extra bag of marijuana and rolling papers she made him throw out the window; they do not find the contents of the ashtray, nor the iron filings from the leg irons and the handcuffs, which she dumped out herself, and they do not find the traces of marijuana and ash which, for good measure, she broomed from the floor and seats after she made him pull Sugaree to the shoulder.

At about this time, a dusty pickup comes to a stop by the side of a lonely stretch of Wyoming state highway, about forty miles to the northwest. "I'll be goddamned," the driver says, looking in his rearview mirror at the object that gleams from the roadside. A moment later he's poking all around it, lifting the lid, peering inside. It's not just in good shape, it's straight-from-the-factory new. It's still got the plastic bag with the warranty in it taped to the back.

"I'll be goddamned," the man says again, after he hoists the brand-new clothes dryer into the bed of his pickup.

Rivera has cut into the seats, the overhead fabric, the pallet. He grows frustrated. He cuts under the seats. The minutes go by. After a while, he looks up and sees the captain's face in the cab window again.

"Rivera, what's going on?"

"Well, I ain't found it yet, but—"

"Rivera, I got fifty trucks out there."

"I scraped some marijuana residue out of the ashtray, and—"

"Rivera, you scraped *residue*? We're going to make a bust for possession of *residue of marijuana*? Fill out the forms, process him, have him arraigned, show up for a hearing to prosecute him for possession of less than a fly dump's worth of pot? I got fifty trucks lined up out here!"

"Sir, I—"

"Rivera, give Mr. Samuelson his license, wish him good day, and suggest that in future he not drive along the highways of Wyoming with a dime bag in his lap. Suggest that he keep the said dime bag hidden away so that he will not have time to chuck it out the window, so you, with your Exacto knife, will be able to find it before cutting your hands off."

"Sir—"

"Rivera—"

"You want me to give him a field sobriety test?"

"Rivera, goddammit, I want you to give him his license!"

"But, Captain, I haven't finished with the trailer."

"How many boxes you look in?"

"I dunno. I'd say about fifty, fifty or sixty."

"How many of 'em had clothes dryers in them?"

"All of them."

The captain turns to go.

"But, sir—"

"Rivera, look at that sonofabitch out there." The captain points through the window at Bear, who has recovered some of his color and stands fidgeting by the side of the truck. "Does he look like an assassin to you?"

Rivera does have a point, although neither of them will ever know it. There are twenty-nine boxes left to inspect, and only twenty-eight of them contain dryers.

CHAPTER 49

The man with the white hair and the dirty raincoat squints at the small American flag before opening the door of the Cody Law Enforcement Center. It flies at half-mast, snapping angrily in the chilly October wind.

"Cold out there," he says a moment later, as he pulls the door behind him.

"Be snow again, up in the mountains tonight," Patrolwoman Kipler answers. She smiles wanly. She wears a black armband.

"Terrible," Mac says, shaking his head. Nothing like this has ever happened in Cody. Six police officers lost: six sons, six brothers, four of them fathers. The town is in shock. On Main Street at any hour of the day, someone has stopped, arm on a neighbor's arm, commiserating. Later a historian at the university will say that not since 1903 has Cody lost so many men in a single day.

Mac introduces himself and asks to speak with someone about the shooting over at the airport yesterday.

"Well, Earl Simpson is our information officer, only he's not around right now."

"Let me talk to the captain then, could I?"

The new captain is in no mood to be interviewed, particularly on the day after Fred Quartarone's murder, and by a man he's never met, who says that he's from a Washington newspaper. He comes to the counter, stands by Patrolwoman Kipler's side, and says, "I'm sorry, sir, this is a confidential federal investigation, and I can't give you any information."

"Tell me one thing, just on background, Captain. How did you guys find her? This gal's from Maryland, and as far as anyone knew, had no contacts to this area. How did you manage to find her?"

"Up at the Buffalo Bill."

"The museum?"

"Yep."

"But—"

"Sir, that's where we found her. And that's the only comment I have."

"Wait, one more—"

The captain is stepping away.

"Just help me out, Captain, whom may I call in the FBI? Who's on the investigation, can you tell me?"

"Why don't you try Mr. Fitch's office. I have a number here."

"No, Captain, Mr. Fitch is the deputy director, he'll never take the call. Is there some agent, somebody on this investigation I can contact, you know? Just a name. Let me have a name and I'll call whomever."

The captain pauses on the threshold.

"Captain, six of your men are down. It's the worst day in the history of this department. And a few things about this case aren't adding up very well. Now, I can go and get the deputy director's canned story. I mean, I can get that. Or you can tell me who is really on this thing, and we can find out who or what killed your men. Give me a hand here. Please."

It's a pretty good speech, all things considered, but the climax is delivered to a swinging door, for the captain has left.

"What the hell is a fugitive doing at a museum, for Chrissake?" Mac shouts, but no one is listening.

Fifteen minutes later, Mac walks up the stone steps and through the door to the museum's lobby, where he buys an eight-dollar ticket.

"So you get a lot of folks through here on an average day?"

"Oh, yes," says Helen Kindle. "More in the summer, but still, it'll be quite busy through the fall."

"My name is Mac, Henry MacPherson," he says. "I'm press. I'm from the *Washington Herald*. I wanted to ask you a few questions, if I could. Were you here the other morning when they caught Louisa Shidler?"

She blanches, catches herself, and her hand strays to her mouth. "Ah, sir, they told us we shouldn't talk to the press. That we should direct any reporters to the FBI."

"I understand, Miss . . ."

A visitor appears, and Helen Kindle turns to take his ticket, leaving the blank unfilled. Then she sits resolutely behind the counter, staring away from the white-haired man whose lips are pursing in and out. "Sir, I'm sorry. They were very particular."

"Ma'am," he says, "I don't intend to quote you or anything. I'm just trying to kind of get a feel for it. You know how police reports are, very dry. I'm trying to get a sense for what it was like when the Cody police spotted her here. Did she put up a fight, try to run away? Had you recognized her?"

Behind Helen, Ginny St. Cloud looks up, surprised, then turns away warily. Her eyes look weary. Patrolman Scott Pates was one of the six killed. He and her Matty played together as boys and Scott's father had taken them on their first elk hunt. She wears an armband too.

Mac steps around the desk and shakes her hand, which feels stiff in response. Ginny avoids his eye. "I'm covering this for the *Washington Herald*. I was just wondering where it was that Cody policemen spotted Louisa Shidler."

Ginny looks away. "Mister, it's like Helen said. You go on and talk to the police." She sighs, and then leans down to hold her head in her hand, and begins to cry.

"What will it be, mister?"

The barmaid at the Irma Hotel's lounge looks impossibly young to him, a baby, a junior-high-schooler. Her brown hair is done in little ringlets, and the curls hang over pudgy cheeks, cheeks that belong to a girl in the cheerleading squad. On her finger is what looks like an engagement ring.

"Just a cup of coffee, please," Mac says.

"Not from around here?"

"No, miss. I guess I picked a bad day to be traveling through on business, too."

"Yeah, you did," she says. "You sure did. Awful day."

There are three men at the long bar. The big room is dark, the dining tables all empty. Except for the rattle of lunch cleanup in the kitchen, it is quiet in the Irma. Only a few patrons sit at the bar. One of them, a tall thin man, with dark hair and a receding chin, wearing a red shirt and tight blue jeans, sits at its far corner, nursing a glass of beer and smoking. His face is craggy, its expression largely hidden beneath a mustache. A couple of stools down from him, an older, shorter man, balding, in blue jeans and a denim jacket, sits before a mixed drink of some kind. "Terrible," he keeps saying, "just terrible." He keeps trying, unsuccessfully, to engage the man in the red shirt in conversation.

The barmaid brings Mac the coffee. "Did you know any of those men?"

She nods sadly. "Some, yeah. Larry Steiner was an awful nice guy."

"That guy Pates spotted them," Mac says.

She shakes her head. "I know a friend of his brother's real well. Their family is taking it awful bad."

"If he hadn't been so alert and spotted her up at the museum, none of this ever would have happened," Mac goes on. "They'd all be alive today."

"Yeah, that's right, that woman would have got away to Canada, people say. But you know, Scott was very serious about his work, and all. He was engaged to a real nice girl, too, Doreen Stalter. They were going to be married New Year's, I think. Was it New Year's, Donnie?"

The older man in the cowboy hat nods. "Yup. That's when they set it for. Terrible. I know her daddy real well too. She's brokenhearted, his little girl."

Then the man in the red shirt interrupts, irritated, and finally says something.

"What, excuse me?" Mac asks.

"Nobody didn't spot her," the man repeats.

"Oh, don't take no notice of him," says the barmaid.

But Mac looks down toward the end of the bar. "I don't follow you, friend," he says.

The man takes a long drag on his cigarette. He stares at the mirror behind the bar. "Nobody didn't spot her," he says again.

"Why do you want to go and say a thing like that, Alfred?" the barmaid demands, turning on him. "Scott Pates was a hero, and you go and—"

"Don't have nothing against Scott Pates," says Alfred, "but he didn't spot her, that's all. She turned herself in."

"What do you mean, she turned herself in?" Mac asks.

"She come up to Helen Kindle, asks her to call Cody PD, says she and her daughter want to turn themselves in. That's the way I heard it."

"Her daughter?" Mac asks.

The man nods.

Mac picks up the coffee cup, and steps toward the quiet man at the end of the bar. "Buy you another beer, friend?" he asks.

Later that afternoon, Henry MacPherson stands on the windswept grass, the west wind beating against his overcoat, the puckers and grimaces playing with particular force across his face. He stands by the hole in the airport's perimeter fence, staring through a camera's long lens at the agents clustered on the tar macadam. One of them is on his hands and knees, scraping something from the runway surface, it looks like. Behind him are a sheriff's deputy's car and two Cody patrol cars. Two more men are measuring something. In the waning light, Mac can't make much out. He sweeps the camera back and forth from the gash in the perimeter fence to the spot where the police officers are working. Once, as the frame passes by, he catches sight of a small black object in the grass. He points the lens back, hunting back and forth across the grass for a moment to find it again. And then it comes into view. He stares for a long time, pretty sure of what it is. And then he presses the shutter. Several times.

Before he leaves the highway shoulder, he makes a further mental note, studying the angle at which the direction of the object intersects the fence. He'd guess it at about sixty degrees, with the object at fifty yards or so away. He studies it carefully, for it will be impossible to find the object in darkness unless he knows exactly where to look.

"Agent Phillips?"

The phone rings just as Gene Phillips is pulling on his coat, about to leave the office. There's nothing like being pulled off a big case for freeing up time. "Yeah?"

"This is MacPherson."

"Christ." Phillips looks up quickly. Two guys are in the office, Bobby Picarro and Paul Robertson, both on the phone. Neither is paying attention. "Look," he says, quietly, "you need to turn yourself in to District police."

"Happy to talk to them, anytime," Mac says. "Just been a little busy lately."

"MacPherson, hang up the damn phone, or I'm going to trace this line."

"Trace it."

"You are wanted in connection with a murder investigation, MacPherson."

"You know that's bullshit, Gene."

"Hang up the phone!"

"Tap it, Gene. This call recorded?"

Phillips sighs, looks around again. "No. Not unless I want it to be."

"Well, Gene, hear me out for a minute."

"Save your breath. I'm off the case."

"What?"

"What I said. I've been reassigned."

"Christ. Off the case? What the hell for?"

Phillips doesn't answer, but sits back down, now, lays his briefcase on the desk. Mac takes a moment to think about it, and then says, "Gene, I think maybe you'd better hear me out anyway. I've talked to the Cody PD information officer and I have the press releases and so on and that's all very interesting. And I have the official story, that six Cody police officers were murdered when Louisa Shidler's accomplices intercepted her transfer to FBI agents, and she escaped. And that's a very interesting story too. It is also complete and utter and demonstrable bullshit. And it looks to me like the FBI must know it's bullshit. *You* must know it's bullshit. Okay? But it is interesting bullshit. Why the FBI is putting out this interesting bullshit is interesting to me. Hell, why they are reassigning you is also interesting. I am *goddamned* interested right now, Gene."

Phillips sighs. "I'm listening."

"Thank you. Now, the story is that an alert Cody police officer spotted her at the Buffalo Bill Historical Center, and that he and five of his buddies were killed when her accomplices swooped in to rescue her. Except, nobody found her at the museum, Gene. She turned herself in. So explain to me why she wanted to turn herself in?"

"Mac . . . Where the hell . . . You up there in Cody?" Phillips checks himself. "Don't answer that. Shit."

"All right, I won't. The other question I won't answer, because I can't, Gene, is this. Why does one conspirator turn herself into police custody so that her coconspirators will have to stage a military operation to set her free?"

If Phillips can answer the question, he doesn't. He has read the reports, which have Patrolman Scott Pates spotting Shidler at the museum while dropping in on a break to say hello to a woman named Virginia St. Cloud. The late Scott Pates, that is, who is unavailable for comment.

"Have you talked to the museum clerk?" Mac asks.

Still no answer from the FBI agent.

"Look, Gene, with all respect, fuck the reassignment. Why don't you call these people yourself?"

"Hmmm," Phillips grunts. After a moment he says, "MacPherson, remember our conversation about Shidler? When you said she made your top five list?"

"Yeah?"

"What did you mean by that?"

"Well, it began when she was a young reporter. She used to submit the damnedest expense account. You'd get the parking voucher and the mileage statement, and then there'd be all this differential calculus to work out some amount to deduct off of that. You know, she'd put in for eighty-seven percent of the mileage and ninety-two percent of the parking, or some goddamn thing. It drove the bookkeepers crazy, and finally the thing bounced up to me. I remember calling her into my office one day, and saying, 'Shidler, what in the Christ is this?' She says to me, 'Well, I ran in to get my cleaning that day on the way to my planning board meeting. And you know, it was four percent of the time that afternoon, so I knocked four percent off of the parking.' Honest to Christ. Now, Gene, you need to understand, junior reporters don't get paid dogshit, and a healthy flexing of the expense account as far as the damn thing will stretch is a constitutional right, as far as I'm concerned. In Vietnam, an expense account almost got me fired, before they figured out that they'd have to come the hell down there themselves to get me out of the bureau. But not Louisa Shidler. It's not in her nature."

Phillips does not tell this newspaper man what he is thinking. He does not mention his suspicions that someone had tapped Shidler's phone and recovered the tap just prior to his visit. He doesn't mention the reaction of the Stillwell campaign to the call from the car phone. He doesn't mention the tape from the Jackson County Sheriff's Department that remains in his desk drawer.

"Hmmm" is the only sound he makes. "Listen, I'm about to start a trace. So you better hang the damn thing up. And, MacPherson?"

"Yeah?"

"Keep in touch."

"I will. But, Gene, I've got a homework assignment for you. Got a pen?"

CHAPTER 50

When you were a kid, did you ever play in the big box that a washing machine or a dryer comes in? Victor Isselstine once made a fort out of one in his backyard and we played in it for almost a week. Until it rained. Well, Mother and I hid in one for a whole day. In the back of Sugaree, Bear's truck, which was about as hot as the inside of a real dryer, and we sat there, bouncing around in a box. Mother made us do it. It was dark and hot and I thought I'd go crazy. But sure enough, she was right, because they put Sugaree through a road block, and the state police tore apart the truck looking for us, and we sat and listened, just waiting for them to find us in the back. First we heard the door latch go, and then the door slide up, and then a little bit of light came into the box. We could hear a man scrambling around the boxes, and this zipping sound, which was his knife, opening them. I was really scared, but I guess he never got to ours. We sat there for a long time, and finally they shut the door and the truck was moving again.

I said, "Mother, can we at least get out of this box?"

She wouldn't let us, not till the truck stopped and Bear opened up the door and hollered up that it was all right to come out. What a strange day that was, when I think of it, my mother smoking grass and then hiding in a box. Oh, I forgot to tell that part. Mother, she and Bear smoked marijuana the night before. That's when we were driving south through Wyoming. They thought I was asleep, but I could see him hand her the joint, and I heard her cough. Pretty strange, like I said.

Well, Bear, he took us to Carter, New Mexico, where he lived, and he got Mother the motorcycle. I rode on the back, and both of us had helmets, so you couldn't tell who it was. The idea of Mother on a motorcycle? That's maybe the one thing about the whole business that if someone had said to me, like, your mother will ride a motorcycle from Carter, New Mexico, to Washington, I would have said, "As if." But she did.

Carter is this little spot on a map. I didn't ever see a town there, only desert, and some gas stations and two bars. Bear lives in an "Earthship"— that's what he calls his house. It's adobe made out of car tires built right into a hill out in the middle of the desert. It was kind of like a cave, a warm cave, with big thick walls. His wife, Becky, and their son, Travis, were home when we got there. They came out of the Earthship, and she didn't look too happy to see us get out of the truck. She stood with one hand on her hip and the other shielding her face from the sun and looked at him like he'd brought home a couple of stray dogs without permission, and she knew she'd be the one to walk them and feed them and clean up their poops. She didn't do much but nod at us. But they let us stay in the Earthship that night.

"Just some friends, Beck," Bear said. "They're passing through."

He went up to kiss her but she turned and just gave him a cheek to kiss.

"Where have you been, Bear?" she asked. "Just where have you been?" And before he could answer her, she was going on about Royall Stillwell being shot and him being out there on the road and did he even pay attention to what was going on in the world and did it occur to him just once, just once, mind you, to give her a call and let her know that he was all right and not facedown in a ditch somewhere having one of his attacks.

"Well," he said, "I don't guess the terrorists would have been after Sugaree, Beck." The way he said it made you think he was the last person on earth who would have been in that shootout in Wyoming.

"That's not the point!" she said. That wasn't the point at all and there he went again trying to change the subject from the point.

Mother and I, we'd been standing over by the truck, kind of exploring the sand with our toes, just making little circles in the sand with our toes and I was paying close attention to the scuff marks on my Reeboks. You didn't think anything at all was alive there, until you looked closely, and then there were these extremely interesting brown ants who were crawling around just below the ground.

Becky, she went on with Bear for a while longer, telling him that wasn't the point. I was listening for Becky to say what the point was, but she never did that I could hear. Some of it was a little snuffly, so I might have missed it. I snuck a peek at Bear. He had put his arms around her to give her a hug, and she turned her face away but I could tell she wanted that hug.

"Best not to get your line all snarled up with it, Beck," he said.

Their son, Travis, stood off to the side, watching this.

Becky kind of disappeared into his beard and his big arms, but she kept saying, he could have called and let her know he was okay. The vice president, he was shot dead by Shiite terrorists, and no one was safe, did he know that? Didn't he think she would be worried? And the price of oil would probably double and then where would Bear be? Where would they all be? Out of work is where and with no money saved and winter coming on.

"Well," he said, "I know they was talking about that on the radio, but I filled up in Pueblo, Beck, and diesel was still a buck twenty-two, like it was last week."

Well, she said, that wasn't the point. Because it was coming. It was going to be bad and it was coming soon. Why, this was the only thing on television night and day. Royall Stillwell shot in his own backyard by terrorists and the election not a month away. It was coming and Bear wasn't paying attention, she said, and this man shot in his own home, and Bear not even checking on *his* own home to see if they were all right. No, he was driving around with hitchhikers.

Mother and I shuddered just a little at the way she said "hitchhikers."

I looked up and Bear was kind of rocking Becky, like you do a child who's fallen down and is crying, and he said, again, "You know how you do when you get your line all snarled up."

This whole business with Bear and Becky outside the truck took a while. Mother and I couldn't do anything but try to shrink into the background, but to tell the truth, there wasn't a lot of background.

It was hot there, and the ground was all rocky and dry, nothing much growing that I could see, with only desert plants in front of the Earthship. There were some old tires out front, and barrels of trash, and it didn't look very tidy. The wind was blowing, and you'd get dust in your nose and eyes just standing around outside. I saw lizards on two of the tires, just sitting motionless on the tires in the sun.

Travis, he was thirteen, and he had a rattail. The rattail was extremely unflattering in my opinion, but of course I didn't say so.

"You like to hunt?" he asked me. He didn't say "Pleased to meet you" or "How do you do?" He just kind of turned sideways, not even looking at me, and said, "You like to hunt?"

We don't exactly do a lot of hunting in Bethesda. I shook my head no, and after that he didn't say too much more to me.

Finally, Becky went inside and Bear said to Mother, "It'll be okay."

"No," she said. "Bear, we've caused you too much trouble already. We should go."

He pulled at his beard a little, thinking about it. "Well," he said, "where do you figure on going?"

There wasn't any answer to that question. So we stood there for a while, kicking at the dust some more, like you do when it's time to leave, but no one is quite ready to make the first move. Then Bear got kind of a strange smile in his face, like a mischievous kind of grin, and said, "Follow me."

He had a little shed where he kept stuff. Mother always says, when she wants me to clean up, that you can tell a lot about someone by her closet. Well, the same is true of sheds, and what you could tell was that Bear wasn't the most organized man in the world. Also, that he never threw anything away. He had old shovels and rakes and stuff in there, and boxes full of *Mother Jones* magazines all yellow and curled, and pails gooped up with adobe, and trowels that he hadn't cleaned, and more pails that were half full of oil. Just sitting there. One of them had a dead mouse, where it had fallen into the oil. He cleared away a lot of rubbish and underneath was this old motorcycle, covered in dirt and old dead bugs and with cobwebs between the handlebars, and a post-hole digger lying across the seat. The seat was torn up and the foam rubber was orange and kind of burned-looking, it was so old. He had to wipe away the dirt on the gas tank so you could see where it said "Triumph."

"This is my bike," he said. "Haven't ridden her in a long time. Not since, well, you know—"

Mother kind of stood there in the doorway, squinting, with her arms folded up. I could tell she was thinking, "What does it have to do with me?"

So Bear, he knew what was on her mind, and he goes, "You said you've got to go back. How do you figure to get back to Washington?" Mother didn't say anything.

Bear fussed with the motorcycle for a while. He tried to pull it out and a roll of old rusty barbed wire fell off a shelf and started to unwind, and then some shovels fell down.

"You wait," he said. "You wait and see. She's a beauty!"

"Bear," Mother said, "I've never been on one of those things."

He got the bike out of the shed, and Becky came outside and stood there with her hands on her hips, scowling at it. Just the sight of that motorcycle got right to her, you could tell. I think she didn't know whether to get on him, scold him for fussing with it instead of coming inside when he's been gone for a week, or whether she was thinking, "Hey, maybe he'll finally get rid of that motorcycle which has been driving me crazy taking up space in my shed for fifteen years."

So she turned and stomped off to the house, and I watched her go. Bear smiled at me, and said, "Becky doesn't like surprises. She'll mellow out, though." He winked at me, and then he got a hose out, and rinsed the bike off. The water came out kind of brownish. They didn't have much pressure out there, but it still helped. Then Travis and him wiped it down with rags, and it didn't look quite so bad anymore, only the chrome was old and had rust all over it.

"Got some gas in here somewhere," he said from inside the shed, and we could hear him scraping around in there. Then he came out with an old gas can that didn't look too much better than the motorcycle.

He walked around the bike with Mother a few times. "Here's your starter," he was saying. "Here's your brakes. Here's your gearshift," stuff like that.

And Mother, she goes, "Where's reverse?"

Bear looked at me and said, "I guess this isn't going to be easy."

He had her ride it around the back of the place, down this dirt road, and then turn and come back. We stood and watched her. "You got to lean!" he'd yell when she got to the turn. "You got to lean!" But she didn't lean, like you're supposed to, when she made a turn. Instead she sat upright and very prim-looking too. She looked like Mary Poppins on a bicycle. Bear, he just shook his head and said, "Isabel, you better get on there with her, and when she turns, lean, okay?"

So I did the leaning.

When she had learned to ride up and down the dirt track well enough, she tried the road. She went down a ways until she went out of sight around a bend.

"She's a biker now," Bear said.

The day we set off back east was a Saturday. It had been a pretty uncomfortable two days in the Earthship, especially that last Friday night. Travis, he didn't pay too much attention to me. Bear was kind of busy with one thing and another, the motorcycle mainly, and also he scrounged up helmets from somewhere. But Becky just sat in front of her television set in the living room, like she wasn't going to leave that TV until we were gone. Once in a while she'd say, "Bear, come on in here and look at this." It was all about the assassination, the assassination. Bear would say, "Now,

Becky, there's nothing we can do about it, nothing the television can do about it either."

All the Earthship's rooms had a window on one side, which got plenty of sun in the daytime. But all their backs had none. It was like a cave. In the living room they had some Navajo rugs on the floor, a few lamps, three stuffed chairs, and an old couch with a crate in front of it to put your feet on. It was all stuff that didn't go together very well, but it was cozy and warm.

Becky was in a big red chair with her knees drawn up and her arms around them, and Mother and I were at the back of the room on the couch, kind of sitting stiffly and afraid to put our feet or hands on anything the way you are when you go to a house in Chevy Chase, or where the people don't have kids. Not that the house was neat, far from it. It was just that we were sure whatever we touched would be wrong. And maybe also that we both had the sense Becky was working up to something.

On the television, they were having one of those shows where the newspeople sit around in a circle and argue with each other. In my opinion, besides being boring, those shows are like four kids eating ice cream out of one bowl. Everybody grabbing and making a mess of it and pretty soon it's all on their faces and they're all yelling at each other.

The first one was saying it didn't add up, that Shiite terrorists never acted this way, secretly assassinating someone. He was saying they always planted bombs in public places: schools, buses, marketplaces. Didn't people remember the World Trade Center, and Tel Aviv, and Beirut? Pan Am 107? And then the other one cut him off and was demanding, Did he doubt the CIA report that the men shot and killed outside Mexico City were from the Guardians of Allah? Did he doubt it, yes or no? And then the first man would say, he just wanted some questions answered. Then the other would go, "Yes or no, just yes or no!" Pretty soon the others would all jump in, and said the first man probably thought Kennedy *was* killed from the grassy knoll and Jimmy Hoffa was alive and a lot of other stuff I didn't quite follow. And then they were all yelling at each other.

"They shouldn't all interrupt like that," I said.

Nobody answered me. Bear and Travis were out back, and Mother and Becky were glued to the television.

Later that night, after the show was over, the TV was kind of doing the same news for the hundredth time, showing the same television footage. Becky turned to Mother and blurted out, "Where are you from, anyway, Patsy?"

Mother and Bear had given her name as Patsy that first day. They didn't make up a name for me, though. I was still Isabel.

"We're from back east," Mother answered.

"*Where* back east?"

It was real quiet then. "I'd rather not say," Mother answered, after thinking about it a little.

"Well, what are you doing running around the country with your little girl?"

I was squirming, wanting to get out of there. Mother didn't answer right away. She looked away, and said, softly, "It has to do with my husband. My ex-husband, anyway."

Mother!, I thought. I'd never heard such lying.

Then Becky turned red, and looked away, not embarrassed red, but upset red, like you are when you want to be incredibly mad but instead you almost cry. "Is there something you and Bear should be telling me?"

Mother went, "What?" I think she didn't get it as soon as I did. Becky had her arms folded and she turned to the window, waiting for an answer.

"Something I should be . . . ?" Then Mother got it, and looked at me, like, what do I do about this? I shrugged.

"No, no, Becky," she said. "There is nothing like that. Nothing like that. I was a hitchhiker, and my daughter and I are in some trouble, and he helped. That's all. Oh, dear."

Becky let it go there, and pretty soon Mother and I went off to bed. You knew that, for each of them, the morning couldn't come fast enough.

When it did, the television was on again. That was Saturday, the day of the funeral of Royall Stillwell. The television pictures were of crowds in Washington, and soldiers. There was a team of black horses drawing a caisson with his casket. The casket had an American flag on it. One horse walked without a rider, and had a boot in one stirrup, backwards. And drums. Just drums and kind of a low buzz along the avenue, and crowds. It looked gray there, and sure enough it began to rain as the caisson was going down Pennsylvania Avenue, and then the crowd alongside Pennsylvania was just a black sea of umbrellas.

"Do you want to watch this?" Bear asked Mother.

"No," Mother said. "No thank you. We have to go." I was surprised. You know, Mother had worked for him and all, and with everything that had happened. Still, she said, "Becky, thank you very much for your kindness. I'm sorry for all the trouble we've been."

Becky mumbled something, not looking away from the TV.

"Sure you don't want to watch this?" Bear asked.

"No," she said. "No, we've stayed much too long already, and we have a long way to go."

We stood by the bike in the yard and she said, "Bear, I'll never forget this, and you'll be paid back every penny."

And he smiled and slipped her something and said, "I know." Becky was standing over by the house with her hands on her hips again, so I said, "Mother, we'd better go." She shook his hand very formally, like it was a business meeting, but you could kind of tell in her eyes she had kind of a soft spot for him. And I gave him a hug and he picked me up off the ground like I was nothing.

When we'd gone down the road a ways I asked her what it was he had given her. You had to shout to be heard and with the helmets and all. I had my hands around her waist and I asked, "What did he give you?" And she said, "What?" And so I shouted it, and she said, "What?" again, and I thought, Oh brother, this is going to be a long ride.

Anyway, it was a bank card. He gave us his bank card, so we wouldn't get caught trying to use the one she had. He could always tell Becky he'd lost it, because she'd believe that. "You'll pay me back," he told Mother when he gave it to her, before she could even say anything.

I guess he'd gotten to know her pretty well.

And so we rode east, Mother and me, with our big motorcycle helmets on so no one could tell who it was. I swear that every time I'd pull that stupid helmet over my ears, I'd see the pictures from the TV again. Right in the visor, I'd see that gray rain, all those soldiers on that dark day, the big wagon wheels rolling and clattering down the asphalt, and that black horse with no rider and the boot stuck backwards in the stirrup. And the raindrops popping up off the flag, and all those silent people by the side of Pennsylvania Avenue. I kept seeing it and seeing it. The thing of it was, we left New Mexico on a clear sunny day. I kept thinking, that's where we're going; we should have been running in the opposite direction, and that was where we were heading, like it was a great big gray magnet and we were a couple of puny filings being sucked right into it. Me and Mother, on an old motorcycle that she couldn't even ride around a turn properly.

We stayed mainly on the state roads, not the big highways, but not tiny roads either. We rode east to Oklahoma City. Personally, I couldn't understand that place. You ride along forever through nothing, and then all of a sudden, suburbs, and then, this city, and then suburbs, and then nothing again, and you think, Why? Why put a city there at all? I couldn't understand it. God, Oklahoma was a long day. Memphis, we rode through Memphis, and stayed at a motel in Tennessee. We rode through the Smoky Mountains into Virginia, and then we rode all night to get to

Washington, and we got there on Tuesday just as the sun was rising, with the whole city peaceful.

And as for motorcycles, I know a lot of girls think they're sexy, but you can take all the motorcycles in the world and drive them to the crusher and make tin cans out of them, as far as I'm concerned. Boy, did our butts ache after a ten-hour day on that thing. We couldn't stand up straight, we kind of scuttled like old people who've lost their walkers.

I remember the motel we stayed at in Oklahoma. I kept having bad dreams and waking up, and I tossed around a little bit, and then I looked up and saw she was sitting on her bed. It was still made, and she was sitting there looking at me.

"Mother," I told her, "you need to sleep."

She didn't say anything, just sat there staring.

"Here," I said, "you can snuggle in with me."

And she climbed into my bed and snuggled up to me like a little child.

CHAPTER 51

The things she has left, Louisa knows she should count the things she has left. She is in a motel room near Brownsville, Tennessee, whose ugliness seems too aggressive to be an accident, whose orange bedspreads, and bright green carpeting, and garish veneer, and print of a forest glen at midnight, must surely emanate from a conscious desire to war with beauty, to ruin it outright. From the lamp comes barely any light at all. Even the sounds are ugly, the hacking, mindless laugh track from the television, the passing roar of trucks on the highway.

She sits at the desk beneath the pale light of the lamp and opens her wallet. What has she left, in this oasis where even the water is sulfurous? Not Samantha Snow's card—a machine ate that somewhere. Bear's card, she has that left. Bear's card, which has paid for the motel rooms and the hamburgers and, where they can find them, the pieces of fruit. And which has paid for her ad in the personals, the ad she's been calling in to Washington daily.

Another burst of canned laughter, and she looks over at Isabel.

"You want me to turn it down?"

Louisa shakes her head, turns back to the desk. She still has her driver's license. Isabel's health-plan card. Her own. Isabel's picture, returned to her by Bear. Toby's. Her membership cards—video rental, American Bar Association, Bethesda Public Library. Credit cards, all canceled. More laughter from the television. Frequent-flyer cards. Still more. Perhaps the audience has seen her wallet and is having a good roaring Hollywood howl. A canned howl, just like the canned politics and the pervasive canning of everything else in this country.

A deck of little plastic playing cards and a few photographs under a dim hotel light. This is your life, playing cards, and . . .

There is another burst from the television—surely the laugh track of American television would make a cruel psychological weapon—and just then the white rectangle flutters out of a leather slot, and falls to the desktop, face up.

FRANCIS J. IANELLA
LIAISON OFFICER

UNITED STATES DEPARTMENT OF COMMERCE

say the printed letters. Except he's not the liaison officer anymore. He scratched it out and was promoted, wasn't he? There it is, "Deputy Sec'y," blue ink scribbled while the loudspeakers pounded and thumped in the Willard ballroom and she just wanted him to take his cloud and go away. My card, Louisa. Frank's own cursive to prove his worth. Deputy Secretary Frank, Commerce Secretary Peter Coburn's Deputy Dog. And Royall's. And I've carried his calling card all over hell and gone. I didn't have one to give back. No promotions recently, or ever, now.

Deputy secretary. But not secretary exactly—he wrote "Sec'y." She holds the card closer to the bulb, stares at the four letters and that odd curlicue of an apostrophe. There is not enough light. She goes to the bathroom, holds the card up against the flickering fluorescent bulb over the sink. She climbs onto the counter, to gather all of the wretched light she can. Now she is standing on the counter, straddling the sink, holding the card up to the bulb. She must have more light. Again from the other room comes a pulse of laughter from the television, which then rises to a mindless crescendo. Except now it could be the full throated bray of ten thousand televisions, and Louisa Shidler, standing on a countertop in a wretched motel bathroom, would not hear it.

"Oh, my God," she says. Her eyes are riveted to the card. Then, "Isabel?"

From the bedroom there is only the television noise.

Later that night, long after she has pulled the envelope from Buster's punctured abdomen, when at last the television is quiet and the room is dark, and the rise and fall of breath tells Louisa that Isabel is sleeping in the other bed, Louisa holds her knees close to her chest, and cries. Was she wrong, was she hasty and wrong again? She sees Royall as he was that last day, in his study, that last time they were together, sees the sadness etched in his face, and hears him say those strange words: *Louisa, I've been looking, and I can't find the solution.*

CHAPTER 52

As we went farther east, Mother became more and more like the old Mother. She'd plan each day's ride: plan the rest stops and the lunch stops and the routes, and then she'd stick to the plan. I'd watch her making little notes on the map.

I asked her could we call Dad, at least, but she said no. She was very particular about it. We couldn't call anybody we knew, because they would have all the phones tapped. It made me cry, that we couldn't even call Dad. And I even threw kind of a tiny tantrum, because a little part of me was thinking she just wouldn't call him because of, well, the problems they had together. But that was extremely inappropriate of me. Because I knew that Mother was right, really.

Somewhere in Tennessee I think it was we stopped for gas, and the man said, "Y'all here for the convention?"

There was a bikers' convention out at a fair grounds, and they were riding east to the Smokies, hundreds of old motorcycle guys and motorcycle mamas. We went to take a look. Mother thought it might be good to fall in with them as far as we could, that it would help us keep inconspicuous. They were kind of funny-looking, with all their leather and their funny little helmets. The men, when they got off their bikes, were shorter than the women, and the men all had potbellies, mostly. And beards. The women were just big all over.

We got to talking to some of them. They didn't think much of our Triumph. Or of me either. One of them said, "Shouldn't she be in school?"

"This is a special project for her," Mother said. "She writes about it in her journal."

We rode with a bunch of them toward Pittsburgh, until we had to turn east. They liked to ride up alongside you, two motorcycles abreast in the lane, but it made Mother nervous. When we got to Knoxville, we split up. They were headed east to North Carolina, and we had to ride northeast to Virginia. We stopped in a gas station in Kingsport, Tennessee. Just before we climbed back on the motorcycle, I said to her, "Mother, you lied to those people about me having a school project!"

She was real thoughtful about it. "Isabel, when this is all over, will you make sure that this lying doesn't become a habit for me?"

I was quite proud the way she asked me that, as if she needed a favor and nobody but me could do it for her. I said, "Yes, Mother, but when will this be over?"

"Well, I don't know," she answered. Then she pulled down the visor on her helmet and started the motorcycle.

CHAPTER 53

Tuesday, October 22, brings proof that the Crab was right: even Smaug, with all her spinning, all her back-channel connections, cannot control the gusting winds of the popular press. The press is all over the story now, and there is Renoir's model, frowning grainily from the cover of *Newsweek* in every newsstand across America, wearing an uncharacteristic expression that a photographer captured in a tense moment during a conference in Brussels. Emblazoned in black across her chest is the question:

Have You Seen This Woman?

In Washington, D.C., a vendor on Twelfth Street reaches into his dirty green smock for change. He hands the coins and the magazine to a woman wearing large sunglasses. As she walks away, his narrowed eyes follow her. He strokes the coarse stubble on his chin. There's something familiar about her, he thinks, before turning to the next customer.

Discipline, discipline. From the road, she has placed a variant of the ad in the *Herald* each day since leaving Carter. She will do it again, before letting herself read the article. Finding a phone booth, she uses Bear's credit card once more and calls it in. The ad will run in the morning, she is assured.

Much-sought-after gal soon to be DWF seeks union with old newshound. I'm a stationary sort of gal. How about lunch today? Ref. 8873.

The air is crisp. It is a bright, mid-autumn day in Washington, with a bit of a breeze, and little puffs of cloud scudding across the sky. Louisa

Shidler has returned to the place where her troubles began, and she walks briskly through the throngs, her pace nervous and brisk, her expression hardened. She has folded the magazine with its back page out, and strides with it toward the Mall. Seeing it on the newsstand was a shock, and she had to struggle to keep herself in check.

She finds an empty bench under the rank of sycamores on the Mall, feeling some security in the crowds of tourists who pass innocently by. She begins the story.

> For as many as seven years, Louisa Catherine Shidler may have led the ultimate double life: Washington bureaucrat by day, conduit for foreign bribes by night. This week, she escaped in a bloody airport shootout in the Wyoming mountains. And then there is the matter of the assassination. Law enforcement officials claim the double assassination last Tuesday of Ambassador Royall Stillwell and Secret Service Agent Thomas Molloy was the work of a shadowy splinter group of radical Shiite Muslims, and deny any connection between the assassination and Stillwell's former trade deputy. Still, too many questions remain unanswered. Among them: did a mere deputy receive the biggest bribe in history without the Trade Representative's knowledge? If so, how? Is her escape related to his assassination? And as the nation searches for the 37-year-old mother from Bethesda, everyone who has ever known her is also asking the question, "Who is Louisa Shidler?"

"Michael!" calls a woman's voice. "Wait!"

Louisa looks up from her reading. A determined four-year-old is dashing up the path, while an anxious young woman pushing a stroller behind hurries to catch up.

"Michael!"

Michael catches sight of Louisa, and veers toward her with a fierce expression on his little face. "Pow!" he shouts, karate kicking the air in front of her.

"Michael! Stop that at once!"

Michael clenches his teeth and issues little explosive sound effects as his red sneakers and busy hands rain karate chops and kicks on the air in front of Louisa. His mother, rushing up behind, saves Louisa from further mayhem by seizing his arm.

"Michael!"

"White Ranger!" shouts Michael.

"Michael, you stop that at once! Stop it! You apologize to this lady!" The woman looks up at Louisa helplessly. "I'm so sorry."

"White—"

"Stop it!"

"It's okay," Louisa smiles. "Nice to meet you, Michael," she says, extending her hand.

"I'm not Michael!"

"Shake the lady's hand, Michael!"

"I'm the White Ranger!"

"Michael, honestly!"

Michael eyes the hand with suspicion, uncertain whether to karate-chop it.

"I'm so sorry," his mother says.

"Who are you?" demands Michael.

"Loui—" she starts, and then, flustered, cuts herself off.

"Excuse me?" the mother asks.

"Lou," she says. "They call me Lou. How old, how old is the baby?" She turns to the carriage.

"Oh," says the young woman, "she's only six months next week."

"She's beautiful," says Louisa. They look down into the stroller, where the baby lies wrapped in a yellow blanket with the perfect calm of an infant in sleep, hair as fine as cornsilk falling from beneath a little stocking cap. You'd never guess she was kin to her fearsome brother.

"Thanks."

"How peacefully she sleeps."

"She hasn't discovered the Power Rangers yet," the mother answers. She turns suddenly. "Michael!"

While Louisa has been looking down at the baby, Michael has gotten hold of the magazine from the park bench.

"I can read!" he says, holding it up.

"I'm so sorry, Louise."

"Lou," Louisa corrects.

"Michael, would you please stop that and give Lou her magazine back!"

"I can read!" Michael proclaims again. He holds the magazine out, unfolded. Louisa's photograph stares out from beneath his chin.

"Once upon a time," Michael begins.

"Honestly—"

"There was a White Ranger and a Megazord, and—"

"Michael!"

"The Megazord said he would blow up the whole world if someone didn't—"

"Michael, give that magazine here at once!"

"Give him a ten thousand million and fifty hundred dollars. And the good—"

Michael's mother snatches the magazine from him, and in the confusion the cover rips off in her hand. She fetches the boy a paddle to the backside before recovering the rest of the magazine.

"Lou, I'm so sorry, I'm so embarrassed, I don't know what I can say. Michael, we are going to go straight back to Gammy's! We are *not* going to see the rocket ships!"

"Mommy!"

"It's all right," Louisa is saying.

"Please, let me pay you for the magazine. I—"

"Mommy!"

"No, really—"

The young mother hands Louisa the magazine and its cover separately. As the cover passes from her hand, the woman's eyes fall across it. She looks up at Louisa. The little syllable "Oh!" slips out, involuntarily.

Louisa takes the magazine. "Funny coincidence, isn't it?" she says.

"Yes. Yes. I'm, I'm sorry we've disturbed you. I'm . . . Michael. Come along!" The woman grabs her son's hand, and pushes the stroller quickly down the path.

Six minutes later, when the park policeman comes to the bench, Louisa and the magazine are gone.

It is early evening when she places the next call. All day Louisa has been starting, turning suddenly, jumping at noises, sure at any moment that she has been discovered. She has one errand to run, and then spends the balance of the afternoon in the Smithsonian, craving the anonymity of the tourist, lingering in the darker corners of the museum's exhibits. As evening comes on and the city's office workers begin to stream onto the avenues, she finds a phone booth. Outside, men and women in suits hurry by to the Metro station.

"Law offices," says the receptionist.

"Joel Krasnowicz, please."

"Please hold."

He picks up a moment later.

"Mr. Krasnowicz, this is Louisa Shidler," she says.

"My God," the lawyer answers. He steps over to close his office door, and then returns to the telephone. "Where are you?"

"Do you really want me to answer that?"

A pause. "No. Not yet."

She answers anyway. "I've just come from the hairdresser's."

"Excuse me?"

"I was a redhead for a while. Now I've gone brunette again. A curly thing, you know, a Nashville look to hide the face of *Newsweek*'s cover girl."

"Louisa, what is going on with you?"

"I'm not sure you'd believe me. I'm not sure I'd believe me. Why don't we start with what you've heard?"

"Me? Two counts of escape, six counts of murder of a police officer, kidnapping—"

"Kidnapping?"

"Yeah. You are wanted for kidnapping Isabel."

"That's . . . well, I almost said that was surprising. But nothing is surprising anymore. All right, I understand."

"Listen, Louisa, you want some advice?"

"As long as it doesn't cost me five thousand dollars, Mr. Krasnowicz."

"Turn yourself in. Walk into the nearest police station and turn yourself in."

"Thanks for the advice. Let me ask you something. Is it possible that your phone is tapped?"

"Why would it be tapped?"

"Because you are the attorney for a missing woman who is wanted for all of these terrible things. Can they do that?"

"No. This phone is not tapped."

"I cannot believe you. Please do this. Walk immediately to the corner of Twelfth and E. There is a phone box there. Immediately."

Louisa is betting that Joel Krasnowicz was wrong about his telephone. Belts, she thinks, belts and suspenders.

Fifteen minutes later, Krasnowicz, the telephone cradled on his shoulder, stands nervously by the phone box outside a bar called Vincent's, looking up and down Twelfth Street. He listens carefully, tells her what he knows about developments since her departure. It is not much.

He has trouble making out her voice. She is calling from a noisy place. There is rockabilly music in the background and she keeps her voice up. The call ends promptly. As Joel Krasnowicz turns to walk back to his office, the door of Vincent's opens and two young couples burst, laughing, onto the street, music spilling out with them. It is the music that stops Krasnowicz in his tracks. It fades quickly away as the door swings to.

Krasnowicz goes to the bar's entrance. When he opens it, he hears the music again. Rockabilly.

Pushing his way past the crowds to one corner of the room, he finds the pay phone. It is on the back wall, about six feet from a window that looks out on the phone box where, a moment ago, Krasnowicz stood.

It is crowded and noisy in the bar. Krasnowicz scans the crowd briefly, doesn't notice her. But perhaps it is better not to know. That is what he is thinking as he turns abruptly to leave. A heavyset man with bad acne enters the bar, shouldering his way past Krasnowicz in the doorway.

"Excuse me," Krasnowicz says as he squeezes past. The man doesn't answer.

Louisa sees Steeves in the instant she emerges from the ladies' room: the man who stood in the helicopter doorway with an automatic weapon, the one who made Isabel scream. He stands near the bouncer about twenty-five feet away, craning his neck around the room, searching for the woman with the Nashville hair. Louisa threw out the line about the hair as a red herring, of course; she has spent the early afternoon having her hair close-cropped and dyed blond. But she had no idea this would happen so fast.

Louisa moves swiftly away, scanning the back of the room for another entrance. There is none. Squeezing between two men at the bar, she turns her back to the doorway. In a moment she sneaks a glance. Steeves has moved about ten paces from the door. She looks again around her, at the bargirl, at the crowd. There is a whoop as a large party moves to the dance floor.

The noise is loud, too loud. She can feel the man behind her, nearby. She smiles nervously, catches the bartender's eye, orders a drink.

That is when she notices the young man sitting alone at the end of the bar. He wears the Washington uniform: white shirt, yellow silk tie, blue suit, well-shined tassel loafers, tortoiseshell glasses. Louisa would put his age at somewhere in the late twenties. He is sipping a beer and staring up at the television. You've seen him before, the young man at the suburban health club, with the neatly trimmed hair and the unlined face. You've noticed his endless fascination with the mirrors there. He's the one who wears tank tops and brown weightlifter's belts and drowns like Narcissus in a mirrored pool of his own biceps, and then dons his blue suit and yellow silk tie to return to the law firm or the consulting firm or the whatever. Not exactly Louisa's type.

His name is Bill Friedman, and it happens that he is in a Vincent's phase. Since joining Ernst & Young some three years ago, his life has taken on a regular pattern, and this phase is a part of it. For six months or so, he lives with his girlfriend, Kelly, a paralegal at a big Washington law firm. At some point, the subject of marriage comes up, and Kelly announces that she sees no point in prolonging a relationship with no future. Either he is in this relationship or he isn't. The conversation grows heated; she trips him up in argument and throws him out.

After expulsion, the Vincent's phase begins. Friedman spends his evenings there, scouting for new prospects. The Vincent's phase usually is short: he has little luck, crawls back and begs forgiveness, and Kelly yields.

"Don't mope around wanting sex from me and then, and then tell me you need *space*!" Kelly said to him two days ago, on the occasion of her most recent ultimatum. "*Space!* That's such bullshit! You want space, go to Mars and leave me alone!"

He cannot manage Mars. But at six-fifteen on this Wednesday evening, Friedman has taken up his post at the end of the bar at Vincent's. He is pretending to watch the football game on the television when the strange woman with the short blond hair is suddenly at his side.

"Hi," she says.

"Hi."

"I've been watching you."

"Really?" he answers. He studies her. Her hair is dyed an unnatural blond color, but her face is kind of pretty. Familiar, somehow. She seems older.

"Yes. I have. And I want to get to know you. I really want to get to know you. What's your name?"

She is looking him straight in the eyes. This seems a little odd; *she* seems a little odd. And this kind of thing never happens to him. But hey! "Bill. Bill Friedman. What's yours?"

"Patsy."

"Patsy what?"

"Just Patsy," she says, touching him on the arm, coming closer to him. "You have beautiful eyes, Bill Friedman. Has anyone told you that?"

Her face is very close to his as he stammers, "Not recently."

"Well, it's true."

"Thank you."

She smiles at him. "You're supposed to compliment *me*, now, Bill Friedman."

"Oh, yeah. You have, you have a nice smile."

"Thank you."

"You look kind of familiar somehow. Have we met?"

"No, I don't think so."

"Sure?"

"Bill, did you take Fine Arts 101?"

"Sorry?"

"College, Bill, college. Take the Fine Arts survey course? Look at the Impressionists?"

"Yeah . . . sure . . ."

"That's why I look familiar."

"I see," he says, but doesn't really.

"Some people think I resemble Renoir's favorite model," she says. "Do you know Renoir?"

"He was a painter, right?"

She smiles. "Only as a boy. As a man, he was an artist."

Poor Bill Friedman doesn't know what to think about that, and has the vague sense that he missed both halves of a double entendre. Nor does he know what to do about the fact that now she has gotten close to him, uncomfortably close, and is pinning his eyes with her own. "I think this introduction is going rather well, don't you?" she says.

Bewildered, the young man answers her smile. They begin to converse, and she wraps her forearm around his.

This woman is coming on to me, thinks Bill Friedman with the beautiful eyes. The thing to do is to be cool about it.

The pair remains at the bar as the crowd thickens around them. Louisa does not look up from the beautiful eyes of Bill Friedman for almost an hour. The noise has grown, thankfully, and the crowd has thickened behind and alongside them. When at last she casts a quick glance over her shoulder, she can no longer see the man with acne.

Belts, she thinks, belts and suspenders.

Belts and suspenders, yes, but she has been through two very near misses, in this her first day back in the capital, and she has nowhere to go

to ground. They have all the bases covered. Within hours of the encounter with little Michael on the Mall, even Krasnowicz's phone was
tapped. That means they have her office acquaintances staked out, the
family, Toby, you name it. Isabel, have they found Isabel? She doesn't dare
think of it. The man with acne is gone, but she knows that he has not
gone far.

Over the din of the bar, which grows ever louder, her animated young
beau is in the middle of a story. She nods, although at this point Louisa is
planning, not listening.

It is a simple enough plan. But she decides she'd better have another
drink. For Toby—unbidden, undeserving, undesirous Toby—intrudes on
her consciousness. She finds that though he has no logical hold on her any
longer, what she now faces is frightening to her, even with this inane
young man. Fidelity has been a refuge for her, and emotionally it is hard
to leave that refuge. For Toby has remained a habit long after he has ceased
being a companion. She tries to concentrate on Bill Friedman, smiling to
encourage him as he continues to prattle on about some inane thing or
other. The drink should help a little, she thinks.

Night has fallen in the desert, and a cold wind blows from the west, so
that Bear puts a jacket on before going outside to get a few sticks for the
woodstove, and thinks, as he does every year, it shouldn't be getting this
cold at night already.

He is back in the kitchen when Becky says, "Bear, come and look at
this."

It is the television again. Over the past week, Bear has grown a little
testy about this obsession she has. He went off for a short haul to Albuquerque and came back the next night, and it was as though she hadn't
moved from the red chair. Maybe she hadn't. She had watched every program she could find on the networks or CNN, the running and rerunning
of the funeral, the endless breathless updates on the murder investigation,
the analysis of its effect on the election, on Middle East politics, on oil, on
Congress, on the economy, on national defense, on the media, on the life
cycle of the three-toed sloth.

Washington can be forgiven for losing its bearings a little. It is decades
since the capital has had to deal with so confusing and urgent a series of
events. Even the mechanisms of government have staggered. Every committee chair in the Congress, it seems, has called for an investigation of
something. The FBI and CIA are quarrelling bitterly and, indeed, openly
over jurisdiction. The Joint Chiefs have each arm of the services on alert.

Statements from President Breed call for calm, but the President himself has retreated to his basement, there to carry out his campaign via television. His brave words on the day of the assassination aside, he will not be seen outside the White House again before Election Day.

In the daily din of the media, Birch Thornacre's throaty voice is in full cry, calling down curses on the heathen. His baying has the usual dreary effect. Near the Auburn University campus, the house of an Iranian scholar is firebombed. That no one is suggesting the complicity of Iran doesn't seem to matter. The Shiite Muslim connection is seen to be explanation enough.

Proctor and Belakis continue to stump, but even they look confused, with one opponent shot and the other in apparent hiding. The last of the presidential debates has been canceled. A CBS poll for the first time shows "undecided" substantially outpacing either of the two major party candidates.

The roiling of Washington has sent wave on wave crashing out through the media-besotted country, so that even in a remote corner like Carter, a middle-aged woman might sit for hours, wide-eyed, before the television.

Bear was away in Albuquerque for only one night. He made sure to telephone Becky this time, but when he did he could hear the television in the background. He asked for her news, but she wanted to know if he'd heard that we had sent three aircraft carriers to the Persian Gulf. Bear tried to change the subject on the phone, and that didn't work, and he tried when he returned to Carter the next night, and that didn't work either.

"Bear?" It is Becky again, calling from the living room.

"Just a minute, I—"

"No, Bear, come right away! Look at this!"

So he goes in, and there it is on the television screen, Louisa's photograph. "In a copyrighted story," the announcer is saying, "*Newsweek* magazine today reports more strong evidence linking the assassination of Royall Stillwell with the strange case of former Stillwell aide Louisa Shidler."

"That's her," says Becky. "That's her, Bear!"

The announcer goes on with it. Shidler recently pleaded guilty on fraud and bribery charges. Federal prosecutors said she had taken a $50 million bribe while working for then Trade Representative Stillwell on foreign trade issues. She escaped from house arrest two days before his murder. Late on October 16 she was again in police custody in northwest Wyoming, but escaped after a bloody shootout left six Wyoming police officers dead. She was well financed, she had a military force at her beck and call, she was Stillwell's former deputy, and she was missing.

"Federal authorities are providing no answers to some disturbing questions," the announcer continues. "Did Ambassador Stillwell know of the bribe? Was he murdered to preserve his silence? Was she involved in his murder? And where is Louisa Shidler today?"

The television report cuts to Justice Department and White House press conferences, where red-faced flaks are denouncing the putative Shidler connection to the assassination as ludicrous, fantasy. The reporters' questions come back so furiously that the press secretary looks almost as if he's dancing behind the podium, like a man burning his bare fingers trying to keep lids on pots that are boiling over.

"Bear, that is *her!*" Becky repeats, when they flash the photograph again.

"That don't look like her. Her hair was different."

"Patsy my eye. We're the damn patsies. That is *her.*"

Now there is a picture of the Bethesda house, and the story has turned to background on Louisa.

"Becky, I don't think—" Bear is saying, when he is interrupted by the announcer.

". . . where until recently she lived with her husband, Toby Higginson, and a daughter, Isabel—"

"Did you hear that!" Becky almost shouts in triumph. "Her daughter, Isabel. Bear, we got to call the police! That was her, and you weren't even paying attention."

She picks up the telephone.

"Beck—"

She has started to punch in the numbers, when the big fingers clamp down on hers.

"Bear!"

"Becky," he says. "Becky, stop. Just stop and listen for a minute."

She does stop, for his grip has surprised her. He replaces the phone in the cradle. Travis has come out into the living room to see what all the commotion is.

"You go on back to your room, Trav," Bear says. The boy's footsteps are heard, then the sound of his door shutting.

"Just hold on a minute," Bear says again. There is a catch in his voice, an agitation, a sound she knows too terribly well, and her eyes widen, watching him. He reaches over and flicks the television off, and then pulls the brown pill bottle from his shirt pocket, unfastens the top, and swallows two pills. He rises unsteadily. She anticipates him, and rushes to the kitchen to fill his glass with water and then help him get it down.

He settles into the couch, sitting in the shadows, and she waits for his breathing to slow.

After a while his voice comes very softly. "Just supposing it was her. Do you want every FBI agent in the world here in an hour and a half, Beck? Do you want 'em all tearing through the shed and the Earthship and Sugaree and God knows what else? Finding every stash I forgot and left someplace sometime?"

He coughs a little, and gets up, slowly, to poke at the fire in the wood stove. "You want 'em all rootin' around in there? I gave her a ride. I gave her my bike, even. What's that make me? I ain't no lawyer, but I'd say they'll find something wrong with all of that. And then it's me on the TV too, and the company hearing about it, and all? Now just think this thing through. If it was her, she's just a little gal on a motorcycle—"

"On your motorcycle, Bear! On your stupid, stupid motorcycle!"

"Which was stole from my shed last week," he announces, as if that will settle things.

Not, on the whole, an elegant solution, but Becky realizes it will have to do. Quiet again descends on the Earthship; outside, the wind whistles forlornly.

"Oh, Bear," she says, "why did you ever pick her up in the first place?"

He takes her hand between his hands, and says to her gently, "She ain't no killer, Beck, no more than I am. Now don't go getting yourself in a snarl over this."

Young Bill Friedman lives in the downstairs apartment of a two-family in northwest Washington. (It was a good investment, he explains. He is extremely interested in good investments.) By eleven, when they arrive there, the streets are mostly deserted. Louisa has learned much about Bill Friedman by this time. It has not been difficult for him to fill the hours with himself; he is, after all, a male in his twenties. And so she has heard rather a lot about accounting, wind surfers, and his views of the relative merits of various professional basketball players.

"What do you do, Patsy?" he finally gets round to asking when he is fumbling for the keys to his front door.

"I'm an artist. A *painter*, you might say." She watches as he works his keys nervously under the porch light. She feels an unexpected calm, and wonders if she is ready for this. And then she wonders if she will be alive by this time tomorrow.

"Really?" he asks.

"Yeah."

"Where, here?"

"No. I live in New Mexico. But I had to come east to see a few people. I've been traveling around, taking a little time off from my . . . painting."

"Seriously?"

She smiles at him as they enter the apartment.

He *is* an accountant, she thinks. Everything is tidy. A spotless beige carpet underfoot, a clean white sofa before, a dusted television beyond. Ah, *another* man who dusts! Except this one dusts everything, not just the television. Perhaps he could drop by Toby's apartment once in a while.

Only the mountain bike, parked inside the door for the usual urban reason, seems even slightly out of place.

"Do you like to ride?" she asks.

"I try to get out on the weekends. When I can."

"Nice bike."

"Yeah, I like the Cannondale. Very comfortable. It has the new Shimano shifters. They're excellent." Louisa fears a parts list coming on, but Bill Friedman stops himself, and comes close to her.

"So, Patsy, how about you? You like to ride too?"

Oh, dear. She might have preferred the parts list to the feeble double entendre of the young accountant. But, still in role, she smiles seductively at him. She has a part to play and, for a moment, an extremely forgiving audience. They embrace, his hands chastely round her shoulders. Different arms, a different body—so much thinner than Toby, she is thinking. It seems strange. As she looks beyond his shoulder it occurs to her that her own life has become such a haphazard thing that, for all the forethought and contrivance of this encounter, she may merely be putting off the inevitable. It seems less important to preserve a—what? a standard?—when every dawn might well be your last. Nevertheless her left brain does a quick tally of the days since her last period; she concludes that the risk, though one that would formerly have been unthinkable, will be the least of the risks she has run in the last twenty-four hours.

"Took you long enough to ask," she whispers.

What takes place in his bedroom is therefore somewhat unexpected. She cannot surrender herself to her role so far as to fall in naturally with it, but it is dark, and his caress is strong, and the ardor of a young man in that darkness, so long unfelt, she has to admit it to herself, is welcome. She did not expect this, and actually feels a confusion in his embrace. The confusion multiplies when he reaches his moment. As he grasps her shoulders and trembles, she closes her eyes, and tries, with some success, to think of better times.

Susan D'Agostino is the last one in the city room. The other monitors have fallen dark as, one by one, the reporters have slipped away. Now it is just she and her screen and the fluorescent lights. She has been living on caffeine for a week, since the previous Tuesday morning when her home phone rang at 7:10 with the news of Stillwell's assassination.

The paper has long since been put to bed, when she looks up to see a familiar shape shuffling across the room toward her.

She squints for a moment: her eyes are dry and she cannot be sure it is him, at first. "Mac?"

"Hey, Suse."

"God, Mac, it's two-fifteen in the morning."

"That it is, Suse."

He comes across the floor to her desk and stands quietly before her.

"You look like a guy who missed the last train."

"I did."

"And made last call."

"Alas, Suse, I didn't."

"You're fired, you know."

"Aye."

"And aren't you, like, a fugitive, or something?"

"Suse, for Chrissake. A fugitive is someone who has escaped. I have not yet been arrested."

She doesn't look quite so comfortable with the distinction. "I'm not sure that's right, but, hell, you're the managing editor. Or, I should say, the former managing editor. So what are you doing? You sure didn't come back here for the coffee."

"Susan, I need that reverse phone directory. You know, numbers to addresses."

"You got a prospect off some bathroom stall, Mac?"

"Something like that. Nexis, too. And the morgue. And the paper."

She laughs, shaking her head. "Christ. You need Nexis at this hour?"

"Yes."

"Mac, what you need is a life."

"Suse, I have enough of a life right now, thanks."

He stands, waiting. But it was the right moment to catch Suse with this unsettling situation. At that hour of the night, nobody cares much about anything.

She sighs. "Mac, tell me this. Would it piss off Voulke to know you were back poking around?"

"I expect so."

"And Ephram, too?"

"Definitely."

"Well, then, make yourself at home. I'm out of here. By the way, you didn't see me." She switches off her monitor and grabs a handbag. Halfway across the room she turns around and trots back to give him a quick peck on the cheek. "We've missed you, you asshole," she says.

Then she hurries for the door.

CHAPTER 54

A shriek in the darkness, and Louisa sits bolt upright and cries out.

But it is only the accountant's alarm clock. She is shaking, breathing hard, as the alarm continues to ring. Her bedmate stirs, punches the clock, and it is silent again. Wide awake, she tries to calm herself as he stirs again. In a moment, Bill Friedman is all accountancy. Suddenly businesslike, he kicks his legs to the floor, rises, and heads for the shower.

She puts a light on, looks at the clock. Six A.M. A few minutes later he hurries across the bedroom, grabs a suit and a shirt from his closet, and goes into the living room, where he flips on the television to *Good Morning America*. A bad sign.

"So, Bill, big day at the office?" she calls out.

She hears no response from Bill, but there is one from the television. "When we return, the latest news on the assassination," says the television host.

"Bill?"

"Yeah?"

"Big day at the office?"

"Yeah . . ." He isn't listening.

Quickly, she grabs a shirt from his closet, throws it on and goes to the threshold. She smiles brightly. "Good morning," she says.

"Hi." He is on his couch, staring at the television.

"So, busy day ahead?" She tries to divert his attention.

"Oh, you know, couple of meetings. I have to meet the audit partner on a big case. I think I've found a real problem with the CFO of one of our Fortune 500 clients," he says, sounding important. But she can't get his attention off the television announcer. Unnamed sources are being quoted for more background on Guardians of Allah. Friedman's eyes are glued to the screen.

"This is incredible," he says.

"Yeah."

"And in a moment, related news on the nationwide search for Ambassador Stillwell's former deputy, the fugitive Louisa Shidler." The television goes to commercial, and Bill Friedman returns to tying his necktie.

Louisa knows she has only a minute or so. She moves softly across the room, comes close to where he sits on the couch. Her back is to the television, blocking his view, as she says, "Let me help you with that tie." Her fingers begin to loosen it. He hesitates for a moment, and then his fingers are unbuttoning the shirt. Her shirt.

A minute or so later, the newscasters return to the television screen with their story that Louisa Shidler has been reported seen in the District. They even flash a pretty good likeness on the screen behind her. Louisa is conscious of many things—the loud voice of the newscaster, the bicycle leaning up against the wall next to the couch, the sound of passing cars. Fortunately, Bill Friedman's consciousness is much more narrowly focused, and not on the television.

She washes for a long time. The sun has come up and the young accountant has gone off to work. Opening the hot-water valve has brought her back to those days when Isabel was a toddler, and it seemed as if only by pulling the shower curtain behind her could Louisa shut herself away from hands clinging to her body. Those were the days when Isabel was always tugging on a leg, and Toby on an arm. Now . . .

Her skin reddens under the blast of hot water. She watches the spray running down her breasts, rubs her hands across her belly, feels her shoulders loosen under the heat, tries to feel a moment of relaxation, of refuge. But her mind is going too fast.

Later, she finds what she needs in the drawers and the closet. She decides to leave a note, and sits down at the computer.

> *Bill, thank you. I had to borrow a few things. I'll return them when I can. Thanks.*
>
> *—Patsy*

Mac is strangely serene, as he sits and sips coffee at his table in the main lobby of Union Station. His view is simple. He has not hidden. He has not attempted to avoid the police. If he has kept his movements secret from computers, he has walked in the light of day. When the police come to ask him questions about Amada, he will answer them.

At noon, he is studying the personal ad again. "Much-sought-after gal" wants "union" with "old newshound." She's a "stationary sort." Union Station?

He sits beneath the overhead screen announcing arrivals and departures. Around him the commuters hurry in shoals as the trains are called. The announcements echo through the station, until the background hubbub resolves into a single, quiet voice.

"Excuse me."

Amazement. Vaguely he noticed her approach him in the crowd, and yet he didn't see her at all. Her hair is now short and an artificial blond color. The Lycra clothing is like nothing he might have guessed she would wear. Only her jaw and cheeks appear genuine, in the midst of this bizarre costume.

"Well, for Chrissake," he says softly.

She doesn't answer, or take a seat. Rather, she places her messenger's bag and bicycle helmet on the table and, putting her left foot on a chair, leans over to tie her shoe. And then she and the messenger's bag and the helmet are gone, melting into the crowd.

But a piece of paper remains on the table. A piece of paper, and a teddy bear whose midriff leaks white stuffing. They must have slipped out of the bag. He picks up the note.

"Phone bank against west wall," it says, "fourth phone from door."

"Have you been followed?" she asks him a moment later, when he has answered her call.

"I don't think so. How are you, Louisa?"

"Day to day. You?"

"I'm a fugitive myself."

"Really?"

"Someone has murdered my cleaning lady, and come pretty close to murdering me as well."

"Murdered your—"

"Yeah."

"Seriously?"

"Oh, yes. Murder exceeds even my capacity for gallows humor."

"My God, what happened?"

"I'm not sure, but I'm guessing she surprised someone going through my files. They found her in the study, apparently. Two shots, very professional."

"Oh, Mac—"

"They may have been there to find the papers I got from Racine's secretary. Anyway, there is now a warrant for my arrest."

"Lord."

"There's some good news, at least. I've been fired."

"Mac, I'm so sorry."

"Christ, I don't guess it's your doing. And the being fired part I like, actually. A journalist has to be fired at least once a decade or he'll lose his self-respect. Fired *at,* I could do without, but so far it hasn't come to that. I didn't like Ephram much, anyway. Where's Isabel?"

"She's okay, I think."

"She's not been harmed?"

"No. Thank heaven, she's all right."

"Louisa, in Cody you turned yourself in, didn't you?"

"Yes. And six police officers were murdered."

"Where have you been since the sixteenth?"

"Lots of places. Listen, Mac, I've come back to town for a reason, and it's not to turn myself in. I got your message. Tell me about Europe."

Mac looks around the station. Throngs of commuters stare up at the screen, waiting for the colored lights to change so that they can find their trains. Two transit cops lean against a phone booth twenty yards away, chatting. The line from Au Bon Pain snakes out into the concourse. Men and women in suits are milling around the newsstand. At a nearby table, a woman is eating popcorn, reading a newspaper. A man is carrying on a vigorous conversation over a cell phone. It is a funny thing about a man in a public place speaking earnestly into a cellular telephone. It used to be he drew attention to himself that way. Now no one pays attention.

"There's a lot to tell," he begins. "And not much time to tell it. But, Louisa, have you heard of a man named Claude Housez?"

Now the silence is at her end, as she tries to think. "Somewhere," she says. "Some kind of wealthy Swiss investor or something?"

"French. But lives in Geneva. He's an arms trader. One of the world's biggest, apparently."

"Is he in pharmaceuticals?"

"Not the legal kind. Not as far as I know."

"So you're saying the bribe wasn't for the pharmaceutical annex at all?"

"I don't think so. It looks as if Racine—the one who sent bank statements to the post office box—worked for Housez."

"Arma virumque cano?"

Mac smiles. "Yes. Best I could do."

"An arms dealer. It was gun running? How?"

"Well," Mac answers, "I don't think it was that either. I think we're talking about legal arms deals. Government-sponsored arms deals."

"Then I don't follow."

"Claude Housez is a broker of legal arms sales. He makes billion-dollar deals between foreign governments and U.S. contractors. He hires on to the foreign government as a consultant, gets a percentage of the deal as a success fee if they secure the sale. Government of Malaysia, of Indonesia, of Turkey, you pick it. He puts together a package with an American seller: all legal under the Arms Export Control Act. When the deals are reviewed by the agencies, Claude's client's deal slides right through. This year he did a big AWACS deal for the Malaysians. Last year, several deals for various clients, Bahrain among them. Ninety-three was the year Commerce approved a one-billion-dollar sale of fighter jets to our dear friends the Indonesians. Other brokers are less successful. Perhaps Mr. Housez has bought a little insurance, to get his deals through."

"And so," Louisa muses quietly, "your Mr. Housez sets up a rainy-day fund for the American diplomats who sign the approvals. Is that it?"

"That's how it looks."

"USTR doesn't give the approvals in arms sales."

"Right," Mac answers. "All of those deals have to be approved by Commerce and Defense. And Housez always has a concierge, a concierge in every city."

"A concierge?"

"That's what his lieutenant called it, when I found him. A concierge. To find all the other things one needs when traveling. To act as go-between."

"Frank Ianella," she says, softly.

"Sorry?"

The words begin to rush from her in a torrent. "That's the Frank Ianella connection. Mac, Frank Ianella was Royall's lieutenant, his right-hand guy on the campaign. But he's also a deputy secretary at Commerce. And I think his handwriting is on the incorporation papers for the company that owns the post office box where the bank statement was sent. It matches some of his handwriting on a business card I have. Frank, Frank must be the go-between between the Frenchman and the secretaries. He can come and go as he pleases, and no one notices."

"Louisa—"

Louisa's mind races on, and she doesn't hear. She cannot see Mac's face, see the way the lips of the old editor are pursing doubtfully, the eyes squinting again. "Mac," she continues, "these guys are like the President. You can't get a *meeting* with the secretary of commerce. Or defense. You can hardly get a phone call that isn't scheduled. They're run by schedulers. And when you get the meeting, or the call, they're never alone. They are surrounded by lieutenants. I mean, the United States secretary of commerce can't just take a call from an arms dealer. So you have a broker. Someone who's in and out of the office all the time. Someone like Frank Ianella. There's your concierge."

"Louisa, nice theory. But how do you know?"

"You remember bank statements were sent to a post office box? The box was owned by a corporation. I got copies of the papers—they're rolled up in an envelope in Buster, and there's handwriting on the form, where it says 'Secretary.' Well, on September sixth, he wrote the same word on a business card he handed me, showing his promotion. It's an abbreviation, actually, but Mac, it's his handwriting. You see Buster?"

"Buster?"

"The bear."

"Oh, yeah, I was going to ask you about that." Mac picks Buster up, turns him over in his hands. The bear smiles bravely.

"The copy of the articles of incorporation is in there. It's my only copy, Mac. I want you to keep it safe."

There is a pause then, which leaves her uncomfortable, as he withdraws the envelope, looks at the photocopy. At length, she hears the doubt in his voice. "What else do you have?"

"Well, like I say, he's got the access . . ." Her voice trails off, and all of a sudden it is Louisa the reporter, having to lay her glorious balloon on the table before the editor, knowing that he will find the one place to make a nasty little prick and then she will have to watch the air whoosh out from it until it is simply a puny strip of rubber lying on the table, and the look on the editor's face is saying, "That's the story?"

"Louisa, that's it?"

"Isn't that enough?"

"What do you think? One word of his handwriting? Make that one abbreviation, four letters and an apostrophe, which I suppose you could have copied off the card he gave you? You don't have the original corporate form, just a copy, right? You think that original won't be deep-sixed, if it hasn't been already?"

He's right, she thinks. He's always right. Damn him.

"What do we have that links the guy to Housez?" Mac goes on.

From her, silence. She has nothing. She bites her lip, looks around the phone bank on the east concourse, where she is standing, and struggles not to slip, to begin the slide to surrender. For there is a vulnerability in the architecture of Louisa's mind, a peculiar susceptibility to the past. She can disguise herself, place a personal ad, study a handwritten word; she can ride a motorcycle and seduce an accountant. She can infer a thrust and plan a parry, and do it all with a logic, almost a certainty. But then if her mind comes upon something too powerful from the past, too puissant a memory of Toby, perhaps, or, as now, a reminder of her own fallibility, straight from the days when she was Mac's eager but green disciple, she feels the mind's superstructure begin to shake.

She waits for him to say something, anything. It seems to her that she waits a long time. Finally he sighs, and says, "Louisa, this is becoming kind of crazy. You're out here running around in your bike suit. You could be found by these people at any moment. Maybe we've got to just trust some police organization or other and have you publicly turn yourself in. Make a loud enough noise and hope nothing can happen to you. I've been working with a guy at the FBI, and he—"

A guy at the FBI. Distracted, for a moment, by a memory of the man in the helicopter's bay, the letters "FBI" on the jacket and the rain pouring down, Louisa answers, "I don't think so."

As far as Mac can see, that leaves but one alternative. Union Station seemed in the morning such a hopeful destination to the man with the personal ad clipped from the paper in his pocket. Suddenly it feels like the last stop. "Then you're going to have to tie this Ianella to Housez," he says.

"Yes," she says. "Yes. All right, Mac. Tell me about Claude Housez. Tell me everything."

It takes him about ten minutes. When he has finished, he waits for her response. Getting none, he prompts, "So. Anything there sound like a lead on Frank Ianella?"

She takes a minute before responding, for although she has digested the information, her mind, jump-started somehow by her memory of the Cody airport, has moved on from the details of Housez's business. She answers Mac quite deliberately. "No. I guess I'll have to ask Mr. Housez himself."

Toby Higginson is bending at the waist, panting, and the sweat is running down his forehead. He has just placed a drop shot and watched his opponent stretch in vain to get to it, and he has gone up 9–8 in the rubber match of his afternoon game. His legs, though, are not what they were, and he is sucking in wind. Squash has been his one escape in this bizarre month of disappearance and stunning surprise, of the revelation that his wife is a thief, and maybe an assassin, and that she has fled with his daughter. The White House has forced him to resign, and so he has been living on the charge accounts, playing a lot of squash. The explosion of the ball off the wall, the burning in his thighs as he plays a shot, the blackening of his gray T-shirt with sweat: it has been the only distraction for this bewildered man.

The little door at the rear of the court opens, and the attendant interrupts to say that there is a call for Mr. Higginson.

"I'll call 'em back, Gordo." Toby takes the squash ball as he lines up the next serve.

"Lady says its urgent. She said you would tell me to take a number and I was to say no, you have to take the call."

Toby looks at Gordo, who shrugs. "Who is she?"

"She didn't say."

"White House? Was it Kristina?"

"She didn't say."

Toby shrugs at his opponent. "Sorry, man," he says.

"It's all right. I'll hit."

"I'll get rid of this and be right back. You are serving eight–nine."

"The hell is this all about, Gordo?" Toby asks the young attendant as they go to the front desk.

He is still breathing heavily as he takes the telephone in a sweaty hand and leans against the counter. "Toby Higginson," he says.

"It's me."

He is silent for a moment, for he is completely stunned by the voice, and then says, "Jesus."

"Toby, I don't have much time."

"Jesus Christ. Weeze, where are you? What the hell are you doing?"

"This isn't the right time to catch up," she says.

"Where is Isabel? Where the hell is Isabel, Louisa?"

Gordo looks up at Higginson's dark, angry face, and then quickly looks away. Toby checks himself, turning his back to the desk.

"Quiet," Louisa says to him. "Listen to me."

Toby whispers now, but it makes no difference. "Where is she?"

"Safe."

"Where?"

She can hear, over the telephone line, the background explosions of the squash balls, the booms and the crash they make when they hit the tin skirting. It makes her flinch a little. "No," she answers him. "If you go to her, or call her, or even *think* about her too much, they'll find her. And if they do that, they'll kill her. If you tell anyone, *anyone,* about this call, they'll know."

"You've got to turn yourself in," he says.

"I tried that once. Toby, if that happens, you'll be a widower before our divorce is final."

"They said . . . Honey, where are you?"

"Never mind. Listen, listen carefully."

"Where are you?" he demands.

"Toby, listen. They took Isabel. They kidnapped her and they would have killed her. And me. I'm sure they are watching you, trying to find me. They will kill us all. You've got to keep out of quiet places. And you've got to help me."

"Weeze, she was with John and Emily. I talked to her. I talked to him."

"No you didn't. She was in Wyoming when you talked to her."

"That guy from the FBI said she hadn't been there, but honest to God, I talked to your father, and to her."

"You didn't, Toby, it only seemed like you did. They had his voice recorded or something, I don't know. But Isabel was in Wyoming. She told me herself."

"Weeze, do you think you're being a little paranoid about this?"

"They killed six men in Wyoming. Do you think we're special, you and me? Play squash again tomorrow. At two o'clock sharp you'll get a call from me in the phone booth diagonally across the street from the club. I'm going to need your help."

"My help?"

"Yes. Starting with some plane tickets, Dulles to New York. I'll give you the details tomorrow."

CHAPTER 55

It is Tuesday, October 29, and the Cat in the Hat has come to America. Standing in the Dulles international terminal with the paper in his hand, surrounded by the crush of travelers hurrying this way and that, he studies the message again, tries to make some sense of it. He frowns, rereads it. The messenger has vanished into the crowd. He has only one Thing with him on this trip, and so far he has been of little help.

Tired and irritable after his long flight from Geneva, he does not like this not being in control. Well, he thinks, it is simply a first-class ticket arranged by Mrs. Stillwell, on a commercial flight to New York, where she evidently wants to meet with him. At a law office there. How much mischief can there be in that? Still, didn't she say she was quite unable to travel? He looks up at the television screen and sees that Flight 62, connecting from Orlando to New York, is on schedule. Uneasily he folds the message, restores it to his jacket pocket, and nods at Thing One. They move off toward Gate 17.

It is early afternoon when he enters the Boeing 737 aircraft from the jetway and finds seat 4-B in the first-class section. It is on the aisle. There was no room in first class for Thing One. He's back in economy.

As Housez hands the flight attendant his suit jacket, he takes brief note of the young woman in the adjacent seat. She has short hair and is in her mid-thirties, he would guess. Attractive, apparently, although it is difficult to tell behind the outsized sunglasses. Her hair is blond, a trifle unnatural in shade. The young woman stares resolutely out the window. Housez takes his seat and pulls out the message from Doolie Stillwell. In a moment, the attendant has done her work, and he is sipping a gin. That makes it a little better. But not much.

His eyes close briefly, as the jet taxis to the runway and holds in the queue. Housez winces at the overhead monitor's relentlessly cheery demonstration of seat-belt clasps and life jackets. Mercifully, it comes to an end and the aircraft makes its turn for the runway. The rising whine of the engines signals takeoff. Just as the wheels lift and Housez's eyes open, he finds that the woman is looking at him.

"Did you have a pleasant flight from Geneva?"

Housez's face registers surprise, and then goes blank. He's getting a little tired of people popping out of nowhere with questions about Geneva. He studies the woman, attempting to guess her motive. Meanwhile, the airplane pulls into its steep climb out of Dulles.

"It seems you are familiar with my travel plans, Miss . . ."

"Don't you recognize me, Mr. Housez?"

"No. I am afraid I do not."

She nods. "Surely you do. I might be the most famous woman in America." She removes her sunglasses and shows him her face for the first time. Her gaze is direct, her eyes a little haggard. "Still no?"

He does not answer. "Was this message from you?" he asks, unfolding the paper.

"Yes."

"So. You are with Mrs. Stillwell? Why this change in plans so suddenly, please? You are sent to escort me, for some reason?"

Louisa smiles. "Not quite. There is no change in her plans."

There is a pause as he digests this. He looks away, rubs his eyes, then looks back at the young woman. It takes a few moments before he can see the obvious, and the obvious provokes in him an equal measure of admiration and fear. He frowns, and examines her more closely. They have to put their heads close together over the armrests, for the aircraft is climbing to its cruising altitude, and the cabin noise overwhelms a whisper.

"You are Louisa Shidler?" he asks.

She smiles.

The Cat settles back into his seat, silent for a moment. He takes a gulp from his gin—rather a large one. After he sips again he says, "Well, this is most diverting. Most dramatic. Most confusing. Why do you go to this length, please?"

"Forgive me, Mr. Housez, but it is difficult to get a meeting with you."

He smiles and claps his hands. "Ah," he says, "precisely so. Yes."

"Particularly on my terms."

"And what are those terms?"

She directs a penetrating look at him. "No guns. No thugs. No kidnappings. Just conversation, between the two of us."

Louisa signals the attendant. "Would you mind bringing him another?" she asks. "And I'll have one, too." She places her hand on his forearm.

"Although I have found it rather an easy thing to meet with your—oh, what shall we call them, your people—it is more difficult to meet with you. I thought it might be good for Gallo-American relations if we got together personally. And I asked myself, how does a person like me ask a man like Mr. Housez to go through a metal detector? An airplane seemed like the right place. So please forgive the somewhat unusual arrangements."

Housez is chuckling throughout the explanation. "I congratulate you, Miss Shidler. Very well done. Alors, since you have arranged this meeting, why don't we call it to order? I don't, by the way, have any idea of what this paranoid discussion about guns and thugs means. But, c'est très amusant. So."

At this point, with the flight under way and the sunglasses off, with the Frenchman's curiosity engaged and with a glass of gin in front of each of them, she embarks on a monologue. It is coherent, but a little pressed, veering toward irrational. "Mr. Housez, I've been arrested, threatened, nearly killed. I have been accused of an assassination. I don't have means, I don't have friends, not anymore, and I don't have time. And so it's the moment for me to be moving on. You can help me with that. Mr. Housez, I want to talk to you about the money."

"The money?"

"Yes, Mr. Housez, the money which seems to have gotten me arrested, my daughter kidnapped, and Royall Stillwell killed. The money."

"This game, Miss Shidler, it is difficult for me to play with you, when I have no idea what it is you are talking about." Only the creases at the corners of his eyes speak at cross purposes to his lips.

"But I'm afraid you do, at least, according to Mr. Racine's file on the account."

She reaches down into her satchel and removes a photocopy of a document, hands it to him.

His eyes anticipate her hands, and she can see that he keeps them away from the document only with difficulty. "What is this?" he asks. "Who is this Racine?"

"Oh, dear, Mr. Housez, how little appreciation you show for your lawyer! Surely you remember his name? The fellow who kept so many files for you." Now that the flight has leveled off, Louisa's voice is a little too loud. It is making Housez nervous, making him bring his head closer to hers, so that she will speak more softly. She seems not to notice; she seems to him a little frayed.

He studies the photocopy of Racine's notes, sees his own initials in the lawyer's careful script, sees his assistant's name, phone number, next to wiring instructions, and the figure "Swfr 6omm."

He is shrugging and shaking his head, and now he is not smiling any-more. "I don't, I don't know what this is, and I am finding this rather tire-some."

"Au contraire, Monsieur Housez. C'est très amusant, non?"

Louisa has seen the way his eyes have retreated to a defensive cast, the way he studies her. He looks down at the paper and remains silent.

"You don't know what that is, Mr. Housez? Don't you think the Swiss authorities will know what it is? Don't you think you and I should speak more candidly?"

He won't answer, but his eyes are fixed on the paper, and he is listen-ing carefully.

"We really need to have a conversation, Mr. Housez." She looks away from him toward the window. The aircraft climbs out of a cloud bank. There isn't much time—they will be in New York soon.

He sits back in his seat, presses the recline button, and pulls the airline magazine from the seat pocket. "Madame, I don't know what you are talking about." She watches him for a moment. He is turning the pages too fast to be reading anything.

"Mr. Housez, I think you need to satisfy yourself about something."

Louisa rises from her seat, and in one swift movement has slipped past him and taken his hand. "Come," she says gently, leading him into the aisle. When he hesitates, she motions him with a subtle nod, and it is the kind of nod that has always been Claude Housez's weakness. He follows, then, as she makes her way toward the rear of the aircraft. Thing One looks up as they pass, but Housez smiles: everything is all right. The at-tendants are busy preparing the drinks cart, and they do not look up when Housez and Louisa pass behind them and reach the tail section.

There, a pregnant woman is pacing up and down, her hand to her back. It appears that she's holding dibs on one of the lavatories. "I'm all done," she says, as Louisa approaches.

"Are you all right?" Louisa asks.

"Oh yeah, a little nausea is all. I'm fine."

"Sure?"

The pair slips past her. Housez feels another tug on his arm, and in the next moment, a lavatory door is snapping shut behind him. And Louisa.

There isn't much space. She leans back against the sink; the closing of the door has pressed his legs against hers.

"Miss Shidler, what on—"

Her look quiets him, as she reaches past to latch the door, then takes his right wrist in her left hand and brings his hand to her collarbone. She grips the wrist tightly there, for a moment, and then, deliberately, begins to guide the hand down her chest, all the while staring at him in silence. The hand reaches her breast.

"As I said, Mr. Housez, it is clear that you need to satisfy yourself."

Housez surrenders domain over his hand. She pushes its now spreading fingers along her rib cage down to her waist, her hip, her flank. She pushes it down, farther, along her leg, until he has to stoop. Then she guides it inward, and begins the return journey along the inside of her thigh.

He stops.

"Keep going," she breathes into his neck.

And so he does.

"Press!" she orders. "But gently."

He complies, and she lets him hear, just above the noise of the aircraft, a sound that is something slightly more than the exhalation of breath.

"You see," she whispers, "I'm not wearing a wire."

He smiles. The body search continues now, but without her direction.

They are sandwiched so closely in the lavatory that she can feel his heart rate quicken. She studies his eyes. They go a little cloudy, and his breathing becomes heavier, as his hands begin to hurry across her torso, pressing and clutching, and then they are behind her, pulling her closer to him. She marks the bellwether of his mood with an inward smile, reaches up and folds her arms around his neck.

For a few moments there is silence, as she uses her fingertips along the break of his shoulder and neck to urge him on. It grows hot in the lavatory.

"What else are you not wearing?" he asks.

"Perhaps when the time is right—"

"Take this off." With a deft twist he has undone the snap and is tugging at her jeans.

"No."

"Come, quickly . . ."

"Not here. We will be in New York soon enough."

"I want you now."

"You get what you want."

"Often."

"Always."

"Always, then."

She pushes his hand away, but holds his chest to hers. "Almost always. But I like that in you. You want Racine dead. He's dead. You want Royall dead. He's dead. You want me dead. Six police officers are murdered, and I, improbably, escape. So, not always."

"You have a vivid imagination."

"Do I?"

"Yes, you do. These are not my doings."

"No? One thing, Claude," she says, her voice turning cold now. "What is it?"

"Don't you ever send people after my daughter again."

He pulls away to look at her, but she pulls him back toward her.

"Never!" she says. "Say it!"

Preoccupied with the business of his hands, he says huskily, "This has not been my business."

"She's only a child."

"For that entire silliness, you had another to blame."

Indirection. She continues to hold him close to her, but lets the conversation wander. Never thrust for the key point, didn't Mac teach her that? Open a door, he used to say, and wait for information to walk in. Information is like a dog. But there isn't much time. They will be in New York soon. The whine of the aircraft is in her ears as she presses her fingertips into his back. So, change tack for a moment.

"You know what I don't understand, Claude? Why the kidnapping at all? Why weren't we murdered in our beds in Bethesda? Wouldn't that have been a lot less complicated?"

"I asked . . . I asked the same question. It was . . ." He searches for the English word, has trouble finding it. "Merde. It was of the, hmm, elle a dit, the noncertainty, the ambiguity of what you knew. The fear of what will be disclosed by others if you are dead. You have said something to them, that the information must come out if you are killed. They are insistent, this must not be happening before the election. Afterwards, after you are in jail, no one pays attention. That is the thinking explained to me. To me, it seems complicated, too complicated. But this is the idea. Vous comprenez?"

But no. Louisa does not understand. She does not understand at all. It was the uncertainty. *Elle a dit.* Not *Il a dit.* He did not say *Il a dit.* Did he? Do the Genevans pronounce French differently? Louisa cannot remember that they do. *Elle a dit. She* said. *She* said it was the uncertainty.

Leave the point. Circle back to it later. "The Concierge . . . said it was the uncertainty?"

"This is what the Concierge says, yes. The daughter would induce you to plead guilty. Then, what you say, after the election, it is a crazy person in a jail saying things. Or maybe you commit suicide there. Something like that. Not a problem, they said."

"And you, you don't care. You have your arms deals, this is just a price of doing business, Claude?"

"I am a businessman."

"Your clients buy a lot of American goods, don't they, Claude?"

"And if they do? Perfectly legal, as you know. Alors, enough talking."

She lets his hands wander, thinking of what he said. *After the election,* it was. When the hands stray too far, she fends them off: "No. Not enough. What has she planned for me, the Concierge?"

"This you must ask the Concierge." No flinching at the pronoun. No breaking of stride. He did say *Elle.*

"Bring me to the Concierge, then."

He pushes back from her and examines her coldly. "And why would I do that, please?"

"So that I don't expose you."

He laughs. "You are a wanted criminal. I do not think you are in a position to expose anything."

"Tell me this—"

"It is not the time to talk of this. You have some reason for dragging me into this stall?"

"I have twenty-five million reasons."

"You have overestimated your value."

"Not my value. The value of my research. Racine's file. I want half the money."

A silence, now, and the Cat in the Hat is all business.

"This is all, this is not my affair. But what is your proposal? Perhaps I can relay it."

"I'll give you the originals of the file. I destroy all of the copies but one. I save one copy. If I or my daughter comes to harm, the last copy emerges."

"And why does one trust such a thing?"

"Because it is better than the alternative for you. And because you know, and I know, that you and your Concierge can leave instructions for my death even if I were to betray you. It is what the arms negotiators used to call mutually assured destruction."

"Yes. We called that MAD."

"That is another name for it."

"And if I do not agree?"

"In the back of seat three-B, there is an air phone. I will return to the seat and telephone the FBI. They will be waiting at the gate in New York to arrest us both."

His eyes search her for signs of bluffing, but he sees none.

"Mr. Housez," she says, quietly, "I have nothing to lose."

"Under your proposal, when, when do I get your file?"

"When I get the twenty-five million. I'll give you the wiring instructions. When I have confirmation of receipt, you get the documents. As I say, Mr. Housez, if something were to happen to me, those documents would emerge. Bad for business."

"How do I trust you? How do we make the exchange?"

"I will arrange for that. We'll use a law firm, if you like. But I need one more thing. I need the Concierge's commitment, too."

"Miss Shidler, you had better lay all of these terms upon the table."

"Of course. I require twenty-five million dollars wired to a British Virgin Islands trust under wiring instructions I shall present. The Concierge will then arrange for evidence to surface clearing me of the murder and kidnapping charges. When that happens, I emerge from hiding, to serve a short sentence for bribery and for escape. Not the ten years the prosecutors were talking about. Six months. At a prison my lawyer says is acceptable. At the conclusion of the sentence, I shall leave the country and claim the money. The prosecutors are not to know about it, of course. And if you and the Concierge do not keep your end of the bargain, my information comes out.

"The matter will die there, Mr. Housez. My agents will retain copies of certain documents. If any harm comes to my daughter, or to me, they will emerge. If I am not exonerated of the other charges, they will emerge. I will continue to presume that, if they emerge outside the terms of our agreement, you and your people will know where to find me. But with this arrangement you buy my silence. Business can carry on, business as usual."

Is it plausible? She has pondered and pondered that question. Why not? Why not assume that to the businessman Claude Housez, all solutions, like all problems, can be measured in dollars? Now it is out there, and she can only brass it out, make it plausible.

"Think of it," she says, "as a capital investment. Think of the money you'll save on helicopter fuel."

The Cat gives her a little half smile. "Well, it's not cheap. All right, I understand the proposal."

Louisa gives him the number to call the following afternoon. He is to be with the Concierge, in Washington. They must call precisely at four-thirty.

"Yes. I understand," he answers, still smiling. "But what makes you think the Concierge is in Washington?"

"Intuition."

Above the sink, a red panel flashes on, directing that passengers return to their seats.

"Quel dommage," she says, slyly stroking his cheek.

"Yes, it's a pity," he answers.

She reaches up and traces, with her lips, a gentle path along his jaw up behind his ear. "Just as a matter of curiosity," she whispers, "which is more expensive, helicopter fuel, the secretary of commerce, or me? Hmmm?"

The Cat laughs softly, a laugh that is something of a purr. "What do you Americans say, one must pay to play? Your commerce secretary costs a lot more than helicopter fuel, I can assure you. But then, he is worth so much more to me. And as for you, we're still negotiating your price, aren't we?"

The pregnant lady must have returned to her seat. A young man, neatly dressed in a pale blue button-down shirt and pressed chinos, is waiting for the lavatory when the two emerge. He turns away, somewhat embarrassed, as the blonde seems to look right through him.

Two businessmen lugging fat garment bags brush past them from behind, and another pair late for a different gate surges toward them from the front. Crowds of travelers throng the terminal at La Guardia Airport, and Louisa tugs Housez's arm until he follows her to a bank of telephones, out of the crush.

"I think it best that we return— Who's he?" She has interrupted herself to inquire about the hulking man with the ponytail who has emerged from the crowd.

"My traveling companion."

"I see. Well, I was going to say I think we should return to Washington separately." She hands Housez a ticket. "I'm afraid I only have one. Where were you planning to stay? The Willard, perhaps?"

He shrugs. "I don't know. I have no reservation."

"Mr. Housez, you underestimate me again. Of course you have a reservation, at the Willard. If you like, I may join you there." She places a hand on his elbow. "Say, about nine P.M. All right? We can make all the other arrangements there."

She smiles inscrutably. Was it over the word "arrangements"? In an instant she has vanished into the crowd.

When she has gone, Claude Housez nods at Thing One and picks up one of the receivers. He has half an hour until the next flight, plenty of time to make one call.

As for the pregnant woman, she is the last passenger to emerge from the jetway into the concourse. Tired and flushed, she drops her carry-on bag and takes a seat in the lounge. There she waits, leafing through a thick legal document until five minutes to three. Her glance flickers upward only once, momentarily, as Housez and Thing One cross the concourse together for the return flight. Some minutes later, she reaches into her bag and removes a cellular phone, punching in a number.

"Hi," she says, "They just closed the gate for the three o'clock to National. He's on board. Is there another guy with him?"

"Yes. I'll be there in a minute."

Louisa Shidler comes out of the crowd to join her friend in the lounge moments later. "How are you feeling?"

"I'm okay," says Marcy Mosseau. "My back is killing me, though." She leans down and pulls the Dictaphone from her bag. It is still white and sticky with adhesive from the duct-tape she used to affix it to the inside of the trash receptacle in the aft lavatory.

"But, shit, anytime you want to be taped making whoopee in an airplane lav, Weezy, I'm your gal."

"Thanks. I'll send you a copy someday. You'll call Toby, right?"

"My next call."

"Isabel, has she been too much of a bother?"

"Well, the girl can't cook, or make a bed, but . . . Weeze, I like her. She's going to be a fox, you know."

"Don't tell me that. Don't tell *her* that. And take care of that baby."

"You take care of yourself, girl."

Louisa kisses her on the cheek. "I can't thank you enough."

"Just gimme that kid of yours for unlimited baby-sitting, and we're square."

"Yes, yes, of course." They embrace.

After Louisa disappears into the crowd, Marcy places one more call, to Toby.

A few minutes later, holding the small of her back, a gesture that is now genuine, Marcy rises and makes painfully toward the ticket counter. "Lester," she says, addressing her belly, "we're never going to make partner if I don't give up this pro bono shit."

At 4:20, Toby Higginson is pacing nervously behind the rank of limousine drivers holding signs outside the airport security barrier at Washington National Airport. He keeps glancing up at the "Arrived" telescreen. Then he sees on the down escalator the two men Marcy

Mosseau has described, the dapper Frenchman with silver hair, wearing a yellow silk tie on a shirt of broad stripes, and, behind him on the escalator, the big man with the ponytail. Housez carries an attaché case and is now visibly tired and cross. He glances once at his watch as he waits for the escalator to reach the floor.

Higginson maneuvers in behind. Moments later, as Housez and his bodyguard step into a cab, Toby hustles across the taxicab rank and climbs into the passenger seat of his Saab.

Mac, at the wheel, follows the cab onto the George Washington Memorial Parkway, slipping behind it in traffic. The cab makes its way across the Potomac and into the city, to the Willard Hotel. Mac follows, then pulls a block ahead, where he drops Toby off.

"Good luck," he says.

Toby Higginson will spend the next hour seated in a brocade armchair in the hotel lobby, his face hidden behind *The Washington Post*. By a curious coincidence, it is the very chair upon which his wife sat almost two months before when she tore open the letter from M. Racine and calculated the exchange rate for Swiss francs. But this evening the hotel is quiet. At five past six, Toby Higginson lowers the newspaper a little and observes a familiar woman at the hotel entrance.

"Jesus," he mutters to himself, quickly raising the newspaper.

When she has walked past, he watches her disappear into the elevator bank.

Fifteen minutes later she returns. Toby remains well concealed behind his newspaper. There is an uncomfortable moment when the woman is spotted by an acquaintance not fifteen yards from where he sits. The women exchange brief pleasantries. There is talk of the election, laughter. The woman's acquaintance wishes her good luck. "Thank you," says the familiar voice. "We may need it." Then she is gone.

At five past nine, Housez is in his hotel suite. He has tried to nap; he has tried to assure himself that the Concierge's calm was merited, he has tried to watch the television, he has tried the newspaper. But he is troubled. He does not like being alone, not controlling the situation. Thing One sits in the corner of the room, intent on the television.

His telephone rings. It is the desk.

"Mr. Housez?"

"Yes."

"A young lady came by to—"

"Well, tell her I'll be down shortly."

"Actually, I'm afraid she said she had to go, sir. But she left something for you. I'll send it up."

Thing One looks on silently as Housez opens the box. Inside is a Dictaphone, containing a tape and a note. The note says, simply, "Copy of this morning's tape. If you fail to deliver Concierge as promised, this goes to the FBI." He turns to the Dictaphone. Unfamiliar with it, he turns it over in his hands several times before operating the switch. When the tape begins, there is too much background noise at first. He has difficulty making out what it is. But something sounds familiar, and then he recognizes the sound of his own voice. In what could only be an airplane lavatory.

The spool fills, as dead air continues. Then, finally, comes a click, a commotion, and a snap.

He hears what sounds like his own voice. "Miss Shidler, what on—"

And then something hard to make out. He thinks he hears "need to satisfy yourself."

He steps over and turns the television off, then listens. There is a background whine, loud, high-pitched, and then there is some noise that is harder to identify, shifting, fumbling.

Minutes go by. Minutes and minutes of confused breathing, muttered words. It's not so bad, he thinks, not so bad. Until he hears the end, words somehow so clear they were elocuted, rather than spoken. "Your commerce secretary costs a lot more than helicopter fuel, I can assure you. But then, he is worth so much more to me."

Claude Housez switches off the machine and curses.

CHAPTER 56

It is Thursday, Halloween, the last day in October. The election is only days away. Louisa goes back and forth on the timing question: Mac's FBI man must have enough time, but not too much. If she gives him too much time, the story will leak out. If the story leaks out, the plan will not work. After some deliberation, she decides on 12:45 P.M. today. She will light the fuse at 12:45. Whether it will explode in her face, or theirs, only the day will show.

Early in the morning, she messengers the instructions to Krasnowicz's office herself. He agrees to man his post at the courthouse. His part seems unlikely to go awry, but the FBI will be a different story. It all depends on the man Phillips. At any rate, it no longer matters. She is determined, now, to carry the plan forward to its conclusion. It should only take ten minutes or so to set it all up, assuming she can find them at their telephones. That will give them an hour to organize things, and an hour to get to the spot. Just enough time, if they hurry.

By an odd coincidence, this is also the day that three women have chosen to meet for lunch at 12:30 at a certain well-frequented H Street restaurant. Old acquaintances, the women wear the uniform of the city's female professional elite. They order designer salads. They have come to gossip: about their families, their careers, the election, the passersby visible through the floor-to-ceiling window that separates their table from the sidewalk. But they find that they have not chatted long before the conversation turns to the woman everyone is talking about, the one who was on the cover of *Newsweek*.

"She was one of those women," the redhead begins. "Let's just say, it doesn't break your heart to find out that everything isn't *quite* so perfect."

"Ooh, catty." Lea Anne Haffenreffer wears a silk scarf around her throat, and earrings, bracelets, rings—a good number of these—a necklace . . . she's *done*. "You want my theory? Post–Goody-Two-Shoes Re-active Disorder. After a lifetime as the teacher's pet, she cracked. You know, a postal-worker thing."

"I think it comes down to having one child," says the third, a brunette who is short and a little plump, and has ordered the most virtuous salad. "You know those people who have only one child, and they drive you crazy with how wonderful their one child is? I'm a perfect little wife, a perfect little Ivy Leaguer, and I have one perfect little child as a result of one perfect night with my perfect man. I do everything once, and per-fectly. And then I go insane."

Chuckles all around. "She went to Duke," says the redhead.

"Whatever. Southern Ivy League. Wisteria League. Same thing."

"And he left her, you know, the perfect husband. Before all the crazi-ness."

"Can you blame him?"

The conversation shifts to the evening's preparations. The Halloween costumes have been ordered from the best catalogues. You can't get a decent one anymore—they're all Disney characters. And the worst of it is, that's what the children want: the women commiserate about trick-or-treating.

"Every year it's the same," says the brunette. "Larry goes, 'Hon, I'll take them trick-or-treating this year.' "

The table itself seems to shake with laughter over this. Husbands al-ways say they'll take the kids out on Halloween this year. Until about noon, when the wives get frantic calls from their husbands' secretaries.

But the conversation does not linger on Halloween, nor even on the children, for the woman they have been discussing exerts a powerful force on the three friends. They come back to her when the coffee arrives.

"Did you believe it, the morning it was in the *Post* and the *Herald*?" the redhead asks.

"What, the bribe business? No, I absolutely did not believe it," an-swers the brunette.

Lea Anne says she believed it.

"No you didn't. You *wanted* to believe it. You were dying for it to be true. But you didn't *believe* it. The woman probably reports frequent flyer miles to the IRS."

"Once she told me she does."

The brunette supposes that *that* is true.

"And what about that air-raid business, or whatever it was at that air-port?" interrupts the redhead, pressing on. "Did you believe that?"

No one wants to be the first to field that question. The women cast their eyes down to their coffees; their fingers fiddle with the Equal packets. As she is stirring her cup, Lea Anne suddenly is distracted by something beyond the window, out on H Street: a shape, or a flash of light, or perhaps just a premonition.

Just beyond the window glass, a very different conversation is under way at the pay telephone. "Mac?"

"Yes."

"We're ready. Go ahead with Agent Phillips. Remember, you want everything in place no later than three."

"All right. I'll see you there."

"God willing," says Louisa Shidler, and hangs up the phone.

Inside the restaurant, Lea Anne's attention has drifted from the conversation. She watches through the window as, outside, the bike messenger hangs up the telephone, near where her bicycle leans against the stanchion of a phone box. The messenger wears the usual impenetrable uniform: helmet, reflective glasses, Spandex, gloves.

"No," says Lea Anne, returning her attention to the lunch. She did not believe the part about the murders in Wyoming.

"No," the brunette agrees, her eyes returning to her coffee. "Not that." She stirs it thoughtfully.

Again Lea Anne looks up from her coffee, past her redheaded friend to the sidewalk outside the window. She feels a chill, realizes she hasn't been concentrating on the conversation.

"Nobody knew her, that was the thing. We all knew her and yet nobody knew her."

"I wonder where she is," the redhead says.

As she turns to mount the bike, she sees them. For a moment, Louisa cannot help but stare in at her old world: the blue suits, the pumps, the handbags, the friends for lunch. She has eaten there. She can almost taste the salad. Looking in at Lea Anne, she catches her eye briefly. It is as though she has shared the glance of something living in a different world. She feels the recognition of a person visiting the zoo and a creature behind zoo glass, except that Louisa, for her part, is not sure which is which. Will she ever rejoin them? The idea seems strange to her now.

Maybe Lea Anne knew it was me, she thinks, as she mounts the bicycle. Louisa has a twenty-mile bicycle ride ahead of her, and she tries to put the thought of Lea Anne out of her mind.

The pieces have been set in motion. Just before one, Mac reaches Eugene Phillips at his desk.

"This is Henry MacPherson."

"Lord, you're like a bad penny, MacPherson."

"I take that as a compliment. How've you been?"

"Middling to fair. You ready to be arrested?"

"Almost. But first, a friend of mine wants to meet you."

"A friend of yours . . . ? Sorry, who's the friend?"

"The friend is shy, Gene, very shy."

"MacPherson, why don't you hold a minute, and I'll—"

"No. I won't hold. Gene, I have a friend anxious to meet *you*. Not your boss."

Phillips stops, thinking. There are a lot of thoughts in his head competing with the silence on the line. Some of them have to do with Sissy, and South Carolina, and his pension. Just not all of them, that's the problem. He looks slowly around the office. Nobody but Picarro, who is firing paper clips at a wastebasket with a rubber band. He returns nonchalantly to the call.

"This might be a lady friend?"

"A friend who is a lady."

"Well, I don't believe that's my case, Mr. MacPherson."

"Gene, I don't want you to go upstairs with this. When she turned herself in to the FBI, six police officers were murdered. When I tried to put a toe into this pond, my maid was murdered, for Chrissake. Stillwell was killed. They kicked your ass off the case. You can't send this upstairs, Gene, because upstairs is dirty, and if you do, you and I and everybody else is dead. You have to put together a team, right away. Gene, there's a group, hostile, probably armed, in an office park about an hour's drive from Washington. You need to be there at three."

"Where?"

"In Maryland. I'll explain later. Look, you get your team, you keep this damn quiet. Four or five capable subordinates, and a bag of tricks, I don't know, guns, body armor, all that sort of stuff, you get them in a vehicle and headed south on Route 5, and you call me. I'll give you more details then."

"Look, MacPherson, if you know where this woman is, you need—"

"Gene, I don't know where she is. I only know where she might come, so long as you do your part. And that's what I plan to tell you. But if you report this upstairs, she won't. Your agency is compromised. You know it and I know it."

"Wait," Phillips is saying, his pencil scribbling the information. Mac gives him the number of his cell phone.

"Wait!"

"Call me when you're headed south on Route 5," Mac repeats. Then the line goes dead.

"Jesus Christ," Phillips says. "Jesus Christ." He looks up to see Bobby Picarro still sitting at his desk.

"The hell's the matter with you, Gene? You look kind of pale—well, you know what I mean. Just get a call from Jimmy Hoffa or something?"

"Picarro," he answers, "Get Rosen and Thibodeau, and meet me back here in ten minutes. Move, boy."

Picarro has never received an order from Phillips before. At first he is not quite sure how to react. But Phillips's dark look leaves no room for quibbling. "Sure," he says.

At about twenty minutes past one, Mark Roth's buzzer rings. He looks up from the indictment he is drafting.

"Yeah?"

"Attorney Krasnowicz to see you, Mark."

"Here?"

"Yes. In the lobby."

Roth fumbles for his calendar. "I don't have anything scheduled. What's this about?"

Roth holds on a minute while the receptionist behind the plate glass in the lounge of the United States Attorney's office makes inquiry of the nervous lawyer seated on the maroon couch with his briefcase balanced on his knees.

"He says it's urgent" is all she can report when she comes back to the line.

When Roth arrives in the lounge, he finds Krasnowicz's fingers drumming rapidly on his briefcase.

"What's up, Joel?"

Krasnowicz jerks to his feet. "Not here," he says, and they step out into the noisy corridor.

"You come here to negotiate another collar?" Roth asks. He's still angry about that one. Nothing so irks a prosecutor as a defendant who defaults because the terms of bail were too light. Particularly if she defaults and then murders six police officers.

"Maybe my client can make it up to you."

"What does that mean? What do you want?"

"A meeting."

"Well, looks like we're having one. What's on the agenda?"

"Not here."

"Where, then?"

"Come with me." Krasnowicz looks nervously around the corridor. His Adam's apple is jumpy.

"Joel, what is this all about? I've got a two-thirty pretrial."

"Get someone to cover for you."

"What are you talking about, Jo—"

"Just come. Now."

"It's Duval, you know how he is." Judge Duval is the most irascible judge in the district. He saves his most vicious tongue lashings for the most trivial offenses, like, say, sending someone else to a pretrial. He once chewed Krasnowicz out in a full courtroom because the page numbers on his brief were on the top, not on the bottom, as the local rules require. People still talk about that.

"Mark. Listen to me." Roth has never seen the man so pale, so quiet, so frightened. "You need to come with me. You need to come with me now."

"Man," Roth says, "I don't know what you're thinking about, but—"

"I have a client who wants to meet you," Joel Krasnowicz says softly.

Roth whirls, more than angry now, his face white with fury, ready to threaten Krasnowicz with anything.

"Where is she, Joel?"

Krasnowicz shakes his head.

"Where? Where is this meeting?"

"Come."

"Joel, you'd better listen to me. You are about ten inches north of an indictment yourself, and you are slipping south fast. If you know where she is, that's not privileged—"

"I understand my ethical duties perfectly well—"

"And I don't know what kind of stunt you have in mind. We are going to call the FBI right now, and you are—"

"Keep your voice down, Mark. I understand my duties. I don't know where my client is. I am instructed to say that she will meet you at a certain time and place, if certain conditions are met. One of those conditions is that you come, now, with me."

"You are part of this?"

"I have been invited to go to a place, with you. If you agree, and certain other things happen, she has told me she will appear."

"Listen, Joel, if you know where she's going to be, it's the same as knowing where she is. Where is she?"

"Mark, the FBI will be there too. Now come on. We don't have much time."

CHAPTER 57

At the small office park in suburban Waldorf, Maryland, the parking lot is almost full. No one is coming or going, and the early departures for Halloween have not quite begun. The "office park" is more of a strip mall than anything else: a long, three-story, gray wooden structure with a bagel shop at one end, and empty retail space at the other. It is separated from the road by a winding asphalt drive. The building's modest central foyer is empty.

Taking care of Robert Gaines proves to be the easy part for Phillips's team. When Gaines is spotted approaching the mall's main entrance, Rosen emerges from Phillips's van. Inside the building, a second agent, receiving his signal from Rosen by headset, steps from behind the corner of a corridor; moments later, Gaines is in the back of an unmarked FBI van, handcuffed, shackled, his mouth taped.

Upstairs, the second-floor hallway is the perfect setting for Bobby Picarro's cameo role in the affair. Attired in youthful "dress-down," he knocks on the door at the end of the corridor that bears the legend "Homepage."

The door opens a crack.

"Hi," says Picarro, "I'm from Burgundy, you know, Burgundy Software upstairs? Sorry, man, we crashed on copy paper. Score some from you?" His eyebrows jiggle.

Inside the door, the man says, "Wait there."

Picarro listens carefully, marking the absence of voices within the office, waiting to hear the footsteps coming back. With his right hand he gives the hold signal to the two other FBI agents who form his team. As the door begins to open and the hand containing the sheaf of paper emerges, Picarro ceases to be a vaguely amiable software engineer. His foot rises and drives the door back, and in the next moment, he, Phillips, and Rosen are on top of young Chris Bragg in the suite's tiny foyer, pinning him to the floor with a weapon at his temple. Seconds later Bragg is in handcuffs. The agents now sweep the rest of the office.

Bragg is alone. Behind a partition is a large room. On the wall are maps of Washington, D.C., and what looks to be western Wyoming. In the center of the room is a white Formica table with four chairs. Behind the table two desks, each one holding a laptop computer, stand side by side before a window overlooking the woods behind the building. Off the back is a second, smaller office, with a desk upon which there is nothing except a laptop computer. At its far end is a walk-in closet. In it Rosen's team finds a file cabinet and a cache of weapons and ammunition.

Bragg is as puzzled as they seem to be when Phillips demands, "Where is Shidler?" For weeks now, Bragg's group has been wondering the same thing. He sits, handcuffed, in a desk chair and says nothing.

Soon, Phillips has examined the back office and the contents of the walk-in closet. "The office is secure," he says into his headset.

Next come Mark Roth and Joel Krasnowicz. Together they make seven; one who understands imperfectly, six who understand not at all and who are beginning to wonder if they are the butt of an elaborate joke.

Phillips looks at a big sail bag that Krasnowicz has hauled up the stairs. "What the hell is all that shit?" he asks.

"She told me to bring it."

The last to labor up the stairs from the lobby, his footsteps pausing at the landing, his tread slow along the corridor to the office, is Henry MacPherson.

"Who are you?" Roth demands as the door opens.

But Phillips interrupts, smiling. "I should have known we'd see you here, MacPherson."

"What are you doing here?" Roth asks him.

"Like the rest of you," Mac answers, "I was invited."

"He's wanted, chief—this is the guy D.C. police want in that Montes case," Picarro says to Phillips. "Isn't it?"

"You can arrest him later," Phillips answers.

Louisa's eight invitees gather around the table in the middle of the room; Krasnowicz, Roth, Phillips, Picarro, and Bragg are seated. Phillips's agents have frisked everyone, and examined Krasnowicz's sail bag and Mac's briefcase. Rosen has taken position outside the door.

The cellular telephone in Joel Krasnowicz's bag rings.

"Mr. Krasnowicz, this is Louisa Shidler."

"It's her," Krasnowicz says to the group.

"It is she," Mac corrects.

"Are you there, Mr. Krasnowicz?"

"Yes."

"Did you bring the items I requested?"

"Yes."

"Good. Please disconnect the office phone and plug in the conference phone. I'll call the office back."

When she does, there are questioning looks all around the room, but they are met only with shrugs, because not even Krasnowicz and Mac know precisely what is going on.

"Let's start with roll call," Louisa's voice begins. "Mac, are you there?"

"Aye, aye."

"Mr. Krasnowicz, still there?"

"Yes, here."

"Will the rest of you identify yourselves, please."

There is something of the schoolteacher in Louisa's voice, methodical, in control, a hint of hurry in it, aware that she must get through the lesson before the school bell rings. Looking somewhat sheepish, they go around the room. The four FBI agents self-consciously start calling out their names.

She cuts in. "Please show your identification to my attorney. Mr. Krasnowicz, will you verify their identities, please?"

They comply, and the roll call continues. When they get to Roth, he says, "Mark Roth, assistant U.S. Attorney."

"Thank you," says Louisa, when it is all finished. "Agent Phillips," she continues, "do you understand that I wish to surrender?"

"I suggest you do so without any more foolishness."

"I plan to do so. I am unarmed. Do you understand?"

"Yes."

"I require your agreement to several conditions before I appear. First, Mr. Roth, will you conference in Judge Freegard?"

"Judge Freegard?"

"Yes. District Judge Helen Freegard. I want her to attend this meeting by telephone."

Roth is poleaxed. "Judge *Freegard*? I can't . . . I can't . . . She's a federal judge. You can't just call her up and say, hey, judge, please join this . . . whatever the hell this is. What is this, anyway?"

No one seems to know.

"Mr. Roth. Call Judge Freegard—"

"I mean, didn't you have procedure in law school? She's a judge, she's judiciary, not executive, it's just not—"

"Mr. Roth. We're not in law school anymore."

"She could be on the bench, she could be . . . you just don't do it."

"I checked her calendar, and she's—"

"You checked her *calendar*?"

Louisa pauses. Belts and suspenders again. It does sound rather odd. "Yes, of course. I checked her calendar. She's not sitting."

"How did you check her calendar?"

"I called the clerk's office."

Roth laughs. "Well, this *is* the Twilight Zone. America's most wanted called the clerk's office. But it doesn't matter, you can't—"

"Mr. Roth. You call up Helen Freegard. You tell her that the subject of an international manhunt wants to surrender herself, right now. And she requires as a condition that Judge Freegard witness the surrender by phone. No Judge Freegard, no Louisa Shidler."

Roth is silent, looking around the room. "Ah, I've gotta run this by my boss, I mean—"

"No!"

It stops him.

"No! One word to Mr. French, and this meeting is over. You will not speak to him—is that understood?—not until this is over."

"All right," Roth says, quietly.

A moment later the room listens to Roth as he says, "Hi, Linda, this is Mark Roth calling. May I speak with the judge, please? . . . Ah, the Shidler case, sort of. . . . No, no, there is no motion—hey, Linda, please, this is an emergency. I need to talk to her. . . . Yeah, an emergency. If she's in a meeting, I need you to interrupt her. I'm sorry, but this is absolutely urgent."

He waits.

"Hello? Mr. Roth?" The judge's voice sounds clearly over the speaker phone, and the men look up from around the Formica table.

"Yes, hello, Judge Freegard. Thanks for taking the call. I, I don't know exactly where to begin this. I'm in an office park in Waldorf, out in suburban Maryland, with four FBI agents, Attorney Joel Krasnowicz, and a newspaperman named MacPherson. We have been brought here because Louisa Shidler has offered to surrender herself to federal authorities. She is not present, but she is on a conference line. She insists, however, that you be, well, I guess that you be on the phone when she surrenders. Maybe she should explain it."

"Good afternoon, Your Honor."

"Is this Louisa Shidler speaking?"

"It is, Your Honor."

"What on earth is going on?"

"Your Honor, at my request, Mr. Roth and the other gentlemen have assembled in an office, as he explained to you. I am prepared to surrender to them. But I will not do so unless certain conditions are met. Among them, I require that I be able to address Mr. Roth, in person, before I am detained by the FBI. Another is that you be present, by phone, and that you hear what I have to say."

"This is completely, completely . . . bizarre. Did you say Attorney Krasnowicz is there?"

"Good afternoon, Your Honor," he pipes up.

"Mr. Krasnowicz, is this some sort of prank?"

"No, Your Honor. This is very serious."

"I am a judge, not an FBI agent, Ms. Shidler, I can't—"

Louisa interrupts. "Judge, if you don't monitor this call, I will not surrender. I'm afraid you are the one person on the law enforcement side of this whole affair on whose integrity I know I can rely. So you can either stay on the line, in which case I surrender, or hang up, in which case I don't. Besides, you promised."

"I *promised?*"

"Yes. You promised. When I appeared for the plea, you said I could talk to the court. Those were your words, remember? Well, now I'm going to take you up on your offer. I want to talk to the court."

The room remains silent for a moment. At length, the judge says, "All right, Mr. Roth, Mr. Krasnowicz, it appears that we are all to become witnesses. I suppose there will be other lawyers and judges when the time comes."

"Very good," Louisa says. Then: "Now, Mr. Phillips. I want your assurance that I will not be stopped on my way in. And I want your agreement that I will be permitted to make a statement before I am arrested and removed from the meeting."

"Ms. Shidler, you are wanted for murder. I'm not going to assume you're unarmed."

"Agent Phillips, your people will see me. They will see that I am not concealing anything. You can post an agent at the Homepage door and frisk me, if need be. I just want to be guaranteed admission."

"You plan on walking in here naked?"

"Almost."

"Well. We're going to search you."

"That's fine, as long as you let me in to the meeting."

"All right," says Phillips.

"And the other thing," Roth says, "you want, you want our permission to make a statement?"

"I want your agreement that I will be permitted to."

He chews over the remark, looking with puzzlement at Krasnowicz. "Doesn't it usually work the other way?"

"Yes," Krasnowicz chimes in. "I have to advise against it."

"I understand, Mr. Krasnowicz. It is your strenuous advice that I make no statement of any kind. All parties to this meeting acknowledge that you have given this advice. In fact, you have given it in front of a federal judge. I'd say you're covered. And, Mr. Roth, aren't you forgetting something?"

"What?"

"You will want the record to show that Agent Phillips has given me Miranda warnings. So, Mr. Roth, do we have an agreement?"

Roth looks over at Phillips, and Phillips nods. "Yes," says Roth, "we have a deal."

"Very good. Mr. Krasnowicz, please open envelope number one."

Krasnowicz does as he is bidden, withdrawing a manila envelope from his satchel. Inside he finds two forms: one a detailed Miranda waiver, acknowledging that Louisa Shidler has been advised that she need not give any statement, and that any statement she gives may be used against her. The second is an acknowledgment that she will be permitted to enter the meeting unmolested and give her statement before being removed or silenced in any fashion.

"Hand them to Mr. Roth, please. Mr. Roth, you will execute these. When you are finished, return them to Mr. Krasnowicz. Mr. Krasnowicz, do they have a fax machine?"

"Yes, they appear to."

"Sorry I made you bring an extra. I had to be sure. When Mr. Roth has signed the agreement, please fax it to Judge Freegard. Agent Phillips, while he's doing that, please contact your outside backup and advise them of the terms of our agreement. Advise me when the judge has the fax and the backup understands the agreement."

Three minutes later, a somewhat bewildered Helen Freegard, sitting in her chambers with the phone crooked on her shoulder, stares in amazement at the wide-eyed young clerk fresh out of the University of Virginia Law School who has handed her a fax containing the signatures as demanded.

"Good," Louisa says at last. "If you would all be so kind as to wait a little longer, I'll be there soon."

Mac and Krasnowicz can tell what Roth and the FBI agents are thinking: This is a setup. We are all about to be made the dupes of some elaborate ruse. It is an extremely nerve-racking few minutes, with the silence scarcely broken by small talk of any kind.

Meanwhile, in the mall's bagel shop, the bike messenger folds her newspaper and rises to go. She exits into the lobby, and begins to climb the stairs.

From the hall, Rosen advises Phillips, "Looks like a messenger is heading up the stairs."

"A messenger? She didn't say anything about a messenger!"

Louisa walks slowly down the corridor, coming face to face with Rosen, posted at the Homepage door.

Through his earpiece Phillips hears Rosen say, "Christ. *She's* the messenger. It's her."

She is dressed in skintight black Lycra bike shorts, a skintight multi-colored cycling jersey, purple reflective sunglasses, and a bike helmet, and she carries a messenger bag. She sets down the bag and removes her helmet and sunglasses, and then, face to face with Agent Rosen, places her hands behind her head.

"Four-Two to Advance One" comes through Phillips's earpiece. "It's her. And she sure isn't hiding anything." But he frisks her anyway.

"She's clean."

"Let her in," says Phillips.

Now she is standing before them. An apparition in Lycra. Short hair, dyed platinum blond with darker roots just beginning to show, her eyes shadowy and tired, and yet, somehow, something in the face, in the quality of the skin, is reminiscent of Renoir's woman. "Good afternoon, gentlemen," she says. "Your Honor, are you there?"

"Still here," Judge Freegard replies over the telephone. "I take it Ms. Shidler has joined the meeting?"

Picarro draws his gun and begins to tell Louisa that she is under arrest.

"Agent Phillips, I understand that I am under arrest and shortly may be detained. But I went to this length to assemble all of you on such short notice for a reason, and as we agreed earlier, you will listen to me before this goes further. Now, please, tell him to put the gun down. As you can see, I am unarmed. You already have two of your men at the door. I scarcely think you have anything to fear from me."

Phillips motions to Picarro to sit down. He whispers into his microphone to Rosen.

"Thank you. Your Honor, gentlemen, I'm here, and you're here, because I no longer know whom to trust. I don't know if I can trust the FBI, or the United States Attorney, or Attorney Krasnowicz. I know that I can trust Mr. MacPherson, but, to paraphrase Stalin, he hasn't any divisions. I am hopeful that there is some one of the rest of you, at least, who is honest. I believe at a minimum that I can trust the court. That is why I asked you to participate, Judge Freegard. You are about to hear a very unusual story. But, at any rate, my theory is that there are now enough of you here so that the truth must come out. And the truth is my only protection, I'm afraid. So I arranged for you all to be witness to this statement."

Like an advocate making a closing argument, she leans up against the table and begins. "On the evening of September sixth, 1996, Royall Stillwell sent me to McLean to meet his wife, Dulaney, and bring her to the Republican National Campaign kickoff party. Mrs. Stillwell, in turn, asked me to go into her husband's study to get a pair of invitations. While in there, I found on the ambassador's desk what I was not supposed to find. A letter addressed to me in care of a Washington post office box which is not mine. I took the letter. It contained a bank statement, from a Swiss bank known as Duclos and Bernard, addressed to me. It was sent by a Swiss lawyer named Henri Racine. Mac, do you have Buster?"

The tired and wounded teddy bear makes his last appearance.

"Excuse me?" asks the judge.

"Your Honor. Buster is my daughter's teddy bear." She looks up at Phillips. "Is there a pair of scissors in that desk?" She returns to the phone. "Inside Buster is a copy of the letter I found that night, along with certain other documents. I hid them there."

Poor Buster: there is not much left of his middle, but what remains is gutted, and white stuffing empties upon the table. Within is the envelope, tightly rolled. Louisa looks at the teddy bear with a tinge of regret. Disemboweled, he still smiles bravely.

"The post office box was number 602334. If you look at the incorporation papers, you can see a note for the state secretary of state's office in the upper right-hand corner. Compare that handwriting to this."

She puts the business card on the table. "Frank Ianella wrote on that card on September sixth."

Roth is looking at the card as she goes on. "Ianella is a campaign aide—or, I should say, *was* an aide—of the ambassador's. He was also a high-ranking official in the Commerce Department, with direct access to Secretary Coburn. The FBI can confirm all of these facts.

"I made two copies of these materials. One I left in a desk drawer in my house. A second I sewed into Buster, here, who used to belong to my daughter, Isabel. I decided to seal the third in an envelope and leave it with Mac. Mr. MacPherson, that is. At the time he was managing editor of the *Washington Herald*."

"Since fired," Mac explains.

"Mac," says Louisa, "why don't you take it from here?"

"Judge, this is Henry MacPherson speaking. I used to be managing editor over at the *Herald*. I've known Louisa since she was about twenty-one, and just out of college. Years ago, she worked for me as a reporter. On September seventeenth, along about eleven or twelve, Louisa showed up in the news room of the *Washington Herald*. She was quite agitated. I hadn't seen her in a number of years. She asked me if she could leave something with me, and handed me an envelope. She said to open it if anything were to happen to her. I told her to call the police. She said that was not possible, and asked me simply to hold the envelope.

"After she had left, I then, I will confess, opened the envelope. I was worried about her. Inside I found these materials she has described and a letter from her explaining what she has now told you—"

"Did you report this to the police?" Phillips interrupts.

"No. I have known Louisa Shidler for a long time. I knew she was a highly—forgive me, Louisa—a highly rational, I might say a conventional, person. I figured that if she was afraid to go to the police, there must be a good reason. But I was intrigued.

"When the news broke about Louisa's arrest, I decided to fly to Geneva and look for this Racine, who had sent the bank statement. I got to meet him by posing as the agent of a wealthy American looking to hide money. I used the same figures that appeared in the Duclos and Bernard statement, and then I mentioned the name of Royall Stillwell. He ended the meeting. The next morning, they found his body in the Rhône. My guess is that he had reported our meeting to whoever was behind the original funds, and that person panicked. But I don't know. I gathered all I could on Racine from the international clipping services."

He spreads the clippings on the table. "There isn't much," he says. Roth begins to look through them.

Krasnowicz explains: "Your Honor, Mr. MacPherson is showing us various newspaper clippings. They are in French. There is a Racine mentioned."

"The next morning," Mac goes on, "I went back to his office. Racine's secretary and two Swiss police officers were there, and I talked her into giving me a copy of Racine's 'Louisa Shidler' file."

"That was convenient," Roth interrupts.

"She thought I was the client," Mac says. "I left his office with the file and drove to Paris, where I posted it to Mr. Krasnowicz, here."

"Judge Freegard, are you hearing this?" Louisa interjects.

"Hearing it, yes. Understanding it, I'm not so sure."

"Very good. Mr. Krasnowicz?"

"On Monday, September thirtieth, I received a package that had been sent via express mail from Paris," says Joel Krasnowicz, taking his cue and opening the package. He hands the sheaf of photocopies to Mac.

"That is the package I sent him from Paris," Mac explains. "It contains the copy of the file I got from Racine's secretary. In it are Racine's notes from his 'Louisa Shidler' file. You'll notice," he continues, paging through the gray photocopies, "the name de Soissons and the initials 'AdS' in these notes here. Through contacts in Paris, I was able to establish that 'AdS' is probably a man named Alain de Soissons.

"I sent another copy of this to my home in Georgetown. I think someone may have been looking for it and was surprised by my cleaning woman, Amada Montes. Gene, you might want to check and see whether it's there. My guess is, it isn't. Haven't been back myself."

He pauses, rubs the back of his neck. "Reminds me, Gene, you need to arrest me at some point."

"We'll get around to it," says Phillips.

Louisa says: "I should add, now being as good a time as any, that I never met Mr. Racine, or anyone from Duclos and Bernard, and I never had any sort of account there, or anywhere else in Switzerland."

"Gene, have your people done your homework assignment?" Mac asks.

Phillips nods. "I have. De Soissons was a career lieutenant of Claude Housez, the industrialist."

"And arms trader," Mac adds. "Correct?"

Phillips nods again.

Mac carries on. "So that part checks out. I met de Soissons. After an eighteen-month stay in a Frankfurt prison, he was feeling less protective of his former boss. He shared something. This."

Mac tosses onto the table a photograph. It shows a group of five men in fatigues, standing in loose formation near an airplane. Two of them hold M-16s.

Roth picks it up and stares at it. "What am I looking at?" he asks.

"That's the team picture, Mr. Roth," Mac answers. "That's the 1965 Laos varsity. Left to right: unknown grundoon number one; Claude Housez; Alain de Soissons; unknown grundoon number two; and, next to him, Air America's own Jimbo Fafard Fitch. Better known to Agent Phillips as Deputy Director James Fitch, FBI."

Roth looks puzzled. "Jim Fitch?" he asks.

"Jim Fitch."

Phillips looks nervous now. He reaches across the table toward the conference phone, then stops. "This could be a doctored photo," he says. "Could be anyone."

"But it's not anyone," says Mac, smiling. "It's Air America captain and all-purpose spook Jim Fitch, Vientiane, 1965. Then he was a crusading anti-Communist. Also a weekend drug smuggler, just to make ends meet. Ever seen his house on Nantucket, by the way? Pretty swell, even for the deputy director of the FBI."

Now Louisa returns to the story. No one in the room is quieter than Mark Roth and the FBI agents. They have ceded all control.

Step by step, Louisa retraces the steps for them; Isabel's kidnapping, the lonely house arrest, her call to Thornacre's show, her own flight westward, her daughter's ordeal with the kidnappers and her escape, the murderous night at Yellowstone Regional.

Finishing, she says, "I read the accounts of the airport incident. They are all false and, I suspect, Agent Phillips, discredited by the physical evidence at the scene. They are also discredited by something else. Mac?"

Mac withdraws a battered black cellular phone and turns it over in his hand. Roth explains, "He's holding a phone, Judge."

Mac says, "Like everybody else, I heard the news of that ambush that night, the sixteenth of October. The next morning, I flew to Salt Lake, rented a car, and got to Cody the next day. I reached the airport in the afternoon. The cops had taped off a big square inside the airfield. They wouldn't let me near it. So I drove along the airport perimeter, parked, and then walked it. There was a chain-link fence running along the highway, broken down in one spot. I looked at the cops through my long lens. I couldn't see much of the crime scene. I was too far away. Two or three Cody police cruisers, a couple of unmarked cars, several guys standing around. I studied it for a while, but couldn't make out more than that. So, as I'm standing there peering through the fence with a camera, suddenly this thing catches my eye. A dark object, about a hundred yards from the fence, poking out of the tall grass, between the perimeter and where the cops were. The grass is long there, so I couldn't be sure. But it looked like a cell phone. That night, I came back."

He lays the telephone on the table.

"Why didn't you turn this over to the authorities?" Roth asks.

"Who are they, Mr. Roth?" Louisa interrupts. "Who are the authorities?"

There is silence in the room, as all eyes examine the phone's battered plastic.

"This phone is a Nokia 997," Mac says. "According to the guy at Radio Shack, it has an embedded speed-dial function. He said this one has some kind of encryption device in it, too. Anyway, you dial pound one, or pound two, et cetera, and it dials a programmed number. The guy gave me a printout of the numbers. It's all in here."

He hands Phillips a document.

"So?" asks Roth.

"So, let's try it," Mac says. He flips on the power and presses pound one. They all hear a busy signal.

"What was that?" the judge asks.

"Your Honor," says Roth, "Mr. MacPherson tried the speed-dial function, and there was a busy signal."

"It was busy," Mac explains, "because we're on the phone. That speed-dial number is the number for this office."

When all have contemplated this remark, Roth says, "That telephone could have come from anywhere."

"Not anywhere, I think," Mac answers. "More likely skittered out the door of a helicopter taking evasive action. You recall that the witnesses talked about a fire, or something, on the copter? Besides, look at this."

He hands them another photograph.

"I took this from the airport perimeter fence. When you blow it up, you'll find it does check out. You've got Park County deputy sheriffs, Cody cops, FBI, all recognizable in the background. See it?"

Roth nods.

"And what do you see in the foreground?"

You could only see a corner, poking out from the grass, but the dark object looked as though it could be the telephone.

Louisa checks her watch. There isn't much time. She begins again, and she tells them the story of her flight from Washington to New York. "Mr. Krasnowicz," she says, "did you bring the Dictaphone?"

The lawyer snaps the tape into the little recorder.

"Agent Phillips," Louisa says, "this tape is difficult to make out. It was recorded in the lavatory of Delta Flight 62 to New York, two days ago. I was with Mr. Housez, and you will find that he made an incriminating statement. He admits to involvement in the helicopter assault."

They listen to the tape for a moment, but the background roar makes the voices all but inaudible.

"I'm sorry," says Judge Freegard, "I can't hear a word of whatever that is."

"It is very difficult to hear," says Louisa. "But Agent Phillips's people have special techniques for filtering out background noise on tapes like this. Mr. Krasnowicz, please give him one of the copies. You have saved another one, correct?"

"Yes, as you instructed."

"Wait a minute," says Roth, who has attempted to master all of this. He is still thinking about his bribe case. "There was a bribe paid, right? The money was paid to your account."

"To an account set up to look like mine, yes," Louisa answers. "As we explained, Housez is an arms trader. We think he was bribing high officials in the departments of commerce and defense to approve applications for U.S. arms sales. These are billion-dollar deals, some of them, and it's worth a lot of money to certain foreign governments to have their transactions approved. Housez was the trader, Secretaries Coburn and Jaeger were probably the beneficiaries of his largesse, and I was a name they used to park the money. But one missing piece of the puzzle is the Concierge, Housez's term for his go-between."

Roth settles again, his hand in his chin. Elaborate tales are never plausible to prosecutors. But he has never seen one presented like this.

"Now then," Louisa says, "we're coming to the conclusion. What is this man's name?" She is looking at the young man who, an hour before, was alone in this office. He turns away from her.

"Bragg," says Phillips.

"Right. Mr. Bragg, when they charge you with conspiracy to commit murder and felony murder, it is likely to go very badly with you. Very badly indeed. But I suspect Mr. Roth here might be inclined to show some restraint if you demonstrated remorse and helped the government identify the people behind this."

"I don't know what you're talking about."

"I think you do. And Mr. Krasnowicz, who is a very skillful lawyer, will tell you that about your best way out of this is to argue that you were too much of a young simpleton to know what was going on around you. Would you concur, Mr. Krasnowicz?"

"Indeed I would."

"Very good. Now, Mr. Bragg, what a good and dutiful young simpleton might do if his telephone rang in the next few minutes is carry on as if none of the people in this room was actually here, wouldn't he, Mr. Roth?"

Roth looks up at her, and now he has caught the thread of her plan. He smiles. "That sounds like a very good idea to me."

"Well, then, we have a little further business with the telephones." Louisa looks at her watch. It's 4:27. She picks up the Nokia, flips it open, and turns the power on. "Agent Phillips, I need to borrow your seat. Mr.

Roth, will you sit closely by me, please. I want you to listen to both ends of this call. I will hold the receiver away from my ear. That cannot, I believe, be construed as a wiretap."

Roth nods his head in concurrence. Federal prosecutors are expert in what is and what is not a wiretap.

"Ms. Shidler and Mr. Roth, the court is now done with this" comes the voice over the speaker phone, and the group in Maryland is reminded that the judge, whom everyone had forgotten, is on the conference line. "I will not be a party to any business, as you put it, with the phones. Ms. Shidler, I have heard what you have to say, and it is most interesting. I can assure you that I will want to hear more. Good-bye."

The sound of the dial tone fills the air. The judge, alas, is a lawyer too. She said she'd be present. She didn't promise for how long. Louisa snaps off the line, frowning, and turns back to Roth.

"Mr. Roth, please be very careful to listen. For what she says, and for what she doesn't say."

She, Roth wonders, as he shifts his chair next to the most wanted woman in America. For her part, Louisa has only to suggest, now, and to let the men act, for they have fallen under her spell. If she should mention that she would like to leave, someone would probably call her a cab.

And then the cell phone rings.

"Yes?" Louisa answers.

"Hello?" It is Housez.

"Hello, Claude. Have you made the arrangements?"

"Yes. I have . . . made the arrangements."

"And you are with the Concierge?"

"Yes."

"I would like to speak with her, please."

"Alas, she is very shy."

Louisa hesitates, looks around at the circle of eyes in the Waldorf office. She was not prepared for this. "I . . . I will not go forward without her," she responds.

"She is very shy about telephones. Why don't you give me the financial instructions?"

In the conference room, the men sit silently. Louisa, taken aback for a moment, can think of nothing but to soldier ahead. "The wire transfer must be made tomorrow, per the instructions I will deliver. When the wire is complete, Brook Bevilaqua will deliver to you the original documents."

"Brook Bevilaqua?"

"Yes."

"Attendez."

In Waldorf, there are inquisitive glances around the conference room. Brook Bevilaqua is one of the best-known law firms in Washington. There is a pause now at the other end of the line, too.

"Louisa, the Concierge is having difficulties to know that you have, er, retained Brook Bevilaqua in this affair."

This Louisa is ready for. She rallies. "It wasn't so hard. They know very little. They know that they have a client, a British Virgin Islands trust. They hold a power of attorney and instructions that they are to deliver the contents of a package of documents as a certain person shall instruct to-morrow. If I get the money, they get the instructions, and deliver the package to you. They also understand that someone may call tomorrow to inspect the package. I expect that you will want to do so in the morning, before you authorize the wire. If they receive a certain phone call, they permit inspection of the package, including their instructions. They have been instructed to show pages to the visitor. They have been told that the visitor must not touch the pages in the package."

"Is there anything else?"

"When Brook Bevilaqua has confirmation that the money has been received by the trust, they release the documents."

"This is very, er, elaborate, is it not, Louisa?"

"Yes. I am very elaborate. And I am also alive."

"Hmmm. Hmmm. Louisa, attendez, please, I discuss this."

He comes back to the telephone in a moment. "Well," he says, "we will need to see copies of these documents before we go any further. Not tomorrow, with the law firm. First. Tonight. Otherwise, we do not know that any of this, how would you say . . ."

Louisa waits, but she fears her antagonist is a better negotiator.

"I have arranged for that tomorrow. At Brook Bevilaqua."

"No. It must be tonight."

"A meeting?"

"Yes."

Her mind racing, Louisa hits on something. There isn't time to test it, so she throws it out and hopes. "All right," she says. "That is agreeable. But the Concierge must be present."

Phillips is shaking his head. He doesn't like this.

"Hmmm," Housez answers after a pause. "Attendez. I need to speak with the Concierge."

After a brief pause, he comes back. "Alas, I am afraid this is not pos-sible."

"Then we have no deal, and my next call is to the FBI."

"I do not think you will do this, not to forfeit the money."

"Listen to me, Claude, this is not about the money. This is about my daughter and myself. Unless I am convinced that the Concierge will honor our agreement, we have no agreement. I must speak with her. Now on the phone, later at the meeting, one or the other."

"This is not possible."

Louisa sighs, and then says, very deliberately, "Claude, did you receive the tape last evening?"

"Yes."

"The Concierge will be at the meeting, or the tape is in the FBI's hands in one hour, along with the information that you are in the District."

There is an extended silence. "Attendez," he says, finally.

This time, when he comes back, he says, "Very well. She suggests a park called Hains Point. You know it?"

"Hains Point? Where, at the end of Potomac Park, by the water there?"

"A giant man in quicksand." It is clear he is echoing someone's description. "A sculpture at the tip of the park . . ."

She knows it, and looks over at Phillips, who now is shaking his head vigorously. Nevertheless, Louisa answers quickly, "All right. When?"

"We cannot meet you right away."

"Seven o'clock?"

"Better say nine. We have some business to arrange first."

"Okay, nine," Louisa says. "Nine o'clock. You and the Concierge. Don't bring anyone else. That thug of yours, the one with the ponytail. Leave him home. I'll have made arrangements about what will be disclosed if anything happens to me. Anything happens to me, the tape will be with the FBI. You understand?"

Louisa switches off the phone, the disappointment plain on her face. In the room there is a silence no one wants to break. "You know she was with him, right?" She looks beseechingly at Roth, rubs her temple. "I thought she would come on the phone. If I don't have her . . ."

But she hasn't time to despair, for now the office phone is ringing. "Wait," she says, "that will be her. Mr. Roth, Mr. Phillips, listen in on this."

Now Bragg feels the stares on him again, as Louisa turns to lean close to him. "Years in prison, Mr. Bragg, years in prison could ride on this conversation," Louisa says.

The phone rings again. Picarro lifts the receiver, places it to Bragg's ear.

"Homepage," he answers, holding the receiver to one side.

"Get me Gaines," says a woman's voice.

Roth's eyebrows, and Louisa's, tell the story. Louisa recognizes the voice instantly. Roth has heard it before, certainly, but is struggling to place it.

"He's not here," Bragg says.

"I told him to be there. Get hold of him immediately and see that he calls me. I must speak with him right away."

At this moment, Bragg decides to earn himself a few extra months off. "Is there anything I can do?"

"Listen, honey, we've just had a conversation with a certain person we've all been anxious to find. She wants to meet me at Hains Point tonight at nine. Personally. With our French friend."

"Are you going to meet her?"

"I don't see how I can let her down. But I need to be properly equipped for this kind of meeting. I want one of you to come to my office immediately with the, ah, equipment. Do you understand?"

"High-caliber?"

"I haven't any idea, really. I want something reliable which will fit in my pocket and which I won't have to fool with. Are we communicating?"

Bragg looks at Phillips, and Phillips is nodding his head.

"Yes," Bragg answers. "Yes, ma'am, we're communicating pretty well."

"Very good. Well, if you can do this, so be it. Otherwise, send Gaines. Six o'clock. Be discreet. Just tell them at the door that you're here from the campaign." The dial tone sounds in the receiver. For a moment, no one speaks.

"Well," Louisa asks, "is that enough? Now do you have her?"

Roth and MacPherson have recognized the woman's voice. Phillips's expression is blank. Roth finds that the eyes of the room are on him. It is his job to know the answer to this question.

"No," he answers, after deliberating.

"No?" Louisa is incredulous. How much more do these people need?

Shaking his head, the prosecutor explains. "It sounds incriminating, but think about what she said. She wants to be equipped. With something reliable that will fit in her pocket. Could be anything. Could be a cell phone."

"What do you mean?" Louisa demands. "You heard her! High-caliber, she said!"

"A really good cell phone," says Krasnowicz.

Louisa, incredulous, is shaking her head, astonished by this. Lawyers! "You're not serious!"

Roth rubs his temple. "Look, I don't know what to believe here. If this is for real, why don't you go ahead with the Brook Bevilaqua thing? Once they wire the money and show up for the documents, maybe there's something to look at—"

Louisa stares at him in disbelief, then at Phillips.

"Something to look at? You'll have something to look at, all right, you'll have a victim to look at. Mr. Roth, I haven't hired Brook Bevilaqua! That's just a story! Do you really think I can get Brook Bevilaqua to close a blackmail transaction?"

"I dunno," mutters Joel Krasnowicz. "Isn't that what they usually do?"

"The point was to get her on the phone. Surely, Mr. Roth . . . ?" Louisa says, ignoring her lawyer. "Surely . . ."

Her eyes search the room, but no one will return the glance. At last she notices that Eugene Phillips is smiling in a patient, distant way, the smile of a fisherman who has watched a prize rainbow strike twice at successive fly casts, and who thinks it is now only a matter of time before the fish is his.

The lawyers see only that the fish is not landed. That is why they are lawyers.

"Mark's right, you can't be sure," Joel Krasnowicz says. With an odd light in his eye, he leans back in his chair, and begins declaiming. "*Assume* it's a gun she wants. It doesn't matter. Members of the jury," he says, "my client had a meeting planned on a dark night in a lonely place with this suspected killer. It was a misguided effort, an imprudent one, but the killer had reached out to her. She thought she could do the republic a service by helping bring this escaped felon, this killer, to justice. Of course she called her private security guards. Of course she asked them to provide her with protection. Wouldn't you?"

Louisa sinks to the table, her head in her hands.

" 'Private security guards'? Joel—"

"Louisa, it's what I do for a living. Usually the facts are worse."

"You can't, you can't just go pick her up?" Louisa implores the prosecutor.

But Mark Roth declines, too. He will not go out on a limb on this one, not with the woman on the other end of the line. "I'll recommend to my boss that we question her."

"And I'll be dead before the recommendation is denied. God! What do we need, another person killed?"

"Louisa—"

"Because that's what you're going to have. You are going to have a dead suspect, a dead suspect with a dead twelve-year-old! Mr. Roth, why do you think this case is in the Eastern District?"

"Sorry?"

"The Eastern District of Virginia, Mr. Roth. Why was I prosecuted there? I live in Maryland, and I worked in the District of Columbia. This case could easily have been brought in either district. Instead, they brought the case in Virginia, on the basis of travel through National Airport. Virginia had the barest relationship with the alleged crimes. So why the Eastern District?"

Roth shrugs. The defense had never raised improper venue. He never gave it any thought. A procedural thing. The FBI wanted him to prosecute maybe. Something trivial: lawyers are always blind to the real explanations of their own good fortune. "The 'rocket docket'?" he asks, referring to the Eastern District's speedy trial rules, notorious among lawyers.

"Are you kidding? Did you *want* a speedy trial? You brought this case in five days. You had to subject yourself to, what was it, Joel, the initial hearing?"

"Preliminary hearing," he says.

"Right, whatever, the hearing, instead of the indictment. You had no time to investigate. Were you ready to try it? I doubt it. The *last* thing you wanted was to be in a hurry to come to trial."

Roth nods. It was true. The direction he received on September eighteenth to obtain an indictment by the twentieth was extraordinary, and proved impossible. He'd stayed up all night on the nineteenth just to get a criminal complaint prepared. "True bill by the weekend," Hanscom said. Roth remembers telling him there was no way to do it, he'd have to go criminal complaint, and thinking, "How the hell will we be ready to go if she doesn't plead?"

Louisa interrupts these reflections. "Mr. Roth, I was indicted in the Eastern District because your *boss* happens to be there. Who dictated that I was to serve ten years? To have the collar? Detention? Remember? Mr. Krasnowicz was stunned at that request, and you would never have negotiated it with him if I hadn't instructed him to do it. I was a first-time offender in a nonviolent crime. Ten years served would have been pretty unusual on a plea. That came from upstairs, didn't it? That's what you told Joel, anyway. Don't you see? She controls upstairs! Just like all the others she controls. She controls Hanscom French, just like she controlled Royall, just like she controls Coburn at Commerce and Jaeger at Defense and all the others. And, indirectly, you."

Roth absorbs this, fearful now, for too much of it is making sense. Louisa is speaking more softly. "Surely, Mark, there's enough. Don't you have enough? Go, make the arrest. You had a lot less reason to arrest me."

Mark Roth shakes his head. Louisa's last statement is true, he admits, but Louisa wasn't . . . well, Louisa wasn't *her*. "Louisa," he answers, slowly, "this has been the most, I don't know, the strangest afternoon of my career. But I know one thing. Mark Roth is not, on the basis of a bizarre two hours in Charles County, Maryland, going to sign an application for an arrest warrant for a woman who—"

"Who's as powerful as—"

"Louisa—"

"That's it, isn't it! That's it. She's intimidated all of you. Remember Charlie, whoever he is? The one who had big ones? That's what you and Joel were laughing about the day I was arraigned. Remember? Well, has any one of you got big ones now?"

A single woman, a woman alone, imploring a room full of silent men. That is what she has become. She begins to glance, distracted, from one to the next.

"Louisa, she hasn't shot anyone," Roth says at length. "All she's done is take a step to protect herself."

The floor is closed to debate. Louisa takes a final count of the ballots, looking first at Roth, then at Krasnowicz, for a sign of reconsideration. But both are pessimists, trained to identify the missing rung, not the sound rungs, of an argument's ladder. At last, she looks over at Mac.

"I'll write it, if you want," he says. "Fuck 'em."

"Bless you, Mac," she says, smiling. "But you're fired, remember? And under arrest, or about to be."

Agent Phillips is nodding, still smiling in a distant sort of way, as Louisa looks his way. And then she hears it again, what Roth let slip.

"What did you say before?"

"All she's done—"

"No, before that. You said she hasn't shot anyone."

She looks at Phillips for a moment, then over at Picarro, slouching against the door. Then she turns and confronts the young man sitting by the phone.

"Mr. Bragg. You've never met her, have you?"

Bragg shakes his head, involuntarily letting go of the truth. Louisa returns to Phillips, with a question in her eye.

"I don't exactly want to drop this, either," says Phillips. "But the lawyers—"

"Never mind the lawyers, Agent Phillips," answers Louisa Shidler. "Didn't you hear what Mr. Roth just said? And Mr. Bragg? I'm going to meet her. And Mr. Bragg isn't feeling well, so someone else is going in his place, to equip her to meet me."

When she has explained her plan, no one speaks, except Phillips. "I don't like it," he says, halfheartedly. "Besides, I'm not sure I can pass for Bragg, here."

"But, chief, you know all us white boys look alike." The big boyish grin of Bobby Picarro again has the floor. He hasn't had fun for at least an hour, and his attention span isn't much longer than that. It's time to have some more.

"Shit, I don't know," Phillips says, shaking his head a few moments later. "You start fooling around with guns, some damn thing always goes wrong."

CHAPTER 58

In the darkness, the limbs seem to claw their way out of the earth. It is as though a giant's corpse were awakening, a giant returned with impatience for All Saints' Eve. Or perhaps it is sinking into the muck there at the junction of the two rivers. The ambiguity of the statue at Hains Point could mean either one. It is a spectral shape, the right arm clutching the air, the foot and hand that have all but sunk, the head, neck-deep in the ground, the mouth frozen in its aluminum scream. It makes them both shiver, the thing looming out of the darkness.

By day the park is busy, but at night it is a lonely place, a spit of land poking into the river across the broad reach of the Potomac from National Airport. The sluggish stream of the Anacostia River empties into the Potomac here, and across the river the yellow pinpoints from the runways and parking lots at National dance through the foggy air like strings of houselights on a rainy Christmas night. Big jets take off and land in rapid succession, and the noise thunders across the river. Once every few minutes, a smaller commuter plane climbs in a northward flight path, crossing the Potomac and the park, its engine noise building to a loud crescendo and then fading.

The pair walk briskly across the access road: Claude Housez and the woman he calls the Concierge. It is cold and damp underfoot and a little foggy. They cross beneath the streetlights to the field, peering ahead at the dark shape.

"Louisa?" she calls, tentatively.

There is no answer. They reach the statue and circle it cautiously. She touches its dark, striated aluminum, afraid someone will dart out from the shadows. But no one does. The statue is deserted.

"Louisa?" she calls out again, as they complete the circle.

Housez's eyes flit back and forth, the exposure of this site making him visibly nervous. They wait, looking back the way they came. A few minutes go by. He reaches for a cigarette and lights it, the match flare making a tiny light in the darkness.

"You think she's not coming? She's frightened and she's not coming?"

"Attendez," Housez answers.

The Concierge lights a cigarette too. The dim light reflects off her fair hair, the hardness of her frown. She paces, nervously, behind Housez. Though utterly confident in almost any setting, even her nerves are stretched by this one, and she glances from imagined shape to imagined shape. A few more minutes go by.

As the Concierge finishes her cigarette, she sees movement in the distance. Seventy-five yards off, someone has come out from beneath the trees by the river's edge, alone in the darkness. The Concierge sees only a dark figure, a shape and the flow of a long coat.

"There," she says.

"Allons-y," Housez answers, and he begins to cross the field.

Near the water's edge, across the darkened field by a cluster of hemlocks, the figure stands motionless. Housez strikes out across the field, the Concierge following. The figure waits, her head wrapped in a scarf. Under her right hand is a manila envelope. Her left hangs empty.

"Louisa?"

Still there is no answer. Housez marches across the grass, the Concierge falling a little bit behind. When they reach a spot about fifteen yards away from the figure, they hear Louisa's voice. "Come no closer, please. Stop there."

Louisa Shidler looks heavy, somehow, but her face is in shadow.

"Louisa . . ."

"I have your package," she says.

The Concierge shows no interest in it, however. "I'm sure you do," she answers, coming up behind Housez.

"Why are your hands in your pockets?" Louisa asks Housez.

"Il fait froid, Louisa."

"Pas mal," she answers. "You see that, except for your package, my hands are empty."

"How thoughtful of you. It happens that ours are not," the Concierge replies.

"You told me—" Louisa's voice is cut off by the roar of a commuter plane's engine, and they stand in silence, waiting for it to pass overhead.

Louisa looks first at one, and then the other. Behind her is the end of Hains Point. Beyond, the greasy water of the Potomac laps darkly against the retaining wall. When the plane's noise begins to diminish, she carries on. "You know that if anything happens to me, if Brook Bevilaqua does not receive certain instructions, copies of those documents will be submitted to the news media tomorrow. And the tape with them."

"Yes. The tape. Well, even if you have made arrangements for it to turn up, dear, it is rather difficult to decipher. I must say, Louisa, you did surprise me with your scandalous behavior. But as to who on earth your companion was, why, that really might be anyone on that tape, don't you think?"

The Concierge takes a step forward, and pulls from her pocket a small handgun. She points it at Louisa. "But Brook Bevilaqua *will* receive instructions," she says. "It will receive them in about fifteen minutes, when the managing partner will be served at home with a subpoena from the U.S. Attorney's office. Brook Bevilaqua will be instructed by a subpoena served by the FBI that the originals of the documents you are holding there are forgeries, that they have been duped by a criminal, an assassin, into complicity in a number of potential federal crimes, and that they are to deliver the originals to the FBI immediately. Mr. Fitch's people will be there to collect the papers."

"God, I was a fool," Louisa mutters.

"Yes," the Concierge answers. "It was good of you to call us."

A long silence, while the Concierge permits Louisa to see how easily she has dismantled the little fence Louisa has erected. Louisa's eyes are drawn to the gun barrel. It is going to be all right, she thinks. There are only blanks behind it. Picarro arranged that. That was the plan, and surely he has carried it out. Surely.

She asks, "Why did this happen to me? Why did you take everything from me? I'm nothing to you."

"Don't take it personally, Louisa."

"Everything. My daughter and my honor and my freedom and my reputation and . . . now, my life. Why are you hounding me? Why? Is it all about the money?"

They do not answer. Housez's expression betrays nothing, except a trace of impatience. If this is to look like a suicide, it has to be at closer range. But there will be problems if they approach: marks of a struggle in the grass. He is calculating. He looks over to the Concierge.

"One question, just one question," Louisa says, her voice catching. "At least tell me, before you do this. Was it just you, Coburn, and Jaeger? Or was Royall a part of it too?"

The mention of the names surprises the Concierge, Louisa can see that. Draw her out, she must draw her out before the shooting of the blanks which she prays that Bobby Picarro loaded in the Concierge's office two hours before. Louisa cannot take her eyes off the gun barrel. She feels herself begin to hyperventilate.

The Concierge's expression, the tone of her voice, has its hard edge back. She has dropped all pretense. "Louisa," she says, "perhaps I underestimated you. I don't know how you've worked that out about dear Messrs. Coburn and Jaeger. You were supposed to be just a safe deposit box, that's all. A safe deposit box that would be easy to explain should it ever be discovered."

"By Royall?"

"No, Louisa. Dear Royall was simply not a reliable man on these matters."

Louisa nods. It is as she feared. He was duped, too. Frank had dropped off the mail, that's what Doolie said that night. Frank. And then when the envelope was missing, Frank whispered in Royall's ear, made him think he had uncovered Louisa's misdeeds. She says, "Royall instructed me to make the change on the pharmaceutical deal—"

"Because Coburn instructed him, Louisa, and Coburn instructed Royall because I instructed Coburn and Jaeger. But that's all beside the point. The pharmaceutical deal was a smoke screen. None of that really mattered, except to explain things, should your account be discovered. The main point is that this wouldn't have been a problem for you if you hadn't gone snooping through other people's mail."

"And you?"

"You *really* don't understand about me, do you? You worked for them and you never understood it. You think I was Royall's girl? Or Coburn's? Or any of them? You think that I work for the politicians? No. I'm the *client,* Louisa. And I remain the client, year in, year out. Well, we do require Republicans in power, of course, and your little adventure threatened to give us a little scare this year, coming as it did right before the election, but now it doesn't matter. Poor dear Royall has been cut down by dreadful Muslim extremists, and we're all rallying behind the President, aren't we?"

"My God—"

"Oh, Louisa, please don't get preachy. Breed would probably appoint me ambassador if he knew the facts, the old fool. You see, Louisa, I deliver the offices they want, and I take my fees. Control the message, control the spin, yes, that's all part of delivering the offices. But the offices cost, Louisa, they cost. If you want it from me, you pay. And they do, all of them, without a whimper. They do as I say, they vote as I say, they make speeches as I say. Frankly, if they want to succeed, they fuck as I say. And, yes, when they do business, it's as I say. But there comes a point when serving the silly little boys becomes rather boring, Louisa. When one decides that it is time for the silly little boys to serve oneself."

From where Louisa stands, the dim light from the statue throws her antagonists into silhouette. Behind Louisa, across the river, another commuter plane lifts off from the runway at National and veers north. The whine of its engine grows.

"Enough," says Housez. "Enough talking. In a moment, someone comes." And now his hand draws a second weapon from underneath his jacket. Louisa feels her throat tighten, as she sees its metallic reflection catch the faint light. Her heart jumps, and she looks from one to the other, her breath suddenly shallow and rapid. Where did he get that?

She forces the conversation on. "The business was selling arms, wasn't it? Selling the approvals. You controlled Coburn, and Coburn controlled multi-billion-dollar arms deals, and Mr. Housez's client got the arms, and he made his cut, and you made yours."

The noise of the approaching airplane is loud, now. Louisa catches something, a subtle flicker from Housez's eyes, and has a sudden revelation: they plan to kill her when the plane is directly overhead.

"Louisa, my dear, a gold star for you. You are *such* a clever girl. Except with a telephone. You just have a way of calling the wrong sort of people. You might have called for help, you know. And instead, you called—"

"The Concierge?" Louisa interrupts.

As the noise of the approaching plane grows louder, Louisa can almost make out the nervous smile in the darkness. Or perhaps it is a flash of light reflected on teeth. "Yes, that's right too. So you've done a lot of homework. Too much. But it's over now, Louisa. You see, school's about to close." She is holding the gun extended, hesitating, her hand shaking a little in the half light.

Louisa makes her last, desperate gambit. "Don't you have the stomach for it, Cynthia?"

But the Concierge doesn't answer, as the noise of the aircraft grows.

"Come then," Housez demands, "down on your knees." He moves quickly toward her.

Louisa's eyes dart toward Housez.

"You don't, do you, Cynthia? You'll hire someone to do it for you!" She steps back, nervously, as Housez comes on.

"Come then!" shouts Housez. "On your knees!"

It is the wrong gun, the wrong gun seeming to rise in slow motion in the Frenchman's hand, while the whine of the commuter engine reaches its angry crescendo. The wrong gun rises toward her, the correct one drops down, as Cynthia Barnett's hand begins to fall to her side, and the commuter jet passes overhead. Claude Housez's plan had been to order Louisa at gunpoint to her knees, to approach her, and to set up the killing at close range. Cynthia would cover her while Housez set up the suicide.

Housez's gun has her in range now. Louisa backs away from him, her eyes wide with fear.

The FBI agents have seen enough. From the direction of the statue, a voice from a megaphone cries, "Freeze!" From the same quarter, suddenly there is a searchlight. In the split-second of Housez's confusion comes the flash and crack as his index finger, one synapse ahead of his consciousness, squeezes the trigger.

Fire leaps in the night. The shot is an instinctive reaction. It cannot be recalled now. It strikes Louisa Shidler squarely above the breastbone, and the force of the blast drives her backward and to the cold ground.

"Goddammit!" a man shouts in the distance.

Panicked, Housez whirls. But not in time: the covering sharpshooter squeezes off two quick rounds, dropping him instantly, and then the agents are upon the two from every side, Phillips's team rushing in on foot, the headlights of the vehicles racing across the field. "You are surrounded! Drop your weapon! Drop your weapon!"

Smaug sees the lights coming at her, the rushing men in the night, feels the noose close around her neck. Her gun slides from her hand, slides and drops into the grass.

Now it is a thicket of drawn weapons around her and Housez. "Get down on your knees, your goddamned knees!" a voice is screaming at Cynthia Barnett.

From Smaug, at first, disbelief. "No!" she calls. "No!" And then she falls to her knees, and a weird wailing sound, almost animal, comes from her throat. "Oh my God, oh my God!" she cries, "what has he done!" Her head is in her hands as she cringes before the high beams of an FBI Suburban, which moments ago has hurtled across the grass. She is melting, a dragon no longer, melting on the grass.

But, in the first moments, most of the attention is paid elsewhere. A pair of agents attends to Housez. Four more crowd around Louisa. She lies on her back, her arms outspread. Anxious fingers feel for a pulse in her throat. A set of hands rips at the coat buttons, tearing the cloth away and pulling at the Velcro straps, ripping, hurling away the double layers of

Kevlar body armor. Only then do the eyes see, gratefully, that the projectile has lodged in the second layer, and only then does Eugene Phillips expel a long breath.

There is no blood, and Louisa's breathing is labored and shallow, but regular. She has sustained the equivalent of a very hard punch to the solar plexus.

As the men minister to her, the Renoir woman slowly opens her eyes. My God, she thinks, I'm still here. In that fiery moment she was sure of her own death. The grass is cold and damp beneath her coat, but she cannot feel anything except the hands of the men. The air is full of sound now, the crackle of radios, the scream of a siren, the clipped, frantic conversation of the men, the roar of an ambulance racing across the field. She feels gentle hands around her slipping a blanket underneath her shoulders. Another pair of headlights is bouncing across the grass.

"Just relax, just relax," someone is saying. "You're going to be all right."

With difficulty, Louisa pushes herself to her elbow, struggling to master her breath. Too many things have happened in one instant, and she continues to hyperventilate.

"Belts," she whispers, "belts—"

"I ought to be fired for letting you pull this stunt! Jesus God, woman!" she hears Phillips say.

"—and suspenders," she returns, softly.

"Let's get a gurney over here," someone is calling.

As Louisa's vision adjusts, she finds herself looking through a fence of flashlight beams at Smaug, now huddled on the ground.

"What are you doing?" Barnett is demanding of the agent who is kneeling to fasten the handcuffs. "She was going to shoot us! She was going to shoot us! She is an assassin, and we thought—"

"Shut up!" somebody says, contemptuously. Smaug falls silent as the handcuffs snap closed.

The men come with the gurney, but Louisa waves it off. "No," she says, "help me up, please. I think I'll be all right."

They grasp Louisa by the arms and lift her to her feet. She takes a step toward the waiting ambulance, then stops. Still out of breath and a little dizzy, Louisa Shidler slowly walks over to Cynthia Barnett. "Just a moment," she says.

Louisa fishes through the shreds of the now-tattered coat, fumbles for a bit, slowly, as if she is determined to relish the fact that, for the first time in as long as she can remember, there is absolutely no hurry. Then she withdraws a metal object from the pocket. The flashlight beams catch it as she holds it unsteadily in her left hand. She wavers a little on her feet.

"I thought you'd want to know," she says to Smaug, half whispering, "that I was armed, too."

All of them—Smaug, the agents and the paramedics standing in a circle, the driver behind the windshield—all of them wait for Louisa Shidler's shaking fingers. They squeeze with excruciating slowness, finally depressing the plastic button. Louisa listens, for a moment, to the satisfying squeak as the tape rewinds, the one that tells you that your Dictaphone has been recording. Then she returns the Dictaphone to the pocket.

"Trick or treat, Cynthia," she says.

"Bitch."

A smile comes to the face of the Renoir woman, a smile that seems to light it in the darkness. "Well," she answers, "a little dog, anyway."

CHAPTER 59

Just before eleven A.M. Saturday, November 2, Louisa Shidler is packing her things and readying herself to check herself out of Veteran's Hospital when Toby arrives at her room. He reaches from behind to touch her
shoulder and kisses her softly on the cheek. She nuzzles him a moment
and smiles.

"How you feeling?"

"I'm fine. Got such a night's sleep, Tobe! The first like that in such a
long time. Did you talk to Isabel?"

"Yes. She's okay. She's waiting for us at Marcy's."

Just the mention of her daughter's name sends Louisa's fingers scurrying, as if by hastening the packing she can advance the moment of seeing
her again.

"I am sorry about your friend's card," Louisa says.

"Who?"

"Samantha Snow. I guess I owe her a few hundred dollars. And her
card was eaten by a machine in, I think it was somewhere in Oklahoma."

"Yeah, it was. But don't worry about it."

"I didn't, much," Louisa answers, smiling frostily. She returns to her
packing.

They are interrupted by a knock. Eugene Phillips peers around the
door. In his hand are a newspaper and a stack of telephone messages.

"Morning," he says.

"Good morning, Agent Phillips," Louisa answers. "This is my husband, Toby Higginson."

"Gene. Mr. Higginson, we've spoken once or twice."

"Yes. Good to know you. And thank you for everything you did."

"How you doing, Louisa?" Phillips asks.

"I'm fine, just fine!" She smiles. "How's your coat?"

"Not too much left of it. Did Sissy give me a going-over! Mmm-hmm!"

They laugh together.

"What's the news?" Louisa asks.

"You're the news. You and Cynthia Barnett and Royall Stillwell and Coburn and—"

"Has he resigned?"

"Coburn? Not yet. Rumor is, today."

"Jaeger?"

"Same thing."

"Fitch?"

"Leave of absence. Effective this morning. Have you seen the paper?"

"No. What about Cynthia?"

"Hired Bert O'Connor," Phillips answers, naming a well-known criminal-defense lawyer.

"Is he going to beat you guys?" asks Louisa.

"Who knows? But things are going well. We executed a search warrant that night, got all of her computers at home and in the office. We've got your tape. Bragg's flipped. French police have de Soissons, and he's already given them quite a statement. Looks like the 'Guardians of Allah' assassination story is bullshit. We may break the case pretty soon. We'll see."

"What happened to Housez?" she asks.

"Going to make it, the doctors are saying."

She sighs. "Good. There's been altogether too much killing. I'm glad none of it was on my side. Hey, have your people cleaned up the tape?"

"Pretty well. You did a good job." Phillips smiles a half smile. "You might have to explain the context a little."

"Yes, well, I expect I will. To myself as well."

She walks to the window and looks out at the parking lot below. "Gene, what happened to Frank Ianella? Has he been arrested?"

"No. He's wanted for questioning, but no one can find him."

"Lord," she says, still staring outside. "Poor Frank. How far is this thing going to go?"

"I don't know. There's already open speculation about Breed."

"And the election?"

"Up for grabs, they're saying. Proctor has scheduled a press conference for this afternoon. Breed's in hiding at Camp David. You know, you're famous. Take a look at this." He extends the newspaper toward her.

But she rejects it, turns toward the bed, zips up her toilet kit, and puts it in her bag. Then she begins to make the bed.

"Hon, they'll do that for you," says Toby.

She ignores him, and goes on with the bed making. "To be honest, I don't really care," she says to Phillips. "Not anymore. I expect I won't vote, this time."

When Louisa finishes the bed, she goes to the mirror, brushing a hand through her hair. "Looks like a cornfield harvested by a farmer in his cups," she says softly. "Gene, maybe I could use that fifty-million-dollar bribe I was supposed to get. I need a serious makeover."

The FBI agent chuckles. "Money's still setting there with Mr. Duclos and Mr. Bernard. Damned if that isn't the *loneliest* fifty million dollars anybody ever heard of. That money's an orphan. Don't belong to *nobody*. Course, if you say it's yours, Bureau might have to rethink things a little."

"No, more's the pity." She fusses in the mirror, pulling at her hair. "My hair alone'll need more help than that, so I guess it doesn't matter. Hope it's put to some good use."

"Oh, I guess the lawyers will get it in the end, that's the usual way of it," says Phillips. "Lawyers from all around the world can argue over this cookie jar—Americans, Swiss, British Channel Islands, British Virgin Islands, Guadaloupian lawyers—I mean, that money made a lot of stops along the way. There'll be quite a number of them arguing about which country oughta claim the cookies, and running up the fees until the cookies are all gone to pay 'em."

But Louisa hasn't been listening, for she isn't really interested in the money. Somber now, she asks the FBI agent, "Gene, why all the elaborate arrangements with me? Do you understand that part?"

"You mean, why didn't they just kill you to begin with?"

"Yes."

He steps across the room and sits down. "I think it's like Housez said on the plane. You remember you told Stillwell that you had information that would implicate him?"

"Yes.

"Ianella was there, right?"

"Yes." She nods. "Yes, he was."

"He was the runner. He reported the news to Cynthia Barnett, and they worried that your information could sabotage the campaign. They could arrange for you to get hit by a truck, but if Stillwell were implicated, the scandal might sink the ticket, and the one thing Barnett and her group needed—really, the only thing—was a Republican reelection. So they had to find some way to keep you quiet through the election. That was the original plan, as far as I can tell."

"All right, I guess that makes sense. So, then, why is Royall assassinated?"

"Well, this part is pretty speculative still. But I think it was MacPherson figured this one out. Once you left home and went out after Isabel, then the story might come out at any time. And when you made that call from the car phone, they figured they had hours, not days, before it was out."

She looks pale, reaches for the bed.

"Are you all right, hon?" Toby asks.

She sits. "I killed him," she says.

"No," Phillips answers. "They killed him. But they killed him because somebody on their team decided to make a bigger bang. And at that point, when they rigged the investigation with this Arab-devils bullshit, you've got terrorists murdering a potential VP, you've got a story guaranteed to submerge everything else. Anything you might say would be so much noise. In all the confusion, Breed would get reelected. That was the idea."

"God in Heaven," she says. "God in Heaven."

Phillips rises. "You may want to think about how you're going to get out of here."

"How do you mean?"

"Louisa, you got about fifty press people in the lobby. Not to mention the calls." He holds up the sheaf of telephone messages. "CBS, NBC, *Times, Post, Globe,* ABC, *Herald, Atlanta Constitution,* CNN, *Winston-Salem Journal,* another one from NBC, St. Pete *Times,* AP, Fox, Birch Thornacre—"

"Birch Thornacre?"

"That's what it says."

"Naaah," she answers. "I've already been on *his* show."

While they are still chuckling, a nurse arrives. "Everything all right, Ms. Shidler?"

Louisa's face falls as the young woman unwraps the sphygmomanometer. "I sort of hoped I was done with that," Louisa says, grimacing at it.

"Last one," the nurse answers. "Want to roll your sleeve up for me? Thanks."

While the nurse measures his wife's blood pressure, Toby sits on the bed, silently leafing through the stack of phone slips. Phillips tells them that AP broke the story on Halloween night.

"AP, not Mac?" she interrupts.

"No, far as we know, some guy named Pierce from France was first. MacPherson has a story today. Of course, it's all over everywhere, now."

"Weren't you supposed to arrest him?" she asks, teasingly.

"Yeah. Never quite got around to it. I'll give him a call."

"Jesus, Weezer," Toby interrupts, looking at a phone message. "Some guy from Creative Artists . . ."

"What's that?"

"Book agent."

She sighs, shaking her head. "Slime. Any other cranks?"

"Yup."

Toby holds up the pink slip for the room to see. "Here's one from Jerry Garcia."

Phillips laughs, and Toby joins him. Even the nurse thinks it funny, and she smiles as she finishes writing up Louisa's blood pressure on her chart.

But Louisa surprises them. "*That* call I'll take."

Toby glances across to Phillips, who stands by the window. Phillips turns from the glass, where he had been looking down at the parking lot, and shrugs. But Louisa is oblivious to this, flushed and so excited that she misdials twice.

"Bear!"

"Hey, that you, Louisa?" He is on the car phone, but his voice is as clear as if he were sitting next to her.

"Bear! Oh, Bear! God it's good to hear you!"

"You all right?"

"I'm good, I'm real good, Bear. Thank you. Thank you for calling."

"Oh, sure, Louisa. Now that you're so famous and all, I had to say hello."

"Where are you?"

"Me and Sugaree are coming up to Flagstaff in about fifteen miles."

"I miss that old truck, Bear.

"She ain't so old. Ain't no older than you."

"I know. Bear, thank you for everything."

"Hey, that's okay."

"How've you been? Are you all right? Becky, Travis, are they—"

"Oh, yeah, everyone's fine. Beck's been watching a lot of TV. She's not quite sure about this latest thing. You being innocent and all."

"Now, what about your motorcycle? How am I going to get that back to you?"

From the foot of the hospital bed, Toby has been staring at his wife with growing astonishment. Phillips has come closer, too. Now Toby mouths, "Motorcycle?"

"Don't worry about it, Louisa," Bear is answering. "Beck wouldn't let me take it back anyway. She's glad to see it gone. It's yours. It do okay for you? Run good?"

"It ran wonderfully, Bear, it—"

"Did you lean? You weren't leaning for shit when you left here."

She laughs. "No. I was too frightened to lean. Isabel leaned."

"How is she?"

"She's all right. I'm on my way to see her now."

"She's a great gal, Louisa. You got a great gal, there."

"I know. Thank you."

"Last night I was thinking," Bear continues, "a kid who could go through that firefight and stay up all night sawing through handcuffs with a hacksaw isn't your average kid, and I—"

There will be a time for these memories, but not now, Louisa thinks, not here in the hospital room. "Bear," she interrupts, "I'll write to you. First thing is, I'm going to get you paid."

"That's all right, you—"

"Nonsense, the fuel to and from Cody alone must have cost you a fortune, and I intend to pay you for it. I'm going to write you a letter, just as soon as I can. And I want to thank you for so many things, but I, I can't really talk right now, okay?"

"Okay."

"I'm with some people and I have to go, but . . ."

"Okay."

"I just wanted to hear your voice. I was so glad you called. You did a lot of things for me, things you don't even know. I'm going to write you, do you hear me?"

"Hell with that. Come smoke some reefer."

Louisa looks over at Agent Phillips.

"We'll have to talk about it," she says. "But maybe. Why the hell not!"

"Hey, Louisa!" Bear says.

"What?"

"I'll be damned!"

"What is it?"

"How's that for timing?"

"*What?*"

"Looks like I got a hitchhiker up ahead."

"Really?" She smiles. "Going to pick him up?"

"I don't know. Got in all kinds of trouble last time I tried that. Had to tell Becky I wouldn't do it anymore. Hold on a minute."

There is a pause. He seems to have put the phone down, which a trucker might do when he needs a hand free for the gear knob. Through the receiver, Louisa hears the rising whine of the engine, a whine that just might be the sound of Bear downshifting.

"Ah, what the hell," he says a moment later. "It's a long damn way to San Diego. Might as well have some company. Don't tell Beck, okay?"

"Promise," she says. "I promise, Bear."

When it is time to go, Louisa takes a last look around the room, at her husband and the chrysanthemums he has brought her, at the FBI agent who has helped save her life.

"There's one thing about Housez," Phillips says. "I forgot to ask you this yesterday. But since two nights ago, I've been curious to know something."

"What's that?"

"How did you get him here—to America?"

Louisa smiles. "Doolie."

"Doolie Stillwell?" Phillips asks, incredulously.

"Yes. She called him for me. I guess she made herself hysterical on the phone, saying that Royall had told her there would be money for her when he was gone, and left her the account numbers, and now she understood the money wasn't available to her. She demanded a meeting, and said she was going straight to *Hard Copy* if he didn't give her the money."

"But she didn't know about the account, right? He didn't know, we don't think."

"Right. But Housez didn't know that. It's true that Doolie didn't know until I told her. But she's a pretty quick study."

Toby asks, "How did you get her to play along?"

Louisa sighs. "Oh, well, Doolie's known me a long time. I don't think she believed the terrorist thing for one minute. And I don't think she believed I'd taken a bribe. When I talked to her, I still thought it was Ianella's deal. But I couldn't prove anything. Thank heaven, it was enough for her. I don't think she much cared for Frank."

"But how did you get to her?"

"I went up to the Old Dominion Golf and Lawn Tennis Club with a message for her. You know, as a bike messenger."

"Come on."

"That's what I did."

"You met her, in person?"

"Sure."

"And she recognized you? What did she say when she recognized you?"

"Well, I had it worked out, at least a little bit. I had a message for her, in a package. They gave her the message, said the messenger was waiting outside for a response. She didn't come outside to meet me until she'd read my story, and I guess it rang true for her. Then she came outside and met me."

"Huh," Phillips says, shaking his head. "And then she went off and made the call. When was that?"

"October twenty-sixth, I think. Saturday. Housez showed up on the twenty-ninth."

"Weren't you worried the story would get out?"

"Oh, I was worried about a lot of things, Gene. But I couldn't think of any other way to do it. All I had was my suspicion. Housez was the only one who could lead me to the Concierge. I just thought that the Concierge was going to be Ianella."

A few minutes later, the last of the forms has been signed. By the desk at the end of the ward, four or five nurses have gathered to wish their famous patient well. A resident waves at her. Toby, Eugene Phillips, and Louisa take the elevator to the basement, and then walk along the corridor toward the delivery entrance. They are just passing through a set of stainless-steel swinging doors when Toby asks, "Weezy, did you really dress up like a messenger and go and see Doolie at the Old Dominion?"

"Really did."

"And she came out on the porch to talk with you?"

"Yep."

"What'd she say? When she first saw you, I mean. Standing there in your Lycra suit on the porch of the Old Dominion? The woman who all the world says is wanted for bribery and six counts of murder. What did she say to you?"

The stainless-steel doors swing shut, and Phillips pauses, for he wants to know too. Louisa places one hand on her hip, and the other in the air, and in a husky drawl, she answers, " 'Louisa, honey, whatever have you done to your *hair*?' "

CHAPTER 60

The package comes six days later, a small parcel wrapped with an old U.S. Geological Survey map. Scotch-taped to it is an envelope addressed to Isabel. Inside, a piece of lined notepaper, torn from a school pad, says:

Dear Isabella,
    I read all about you and your Mom and was pretty amazed by it, I can tell you. Anyway, hope you're okay, and just want you to know, you're a much better outdoorsman, outdoorswoman I should say (!) than I thought you'd be when I saw you come into camp. You and your family are welcome to come out to Wyoming some time, and pack in with us, we'll show you God's own country, that's for sure. And next time you won't have to walk. I'll save Rhonda for you.
                                        Your friend,
                                        Johnny Trapp

      ps Isabel   *Just kidding about Isabella, did you get it?*
      pps   *Get rid of those sneakers and get you some boots!*
      ppps   *The present's to keep with you for next time you get kidnapped*
                                        Your friend,
                                        J.T.

And inside the box, of course, is his compass.

From the corner of the room, Louisa watches Isabel as she reads the letter. Isabel puts it down, then turns the compass over in her hands as though it were a string of pearls. She's quiet only for a minute, and then she begins breathlessly to recount for her mother all the mysteries of ori-enteering, and taking bearings, and contour lines, and true north, and magnetic north. Louisa doesn't hear much of it. She is too distracted by the blush on her daughter's cheeks, the brightness in her eye, and the presence, on her young face, of a new kind of smile—one Louisa hasn't seen before.

They walk out to the alfalfa field, jackets buttoned against the wind, feet crunching over close-cropped grass just beginning to crackle with frost. The sun is setting, and a chilly breeze is coming out of the north from across the Yadkin. She reaches to him and slips her hand into his, and they jostle and bump together as they walk across the rough ground of the field. The herd is down in the hollow by the oak tree and the aluminum gate. They have trodden the ground into cold muddy badlands. The cows look up at them with sweet stupidity, shying from the pair as they come near.

Toby makes faces at number 24, and the cow stares back at him, her wide brown eyes a blank. Louisa climbs the gate into the alfalfa field, Toby beside her, and together they follow the barbed-wire fence up to the hilltop, and then down the other side toward the river field, looking, as they walk, at the broad, brown Yadkin out beyond the swamp willows.

"Isn't it peaceful, Toby?"

"Yeah, it is, Weeze."

She stops and stands with her arms wrapped tightly round her chest and a wide smile on her face. Her hair is still close-cropped, but it has its own color back, and there is again about her face the promise of the Renoir woman. "It's good to be home," she says.

"Louisa," he says, "I—"

She interrupts him. The trouble with marriage, even after it's over, is that there are so few surprises. She knows what he is laboring to say, and decides to save him the awkwardness of it.

"Oh, Toby, I don't think so. You know, you helped save my life. I never could have managed that whole business with Claude Housez and the airplane without you and Marcy and Mac. But it doesn't mean—"

"Why not?" he asks. "Why not?"

She shakes her head.

He continues, "Weeze, I've learned a lot from this, and I know I've done some dumb things, but why can't we—"

"Toby," she says, and she is smiling brightly now, "you haven't done anything *dumb,* and you haven't learned anything from this, not that will change you, anyway. You've just been Toby."

"Weeze—"

"You're not going to change!" She stands on her tiptoes and kisses his nose, and when she draws away the happy look in her eyes perplexes him. He stares off at the river.

"Might as well ask Brutus over there"—she indicates the cattle barn on the facing hilltop, behind which is the bull's field—"to keep off the herd. It's in his nature. And yours. Don't be sad. You're a charming partner, and a good father. A little indulgent, but a responsible parent. Just not a good husband, that's all. It's not so awful. There will be another and another and another. But that's all right. I understand it now. I accept it. In a sneaking way, I'm proud of it, isn't that terrible? And don't you dare tell Isabel I said that!"

It is a strange thing to have said. But her love for him has changed, and now it is more that of a sister for a rascal brother, than of a wife for a husband. She draws him to her and says, "I love you better now, Toby, better than I ever did before. Because now I accept you, do you see?"

He nods, but doesn't really, and holds her tightly around the waist.

"Toby, I think I'm much fonder of you from a distance. We'll have lovely one-night stands, once in a blue moon," she teases. "When you can work me in!"

Under her teasing, he finds his solemnity cracking, the pained, sorrowful affect he has so often practiced. They know each other too well, after all. He smiles at her.

"Weeze, there's no one like you. And I can, honest, I can grow up. I feel puberty coming on, real soon. I'll be an adult in a couple of weeks."

But she puts her fingers to his lips and whispers, "No."

For a little longer they remain there, side by side in the cold, and the reddening of the western sky deepens to purple, while the brown river begins to fade to black. The herd has begun lowing.

"You may be a hunk," she whispers, "but you can't fix a tractor."

"I can learn," he says. "They're not exactly looking to hire me in the Proctor administration."

She shakes her head and takes his hand again, and they turn back toward the house on the next hillside. "It'll bounce back. Maybe you'll have a chance to run yourself, someday."

Evening is coming on quickly, now, and they walk back down the hill. "You must promise me only one thing," she says, as she clambers over the aluminum gate.

"Yeah?"

"Don't chase the youngest ones for too much longer. Don't be one of those sixty-year-old lechers leading cheerleaders around at society balls."

She winks at him, hopping down from the gate, and threads her way through the herd again. He is laughing as he runs to catch up with her, and two cows start nervously and back away. Louisa and Toby stride quickly now, feeling the cold, eager to be up the hill and in the farm-house.

"Why do you care, Weeze?"

"I just couldn't bear to see you make yourself ridiculous, Tobe."

They reach the upper pasture, and can see Isabel peering out the big windows in the living room. He asks it, putting in the form of a question what he knows is better said in the declarative. "So you're going to stay?"

She should, for his sake, better contain her joy. But she cannot. And perhaps the way she answers gives even her disappointed husband a small measure of happiness. "Yes, I'm going to stay. Toby, I'm home."

About the Author

Sabin Willett is a partner with the Boston law firm Bingham Dana LLP. *The Betrayal* is his second novel. He graduated from Harvard and Harvard Law School and lives outside Boston.